HERMAN MELVILLE
HENRY JAMES
STEPHEN CRANE
EDITH WHARTON
SHERWOOD ANDERSON
WILLIAM FAULKNER
FLANNERY O'CONNOR
WILLIAM STYRON

are the authors represented in Philip Rahv's anthology of great American short novels. Written between the years 1853 and 1952, these eight novels display the talents of some of America's foremost writers in the short novel form.

Eight
Great American
Short Novels

Edited and with an Introduction by
PHILIP RAHV

A BERKLEY MEDALLION BOOK
published by
BERKLEY PUBLISHING CORPORATION

ACKNOWLEDGMENTS

False Dawn, by Edith Wharton. Copyright 1924, by
D. Appleton Co. Copyright renewed 1952, by William R. Tyler.
Reprinted by permission of A. Watkins, Inc.

The Man Who Became a Woman, by Sherwood Anderson.
Copyright 1923, by B. W. Huebsch, Inc. Copyright
renewed 1951, by Eleanor Anderson. Reprinted by
permission of Harold Ober Associates, Inc.

Red Leaves, by William Faulkner. Copyrighted 1930
and renewed 1958, by William Faulkner. Reprinted
from *Collected Stories of William Faulkner* by
permission of Random House, Inc.

Wise Blood, by Flannery O'Connor. Copyright
1949, 1952, © 1962, by Flannery O'Connor. Reprinted
by permission of Farrar, Straus & Company, Inc.

The Long March, by William Styron. Copyright 1952,
by William Styron. Reprinted by permission
of McIntosh & McKee.

BERKLEY MEDALLION EDITION, APRIL, 1963
SIXTH PRINTING

SBN 425-02815-1

BERKLEY MEDALLION BOOKS are published by
Berkley Publishing Corporation
200 Madison Avenue, New York, N. Y. 10016

BERKLEY MEDALLION BOOKS ® TM 757,375

Printed in the United States of America

CONTENTS

EIGHT
GREAT AMERICAN
SHORT NOVELS

INTRODUCTION

by Philip Rahv

American literature is rich in examples of the short novel or novella, though it is only within the past four or five decades that some of our foremost writers have taken to this form with gusto and creative intelligence. In the earlier part of the nineteenth century Melville seems to stand alone in his mastery of this form; after him there was to be a long gap until Henry James, in the last quarter of the century, triumphantly demonstrated its high and wonderful vitality in an entire series of novellas of unsurpassed excellence, ranging from *Daisy Miller* in 1878 to *The Turn of the Screw* in 1898. James is no doubt the greatest practitioner of "the beautiful and blest *nouvelle*," as he was wont to call it, in the English language, and he lamented its neglect on both sides of the Atlantic, among writers in England as well as in America. He saw in the *nouvelle* the possibility of the complete integration within a determinate framework of pattern and plot, picture and drama. Its consistent exclusion from the favor of magazine-editors, who much preferred to serialize long novels, he ascribed to "the blank misery of our Anglo-Saxon sense in such matters," meaning of course the matter of the application of artistic standards to the prose-medium in general and, more particularly, the exercise of the strict compositional economy that the short novel demands. However, since the time of James's strictures America's writers have happily overcome the earlier deficiency by enriching our literature in this genre with not a few narratives of significant literary value and imaginative authority.

In this collection the reader will not come upon such famous examples of the novella as James's *Turn of the Screw* and *Washington Square* or F. Scott Fitzgerald's *The Great Gatsby,* the reason being that these works are now readily available in any number of editions, reprints, and anthologies. Instead the selection in this volume brings forward a number of lesser known works that are perhaps in most instances of equal creative stature.

The first item in this collection, Melville's *Bartleby the Scrivener*, was originally published anonymously in the November, 1855 issue of *Putnam's Monthly Magazine* and then reprinted three years later under the author's name in his volume of shorter fiction *The Piazza Tales*. In its appalling queerness and compelling suggestiveness, *Bartleby* is one of the most singular narratives in American letters. If there is any single tale in world literature that it reminds us of it is of course Nikolay Gogol's *The Overcoat*, in which the life and death of a petty little copying clerk in a St. Petersburg office is likewise transformed into something rich and strange. In both stories realistic and symbolic elements are fused into grotesque phantasies of human loss, inconsequence, and deepest alienation. But Melville's protagonist Bartleby, looking out upon the blank brick wall of his employer's Wall Street office, is in far more desperate straits than Gogol's clerk, who before going under proves himself capable at least of one act —the acquisition of the longed-for overcoat—that is meant to salvage his crushed ego and to restore him to the human norm. Not so poor Bartleby, who is beyond any effort at self-regeneration and who, in his mad obdurate refusal to come to terms with the demands of life, dies alone under a prison-wall. His is the courage of ultimate despair and negation, the courage not to be. Critics of Melville, such as Newton Arvin and Richard Chase, have recognized in *Bartleby* a truly inspired intuitive study of schizophrenia at the same time that they have noted its transcendence of clinical associations in dramatizing what is nothing less than "the bitter metaphysical pathos of the human situation itself."

In the last but one paragraph of the tale we are told that Bartleby is rumored to have served at one time as a clerk in the Dead Letter Office at Washington—a detail that has been rightly taken as indicative of Melville's at least partial identification with his protagonist, for at the time of the composition of the narrative he felt himself to be in dire straits, reduced to a state of extreme isolation, having seen his most sustained and valiant efforts at communicating with the world—the epical prose-poem *Moby Dick* and the novel *Pierre*—meet with virtually no response and no understanding. After all, he too was in a sense a scrivener and like Bartleby a failure and an outcast from life. He must have then conceived of himself, as he conceived of Bartleby, as someone "by nature and misfortune prone to a pallid helplessness," doomed to handle dead "letters" and feeding them to the flames. ("On errands of life, these letters speed to death.") But though this subjective reference of the tale is of interest in relation to its author's biography, it in no way affects its objectively-wrought meaning and universal import.

An International Episode (1878) is one of the least re-printed and least known of Henry James's short novels. It surely deserves to be better known. A companion-piece to *Daisy Miller* and written in the same year, it is quite as brilliant a rendering of the author's favorite theme of trans-atlantic relations. It has the characteristic clarity of contour and lightness and wit of phrasing of James's earlier period, qualities which in his later work gave way to effects of a more complex and difficult order. A captivating feature of *An International Episode* is its charm of time and place, as in the description of summertime New York and of Newport as observed through the eyes of two visiting Englishmen, Lord Lambeth and his friend Mr. Beaumont, who are destined to be immensely surprised by what the manner of Americans conceals and what their self-respect dictates. Bessie Alden, the heroine of the narrative, exhibits a remarkable sense of herself as a product of native conditions by turning down the proposal of Lord Lambeth, even though she likes him well enough to marry him and is highly sensitive to "the mementoes and reverberations of greatness" in the life of old European aristocracies. In this refusal Bessie Alden an-ticipates bravely the even more meaningful refusal of a "great personage" (Lord Warburton) by a more formidable Jamesian heroine—Isabel Archer in *The Portrait of a Lady* (1880). It is worth recalling that Bessie's proud behavior was looked at askance by English readers, just as the be-havior of Daisy Miller, in its "inscrutable combination of audacity and innocence," was initially resented by American readers, who saw in it a slanderous account of American girlhood. James was no end pleased by the liveliness and eloquent symptomatic nature of this polar response, for it confirmed his faith in the "international situation" as a theme offering a fullness of resource for the portrayal of manners and morals through the novelistic exploitation of national differences.

Stephen Crane's *The Blue Hotel* contains elements locating it at the very starting-point of the more typically modern line in American fiction. Its theme of violence and sudden death, as well as the detached irony of its narrative manner and the concentration on external detail and circumstance scrupu-lously selected so as to convey meaning without resort to other means, are among the leading characteristics more fully developed by later American writers, as for example Ernest Hemingway, who has in faet singled out *The Blue Hotel* as the very best of Crane's work. Published in *Collier's Weekly* for November 26, 1898, it is one of a series of western stories the material of which Crane accumulated during the year (he was then twenty-three years of age) he spent in the Far West and Mexico. What is most striking about *The Blue Hotel* is its wonderful unity and concreteness of effect achieved through the mastery of particulars and their presentation in an impressionist idiom of great verve and color. The light blue of the Palace Hotel at Fort Romper, a desolate frontier town, "was always screaming and howling in a way that made the dazzling winter landscape of Nebraska seem only a grey swampish hush." This opening chord, struck in the very first paragraph of the novella, announces as it were the imminent death of the paranoiac Swede, shaky and quick-eyed, as he alights from the train holding a great shining cheap valise in his hands. Note, too, the aptness and wit of Crane's imagery, as in the climactic sentence towards the end, telling us that "the corpse of the Swede, alone in the saloon, had its eyes fixed upon a dreadful legend that dwelt atop of the cash machine: 'This registers the amount of your purchase.' "

False Dawn is the first of four short novels, intimately recovering through the medium of fiction the life of upper-class New York from the 1840's through the 1870's, which Edith Wharton brought out in 1924 under the collective title *Old New York*. These novellas, together with her important novel *The Age of Innocence* (1920), dealing with a frustrated love-affair of fashionable New Yorkers in the late Victorian era, comprise a group of fictions invaluable for the opportunity they afford us to savor the distinctive qualities of the American past in its realness, free of the indulgences of legend, patriotic sentiment, and easy notions of the picturesque. So much of the older American literature is given over to fanciful romance and allegory remote from the actualities of time and place that one cannot but be gratefully conscious of those few of our older writers (e.g., Henry James in *Washington Square*, Hawthorne in a small part of his work) whose imagination was not repelled but quickened by the indiginous in its typical and ordinary aspects. The accomplished art of *False Dawn* regains a segment of New York's history—the 1840's—and recreates with sufficient realism the ideas and habits of life, the social conventions and expectations, of the Raycie family, whose outlook and mode of behavior are so wholly characteristic of the entire patrician caste of New York in that old time. It is not a pretty picture and scarcely one that native snobs and antiquarians are likely to relish.

Edmund Wilson has observed of Edith Wharton that "her work is the record of a struggle between wealth and its advantages on the one hand, and aesthetic and moral values on the other." This insight is perfectly exemplified in *False Dawn,* in which is recounted the tragicomedy of the ruinous conflict that ensues between Halston Raycie, who is the embodiment of conventional attitudes and the cult of the superior "family," and his son Lewis, whom he expects to follow in his footsteps and to put heirlooms, entailed estates, and all the ritual of the traditions of the British gentry above all else in life. Lewis, however, disappoints his father horribly by turning out, upon his return from the Grand Tour of Europe, to have been converted to advanced views of art and to have catastrophically failed in his mission of bringing back a sampling of reputable Old Masters to form the nucleus of the Raycie Gallery that his parent so fondly dreams of; for he has returned laden with the wrong kind of pictures, the kind that his father had never heard of and is ashamed to own. No Dolmenichinos, no Albanos, no Carlo Dolcis, no Guerinos or Marattas, and not even a single "noble landscape" by Salvator Rosa; Lewis had committed the unforgivable sin of striking out on his own and had purchased a Piero della Francesca and other pictures to whose appeal he had succumbed under the influence of the young and ever so persuasive John Ruskin, encountered by chance in the shadow of Mont Blanc. This fiasco is the end of Lewis as a respectable member of New York society, and there is no more genuine scene of pathos than the sight of him shivering among his spurned treasures in the "Gallery of Christian Art" that he had so quixotically set up in his shabby house on the corner of Third Avenue and Tenth Street. Thus what this novella throws into dramatic relief is the pathetic limitedness and impregnable complacency of the social caste of which old Mr. Raycie is an ornament and also the great odds against which the emergent imaginative faculty was fated to struggle in that old provincial America with its upper crust that regarded itself as the salt of the earth.

We enter a radically different world, a world from which all gentility and decorum had departed, in Sherwood Anderson's *The Man Who Became a Woman* (1923). Thoroughly expressive of its author's Romantic primitivism, this short novel is among the very best of Anderson's writings and one of his most daring. The scene of the race track and of its men and horses is recreated with the sure feeling that can come only out of the identification of love, and the theme of latent homosexuality is developed on a level of creative insight and sheer intuition removing it from all dependence on reports of "clinical cases" and on ideas derived from psychoanalytic texts. To an imaginative writer such ready-made ideas are largely useless because they cannot but enter the process of his art as abstraction; and abstraction is the ruin of art. As a storyteller Anderson's stance is that of identifying himself with the very perplexity of his characters and seeing them through, as it were, the successive stages of their ignorance; the revelation that ultimately awaits the reader, though verbally inarticulate, is all the more effective when he finally grasps it. And the revelation so gained is indeed the secret of the strength of Anderson's more successful fiction, in which he consistently adheres to a creative method that might be described as one of humility not unmixed with craft in both senses of the word. In *The Man Who Became a Woman*, written in the first person singular, the protagonist who serves as narrator tells us right out what this method is when he says: "I'm puzzled you see, just how to make you feel as I felt that night. I suppose, having undertaken to write this story, that's what I'm up against, trying to do that. I'm not claiming to be able to inform you or do you any good. I'm just trying to make you understand some things about me, as I would like to understand some things about you, or anyone, if I had the chance."

William Faulkner's *Red Leaves* is an astounding performance. Included in his first volume of stories, *These Thirteen*, that appeared in 1931, it is a story of the Chickasaw Indians and their Negro slaves in northern Mississippi in the early years of the nineteenth century when the Indians had not yet lost all their land to the whites. There is nothing quite like this story in American literature, and what is most admirable about it is the capacity shown in it by its author to think himself back, as it were, to a remote and in a sense almost pre-historical period in the history of the South, and to imagine the unimaginable. The mastery of physical detail that Faulkner here demonstrates is virtually absolute, and it is precisely this mastery, or complete immersion, that makes it possible for him to modulate, control, and give inviolable artistic shape to the wildness of imagination that has gone into the conception of the tale. To be sure, in some of his works Faulkner was unable to control this wildness of imagination, and the result was a certain opacity of value and meaning that critics have tried to penetrate by bringing to bear their tools of analysis and explication. But a narrative like *Red Leaves* attains such completeness of realization that the attempt to analyse it would be plainly superrogatory.

Flannery O'Connor's *Wise Blood* belongs to the fictional genre of the Southern Gothic or Grotesque which in the wake of Faulkner's ever so provocative and instructive career has in recent decades turned the Southern countryside and small town into a veritable literary landscape. Most of the writings in this genre, striving for few effects beyond those of the macabre, are of superficial interest. One reflects that most of the writers who go in for it are mainly concerned with exploiting the South because of the extravagant novelistic associations it so readily offers; few bring an original vision to bear upon it. Now *Wise Blood,* which first appeared in 1952 arousing but little critical attention, differs significantly and decisively from the all-too-familiar products of regional sensationalism. What it leaves us with is an emotion of extreme poignancy rather than mere piquancy; its uncommon virulence has an imaginative logic that is profoundly convincing; and it contains suggestions of meaning and value that are far beyond the reach of nearly all the writers of the post-Faulkner generation who have attempted to subdue the South to literary use. Miss O'Connor, a native of Georgia, is the author of a number of novels, but I think that in *Wise Blood* she is at her very best. It seems to me that in this short novel, the action of which takes place in Tennessee, she has created a small masterpiece of life in the Southern hinterland which has a distinct affinity with that mordant masterpiece of modern urban life, Nathanael West's *Miss Lonelyhearts.* The parallel, in the employment of fantasy and surrealistic devices, is close. Moreover, Miss O'Connor's story is a regional statement of positively the same theme as that of Nathanael West—the theme summed up by Hazel Motes, self-styled evangelist and protagonist of *Wise Blood,* in one definite sentence: "Nothing matters but that Jesus don't exist;" and driven by this discovery Motes sets out to preach a new church—"the church of truth without Jesus Christ Crucified." Motes—a "Jesus-lover" in spite of the shattering heresy into which he precipitates himself—is a kind of clodhopper version, strangely enough, of several dominant characters in Dostoevsky, such as Kirillov in *The Possessed* for instance, who is also in his own way a saint turned inside out whose truly religious atheism and/or religious paranoia dooms him to self-immolation.

William Styron is an outstanding younger novelist who came of literary age after the second World War. It might be said of him that he is one of the few truly gifted members of his generation in this rather meager period of American writing who appears to command the resources for a creative career of significant value. That he has been influenced by Faulkner is scarcely open to question. The indebtedness is to be detected both in the form and substance of Styron's fiction, and it has been all to the good in so far as it has allowed him to go in for an elaboration of language uncommon among his contemporaries and to employ narrative techniques designed to extract from his subject-matter its fullest implications.

The Long March is notable as a study of military psychology in its more mordant forms and as an acute though indirect comment on the state of mind of the author's own generation in present-day America. (What this state of mind comes to can surely be summed up as the predicament of men bred in an idealist tradition but unable to find a cause to which to attach their idealism.) The physical agony of the forced march which the Marines in training go through—a march that takes thirteen hours and extends for thirty-six miles—is brilliantly recorded in this novella, and so is its shattering effect on the emotions of the two officers, Lieutenant Culver and Captain Mannix, who are the chief protagonists of the action. Mannix regards the march as an outrage, a futile and cruel undertaking, but his humane rebelliousness, his attempt to break through the barriers of the harshly impersonal military code, are judged to be equally futile by Lieutenant Culver, the narrator upon whose "point of view" the meaning of the story turns: "But underneath his rebellion, Culver finally knew, Mannix—like all of them—was really resigned. Born into a generation of conformists, even Mannix (so Culver sensed) was aware that his gestures were not symbolic, but individual, therefore hopeless, maybe even absurd, and that he was trapped like all of them in a predicament which one personal insurrection could, if anything, only make worse." Thus *The Long March* impresses us not merely as an extraordinarily vivid account of a physical ordeal but as a vehicle discovering and exploring a new theme, that of the rebellion of those "born into a generation of conformists." That this theme is paradoxical goes without saying; but it is also true to remark of it that it is genuine and of extreme pertinence to the situation of Americans in an age of moral confusion, deflated ideals, and unprecedented danger.

HERMAN MELVILLE

Bartleby The Scrivener

A STORY OF WALL STREET

I AM a rather elderly man. The nature of my avocations for the last thirty years has brought me into more than ordinary contact with what would seem an interesting and somewhat singular set of men, of whom as yet nothing that I know of has ever been written:—I mean the law-copyists or scriveners. I have known very many of them, professionally and privately, and if I pleased, could relate divers histories, at which good-natured gentlemen might smile, and sentimental souls might weep. But I waive the biographies of all other scriveners for a few passages in the life of Bartleby, who was a scrivener the strangest I ever saw or heard of. While of other law-copyists I might write the complete life, of Bartleby nothing of that sort can be done. I believe that no materials exist for a full and satisfactory biography of this man. It is an irreparable loss to literature. Bartleby was one of those beings of whom nothing is ascertainable, except from the original sources, and in his case those are very small. What my own astonished eyes saw of Bartleby, *that* is all I know of him, except, indeed, one vague report which will appear in the sequel.

Ere introducing the scrivener, as he first appeared to me, it is fit I make some mention of myself, my *employés*, my business, my chambers, and general surroundings; because some such description is indispensable to an adequate understanding of the chief character about to be presented.

Imprimis: I am a man who, from his youth upward, has been filled with a profound conviction that the easiest way of life is the best. Hence, though I belong to a profession proverbially energetic and nervous, even to turbulence, at times, yet nothing of that sort have I ever suffered to invade my peace. I am one of those unambitious lawyers who never addresses a jury, or in any way draws down public applause; but in the cool tranquillity of a snug retreat, do a snug business among rich men's bonds and mortgages and title-deeds. All who know me, consider me an eminently *safe* man. The late John Jacob Astor, a personage little given to poetic enthusiasm, had no hesitation in pronouncing my first grand point to be prudence; my next, method. I do not speak it in vanity, but simply record the fact, that I was not unemployed in my profession by the late John Jacob Astor; a name which, I admit, I love to repeat, for it hath a rounded and orbicular sound to it, and rings like unto bullion. I will freely add, that I was not insensible to the late John Jacob Astor's good opinion.

Some time prior to the period at which this little history begins, my avocations had been largely increased. The good old office, now extinct in the State of New York, of a Master in Chancery, had been conferred upon me. It was not a very arduous office, but very pleasantly remunerative. I seldom lose my temper; much more seldom indulge in dangerous indignation at wrongs and outrages; but I must be permitted to be rash here and declare, that I consider the sudden and violent abrogation of the office of Master in Chancery, by the new Constitution, as a —— premature act; inasmuch as I had counted upon a life-lease of the profits, whereas I only received those of a few short years. But this is by the way.

My chambers were upstairs at No. —— Wall street. At one end they looked upon the white wall of the interior of a spacious sky-light shaft, penetrating the building from top to bottom. This view might have been considered rather tame than otherwise, deficient in what landscape painters call "life." But if so, the view from the other end of my chambers offered, at least, a contrast, if nothing more. In that direction my windows commanded an unobstructed view of a lofty brick wall, black by age and everlasting shade; which wall required no spy-glass to bring out its lurking beauties, but for the benefit of all near-sighted spectators, was pushed up to within ten feet of my window panes. Owing to the great height of the surrounding buildings, and my chambers being on the second floor, the interval between this wall and mine not a little resembled a huge square cistern.

At the period just preceding the advent of Bartleby, I had two persons as copyists in my employment, and a promising lad as an office-boy. First, Turkey; second, Nippers; third,

Ginger Nut. These may seem names, the like of which are not usually found in the Directory. In truth they were nicknames, mutually conferred upon each other by my three clerks, and were deemed expressive of their respective persons or characters. Turkey was a short, pursy Englishman of about my own age, that is, somewhere not far from sixty. In the morning, one might say, his face was of a fine florid hue, but after twelve o'clock, meridian—his dinner hour—it blazed like a grate full of Christmas coals; and continued blazing— but, as it were, with a gradual wane—till 6 o'clock P.M. or thereabouts, after which I saw no more of the proprietor of the face, which, gaining its meridian with the sun, seemed to set with it, to rise, culminate, and decline the following day, with the like regularity and undiminished glory. There are many singular coincidences I have known in the course of my life, not the least among which was the fact, that exactly when Turkey displayed his fullest beams from his red and radiant countenance, just then, too, at that critical moment, began the daily period when I considered his business capacities as seriously disturbed for the remainder of the twenty-four hours. Not that he was absolutely idle, or averse to business then; far from it. The difficulty was, he was apt to be altogether too energetic. There was a strange, inflamed, flurried, flighty recklessness of activity about him. He would be incautious in dipping his pen into his inkstand. All his blots upon my documents, were dropped there after twelve o'clock, meridian. Indeed, not only would he be reckless and sadly given to making blots in the afternoon, but some days he went further, and was rather noisy. At such times, too, his face flamed with augmented blazonry, as if cannel coal had been heaped on anthracite. He made an unpleasant racket with his chair; spilled his sand-box; in mending his pens, impatiently split them all to pieces, and threw them on the floor in a sudden passion; stood up and leaned over his table, boxing his papers about in a most indecorous manner, very sad to behold in an elderly man like him. Nevertheless, as he was in many ways a most valuable person to me, and all the time before twelve o'clock, meridian, was the quickest, steadiest creature, too, accomplishing a great deal of work in a style not easy to be matched—for these reasons, I was willing to overlook his eccentricities, though indeed, occasionally, I remonstrated with him. I did this very gently, however, because, though the civilest, nay, the blandest and most reverential of men in the morning, yet in the afternoon he was disposed, upon provocation, to be slightly rash with his tongue, in fact, insolent. Now, valuing his morning services as I did, and resolving not to lose them—yet, at the same time, made uncomfortable by his inflamed ways after twelve o'clock; and being a man of peace, unwilling by my admonitions to call forth unseemly retorts from him—I took upon me, one Saturday noon (he was always worse on Saturdays), to hint to him, very kindly, that perhaps now that he was growing old, it might be well to abridge his labours; in short, he need not come to my chambers after twelve o'clock, but, dinner over, had best go home to his lodgings and rest himself till tea-time. But no; he insisted upon his afternoon devotions. His countenance became intolerably fervid, as he oratorically assured me—gesticulating, with a long ruler, at the other side of the room—that if his services in the morning were useful, how indispensable, then, in the afternoon?

"With submission, sir," said Turkey on this occasion, "I consider myself your right-hand man. In the morning I but marshal and deploy my columns; but in the afternoon I put myself at their head, and gallantly charge the foe, thus!"—and he made a violent thrust with the ruler.

"But the blots, Turkey," intimated I.

"True,—but, with submission, sir, behold these hairs! I am getting old. Surely, sir, a blot or two of a warm afternoon is not to be severely urged against grey hairs. Old age —even if it blot the page—is honourable. With submission, sir, we *both* are getting old."

This appeal to my fellow-feeling was hardly to be resisted. At all events, I saw that go he would not. So I made up my mind to let him stay, resolving, nevertheless, to see to it, that during the afternoon he had to do with my less important papers.

Nippers, the second on my list, was a whiskered, sallow, and, upon the whole, rather piratical-looking young man of about five and twenty. I always deemed him the victim of two evil powers—ambition and indigestion. The ambition was evinced by a certain impatience of the duties of a mere copyist—an unwarrantable usurpation of strictly professional affairs, such as the original drawing up of legal documents. The indigestion seemed betokened in an occasional nervous testiness and grinning irritability, causing the teeth to audibly grind together over mistakes committed in copying; unnecessary maledictions, hissed, rather than spoken, in the heat of business; and especially by a continual discontent with the height of the table where he worked. Though of a very ingenious mechanical turn, Nippers could never get this table to suit him. He put chips under it, blocks of various sorts, bits of pasteboard, and at last went so far as to attempt an exquisite adjustment by final pieces of folded blotting-paper. But no invention would answer. If, for the sake of easing his back, he brought the table lid at a sharp angle well up toward his chin, and wrote there like a man using the steep roof of a Dutch house for his desk—then he declared that it stopped the circulation in his arms. If now he lowered the table to his waistbands, and stooped over it in writing, then there was a sore aching in his back. In short, the truth of the matter was, Nippers knew not what he wanted. Or, if he wanted anything, it was to be rid of a scrivener's table altogether. Among the manifestations of his diseased ambition was a fondness he had for receiving visits from certain ambiguous-looking fellows in seedy coats, whom he called his clients. Indeed I was aware that not only was he, at times, considerable of a ward-politician, but he occasionally did a little business at the Justices' courts, and was not unknown on the steps of the Tombs. I have good reason to believe, however, that one individual who called upon him at my chambers, and who, with a grand air, he insisted was his client, was no other than a dun, and the alleged title-deed, a bill. But with all his failings, and the annoyances he caused me, Nippers, like his compatriot Turkey, was a very useful man to me; wrote a neat, swift hand; and, when he chose, was not deficient in a gentlemanly sort of deportment. Added to this, he always dressed in a gentlemanly sort of way; and so, incidentally, reflected credit upon my chambers. Whereas with respect to Turkey, I had much ado to keep him from being a reproach to me. His clothes were apt to look oily and smell of eating-houses. He wore his pantaloons very loose and baggy in summer. His coats were execrable; his hat not to be handled. But while the hat was a thing of indifference to me, inasmuch as his natural civility and deference, as a dependent Englishman, always led him to doff it the moment he entered the room, yet his coat was another matter. Concerning his coats, I reasoned with him; but with no effect. The truth was, I suppose, that a man with so small an income, could not afford to sport such a lustrous face and a lustrous coat at one and the same time. As Nippers once observed, Turkey's money went chiefly for red ink. One winter day I presented Turkey with a highly-respectable looking coat of my own, a padded grey coat, of a most comfortable warmth, and which buttoned straight up

from the knee to the neck. I thought Turkey would appreciate the favour, and abate his rashness and obstreperousness
of afternoons. But no. I verily believe that buttoning himself
up in so downy and blanket-like a coat had a pernicious
effect upon him; upon the same principle that too much oats
are bad for horses. In fact, precisely as a rash, restive horse
is said to feel his oats, so Turkey felt his coat. It made him
insolent. He was a man whom prosperity harmed.

Though concerning the self-indulgent habits of Turkey I
had my own private surmises, yet touching Nippers I was
well persuaded that whatever might be his faults in other
respects, he was, at least, a temperate young man. But, indeed, nature herself seemed to have been his vintner, and
at his birth charged him so thoroughly with an irritable,
brandy-like disposition, that all subsequent potations were
needles. When I consider how, amid the stillness of my
chambers, Nippers would sometimes impatiently rise from
his seat, and stooping over his table, spread his arms wide
apart, seize the whole desk, and move it, and jerk it, with
a grim, grinding motion on the floor, as if the table were a
perverse voluntary agent, intent on thwarting and vexing
him; I plainly perceive that for Nippers, brandy and water
were altogether superfluous.

It was fortunate for me that, owing to its peculiar cause
—indigestion—the irritability and consequent nervousness
of Nippers, were mainly observable in the morning, while
in the afternoon he was comparatively mild. So that Turkey's paroxysms only coming on about twelve o'clock, I
never had to do with their eccentricities at one time. Their
fits relieved each other like guards. When Nipper's was on,
Turkey's was off; and *vice versa*. This was a good natural
arrangement under the circumstances.

Ginger Nut, the third on my list, was a lad some twelve
years old. His father was a carman, ambitious of seeing his
son on the bench instead of a cart, before he died. So he
sent him to my office as student at law, errand boy, and
cleaner and sweeper, at the rate of one dollar a week. He
had a little desk to himself, but he did not use it much.
Upon inspection, the drawer exhibited a great array of the
shells of various sorts of nuts. Indeed, to this quick-witted
youth the whole noble science of the law was contained in a
nut-shell. Not the least among the employments of Ginger
Nut, as well as one which he discharged with the most alac-
rity, was his duty as cake and apple purveyor for Turkey
and Nippers. Copying law papers being proverbially a dry,

husky sort of business, my two scriveners were fain to moisten their mouths very often with Spitzenbergs to be had at the numerous stalls nigh the Custom House and Post Office. Also, they sent Ginger Nut very frequently for that peculiar cake—small, flat, round, and very spicy—after which he had been named by them. Of a cold morning, when business was but dull, Turkey would gobble up scores of these cakes, as if they were mere wafers—indeed they sell them at the rate of six or eight for a penny—the scrape of his pen blending with the crunching of the crisp particles in his mouth. Of all the fiery afternoon blunders and flurried rashness of Turkey, was his once moistening a ginger-cake between his lips, and clapping it on to a mortgage for a seal. I came within an ace of dismissing him then. But he mollified me by making an oriental bow and saying—"With submission, sir, it was generous of me to find you in stationery on my own account."

Now my original business—that of a conveyancer and title hunter, and drawer-up of recondite documents of all sorts—was considerably increased by receiving the master's office. There was now great work for scriveners. Not only must I push the clerks already with me, but I must have additional help. In answer to my advertisement, a motionless young man one morning stood upon my office threshold, the door being open, for it was summer. I can see that figure now—pallidly neat, pitiably respectable, incurably forlorn! It was Bartleby.

After a few words touching his qualifications, I engaged him, glad to have among my corps of copyists a man of so singularly sedate an aspect, which I thought might operate beneficially upon the flighty temper of Turkey, and the fiery one of Nippers.

I should have stated before that ground glass folding-doors divided my premises into two parts, one of which was occupied by my scriveners, the other by myself. According to my humour I threw open these doors, or closed them. I resolved to assign Bartleby a corner by the folding-doors, but on my side of them, so as to have this quiet man within easy call, in case any trifling thing was to be done. I placed his desk close up to a small side-window in that part of the room, a window which originally had afforded a lateral view of certain grimy back-yards and bricks, but which, owing to subsequent erections, commanded at present no view at all, though it gave some light. Within three feet of the panes was a wall, and the light came down from far above, between two lofty buildings, as from a very small opening in a dome. Still further to a satisfactory arrangement, I procured a high green folding screen, which might entirely isolate Bartleby from my sight, though not remove him from my voice. And thus, in a manner, privacy and society were conjoined.

At first Bartleby did an extraordinary quantity of writing. As if long famishing for something to copy, he seemed to gorge himself on my documents. There was no pause for digestion. He ran a day and night line, copying by sun-light and by candle-light. I should have been quite delighted with his application, had he been cheerfully industrious. But he wrote on silently, palely, mechanically.

It is, of course, an indispensable part of a scrivener's business to verify the accuracy of his copy, word by word. Where there are two or more scriveners in an office, they assist each other in this examination, one reading from the copy, the other holding the original. It is a very dull, wearisome, and lethargic affair. I can readily imagine that to some sanguine temperaments it would be altogether intolerable. For example, I cannot credit that the mettlesome poet Byron would have contentedly sat down with Bartleby to examine a law document of, say five hundred pages, closely written in a crimpy hand.

Now and then, in the haste of business, it had been my habit to assist in comparing some brief document myself, calling Turkey or Nippers for this purpose. One object I had in placing Bartleby so handy to me behind the screen, was to avail myself of his services on such trivial occasions. It was on the third day, I think, of his being with me, and before any necessity had arisen for having his own writing examined, that, being much hurried to complete a small affair I had in hand, I abruptly called to Bartleby. In my haste and natural expectancy of instant compliance, I sat with my head bent over the original on my desk, and my right hand sideways, and somewhat nervously extended with the copy, so that immediately upon emerging from his retreat, Bartleby might snatch it and proceed to business without the least delay.

In this very attitude did I sit when I called to him, rapidly stating what it was I wanted him to do—namely, to examine a small paper with me. Imagine my surprise, nay, my consternation, when without moving from his privacy, Bartleby in a singularly mild, firm voice, replied, "I would prefer not to."

I sat awhile in perfect silence, rallying my stunned faculties. Immediately it occurred to me that my ears had deceived me, or Bartleby had entirely misunderstood my meaning. I repeated my request in the clearest tone I could assume. But in quite as clear a one came the previous reply, "I would prefer not to."

"Prefer not to," echoed I, rising in high excitement, and crossing the room with a stride. "What do you mean? Are you moon-struck? I want you to help me compare this sheet here—take it," and I thrust it toward him.

"I would prefer not to," said he.

I looked at him steadfastly. His face was leanly composed; his grey eye dimly calm. Not a wrinkle of agitation rippled him. Had there been the least uneasiness, anger, impatience or impertinence in his manner; in other words, had there been anything ordinarily human about him; doubtless I should have violently dismissed him from the premises. But as it was, I should have as soon thought of turning my pale plaster-of-paris bust of Cicero out of doors. I stood gazing at him awhile, as he went on with his own writing, and then reseated myself at my desk. This is very strange, thought I. What had one best do? But my business hurried me. I concluded to forget the matter for the present, reserving it for my future leisure. So calling Nippers from the other room, the paper was speedily examined.

A few days after this, Bartleby concluded four lengthy documents, being quadruplicates of a week's testimony taken before me in my High Court of Chancery. It became necessary to examine them. It was an important suit, and great accuracy was imperative. Having all things arranged, I called Turkey, Nippers and Ginger Nut from the next room, meaning to place the four copies in the hands of my four clerks, while I should read from the original. Accordingly Turkey, Nippers and Ginger Nut had taken their seats in a row, each with his document in hand, when I called to Bartleby to join this interesting group.

"Bartleby! quick, I am waiting."

I heard a slow scrape of his chair legs on the uncarpeted floor, and soon he appeared standing at the entrance of his hermitage.

"What is wanted?" said he mildly.

"The copies, the copies," said I hurriedly. "We are going to examine them. There"—and I held toward him the fourth quadruplicate.

"I would prefer not to," he said, and gently disappeared behind the screen.

For a few moments I was turned into a pillar of salt, standing at the head of my seated column of clerks. Recovering myself, I advanced toward the screen, and demanded the reason for such extraordinary conduct.

"*Why* do you refuse?"

"I would prefer not to."

With any other man I should have flown outright into a dreadful passion, scorned all further words, and thrust him ignominiously from my presence. But there was something about Bartleby that not only strangely disarmed me, but in a wonderful manner touched and disconcerted me. I began to reason with him.

"These are your own copies we are about to examine. It is labour saving to you, because one examination will answer for your four papers. It is common usage. Every copyist is bound to help examine his copy. Is it not so? Will you not speak? Answer!"

"I prefer not to," he replied in a flute-like tone. It seemed to me that while I had been addressing him, he carefully revolved every statement that I made; fully comprehended the meaning; could not gainsay the irresistible conclusion; but, at the same time, some paramount consideration prevailed with him to reply as he did.

"You are decided, then, not to comply with my request —a request made according to common usage and common sense?"

He briefly gave me to understand that on that point my judgment was sound. Yes: his decision was irreversible.

It is not seldom the case that when a man is browbeaten in some unprecedented and violently unreasonable way, he begins to stagger in his own plainest faith. He begins, as it were, vaguely to surmise that, wonderful as it may be, all the justice and all the reason are on the other side. Accordingly, if any disinterested persons are present, he turns to them for some reinforcement for his own faltering mind.

"Turkey," said I, "what do you think of this? Am I not right?"

"With submission, sir," said Turkey, with his blandest tone, "I think that you are."

"Nippers," said I, "what do *you* think of it?"

"I think I should kick him out of the office."

(The reader of nice perceptions will here perceive that, it being morning, Turkey's answer is couched in polite and tranquil terms but Nippers's reply in ill-tempered ones. Or, to repeat a previous sentence, Nippers's ugly mood was on duty, and Turkey's off.)

"Ginger Nut," said I, willing to enlist the smallest suffrage in my behalf, "what do *you* think of it?"

"I think, sir he's a little *luny*," replied Ginger Nut, with a grin.

"You hear what they say," said I, turning towards the screen, "come forth and do your duty."

But he vouchsafed no reply. I pondered a moment in sore perplexity. But once more business hurried me. I determined again to postpone the consideration of this dilemma to my future leisure. With a little trouble we made out to examine the papers without Bartleby, though at every page or two, Turkey deferentially dropped his opinion that this proceeding was quite out of the common; while Nippers, twitching in his chair with a dyspeptic nervousness, ground out between his set teeth occasional hissing maledictions against the stubborn oaf behind the screen. And for his (Nippers's) part, this was the first and the last time he would do another man's business without pay.

Meanwhile Bartleby sat in his hermitage, oblivious to everything but his own peculiar business there.

Some days passed, the scrivener being employed upon another lengthy work. His late remarkable conduct led me to regard his ways narrowly. I observed that he never went to dinner; indeed that he never went any where. As yet I had never of my personal knowledge known him to be outside of my office. He was a perpetual sentry in the corner. At about eleven o'clock though, in the morning, I noticed that Ginger Nut would advance towards the opening in Bartleby's screen, as if silently beckoned thither by a gesture invisible to me where I sat. The boy would then leave the office jingling a few pence, and reappear with a handful of ginger-nuts which he delivered in the hermitage, receiving two of the cakes for his trouble.

He lives, then, on ginger-nuts, thought I; never eats a dinner, properly speaking; he must be a vegetarian then; but no; he never eats even vegetables, he eats nothing but ginger-nuts. My mind then ran on in reveries concerning the probable effects upon the human constitution of living entirely on ginger-nuts. Ginger-nuts are so called because they contain ginger as one of their peculiar constituents, and the final flavouring one. Now what was ginger? A hot, spicy thing. Was Bartleby hot and spicy? Not at all. Ginger, then, had no effect upon Bartleby. Probably he preferred it should have none.

Nothing so aggravates an earnest person as a passive resistance. If the individual so resisted be of a not inhumane temper, and the resisting one perfectly harmless in his passivity; then, in the better moods of the former, he will endeavour charitably to construe to his imagination what proves impossible to be solved by his judgment. Even so, for the most part, I regarded Bartleby and his ways. Poor fellow! thought I, he means no mischief; it is plain he intends no insolence; his aspect sufficiently evinces that his eccentricities are involuntary. He is useful to me. I can get along with him. If I turn him away, the chances are he will fall in with some less indulgent employer, and then he will be rudely treated, and perhaps driven forth miserably to starve. Yes. Here I can cheaply purchase a delicious self-approval. To befriend Bartleby; to humour him in his strange wilfulness, will cost me little or nothing, while I lay up in my soul what will eventually prove a sweet morsel for my conscience. But this mood was not invariable with me. The passiveness of Bartleby sometimes irritated me. I felt strangely goaded on to encounter him in new opposition, to elicit some angry spark from him answerable to my own. But indeed I might as well have essayed to strike fire with my knuckles against a bit of Windsor soap. But one afternoon the evil impulse in me mastered me, and the following little scene ensued:

"Bartleby," said I, "when those papers are all copied, I will compare them with you."

"I would prefer not to."

"How? Surely you do not mean to persist in that mulish vagary?"

No answer.

I threw open the folding-doors near by, and turning upon Turkey and Nippers, exclaimed in an excited manner:

"He says, a second time, he won't examine his papers. What do you think of it, Turkey?"

It was afternoon, be it remembered. Turkey sat glowing like a brass boiler, his bald head steaming, his hands reeling among his blotted papers.

"Think of it?" roared Turkey; "I think I'll just step behind his screen, and black his eyes for him!"

So saying, Turkey rose to his feet and threw his arms into a pugilistic position. He was hurrying away to make good his promise, when I detained him, alarmed at the effect of incautiously rousing Turkey's combativeness after dinner.

"Sit down, Turkey," said I, "and hear what Nippers has to say. What do you think of it, Nippers? Would I not be justified in immediately dismissing Bartleby?"

"Excuse me, that is for you to decide, sir. I think his conduct quite unusual, and indeed unjust, as regards Turkey and myself. But it may only be a passing whim."

"Ah," exclaimed I, "you have strangely changed your mind then—you speak very gently of him now."

"All beer," cried Turkey; "gentleness is effects of beer—Nippers and I dined together to-day. You see how gentle *I* am, sir. Shall I go and black his eyes?"

"You refer to Bartleby, I suppose. No, not to-day, Turkey," I replied; "pray, put up your fists."

I closed the doors, and again advanced towards Bartleby. I felt additional incentives tempting me to my fate. I burned to be rebelled against again. I remembered that Bartleby never left the office.

"Bartleby," said I, "Ginger Nut is away; just step round to the Post Office, won't you? (it was but a three minutes' walk), and see if there is anything for me."

"I would prefer not to."

"You *will* not?"

"I *prefer* not."

I staggered to my desk, and sat there in a deep study. My blind inveteracy returned. Was there any other thing in which I could procure myself to be ignominiously repulsed by this lean, penniless wight?—my hired clerk? What added thing is there, perfectly reasonable, that he will be sure to refuse to do?

"Bartleby!"

No answer.

"Bartleby," in a louder tone.

No answer.

"Bartleby," I roared.

Like a very ghost, agreeably to the laws of magical invocation, at the third summons, he appeared at the entrance of his hermitage.

"Go to the next room, and tell Nippers to come to me."

"I prefer not to," he respectfully and slowly said, and mildly disappeared.

"Very good, Bartleby," said I, in a quiet sort of serenely severe self-possessed tone, intimating the unalterable purpose of some terrible retribution very close at hand. At the moment I half intended something of the kind. But upon

the whole, as it was drawing towards my dinner-hour, I
thought it best to put on my hat and walk home for the day,
suffering much from perplexity and distress of mind.

Shall I acknowledge it? The conclusion of this whole
business was, that it soon became a fixed fact of my chambers, that a pale young scrivener, by the name of Bartleby,
had a desk there; that he copied for me at the usual rate
of four cents a folio (one hundred words); but he was
permanently exempt from examining the work done by him,
that duty being transferred to Turkey and Nippers, out of
compliment doubtless to their superior acuteness; moreover,
said Bartleby was never on any account to be despatched on
the most trivial errand of any sort; and that even if entreated to take upon him such a matter, it was generally
understood that he would prefer not to—in other words,
that he would refuse point-blank.

As days passed on, I became considerably reconciled to
Bartleby. His steadiness, his freedom from all dissipation,
his incessant industry (except when he chose to throw himself into a standing revery behind his screen), his great stillness, his unalterableness of demeanour under all circumstances, made him a valuable acquisition. One prime
thing was this,—*he was always there;*—first in the morning,
continually through the day, and the last at night. I had a
singular confidence in his honesty. I felt my most precious
papers perfectly safe in his hands. Sometimes to be sure I
could not, for the very soul of me, avoid falling into sudden
spasmodic passions with him. For it was exceeding difficult
to bear in mind all the time those strange peculiarities, privileges, and unheard of exemptions, forming the tacit stipu-
lations on Bartleby's part under which he remained in my
office. Now and then, in the eagerness of despatching pressing business, I would inadvertently summon Bartleby, in a
short, rapid tone, to put his finger, say, on the incipient tie
of a bit of red tape with which I was about compressing some
papers. Of course, from behind the screen the usual answer, "I prefer not to," was sure to come; and then, how
could a human creature with the common infirmities of our
nature, refrain from bitterly exclaiming upon such perverseness—such unreasonableness. However, every added repulse
of this sort which I received only tended to lessen the prob-
ability of my repeating the inadvertence.

Here it must be said, that according to the custom of
most legal gentlemen occupying chambers in densely-popu-
lated law buildings, there were several keys to my door.

One was kept by a woman residing in the attic, which person weekly scrubbed and daily swept and dusted my apartments. Another was kept by Turkey for convenience sake. The third I sometimes carried in my own pocket. The fourth I knew not who had.

Now, one Sunday morning I happened to go to Trinity Church, to hear a celebrated preacher, and finding myself rather early on the ground, I thought I would walk round to my chambers for awhile. Luckily I had my key with me; but upon applying it to the lock, I found it resisted by something inserted from the inside. Quite surprised, I called out; when to my consternation a key was turned from within; and thrusting his lean visage at me, and holding the door ajar, the apparition of Bartleby appeared, in his shirt sleeves, and otherwise in a strangely tattered dishabille, saying quietly that he was sorry, but he was deeply engaged just then, and—preferred not admitting me at present. In a brief word or two, he moreover added, that perhaps I had better walk round the block two or three times, and by that time he would probably have concluded his affairs.

Now, the utterly unsurmised appearance of Bartleby, tenanting my law-chambers of a Sunday morning, with his cadaverously gentlemanly *nonchalance*, yet withal firm and self-possessed, had such a strange effect upon me, that incontinently I slunk away from my own door, and did as desired. But not without sundry twinges of impotent rebellion against the mild effrontery of this unaccountable scrivener. Indeed, it was his wonderful mildness chiefly, which not only disarmed me, but unmanned me, as it were. For I consider that one, for the time, is in a way unmanned when he tranquilly permits his hired clerk to dictate to him, and order him away from his own premises. Furthermore, I was full of uneasiness as to what Bartleby could possibly be doing in my office in his shirt sleeves, and in an otherwise dismantled condition of a Sunday morning. Was anything amiss going on? Nay, that was out of the question. It was not to be thought of for a moment that Bartleby was an immoral person. But what could he be doing there—copying? Nay again, whatever might be his eccentricities, Bartleby was an eminently decorous person. He would be the last man to sit down to his desk in any state approaching to nudity. Besides, it was Sunday; and there was something about Bartleby that forbade the supposition that he would by any secular occupation violate the proprieties of the day.

Nevertheless, my mind was not pacified; and full of a

restless curiosity, at last I returned to the door. Without hindrance I inserted my key, opened it, and entered. Bartleby was not to be seen. I looked round anxiously, peeped behind his screen; but it was very plain that he was gone. Upon more closely examining the place, I surmised that for an indefinite period Bartleby must have ate, dressed, and slept in my office, and that too without plate, mirror, or bed. The cushioned seat of a ricketty old sofa in one corner bore the faint impress of a lean, reclining form. Rolled away under his desk, I found a blanket; under the empty grate, a blacking box and brush; on a chair, a tin basin, with soap and a ragged towel; in a newspaper a few crumbs of ginger-nuts and a morsel of cheese. Yes, thought I, it is evident enough that Bartleby has been making his home here, keeping bachelor's hall all by himself. Immediately then the thought came sweeping across me, What miserable friendlessness and loneliness are here revealed! His poverty is great; but his solitude, how horrible! Think of it. Of a Sunday, Wall street is deserted as Petra; and every night of every day it is an emptiness. This building too, which of week-days hums with industry and life, at nightfall echoes with sheer vacancy, and all through Sunday is forlorn. And here Bartleby makes his home; sole spectator of a solitude which he has seen all populous—a sort of innocent and transformed Marius brooding among the ruins of Carthage!

For the first time in my life a feeling of overpowering stinging melancholy seized me. Before, I had never experienced aught but a not-unpleasing sadness. The bond of a common humanity now drew me irresistibly to gloom. A fraternal melancholy! For both I and Bartleby were sons of Adam. I remembered the bright silks and sparkling faces I had seen that day, in gala trim, swan-like sailing down the Mississippi of Broadway; and I contrasted them with the pallid copyist, and thought to myself, Ah, happiness courts the light, so we deem the world is gay; but misery hides aloof, so we deem that misery there is none. These sad fancyings—chimeras, doubtless, of a sick and silly brain —led on to other and more special thoughts, concerning the eccentricities of Bartleby. Presentiments of strange discoveries hovered round me. The scrivener's pale form appeared to me laid out, among uncaring strangers, in its shivering winding sheet.

Suddenly I was attracted by Bartleby's closed desk, the key in open sight left in the lock.

I mean no mischief, seek the gratification of no heartless

curiosity, thought I; besides, the desk is mine, and its contents, too, so I will make bold to look within. Everything was methodically arranged, the papers smoothly placed. The pigeon holes were deep, and, removing the files of documents, I groped into their recesses. Presently I felt something there, and dragged it out. It was an old bandana handkerchief, heavy and knotted. I opened it, and saw it was a savings' bank.

I now recalled all the quiet mysteries which I had noted in the man. I remembered that he never spoke but to answer; that though at intervals he had considerable time to himself, yet I had never seen him reading—no, not even a newspaper; that for long periods he would stand looking out, at his pale window behind the screen, upon the dead brick wall; I was quite sure he never visited any refectory or eating-house; while his pale face clearly indicated that he never drank beer like Turkey, or tea and coffee even, like other men; that he never went anywhere in particular that I could learn; never went out for a walk, unless indeed that was the case at present; that he had declined telling who he was, or whence he came, or whether he had any relatives in the world; that though so thin and pale, he never complained of ill health. And more than all, I remembered a certain unconscious air of pallid—how shall I call it?—of pallid haughtiness, say, or rather an austere reserve about him, which had positively awed me into my tame compliance with his eccentricities, when I had feared to ask him to do the slightest incidental thing for me, even though I might know, from his long-continued motionlessness, that behind his screen he must be standing in one of those dead-wall reveries of his.

Revolving all these things, and coupling them with the recently discovered fact that he made my office his constant abiding place and home, and not forgetful of his morbid moodiness; revolving all these things, a prudential feeling began to steal over me. My first emotions had been those of pure melancholy and sincerest pity; but just in proportion as the forlornness of Bartleby grew and grew to my imagination, did that same melancholy merge into fear, that pity into repulsion. So true it is, and so terrible, too, that up to a certain point the thought or sight of misery enlists our best affections; but, in certain special cases, beyond that point it does not. They err who would assert that invariably this is owing to the inherent selfishness of the human heart. It rather proceeds from a certain hopelessness of remedying excessive and organic ill. To a sensitive being, pity is not seldom pain. And when at last it is perceived that such pity cannot lead to effectual succour, common sense bids the soul be rid of it. What I saw that morning persuaded me that the scrivener was the victim of innate and incurable disorder. I might give alms to his body; but his body did not pain him; it was his soul that suffered, and his soul I could not reach.

I did not accomplish the purpose of going to Trinity Church that morning. Somehow, the things I had seen disqualified me for the time from church-going. I walked homeward, thinking what I would do with Bartleby. Finally, I resolved upon this:—I would put certain calm questions to him the next morning, touching his history, &c., and if he declined to answer them openly and unreservedly (and I supposed he would prefer not), then to give him a twenty dollar bill over and above whatever I might owe him, and tell him his services were no longer required; but that if in any other way I could assist him, I would be happy to do so, especially if he desired to return to his native place, wherever that might be, I would willingly help to defray the expenses. Moreover, if, after reaching home, he found himself at any time in want of aid, a letter from him would be sure of a reply.

The next morning came.

"Bartleby," said I, gently calling to him behind his screen. No reply.

"Bartleby," said I, in a still gentler tone, "come here; I am not going to ask you to do anything you would prefer not to do—I simply wish to speak to you."

Upon this he noiselessly slid into view.

"Will you tell me, Bartleby, where you were born?"

"I would prefer not to."

"Will you tell me *anything* about yourself?"

"I would prefer not to."

"But what reasonable objection can you have to speak to me? I feel friendly towards you."

He did not look at me while I spoke, but kept his glance fixed upon my bust of Cicero, which, as I then sat, was directly behind me, some six inches above my head.

"What is your answer, Bartleby?" said I, after waiting a considerable time for a reply, during which his countenance remained immovable, only there was the faintest conceivable tremor of the white attenuated mouth.

"At present I prefer to give no answer," he said, and retired into his hermitage.

It was rather weak in me I confess, but his manner on this occasion nettled me. Not only did there seem to lurk in it a certain calm disdain, but his perverseness seemed ungrateful, considering the undeniable good usage and indulgence he had received from me.

Again I sat ruminating what I should do. Mortified as I was at his behaviour, and resolved as I had been to dismiss him when I entered my office, nevertheless I strangely felt something superstitious knocking at my heart, and forbidding me to carry out my purpose, and denouncing me for a villain if I dared to breathe one bitter word against this forlornest of mankind. At last, familiarly drawing my chair behind his screen, I sat down and said: "Bartleby, never mind then about revealing your history; but let me entreat you, as a friend, to comply as far as may be with the usages of this office. Say now you will help to examine papers tomorrow or next day: in short, say now that in a day or two you will begin to be a little reasonable:—say so, Bartleby."

"At present I would prefer not to be a little reasonable," was his mildly cadaverous reply.

Just then the folding-doors opened, and Nippers approached. He seemed suffering from an unusually bad night's rest, induced by severer indigestion than common. He overheard those final words of Bartleby.

"*Prefer not,* eh?" gritted Nippers—"I'd *prefer* him, if I were you, sir," addressing me—"I'd *prefer* him; I'd give him preferences, the stubborn mule! What is it, sir, pray, that he *prefers* not to do now?"

Bartleby moved not a limb.

"Mr. Nippers," said I, "I'd prefer that you would withdraw for the present."

Somehow, of late I had got into the way of involuntarily using this word "prefer" upon all sorts of not exactly suitable occasions. And I trembled to think that my contact with the scrivener had already and seriously affected me in a mental way. And what further and deeper aberration might it not yet produce? This apprehension had not been without efficacy in determining me to summary means.

As Nippers, looking very sour and sulky, was departing, Turkey blandly and deferentially approached.

"With submission, sir," said he, "yesterday I was thinking about Bartleby here, and I think that if he would but prefer to take a quart of good ale every day, it would do much towards mending him, and enabling him to assist in examining his papers."

"So you have got the word, too," said I, slightly excited.

"With submission, what word, sir," asked Turkey, respectfully crowding himself into the contracted space behind the screen, and by so doing, making me jostle the scrivener. "What word, sir?"

"I would prefer to be left alone here," said Bartleby, as if offended at being mobbed in his privacy.

"*That's* the word, Turkey," said I—"*that's* it."

"Oh, *prefer?* oh, yes—queer word. I never use it myself. But, sir, as I was saying, if he would but prefer—"

"Turkey," interrupted I, "you will please withdraw."

"Oh certainly, sir, if you prefer that I should."

As he opened the folding-door to retire, Nippers at his desk caught a glimpse of me, and asked whether I would prefer to have a certain paper copied on blue paper or white. He did not in the least roguishly accent the word prefer. It was plain that it involuntarily rolled from his tongue. I thought to myself, surely I must get rid of a demented man, who already has in some degree turned the tongues, if not the heads, of myself and clerks. But I thought it prudent not to break the dismission at once.

The next day I noticed that Bartleby did nothing but stand at his window in his dead-wall revery. Upon asking him why he did not write, he said that he had decided upon doing no more writing.

"Why, how now? what next?" exclaimed I, "do no more writing?"

"No more."

"And what is the reason?"

"Do you not see the reason for yourself?" he indifferently replied.

I looked steadfastly at him, and perceived that his eyes looked dull and glazed. Instantly it occurred to me, that his unexampled diligence in copying by his dim window for the first few weeks of his stay with me might have temporarily impaired his vision.

I was touched. I said something in condolence with him. I hinted that, of course, he did wisely in abstaining from writing for a while, and urged him to embrace that opportunity of taking wholesome exercise in the open air. This, however, he did not do. A few days after this, my other clerks being absent, and being in a great hurry to despatch certain letters by the mail, I thought that, having nothing else earthly to do, Bartleby would surely be less inflexible than usual, and carry these letters to the Post Office. But he blankly declined. So, much to my inconvenience, I went myself.

Still added days went by. Whether Bartleby's eyes improved or not, I could not say. To all appearance, I thought they did. But when I asked him if they did, he vouchsafed no answer. At all events, he would do no copying. At last, in reply to my urgings, he informed me that he had permanently given up copying.

"What!" exclaimed I; "suppose your eyes should get entirely well—better than ever before—would you not copy then?"

"I have given up copying," he answered and slid aside.

He remained, as ever, a fixture in my chamber. Nay—if that were possible—he became still more of a fixture than before. What was to be done? He would do nothing in the office: why should he stay there? In plain fact, he had now become a millstone to me, not only useless as a necklace, but afflictive to bear. Yet I was sorry for him. I speak less than truth when I say that, on his own account, he occasioned me uneasiness. If he would but have named a single relative or friend, I would instantly have written, and urged their taking the poor fellow away to some convenient retreat. But he seemed alone, absolutely alone in the universe. A bit of wreckage in the mid-Atlantic. At length, necessities connected with my business tyrannized over all other considerations. Decently as I could, I told Bartleby that in six days' time he must unconditionally leave the office. I warned him to take measures, in the interval, for procuring some other abode. I offered to assist him in this endeavour, if he himself would but take the first step towards a removal. "And when you finally quit me, Bartleby," added I, "I shall see that you go away not entirely unprovided. Six days from this hour, remember."

At the expiration of that period, I peeped behind the screen, and lo! Bartleby was there.

I buttoned up my coat, balanced myself; advanced slowly towards him, touched his shoulder, and said, "The time has come; you must quit this place; I am sorry for you; here is money; but you must go."

"I would prefer not," he replied, with his back still towards me.

"You *must*."

He remained silent.

Now I had an unbounded confidence in this man's common honesty. He had frequently restored to me sixpences and shillings carelessly dropped upon the floor, for I am apt to be very reckless in such shirt-button affairs. The proceeding then which followed will not be deemed extraordinary.

"Bartleby," said I, "I owe you twelve dollars on account; here are thirty-two; the odd twenty are yours.—Will you take it?" and I handed the bills towards him.

But he made no motion.

"I will leave them here then," putting them under a weight on the table. Then taking my hat and cane and going to the door, I tranquilly turned and added—"After you have removed your things from these offices, Bartleby, you will of course lock the door—since every one is now gone for the day but you—and if you please, slip your key underneath the mat, so that I may have it in the morning. I shall not see you again; so good-bye to you. If hereafter in your new place of abode I can be of any service to you, do not fail to advise me by letter. Good-bye, Bartleby, and fare you well."

But he answered not a word; like the last column of some ruined temple, he remained standing mute and solitary in the middle of the otherwise deserted room.

As I walked home in a pensive mood, my vanity got the better of my pity. I could not but highly plume myself on my masterly management in getting rid of Bartleby. Masterly I call it, and such it must appear to any dispassionate thinker. The beauty of my procedure seemed to consist in its perfect quietness. There was no vulgar bullying, no bravado of any sort, no choleric hectoring, no striding to and fro across the apartment, jerking out vehement commands for Bartleby to bundle himself off with his beggarly traps. Nothing of the kind. Without loudly bidding Bartleby depart—as an inferior genius might have done—I *assumed* the ground that depart he must; and upon that assumption built all I had to say. The more I thought over my procedure, the more I was charmed with it. Nevertheless, next morning, upon awakening, I had my doubts,—I had somehow slept off the fumes of vanity. One of the coolest and wisest hours a man has, is just after he awakes in the morning. My procedure seemed as sagacious as ever,—but only in theory. How it would prove in practice—there was the rub. It was truly a beautiful thought to have assumed Bartleby's departure; but, after all, that assumption was simply my own, and none of Bartleby's. The great point was, not whether I had assumed that he would quit me, but whether he would prefer so to do. He was more a man of preferences than assumptions.

After breakfast, I walked down town, arguing the probabilities *pro* and *con*. One moment I thought it would prove a miserable failure, and Bartleby would be found all alive at my office as usual; the next moment it seemed certain that I should see his chair empty. And so I kept veering about. At the corner of Broadway and Canal Street, I saw quite an excited group of people standing in earnest conversation.

"I'll take odds he doesn't," said a voice as I passed.

"Doesn't go?—done!" said I, "put up your money."

I was instinctively putting my hand in my pocket to produce my own, when I remembered that this was an election day. The words I had overheard bore no reference to Bartleby, but to the success or non-success of some candidate for the mayoralty. In my intent frame of mind, I had, as it were, imagined that all Broadway shared in my excitement, and were debating the same question with me. I passed on, very thankful that the uproar of the street screened my momentary absent-mindedness.

As I had intended, I was earlier than usual at my office door. I stood listening for a moment. All was still. He must be gone. I tried the knob. The door was locked. Yes, my procedure had worked to a charm; he indeed must be vanished. Yet a certain melancholy mixed with this: I was almost sorry for my brilliant success. I was fumbling under the door mat for the key, which Bartleby was to have left there for me, when accidentally my knee knocked against a panel, producing a summoning sound, and in response a voice came to me from within—"Not yet; I am occupied."

It was Bartleby.

I was thunderstruck. For an instant I stood like the man who, pipe in mouth, was killed one cloudless afternoon long ago in Virginia, by summer lightning; at his own warm open window he was killed, and remained leaning out there upon the dreamy afternoon, till some one touched him, and he fell.

"Not gone!" I murmured at last. But again obeying that wondrous ascendency which the inscrutable scrivener had over me—and from which ascendency, for all my chafing, I could not completely escape—I slowly went down stairs and out into the street, and while walking round the block, considered what I should next do in this unheard-of perplexity. Turn the man out by an actual thrusting I could

not; to drive him away by calling him hard names would
not do; calling in the police was an unpleasant idea; and yet,
permit him to enjoy his cadaverous triumph over me,—this
too I could not think of. What was to be done? or, if nothing
could be done, was there anything further that I could *assume* in the matter? Yes, as before I had prospectively assumed that Bartleby would depart, so now I might retro-
spectively assume that departed he was. In the legitimate
carrying out of this assumption, I might enter my office in
a great hurry, and pretending not to see Bartleby at all,
walk straight against him as if he were air. Such a proceeding would in a singular degree have the appearance of a
home-thrust. It was hardly possible that Bartleby could with-
stand such an application of the doctrine of assumptions.
But, upon second thought, the success of the plan seemed
rather dubious. I resolved to argue the matter over with him
again.

"Bartleby," said I, entering the office, with a quietly severe
expression, "I am seriously displeased. I am pained, Bartleby. I had thought better of you. I had imagined you of
such a gentlemanly organization, that in any delicate dilemma a slight hint would suffice—in short, an assumption;
but it appears I am deceived. Why," I added, unaffectedly
starting, "you have not even touched that money yet," pointing to it, just where I had left it the evening previous.

He answered nothing.

"Will you, or will you not, quit me?" I now demanded
in a sudden passion, advancing close to him.

"I would prefer *not* to quit you," he replied, gently em-
phasizing the *not*.

"What earthly right have you to stay here? Do you pay
any rent? Do you pay my taxes? Or is this property yours?"

He answered nothing.

"Are you ready to go on and write now? Are your eyes
recovered? Could you copy a small paper for me this morning? or help examine a few lines? or step round to the Post
Office? In a word, will you do any thing at all, to give a
colouring to your refusal to depart the premises?"

He silently retired into his hermitage.

I was now in such a state of nervous resentment that I
thought it but prudent to check myself, at present, from
further demonstrations. Bartleby and I were alone. I remembered the tragedy of the unfortunate Adams and the
still more unfortunate Colt in the solitary office of the latter; and how poor Colt, being dreadfully incensed by Adams,

and imprudently permitting himself to get wildly excited, was at unawares hurried into his fatal act—an act which certainly no man could possibly deplore more than the actor himself. Often it had occurred to me in my ponderings upon the subject, that had that altercation taken place in the public street, or at a private residence, it would not have terminated as it did. It was the circumstance of being alone in a solitary office, upstairs, of a building entirely unhallowed by humanizing domestic associations—an uncarpeted office, doubtless, of a dusty, haggard sort of appearance;—this it must have been, which greatly helped to enhance the irritable desperation of the hapless Colt.

But when this old Adam of resentment rose in me and tempted me concerning Bartleby, I grappled him and threw him. How? Why, simply by recalling the divine injunction: "A new commandment give I unto you, that ye love one another." Yes, this it was that saved me. Aside from higher considerations, charity often operates as a vastly wise and prudent principle—a great safeguard to its possessor. Men have committed murder for jealousy's sake, and anger's sake, and hatred's sake, and selfishness' sake, and spiritual pride's sake; but no man that ever I heard of, ever committed a diabolical murder for sweet charity's sake. Mere self-interest, then, if no better motive can be enlisted, should, especially with high-tempered men, prompt all beings to charity and philanthropy. At any rate, upon the occasion in question, I strove to drown my exasperated feelings toward the scrivener by benevolently construing his conduct. Poor fellow, poor fellow! thought I, he doesn't mean any thing; and besides, he has seen hard times, and ought to be indulged.

I endeavoured also immediately to occupy myself, and at the same time to comfort my despondency. I tried to fancy that in the course of the morning, at such time as might prove agreeable to him, Bartleby, of his own free accord, would emerge from his hermitage, and take up some decided line of march in the direction of the door. But no. Half-past twelve o'clock came; Turkey began to glow in the face, overturn his inkstand, and become generally obstreperous; Nippers abated down into quietude and courtesy; Ginger Nut munched his noon apple; and Bartleby remained standing at his window in one of his profoundest dead-wall reveries. Will it be credited? Ought I to acknowledge it? That afternoon I left the office without saying one further word to him.

Some days now passed, during which at leisure intervals

I looked a little into "Edwards on the Will," and "Priestley on Necessity." Under the circumstances, those books induced a salutary feeling. Gradually I slid into the persuasion that these troubles of mine, touching the scrivener, had been all predestinated from eternity, and Bartleby was billeted upon me for some mysterious purpose of an all-wise Providence, which it was not for a mere mortal like me to fathom. Yes, Bartleby, stay there behind your screen, thought I; I shall persecute you no more; you are harmless and noiseless as any of these old chairs; in short, I never feel so private as when I know you are here. At least I see it, I feel it; I penetrate to the predestinated purpose of my life. I am content. Others may have loftier parts to enact; but my mission in this world, Bartleby, is to furnish you with office room for such period as you may see fit to remain.

I believe that this wise and blessed frame of mind would have continued with me had it not been for the unsolicited and uncharitable remarks obtruded upon me by my professional friends who visited the rooms. But thus it often is, that the constant friction of illiberal minds wears out at last the best resolves of the more generous. Though to be sure, when I reflected upon it, it was not strange that people entering my office should be struck by the peculiar aspect of the unaccountable Bartleby, and so be tempted to throw out some sinister observations concerning him. Sometimes an attorney having business with me, and calling at my office, and finding no one but the scrivener there, would undertake to obtain some sort of precise information from him touching my whereabouts; but without heeding his idle talk, Bartleby would remain standing immovable in the middle of the room. So, after contemplating him in that position for a time, the attorney would depart, no wiser than he came.

Also, when a Reference was going on, and the room full of lawyers and witnesses and business was driving fast, some deeply occupied legal gentleman present, seeing Bartleby wholly unemployed, would request him to run round to his (the legal gentleman's) office and fetch some papers for him. Thereupon, Bartleby would tranquilly decline, and yet remain idle as before. Then the lawyer would give a great stare, and turn to me. And what could I say? At last I was made aware that all through the circle of my professional acquaintance, a whisper of wonder was running round, having reference to the strange creature I kept at my office. This worried me very much. And as the idea came upon me of his possibly turning out a long-lived man, and keep occupying my chambers, and denying my authority; and perplexing my visitors; and scandalizing my professional reputation; and casting a general gloom over the premises; keeping soul and body together to the last upon his savings (for doubtless he spent but half a dime a day), and in the end perhaps outlive me, and claim possession of my office by right of his perpetual occupancy: as all these dark anticipations crowded upon me more and more, and my friends continually intruded their relentless remarks upon the apparition in my room, a great change was wrought in me. I resolved to gather all my faculties together, and for ever rid me of this intolerable incubus.

Ere revolving any complicated project, however, adapted to this end, I first simply suggested to Bartleby the propriety of his permanent departure. In a calm and serious tone, I commended the idea to his careful and mature consideration. But having taken three days to meditate upon it, he apprised me that his original determination remained the same; in short, that he still preferred to abide with me.

What shall I do? I now said to myself, buttoning up my coat to the last button. What shall I do? what ought I to do? what does conscience say I *should* do with this man, or rather ghost? Rid myself of him, I must; go, he shall. But how? You will not thrust him, the poor, pale, passive mortal, —you will not thrust such a helpless creature out of your door? you will not dishonour yourself by such cruelty? No, I will not, I cannot do that. Rather would I let him live and die here, and then mason up his remains in the wall. What then will you do? For all your coaxing, he will not budge. Bribes he leaves under your own paper-weight on your table; in short, it is quite plain that he prefers to cling to you.

Then something severe, something unusual must be done. What! surely you will not have him collared by a constable, and commit his innocent pallor to the common jail? And upon what ground could you procure such a thing to be done?—a vagrant, is he? What! he a vagrant, a wanderer, who refuses to budge? It is because he will *not* be a vagrant, then, that you seek to count him *as* a vagrant. That is too absurd. No visible means of support: there I have him. Wrong again: for indubitably he *does* support himself, and that is the only unanswerable proof that any man can show of his possessing the means so to do. No more then. Since he will not quit me, I must quit him. I will change my offices; I will move elsewhere; and give him fair notice, that if I find him on my new premises I will then proceed against him as a common trespasser.

Acting accordingly, next day I thus addressed him: "I find these chambers too far from the City Hall; the air is unwholesome. In a word, I propose to remove my offices next week, and shall no longer require your services. I tell you this now, in order that you may seek another place."

He made no reply, and nothing more was said.

On the appointed day I engaged carts and men, proceeded to my chambers, and having but little furniture, everything was removed in a few hours. Throughout all, the scrivener remained standing behind the screen, which I directed to be removed the last thing. It was withdrawn; and being folded up like a huge folio, left him the motionless occupant of a naked room. I stood in the entry watching him a moment, while something from within me upbraided me.

I re-entered, with my hand in my pocket—and—and my heart in my mouth.

"Good-bye, Bartleby; I am going—good-bye, and God some way bless you; and take that," slipping something in his hand. But it dropped upon the floor and then—strange to say—I tore myself from him whom I had so longed to be rid of.

Established in my new quarters, for a day or two I kept the door locked, and started at every footfall in the passages. When I returned to my rooms after any little absence, I would pause at the threshold for an instant, and attentively listen, ere applying my key. But these fears were needless. Bartleby never came nigh me.

I thought all was going well, when a perturbed looking stranger visited me, inquiring whether I was the person who had recently occupied rooms at No. —— Wall street.

Full of forebodings, I replied that I was.

"Then sir," said the stranger, who proved a lawyer, "you are responsible for the man you left there. He refuses to do any copying, he refuses to do anything; and he says he prefers not to; and he refuses to quit the premises."

"I am very sorry, sir," said I, with assumed tranquillity, but an inward tremor, "but, really, the man you allude to is nothing to me—he is no relation or apprentice of mine, that you should hold me responsible for him."

"In mercy's name, who is he?"

"I certainly cannot inform you. I know nothing about him. Formerly I employed him as a copyist; but he has done nothing for me now for some time past."

"I shall settle him then,—good morning, sir."

Several days passed, and I heard nothing more; and though I often felt a charitable prompting to call at the place and see poor Bartleby, yet a certain squeamishness of I know not what withheld me.

All is over with him, by this time, thought I at last, when through another week no further intelligence reached me. But coming to my room the day after, I found several persons waiting at my door in a high state of nervous excitement.

"That's the man—here he comes," cried the foremost one, whom I recognized as the lawyer who had previously called upon me alone.

"You must take him away, sir, at once," cried a portly person among them, advancing upon me, and whom I knew to be the landlord of No. —— Wall street. "These gentlemen, my tenants, cannot stand it any longer; Mr. B——," pointing to the lawyer, "has turned him out of his room, and he now persists in haunting the building generally, sitting upon the banisters of the stairs by day, and sleeping in the entry by night. Everybody here is concerned; clients are leaving the offices; some fears are entertained of a mob; something you must do, and that without delay."

Aghast at this torrent, I feel back before it, and would fain have locked myself in my new quarters. In vain I persisted that Bartleby was nothing to me—no more than to any one else there. In vain:—I was the last person known to have anything to do with him, and they held me to the terrible account. Fearful then of being exposed in the papers (as one person present obscurely threatened) I considered the matter, and at length said, that if the lawyer would give me a confidential interview with the scrivener, in his (the lawyer's) own room, I would that afternoon strive my best to rid them of the nuisance they complained of.

Going up stairs to my old haunt, there was Bartleby silently sitting upon the banister at the landing.

"What are you doing here, Bartleby?" said I.

"Sitting upon the banister," he mildly replied.

I motioned him into the lawyer's room, who then left us.

"Bartleby," said I, "are you aware that you are the cause of great tribulation to me, by persisting in occupying the entry after being dismissed from the office?"

No answer.

"Now one of two things must take place. Either you must do something, or something must be done to you. Now what sort of business would you like to engage in? Would you like to re-engage in copying for some one?"

"No; I would prefer not to make any change."

"Would you like a clerkship in a dry-goods store?"

"There is too much confinement about that. No, I would not like a clerkship; but I am not particular."

"Too much confinement," I cried, "why you keep yourself confined all the time!"

"I would prefer not to take a clerkship," he rejoined, as if to settle that little item at once.

"How would a bartender's business suit you? There is no trying of the eyesight in that."

"I would not like it at all; though, as I said before, I am not particular."

His unwonted wordiness inspirited me. I returned to the charge.

"Well then, would you like to travel through the country collecting bills for the merchants? That would improve your health."

"No, I would prefer to be doing something else."

"How then would going as a companion to Europe to entertain some young gentleman with your conversation,—how would that suit you?"

"Not at all. It does not strike me that there is anything definite about that. I like to be stationary. But I am not particular."

"Stationary you shall be then," I cried, now losing all patience, and for the first time in all my exasperating connection with him fairly flying into a passion. "If you do not go away from these premises before night, I shall feel bound —indeed I *am* bound—to—to—to quit the premises myself!" I rather absurdly concluded, knowing not with what possible threat to try to frighten his immobility into compliance. Despairing of all further efforts, I was precipitately leaving him, when a final thought occurred to me— one which had not been wholly unindulged before.

"Bartleby," said I, in the kindest tone I could assume under such exciting circumstances, "will you go home with me now—not to my office, but my dwelling—and remain there till we can conclude upon some convenient arrangement for you at our leisure? Come, let us start now, right away."

"No: at present I would prefer not to make any change at all."

I answered nothing; but effectually dodging every one by

the suddenness and rapidity of my flight, rushed from the building, ran up Wall street toward Broadway, and then jumping into the first omnibus was soon removed from pursuit. As soon as tranquillity returned I distinctly perceived that I had now done all that I possibly could, both in respect to the demands of the landlord and his tenants, and with regard to my own desire and sense of duty, to benefit Bartleby, and shield him from rude persecution. I now strove to be entirely care-free and quiescent; and my conscience justified me in the attempt; though indeed it was not so successful as I could have wished. So fearful was I of being again hunted out by the incensed landlord and his exasperated tenants, that, surrendering my business to Nippers, for a few days I drove about the upper part of the town and through the suburbs, in my rockaway; crossed over to Jersey City and Hoboken, and paid fugitive visits to Manhattanville and Astoria. In fact I almost lived in my rockaway for the time.

When again I entered my office, lo, a note from the landlord lay upon the desk. I opened it with trembling hands. It informed me that the writer had sent to the police, and had Bartleby removed to the Tombs as a vagrant. Moreover, since I knew more about him than any one else, he wished me to appear at that place, and make a suitable statement of the facts. These tidings had a conflicting effect upon me. At first I was indignant; but at last almost approved. The landlord's energetic, summary disposition had led him to adopt a procedure which I do not think I would have decided upon myself; and yet as a last resort, under such peculiar circumstances, it seemed the only plan.

As I afterwards learned, the poor scrivener, when told that he must be conducted to the Tombs, offered not the slightest obstacle, but in his own pale, unmoving way silently acquiesced.

Some of the compassionate and curious bystanders joined the party; and headed by one of the constables, arm-in-arm with Bartleby the silent procession filed its way through all the noise, and heat, and joy of the roaring thoroughfares at noon.

The same day I received the note I went to the Tombs, or, to speak more properly, the Halls of Justice. Seeking the right officer, I stated the purpose of my call, and was informed that the individual I described was indeed within. I then assured the functionary that Bartleby was a perfectly honest man, and greatly to be a compassionated (however unaccountable) eccentric. I narrated all I knew, and closed by suggesting the idea of letting him remain in as indulgent confinement as possible till something less harsh might be done—though indeed I hardly knew what. At all events, if nothing else could be decided upon, the alms-house must receive him. I then begged to have an interview.

Being under no disgraceful charge, and quite serene and harmless in all his ways, they had permitted him freely to wander about the prison, and especially in the inclosed grass-platted yards thereof. And so I found him there, standing all alone in the quietest of the yards, his face toward a high wall —while all around, from the narrow slits of the jail windows, I thought I saw peering out upon him the eyes of murderers and thieves.

"Bartleby!"

"I know you," he said, without looking round,—"and I want nothing to say to you."

"It was not I that brought you here, Bartleby," said I, keenly pained at his implied suspicion. "And to you, this should not be so vile a place. Nothing reproachful attaches to you by being here. And see, it is not so sad a place as one might think. Look, there is the sky and here is the grass."

"I know where I am," he replied, but would say nothing more, and so I left him.

As I entered the corridor again a broad, meat-like man in an apron accosted me, and jerking his thumb over his shoulder said—"Is that your friend?"

"Yes."

"Does he want to starve? If he does, let him live on the prison fare, that's all."

"Who are you?" asked I, not knowing what to make of such an unofficially speaking person in such a place.

"I am the grub-man. Such gentlemen as have friends here, hire me to provide them with something good to eat."

"Is this so?" said I, turning to the turnkey.

He said it was.

"Well then," said I, slipping some silver into the grub-man's hands (for so they called him), "I want you to give particular attention to my friend there; let him have the best dinner you can get. And you must be as polite to him as possible."

"Introduce me, will you?" said the grub-man, looking at me with an expression which seemed to say he was all impatience for an opportunity to give a specimen of his breeding.

Thinking it would prove of benefit to the scrivener, I

acquiesced; and asking the grub-man his name, went up with him to Bartleby.

"Bartleby, this is Mr. Cutlets; you will find him very useful to you."

"Your sarvant, sir, your sarvant," said the grub-man, making a low salutation behind his apron. "Hope you find it pleasant here, sir;—spacious grounds—cool apartments, sir —hope you'll stay with us some time—try to make it agreeable. May Mrs. Cutlets and I have the pleasure of your company to dinner, sir, in Mrs. Cutlets' private room?"

"I prefer not to dine to-day," said Bartleby, turning away. "It would disagree with me; I am unused to dinners." So saying, he slowly moved to the other side of the inclosure and took up a position fronting the dead-wall.

"How's this?" said the grub-man, addressing me with a stare of astonishment. "He's odd, ain't he?"

"I think he is a little deranged," said I, sadly.

"Deranged? deranged is it? Well now, upon my word, I thought that friend of yourn was a gentleman forger; they are always pale and genteel-like, them forgers. I can't help pity 'em—can't help it, sir. Did you know Monroe Edwards?" he added touchingly, and paused. Then, laying his hand pityingly on my shoulder, sighed, "he died of the consumption at Sing-Sing. So you weren't acquainted with Monroe?"

"No, I was never socially acquainted with any forgers. But I cannot stop longer. Look to my friend yonder. You will not lose by it. I will see you again."

Some few days after this, I again obtained admission to the Tombs, and went through the corridors in quest of Bartleby; but without finding him.

"I saw him coming from his cell not long ago," said a turnkey, "maybe he's gone to loiter in the yards."

So I went in that direction.

"Are you looking for the silent man?" said another turnkey passing me. "Yonder he lies—sleeping in the yard there. 'Tis not twenty minutes since I saw him lie down."

The yard was entirely quiet. It was not accessible to the common prisoners. The surrounding walls, of amazing thickness, kept off all sounds behind them. The Egyptian character of the masonry weighed upon me with its gloom. But a soft imprisoned turf grew under foot. The heart of the eternal pyramids, it seemed, wherein by some strange magic, through the clefts grass-seed, dropped by birds, had sprung. Strangely huddled at the base of the wall—his knees

drawn up, and lying on his side, his head touching the cold
stones—I saw the wasted Bartleby. But nothing stirred. I
paused; then went close up to him; stooped over, and saw
that his dim eyes were open; otherwise he seemed profoundly
sleeping. Something prompted me to touch him. I felt his
hand, when a tingling shiver ran up my arm and down my
spine to my feet.

The round face of the grub-man peered upon me now.
"His dinner is ready. Won't he dine to-day, either? Or does
he live without dining?"

"Lives without dining," said I, and closed the eyes.

"Eh!—He's asleep, ain't he?"

"With kings and counsellors," murmured I.

There would seem little need for proceeding further in
this history. Imagination will readily supply the meagre
recital of poor Bartleby's interment. But ere parting with the
reader, let me say, that if this little narrative has sufficiently
interested him, to awaken curiosity as to who Bartleby
was, and what manner of life he led prior to the present
narrator's making his acquaintance, I can only reply, that
in such curiosity I fully share—but am wholly unable to
gratify it. Yet here I hardly know whether I should divulge
one little item of rumour, which came to my ear a few
months after the scrivener's decease. Upon what basis it
rested, I could never ascertain; and hence, how true it is I
cannot now tell. But inasmuch as this vague report has not
been without a certain strange suggestive interest to me, however said, it may prove the same with some others; and so I
will briefly mention it. The report was this: that Bartleby
had been a subordinate clerk in the Dead Letter Office at
Washington, from which he had been suddenly removed by
a change in the administration. When I think over this
rumour I cannot adequately express the emotions which
seize me. Dead letters! does it not sound like dead men?
Conceive a man by nature and misfortune prone to a pallid
hopelessness: can any business seem more fitted to heighten
it than that of continually handling these dead letters, and
assorting them for the flames? For by the cartload they are
annually burned. Sometimes from out the folded paper the
pale clerk takes a ring:—the finger it was meant for, perhaps, moulders in the grave; a bank-note sent in swiftest
charity:—he whom it would relieve, nor eats nor hungers any
more; pardon for those who died despairing; hope for those

who died unhoping; good tidings for those who died stifled by unrelieved calamities. On errands of life, these letters speed to death.

Ah Bartleby! Ah humanity!

HENRY JAMES

An International Episode

PART I

FOUR YEARS ago, in 1874, two young Englishmen had occasion to go to the United States. They crossed the ocean at midsummer, and, arriving in New York on the first day of August, were much struck with the fervid temperature of that city. Disembarking upon the wharf, they climbed into one of those huge high-hung coaches which convey passengers to the hotels, and, with a great deal of bouncing and bumping, took their course through Broadway. The midsummer aspect of New York is not, perhaps, the most favorable one; still, it is not without its picturesque and even brilliant side. Nothing could well resemble less a typical English street than the interminable avenue, rich in incongruities, through which our two travellers advanced—looking out on each side of them at the comfortable animation of the sidewalks, the high-colored, heterogeneous architecture, the huge, white marble façades glittering in the strong, crude light, and bedizened with gilded lettering, the multifarious awnings, banners, and streamers, the extraordinary number of omnibuses, horse-cars, and other democratic vehicles, the venders of cooling fluids, the white trousers and big straw-hats of the policemen, the tripping gait of the modish young persons on the pavement, the general brightness, newness, juvenility, both of people and things. The young men had exchanged few observations; but in crossing Union Square, in front of the monument to Washington—in the very shadow, indeed, projected by the image of the *pater patriæ*—one of them remarked to the other, "It seems a rum-looking place."

"Ah, very odd, very odd," said the other, who was the clever man of the two.

"Pity it's so beastly hot," resumed the first speaker, after a pause.

"You know we are in a low latitude," said his friend.

"I dare say," remarked the other.

"I wonder," said the second speaker, presently, "if they can give one a bath?"

"I dare say not," rejoined the other.

"Oh, I say!" cried his comrade.

This animated discussion was checked by their arrival at the hotel, which had been recommended to them by an American gentleman whose acquaintance they made—with whom, indeed, they became very intimate—on the steamer, and who had proposed to accompany them to the inn and introduce them, in a friendly way, to the proprietor. This plan, however, had been defeated by their friend's finding that his "partner" was awaiting him on the wharf, and that his commercial associate desired him instantly to come and give his attention to certain telegrams received from St. Louis. But the two Englishmen, with nothing but their national prestige and personal graces to recommend them, were very well received at the hotel, which had an air of capacious hospitality. They found that a bath was not unattainable, and were indeed struck with the facilities for prolonged and reiterated immersion with which their apartment was supplied. After bathing a good deal—more, indeed, than they had ever done before on a single occasion—they made their way into the dining-room of the hotel, which was a spacious restaurant, with a fountain in the middle, a great many tall plants in ornamental tubs, and an array of French waiters. The first dinner on land after a sea-voyage is, under any circumstances, a delightful occasion, and there was something particularly agreeable in the circumstances in which our young Englishmen found themselves. They were extremely good-natured young men; they were more observant than they appeared; in a sort of inarticulate, accidentally dissimulative fashion, they were highly appreciative. This was, perhaps, especially the case with the elder, who was also, as I have said, the man of talent. They sat down at a little table, which was a very different affair from the great clattering see-saw in the saloon of the steamer. The wide doors and windows of the restaurants stood open, beneath large awnings, to a wide pavement, where there were other plants in tubs and rows of spreading trees, and beyond which there was a large, shady square, without any palings, and with marble-paved walks. And above the vivid verdure rose other façades of white marble and of pale chocolate-colored stone, squaring themselves against the deep blue sky. Here, outside, in the light and the shade and the heat, there was a great tinkling of the bells of innumerable street-cars, and a constant strolling and shuffling and rustling of many pedestrians, a large proportion of whom were young women in Pompadour-looking dresses. Within, the place was cool and vaguely lighted, with the plash of water, the odor of flowers, and the flitting of French waiters, as I have said, upon soundless carpets.

"It's rather like Paris, you know," said the younger of our two travellers.

"It's like Paris—only more so," his companion rejoined.

"I suppose it's the French waiters," said the first speaker. "Why don't they have French waiters in London?"

"Fancy a French waiter at a club," said his friend.

The young Englishman stared a little, as if he could not fancy it. "In Paris I'm very apt to dine at a place where there's an English waiter. Don't you know what's-his-name's, close to the thingumbob? They always set an English waiter at me. I suppose they think I can't speak French."

"Well, you can't." And the elder of the young Englishmen unfolded his napkin.

His companion took no notice whatever of this declaration. "I say," he resumed, in a moment, "we must learn to speak American. I suppose we must take lessons."

"I can't understand them," said the clever man.

"What the deuce is *he* saying?" asked his comrade, appealing from the French waiter.

"He is recommending some soft-shell crabs," said the clever man.

And so, in desultory observation of the idiosyncrasies of the new society in which they found themselves, the young Englishmen proceeded to dine—going in largely, as the phrase is, for cooling draughts and dishes, of which their attendant offered them a very long list. After dinner they went out and slowly walked about the neighboring streets. The early dusk of waning summer was coming on, but the heat was still very great. The pavements were hot even to the stout boot soles of the British travellers, and the trees along the curbstone emitted strange exotic odors. The young men wandered through the adjoining square—that queer place without palings, and with marble walks arranged in black and white lozenges. There were a great many benches crowded with shabby-looking people, and the travellers remarked, very justly, that it was not much like Belgrave Square. On one side was an enormous hotel, lifting up into the hot darkness an immense array of open, brightly lighted windows. At the base of this populous structure was an eternal jangle of horse-cars, and all round it, in the upper dusk, was a sinister hum of mosquitoes. The ground-floor of the hotel seemed to be a huge transparent cage, flinging a wide glare of gaslight into the street, of which it formed a sort of public adjunct, absorbing and emitting the passers-by promiscuously. The young Englishmen went in with every one else, from curiosity, and saw a couple of hundred men sitting on divans along a great marble-paved corridor, with their legs stretched out, together with several dozen more standing in a *queue*, as at the ticket-office of a railway station, before a brilliantly illuminated counter of vast extent. These latter persons, who carried portmanteaus in their hand, had a dejected, exhausted look; their garments were not very fresh, and they seemed to be rendering some mysterious tribute to a magnificent young man with a waxed mustache, and a shirt-front adorned with diamond buttons, who every now and then dropped an absent glance over their multitudinous patience. They were American citizens doing homage to a hotel clerk.

"I'm glad he didn't tell us to go there," said one of our Englishmen, alluding to their friend on the steamer, who had told them so many things. They walked up Fifth Avenue, where, for instance, he had told them that all the first families lived. But the first families were out of town, and our young travellers had only the satisfaction of seeing some of the second—or, perhaps, even the third—taking the evening air upon balconies and high flights of doorsteps, in the streets which radiate from the more ornamental thoroughfare. They went a little way down one of these side streets, and they saw young ladies in white dresses—charming-looking persons—seated in graceful attitudes on the chocolate-colored steps. In one or two places these young ladies were conversing across the street with other young ladies seated in similar postures and costumes in front of the opposite houses, and in the warm night air their colloquial tones sounded strange in the ears of the young Englishmen. One of our friends, nevertheless—the younger one—intimated that he felt a disposition to interrupt a few of these soft familiarities; but his companion observed, pertinently enough, that he had better be careful. "We must not begin with making mistakes," said his companion.

"But he told us, you know—he told us," urged the young man, alluding again to the friend on the steamer.

"Never mind what he told us!" answered his comrade, who, if he had greater talents, was also apparently more of a moralist.

By bedtime—in their impatience to taste of a terrestrial couch again, our seafarers went to bed early—it was still insufferably hot, and the buzz of the mosquitoes at the open windows might have passed for an audible crepitation of the temperature. "We can't stand this, you know," the young Englishmen said to each other; and they tossed about all night more boisterously than they had tossed upon the Atlantic billows. On the morrow their first thought was that they would re-embark that day for England; and then it occurred to them that they might find an asylum nearer at hand. The cave of Æolus became their ideal of comfort, and they wondered where the Americans went when they wished to cool off. They had not the least idea, and they determined to apply for information to Mr. J. L. Westgate. This was the name inscribed in a bold hand on the back of a letter carefully preserved in the pocket-book of our junior traveller. Beneath the address, in the left-hand corner of the envelope, were the words, "Introducing Lord Lambeth and Percy Beaumont, Esq." The letter had been given to the two Englishmen by a good friend of theirs in London, who had been in America two years previously, and had singled out Mr. J. L. Westgate from the many friends he had left there as the consignee, as it were, of his compatriots. "He is a capital fellow," the Englishman in London had said, "and he has got an awfully pretty wife. He's tremendously hospitable —he will do everything in the world for you; and as he knows every one over there, it is quite needless I should give you any other introduction. He will make you see every one; trust to him for putting you into circulation. He has got a tremendously pretty wife." It was natural that in the hour of tribulation Lord Lambeth and Mr. Percy Beaumont should have bethought themselves of a gentleman whose attractions had been thus vividly depicted—all the more so that he lived in Fifth Avenue, and that Fifth Avenue, as they had ascertained the night before, was contiguous to their hotel. "Ten to one he'll be out of town," said Percy Beaumont; "but we can at least find out where he has gone, and we can immediately start in pursuit. He can't possibly have gone to a hotter place, you know."

"Oh, there's only one hotter place," said Lord Lambeth, "and I hope he hasn't gone there."

They strolled along the shady side of the street to the number indicated upon the precious letter. The house presented an imposing chocolate-colored expanse, relieved by facings and window cornices of florid sculpture, and by a couple of dusty rose-trees which clambered over the balconies and the portico. This last-mentioned feature was approached by a monumental flight of steps.

"Rather better than a London house," said Lord Lambeth, looking down from this altitude, after they had rung the bell.

"It depends upon what London house you mean," replied his companion. "You have a tremendous chance to get wet between the house door and your carriage."

"Well," said Lord Lambeth, glancing at the burning heavens, "I 'guess' it doesn't rain so much here!"

The door was opened by a long negro in a white jacket, who grinned familiarly when Lord Lambeth asked for Mr. Westgate.

"He ain't at home, sah; he's down-town at his o'fice."

"Oh, at his office?" said the visitor. "And when will he be at home?"

"Well, sah, when he goes out dis way in the mo'ning, he ain't liable to come home all day."

This was discouraging; but the address of Mr. Westgate's office was freely imparted by the intelligent black, and was taken down by Percy Beaumont in his pocket-book. The two gentlemen then returned, languidly, to their hotel, and sent for a hackney-coach, and in this commodious vehicle they rolled comfortably down-town. They measured the whole length of Broadway again, and found it a path of fire; and then, deflecting to the left, they were deposited by their conductor before a fresh, light, ornamental structure, ten stories high, in a street crowded with keen-faced, light-limbed young men, who were running about very quickly, and stopping each other eagerly at corners and in doorways. Passing into this brilliant building, they were introduced by one of the keen-faced young men—he was a charming fellow, in wonderful cream-colored garments and a hat with a blue ribbon, who had evidently perceived them to be aliens and helpless—to a very snug hydraulic elevator, in which they took their place with many other persons, and which, shooting upward in its vertical socket, presently projected them into the seventh horizontal compartment of the edifice. Here, after brief delay, they found themselves face to face with the friend of their friend in London. His office was composed of several different rooms, and they waited very silently in one of them after they had sent in their letter and their cards. The letter was not one which it would take Mr. Westgate very long to read, but he came out to speak to them more instantly than they could have expected; he had evidently jumped up from his work. He was a tall, lean personage, and was dressed all in fresh white linen; he had a thin, sharp, familiar face, with an expression that was at one and the same time sociable and business-like, a quick, intelligent eye, and a large brown mustache, which concealed his mouth and made his chin beneath it look small. Lord Lambeth thought he looked tremendously clever.

"How do you do, Lord Lambeth—how do you do, sir?" he said, holding the open letter in his hand. "I'm very glad to see you; I hope you're very well. You had better come in here; I think it's cooler," and he led the way into another room, where there were law-books and papers, and windows wide open beneath striped awning. Just opposite one of the windows, on line with his eyes, Lord Lambeth observed the weather-vane of a church steeple. The uproar of the street sounded infinitely far below, and Lord Lambeth felt very high in the air. "I say it's cooler," pursued their host, "but everything is relative. How do you stand the heat?"

"I can't say we like it," said Lord Lambeth; "but Beaumont likes it better than I."

"Well, it won't last," Mr. Westgate very cheerfully declared; "nothing unpleasant lasts over here. It was very hot when Captain Littledale was here; he did nothing but drink sherry-cobblers. He expresses some doubt in his letter whether I will remember him—as if I didn't remember making six sherry-cobblers for him one day in about twenty minutes. I hope you left him well, two years having elapsed since then."

"Oh yes, he's all right," said Lord Lambeth.

"I am always very glad to see your countrymen," Mr. Westgate pursued. "I thought it would be time some of you should be coming along. A friend of mine was saying to me only a day or two ago, 'It's time for the watermelons and the Englishmen.' "

"The Englishmen and the watermelons just now are about the same thing," Percy Beaumont said, wiping his dripping forehead.

"Ah, well, we'll put you on ice, as we do the melons. You must go down to Newport."

"We'll go anywhere," said Lord Lambeth.

"Yes, you want to go to Newport; that's what you want to do," Mr. Westgate affirmed. "But let's see—when did you get here?"

"Only yesterday," said Percy Beaumont.

"Ah, yes, by the *Russia*. Where are you staying?"

"At the Hanover, I think they call it."

"Pretty comfortable?" inquired Mr. Westgate.

"It seems a capital place, but I can't say we like the gnats," said Lord Lambeth.

Mr. Westgate stared and laughed. "Oh no, of course you don't like the gnats. We shall expect you to like a good many things over here, but we sha'n't insist upon your liking the gnats; though certainly you'll admit that, as gnats, they are fine, eh? But you oughtn't to remain in the city."

"So we think," said Lord Lambeth. "If you would kindly suggest something——"

"Suggest something, my dear sir?" and Mr. Westgate looked at him, narrowing his eyelids. "Open your mouth and shut your eyes! Leave it to me, and I'll put you through. It's a matter of national pride with me that all Englishmen should have a good time; and as I have had considerable practice, I have learned to minister to their wants. I find they generally want the right thing. So just please to consider yourselves my property; and if any one should try to appropriate you, please to say, 'Hands off; too late for the market.' But let's see," continued the American, in his slow, humorous voice, with a distinctness of utterance which appeared to his visitors to be a part of a humorous intention—a strangely leisurely speculative voice for a man evidently so busy and, as they felt, so professional—"let's see; are you going to make something of a stay, Lord Lambeth?"

"Oh dear no," said the young Englishman; "my cousin was coming over on some business, so I just came across, at an hour's notice, for the lark."

"Is it your first visit to the United States?"

"Oh dear yes."

"I was obliged to come on some business," said Percy Beaumont, "and I brought Lambeth along."

"And *you* have been here before, sir?"

"Never—never."

"I thought, from your referring to business——" said Mr. Westgate.

"Oh, you see I'm by way of being a barrister," Percy Beaumont answered. "I know some people that think of bringing a suit against one of your railways, and they asked me to come over and take measures accordingly."

Mr. Westgate gave one of his slow, keen looks again. "What's your railroad?" he asked.

"The Tennessee Central."

The American tilted back his chair a little, and poised it an instant. "Well, I'm sorry you want to attack one of our institutions," he said, smiling. "But I guess you had better enjoy yourself *first*!"

"I'm certainly rather afraid I can't work in this weather," the young barrister confessed.

"Leave that to the natives," said Mr. Westgate. "Leave the Tennessee Central to me, Mr. Beaumont. Some day we'll talk it over, and I guess I can make it square. But I didn't know you Englishmen ever did any work, in the upper classes."

"Oh, we do a lot of work; don't we, Lambeth?" asked Percy Beaumont.

"I must certainly be at home by the 19th of September," said the younger Englishman, irrelevantly but gently.

"For the shooting, eh? or is it the hunting, or the fishing?" inquired his entertainer.

"Oh, I must be in Scotland," said Lord Lambeth, blushing a little.

"Well, then," rejoined Mr. Westgate, "you had better amuse yourself first, also. You must go down and see Mrs. Westgate."

"We should be so happy, if you would kindly tell us the train," said Percy Beaumont.

"It isn't a train—it's a boat."

"Oh, I see. And what is the name of—a—the—a—town?"

"It isn't a town," said Mr. Westgate, laughing. "It's a—well, what shall I call it? It's a watering-place. In short, it's Newport. You'll see what it is. It's cool; that's the principal thing. You will greatly oblige me by going down there and putting yourself into the hands of Mrs. Westgate. It isn't perhaps for me to say it, but you couldn't be in better hands. Also in those of her sister, who is staying with her. She is very fond of Englishmen. She thinks there is nothing like them."

"Mrs. Westgate or—a—her sister?" asked Percy Beaumont, modestly, yet in the tone of an inquiring traveller.

"Oh, I mean my wife," said Mr. Westgate. "I don't suppose my sister-in-law knows much about them. She has always led a very quiet life; she has lived in Boston."

Percy Beaumont listened with interest. "That, I believe," he said, "is the most—a—intellectual town?"

"I believe it is very intellectual. I don't go there much," responded his host.

"I say, we ought to go there," said Lord Lambeth to his companion.

"Oh, Lord Lambeth, wait till the great heat is over," Mr. Westgate interposed. "Boston in this weather would be very trying; it's not the temperature for intellectual exertion. At Boston, you know, you have to pass an examination at the city limits; and when you come away they give you a kind of degree."

Lord Lambeth stared, blushing a little; and Percy Beaumont stared a little also—but only with his fine natural complexion—glancing aside after a moment to see that his companion was not looking too credulous, for he had heard a great deal of American humor. "I dare say it is very jolly," said the younger gentleman.

"I dare say it is," said Mr. Westgate. "Only I must impress upon you that at present—to-morrow morning, at an early hour—you will be expected at Newport. We have a house there; half the people of New York go there for the summer. I am not sure that at this very moment my wife can take you in; she has got a lot of people staying with her; I don't know who they all are; only she may have no room. But you can begin with the hotel, and meanwhile you can live at my house. In that way—simply sleeping at the hotel—you will find it tolerable. For the rest, you must make yourself at home at my place. You mustn't be shy, you know; if you are only here for a month, that will be a great waste of time. Mrs. Westgate won't neglect you, and you had better not try to resist her. I know something about that. I expect you'll find some pretty girls on the premises. I shall write to my wife by this afternoon's mail, and to-morrow morning she and Miss Alden will look out for you. Just walk right in and make yourself comfortable. Your steamer leaves from this part of the city, and I will immediately send out and get you a cabin. Then, at half-past four o'clock, just call for me here, and I will go with you and put you on board. It's a big boat; you might get lost. A few days hence, at the end of the week, I will come down to Newport, and see how you are getting on."

The two young Englishmen inaugurated the policy of not resisting Mrs. Westgate by submitting, with great docility and thankfulness, to her husband. He was evidently a very good fellow, and he made an impression upon his visitors; his hospitality seemed to recommend itself consciously—with a friendly wink, as it were—as if it hinted, judiciously, that you could not possibly make a better bargain. Lord Lambeth and his cousin left their entertainer to his labors and returned to their hotel, where they spent three or four hours in their respective shower-baths. Percy Beaumont had suggested that they ought to see something of the town; but "Oh, d—n the town!" his noble kinsman had rejoined. They returned to Mr. Westgate's office in a carriage, with their luggage, very punctually; but it must be reluctantly recorded that, this time, he kept them waiting so long that they felt themselves missing the steamer, and were deterred only by an amiable modesty from dispensing with his attendance, and starting on a hasty scramble to the wharf. But when at last he appeared, and the carriage plunged into the purlieus of Broadway, they jolted to such good purpose that they reached the huge white vessel while the bell for departure was still ringing, and the absorption of passengers still active. It was indeed, as Mr. Westgate had said, a big boat, and his leadership in the innumerable and interminable corridors and cabins, with which he seemed perfectly acquainted, and of which any one and every one appeared to have the entrée, was very grateful to the slightly bewildered voyagers. He showed them their state-room—a spacious apartment, embellished with gas-lamps, mirrors *en pied*, and sculptured furniture—and then, long after they had been intimately convinced that the steamer was in motion and launched upon the unknown stream that they were about to navigate, he bade them a sociable farewell.

"Well, good-bye, Lord Lambeth," he said; "good-bye, Mr. Percy Beaumont. I hope you'll have a good time. Just let them do what they want with you. I'll come down by-and-by and look after you."

The young Englishmen emerged from their cabin and amused themselves with wondering about the immense labyrinthine steamer, which struck them as an extraordinary mixture of a ship and a hotel. It was densely crowded with passengers, the larger number of whom appeared to be ladies and very young children; and in the big saloons, ornamented in white and gold, which followed each other in surprising succession, beneath the swinging gas-light, and among the small side passages where the negro domestics of both sexes assembled with an air of philosophic leisure, every one was moving to and fro and exchanging loud and familiar observations. Eventually, at the instance of a discriminating black, our young men went and had some "supper" in a wonderful place arranged like a theatre, where, in a gilded gallery, upon which little boxes appeared to open, a large orchestra was playing operatic selections, and, below, people were handing about bills of fare, as if they had been programmes. All this was sufficiently curious; but the agreeable thing, later, was to sit out on one of the great white decks of the steamer, in the warm, breezy darkness, and, in the vague starlight, to make out the line of low, mysterious coast. The young Englishmen tried American cigars—those of Mr. Westgate—and talked together as they usually talked, with many odd silences, lapses of logic, and incongruities of transition, like people who have grown old together, and learned to supply each other's missing phrases; or, more especially, like people thoroughly conscious of a common point of view, so that a style of conversation superficially lacking in finish might suffice for reference to a fund of associations in the light of which everything was all right.

"We really seem to be going out to sea," Percy Beaumont observed. "Upon my word, we are going back to England. He has shipped us off again. I call that 'real mean.' "

"I suppose it's all right," said Lord Lambeth. "I want to see those pretty girls at Newport. You know he told us the place was an island; and aren't all islands in the sea?"

"Well," resumed the elder traveller after a while, "if his house is as good as his cigars, we shall do very well indeed."

"He seems a very good fellow," said Lord Lambeth, as if this idea just occurred to him.

"I say, we had better remain at the inn," rejoined his companion, presently. "I don't think I like the way he spoke of his house. I don't like stopping in the house with such a tremendous lot of women."

"Oh, I don't mind," said Lord Lambeth. And then they smoked a while in silence. "Fancy his thinking we do no work in England!" the young man resumed.

"I dare say he didn't really think so," said Percy Beaumont.

"Well I guess they don't know much about England over here!" declared Lord Lambeth, humorously. And then there was another long pause. "He was devilish civil," observed the young nobleman.

"Nothing, certainly, could have been more civil," rejoined his companion.

"Littledale said his wife was great fun," said Lord Lambeth.

"Whose wife—Littledale's?"

"This American's—Mrs. Westgate. What's his name? J. L."

Beaumont was silent a moment. "What was fun to Little-dale," he said at last, rather sententiously, "may be death to us."

"What do you mean by that?" asked his kinsman. "I am as good a man as Littledale."

"My dear boy, I hope you won't begin to flirt," said Percy Beaumont.

"I don't care. I dare say I sha'n't begin."

"With a married woman, if she's bent upon it, it's all very well," Beaumont expounded. "But our friend mentioned a young lady—a sister, a sister-in-law. For God's sake, don't get entangled with her!"

"How do you mean entangled?"

"Depend upon it she will try to hook you."

"Oh, bother!" said Lord Lambeth.

"American girls are very clever," urged his companion.

"So much the better," the young man declared.

"I fancy they are always up to some game of that sort," Beaumont continued.

"They can't be worse than they are in England," said Lord Lambeth, judicially.

"Ah, but in England," replied Beaumont, "you have got your natural protectors. You have got your mother and sisters."

"My mother and sisters——" began the young nobleman, with a certain energy. But he stopped in time, puffing at his cigar.

"Your mother spoke to me about it, with tears in her eyes," said Percy Beaumont. "She said she felt very nervous. I promised to keep you out of mischief."

"You had better take care of yourself," said the object of maternal and ducal solicitude.

"Ah," rejoined the young barrister, "I haven't the expectation of a hundred thousand a year, not to mention other attractions."

"Well," said Lord Lambeth, "don't cry out before you're hurt!"

It was certainly very much cooler at Newport, where our travellers found themselves assigned to a couple of diminutive bedrooms in a far-away angle of an immense hotel. They had gone ashore in the early summer twilight, and had very promptly put themselves to bed; thanks to which circumstance, and to their having, during the previous hours in

their commodious cabin slept the sleep of youth and health,
they began to feel, towards eleven o'clock, very alert and
inquisitive. They looked out of their windows across a row
of small green fields, bordered with low stone walls of rude
construction, and saw a deep blue ocean lying beneath a deep
blue sky, and flecked now and then with scintillating patches
of foam. A strong, fresh breeze came in through the curtain-
less casements, and prompted our young men to observe
generally that it didn't seem half a bad climate. They made
other observations after they had emerged from their rooms
in pursuit of breakfast—a meal of which they partook in a
huge bare hall, where a hundred negroes in white jackets were
shuffling about upon an uncarpeted floor; where the flies
were superabundant, and the tables and dishes covered over
with a strange, voluminous integument of coarse blue gauze;
and where several little boys and girls, who had risen late,
were seated in fastidious solitude at the morning repast.
These young persons had not the morning paper before them,
but they were engaged in languid perusal of the bill of fare.

The latter document was a great puzzle to our friends, who,
on reflecting that its bewildering categories had relation to
breakfast alone, had uneasy prevision of an encyclopædic
dinner list. They found a great deal of entertainment at the
hotel, an enormous wooden structure, for the erection of
which it seemed to them that the virgin forests of the West
must have been terribly deflowered. It was perforated from
end to end with immense bare corridors, through which a
strong draught was blowing—bearing along wonderful figures
of ladies in white morning-dresses and clouds of valenciennes
lace, who seemed to float down the long vistas with ex-
panded furbelows like angels spreading their wings. In front
was a gigantic veranda, upon which an army might have en-
camped—a vast wooden terrace, with a roof as lofty as the
nave of a cathedral. Here our young Englishmen enjoyed, as
they supposed, a glimpse of American society, which was
distributed over the measureless expanse in a variety of
sedentary attitudes, and appeared to consist largely of pretty
young girls, dressed as if for a *fête champêtre,* swaying to
and fro in rocking chairs, fanning themselves with large
straw fans, and enjoying an enviable exemption from social
cares. Lord Lambeth had a theory, which it might be interesting to trace to its origin, that it would be not only agreeable, but easily possible, to enter into relations with one of
these young ladies; and his companion (as he had done a

couple of days before) found occasion to check the young
nobleman's colloquial impulses.

"You had better take care," said Percy Beaumont, "or
you will have an offended father or brother pulling out a
bowie-knife."

"I assure you it is all right," Lord Lambeth replied. "You
know the Americans come to these big hotels to make ac-
quaintances."

"I know nothing about it, and neither do you," said his
kinsman, who, like a clever man, had begun to perceive that
the observation of American society demanded a readjust-
ment of one's standard.

"Hang it, then, let's find out!" cried Lord Lambeth, with
some impatience. "You know I don't want to miss anything."

"We will find out," said Percy Beaumont, very reasonably.
"We will go and see Mrs. Westgate, and make all the proper
inquiries."

And so the two inquiring Englishmen, who had this lady's
address inscribed in her husband's hand upon a card, descended from the veranda of the big hotel and took their
way, according to direction, along a large, straight road, past
a series of fresh-looking villas embosomed in shrubs and
flowers, and enclosed in an ingenious variety of wooden
palings. The morning was brilliant and cool, the villas were
smart and snug, and the walk of the young travellers was
very entertaining. Everything looked as if it had received a
coat of fresh paint the day before—the red roofs, the green
shutters, the clean, bright browns and buffs of the house
fronts. The flower beds on the little lawns seemed to sparkle
in the radiant air, and the gravel in the short carriage sweeps
to flash and twinkle. Along the road came a hundred little
basket-phaetons, in which, almost always, a couple of ladies
were sitting—ladies in white dresses and long white gloves,
holding the reins and looking at the two Englishmen—whose
nationality was not elusive—through thick blue veils tied
tightly about their faces, as if to guard their complexions. At
last the young men came within sight of the sea again, and
then, having interrogated a gardener over the paling of a
villa, they turned into an open gate. Here they found themselves face to face with the ocean and with a very picturesque
structure, resembling a magnified chalet, which was perched
upon a green embankment just above it. The house had a
veranda of extraordinary width all around it, and a great
many doors and windows standing open to the veranda.
These various apertures had, in common, such an accessible,

hospitable air, such a breezy flutter within of light curtains, such expansive thresholds and reassuring interiors, that our friends hardly knew which was the regular entrance, and, after hesitating a moment, presented themselves at one of the windows. The room within was dark, but in a moment a graceful figure vaguely shaped itself in the rich-looking gloom, and a lady came to meet them. Then they saw that she had been seated at a table writing, and that she had heard them and had got up. She stepped out into the light; she wore a frank, charming smile, with which she held out her hand to Percy Beaumont.

"Oh, you must be Lord Lambeth and Mr. Beaumont," she said. "I have heard from my husband that you would come. I am extremely glad to see you." And she shook hands with each of her visitors. Her visitors were a little shy, but they had very good manners; they responded with smiles and exclamations, and they apologized for not knowing the front door. The lady rejoined, with vivacity, that when she wanted to see people very much she did not insist upon these distinctions, and that Mr. Westgate had written to her of his English friends in terms that made her really anxious. "He said you were so terribly prostrated," said Mrs. Westgate.

"Oh, you mean by the heat?" replied Percy Beaumont. "We were rather knocked up, but we feel wonderfully better. We had such a jolly—a—voyage down here. It's so very good of you to mind."

"Yes, it's so very kind of you," murmured Lord Lambeth.

Mrs. Westgate stood smiling; she was extremely pretty. "Well, I did mind," she said; "and I thought of sending for you this morning to the Ocean House. I am very glad you are better, and I am charmed you have arrived. You must come round to the other side of the piazza." And she led the way, with a light, smooth step, looking back at the young men and smiling.

The other side of the piazza was, as Lord Lambeth presently remarked, a very jolly place. It was of the most liberal proportions, and with its awnings, its fanciful chairs, its cushions and rugs, its view of the ocean, close at hand, tumbling along the base of the low cliffs whose level tops intervened in lawn-like smoothness, it formed a charming complement to the drawing-room. As such it was in course of use at the present moment; it was occupied by a social circle. There were several ladies and two or three gentlemen, to whom Mrs. Westgate proceeded to introduce the distinguished strangers. She mentioned a great many names very freely and distinctly; the young Englishmen, shuffling about and bowing, were rather bewildered. But at last they were provided with chairs—low, wicker chairs, gilded, and tied with a great many ribbons—and one of the ladies (a very young person, with a little snub-nose and several dimples) offered Percy Beaumont a fan. The fan was also adorned with pink love-knots; but Percy Beaumont declined it, although he was very hot. Presently, however, it became cooler; the breeze from the sea was delicious, the view was charming, and the people sitting there looked exceedingly fresh and comfortable. Several of the ladies seemed to be young girls, and the gentlemen were slim, fair youths, such as our friends had seen the day before in New York. The ladies were working upon bands of tapestry, and one of the young men had an open book in his lap. Beaumont afterwards learned from one of the ladies that this young man had been reading aloud; that he was from Boston, and was very fond of reading aloud. Beaumont said it was a great pity that they had interrupted him; he should like so much (from all he had heard) to hear a Bostonian read. Couldn't the young man be induced to go on?

"Oh no," said his informant, very freely; "he wouldn't be able to get the young ladies to attend to him now."

There was something very friendly, Beaumont perceived, in the attitude of the company; they looked at the young Englishmen with an air of animated sympathy and interest; they smiled, brightly and unanimously, at everything either of the visitors said. Lord Lambeth and his companion felt that they were being made very welcome. Mrs. Westgate seated herself between them, and, talking a great deal to each, they had occasion to observe that she was as pretty as their friend Littledale had promised. She was thirty years old, with the eyes and the smile of a girl of seventeen, and she was extremely light and graceful—elegant, exquisite. Mrs. Westgate was extremely spontaneous. She was very frank and demonstrative, and appeared always—while she looked at you delightedly with her beautiful young eyes—to be making sudden confessions and concessions after momentary hesitations.

"We shall expect to see a great deal of you," she said to Lord Lambeth, with a kind of joyous earnestness. "We are very fond of Englishmen here—that is, there are a great many we have been fond of. After a day or two you must come and stay with us; we hope you will stay a long time. Newport's a very nice place when you come really to know it—when you know plenty of people. Of course you and Mr. Beaumont will have no difficulty about that. Englishmen are very well received here; there are almost always two or three of them about. I think they always like it, and I must say I should think they would. They receive ever so much attention. I must say I think they sometimes get spoiled; but I am sure you and Mr. Beaumont are proof against that.

"My husband tells me you are a friend of Captain Littledale. He was such a charming man: he made himself most agreeable here, and I am sure I wonder he didn't stay. It couldn't have been pleasanter for him in his own country, though, I suppose, it is very pleasant in England—for English people. I don't know myself; I have been there very little. I have been a great deal abroad, but I am always on the Continent. I must say I am extremely fond of Paris; you know we Americans always are; we go there when we die. Did you ever hear that before? That was said by a great wit—I mean the good Americans; but we are all good; you'll see that for yourself.

"All I know of England is London, and all I know of London is that place on that little corner, you know, where you buy jackets—jackets with that coarse braid and those big buttons. They made very good jackets in London; I will do you the justice to say that. And some people like the hats; but about the hats I was always a heretic; I always got my hats in Paris. You can't wear an English hat—at least, I never could—unless you dress your hair *à l'Anglaise;* and I must say that is a talent I never possessed. In Paris they will make things to suit your peculiarities; but in England I think you like much more to have—how shall I say it?—one thing for everybody. I mean as regards dress. I don't know about other things; but I have always supposed that in other things everything was different. I mean according to the people—according to the classes, and all that. I am afraid you will think that I don't take a very favorable view; but you know you can't take a very favorable view in Dover Street in the month of November. That has always been my fate.

"Do you know Jones's Hotel, in Dover Street? That's all I know of England. Of course every one admits that the English hotels are your weak point. There was always the most frightful fog; I couldn't see to try my things on. When I got over to America—into the light—I usually found they were twice too big. The next time I mean to go in the season; I think I shall go next year. I want very much to take my sister; she has never been to England. I don't know whether you know what I mean by saying that the Englishmen who come here sometimes get spoiled. I mean that they take things as a matter of course—things that are done for them. Now, naturally, they are only a matter of course when the Englishmen are very nice. But, of course, they are almost always very nice. Of course this isn't nearly such an interesting country as England; there are not nearly so many things to see, and we haven't your country life. I have never seen anything of your country life; when I am in Europe I am always on the Continent. But I have heard a great deal about it; I know that when you are among yourselves in the country you have the most beautiful time. Of course we have nothing of that sort; we have nothing on that scale.

"I don't apologize, Lord Lambeth; some Americans are always apologizing; you must have noticed that. We have the reputation of always boasting and bragging and waving the American flag; but I must say that what strikes me is that we are perpetually making excuses and trying to smooth things over. The American flag has quite gone out of fashion; it's very carefully folded up like an old table-cloth. Why should we apologize? The English never apologize—do they? No; I must say I never apologize. You must take us as we come—with all our imperfections on our heads. Of course we haven't your country life, and your old ruins, and your great estates, and your leisure class, and all that. But if we haven't, I should think you might find it a pleasant change —I think any country is pleasant where they have pleasant manners.

"Captain Littledale told me he had never seen such pleasant manners as at Newport, and he had been a great deal in European society. Hadn't he been in the diplomatic service? He told me the dream of his life was to get appointed to a diplomatic post at Washington. But he doesn't seem to have succeeded. I suppose that in England promotion—and all that sort of thing—is fearfully slow. With us, you know, it's a great deal too fast. You see, I admit our drawbacks. But I must confess I think Newport is an ideal place. I don't know anything like it anywhere. Captain Littledale told me he didn't know anything like it anywhere. It's entirely different from most watering-places; it's a most charming life. I must say I think that when one goes to a foreign country one ought to enjoy the differences. Of course there are differences, otherwise what did one come abroad for? Look for your pleasure in the differences, Lord Lambeth; that's the way to do it; and then I am sure you will find American society—at least, Newport society—most charming and interesting. I wish very much my husband were here; but he's dreadfully confined to New York. I suppose you think that is very strange—for a gentleman. But you see we haven't any leisure class."

Mrs. Westgate's discourse, delivered in a soft, sweet voice, flowed on like a miniature torrent, and was interrupted by a hundred little smiles, glances, and gestures, which might have figured the irregularities and obstructions of such a stream. Lord Lambeth listened to her with, it must be confessed, a rather ineffectual attention, although he indulged in a good many little murmurs and ejaculations of assent and deprecation. He had no great faculty for apprehending generalizations. There were some three or four indeed which, in the play of his own intelligence, he had originated, and which had seemed convenient at the moment; but at the present time he could hardly have been said to follow Mrs. Westgate as she darted gracefully about in the sea of speculation. Fortunately, she asked for no special rejoinder, for she looked about at the rest of the company as well, and smiled at Percy Beaumont, on the other side of her, as if he, too, must understand her and agree with her. He was rather more successful than his companion; for besides being, as we know, cleverer, his attention was not vaguely distracted by close scrutiny to a remarkably interesting young girl with dark hair and blue eyes. This was the case with Lord Lambeth, to whom it occurred after a while that the young girl with blue eyes and dark hair was the pretty sister of whom Mrs. Westgate had spoken. She presently turned to him with a remark which established her identity.

"It's a great pity you couldn't have brought my brother-in-law with you. It's a great shame he should be in New York in these days."

"Oh yes! it's so very hot," said Lord Lambeth.

"It must be dreadful," said the young girl.

"I dare say he is very busy," Lord Lambeth observed.

"The gentlemen in America work too much," the young girl went on.

"Oh, do they? I dare say they like it," said her interlocutor.

"I don't like it. One never sees them."

"Don't you, really?" asked Lord Lambeth. "I shouldn't have fancied that."

"Have you come to study American manners?" asked the young girl.

"Oh, I don't know. I just came over for a lark. I haven't got long." Here there was a pause, and Lord Lambeth began again. "But Mr. Westgate will come down here, will he not?"

"I certainly hope he will. He must help to entertain you and Mr. Beaumont."

Lord Lambeth looked at her a little with his handsome brown eyes. "Do you suppose he would have come down with us if we had urged him?"

Mr. Westgate's sister-in-law was silent a moment, and then, "I dare say he would," she answered.

"Really!" said the young Englishman. "He was immensely civil to Beaumont and me," he added.

"He is a dear, good fellow," the young lady rejoined, "and he is a perfect husband. But all Americans are that," she continued, smiling.

"Really!" Lord Lambeth exclaimed again, and wondered whether all American ladies had such a passion for generalizing as these two.

He sat there a good while: there was a great deal of talk; it was all very friendly and lively and jolly. Every one present, sooner or later, said something to him, and seemed to make a particular point of addressing him by name. Two or three other persons came in, and there was a shifting of seats and changing of places; the gentlemen all entered into intimate conversation with the two Englishmen, made them urgent offers of hospitality, and hoped they might frequently be of service to them. They were afraid Lord Lambeth and Mr. Beaumont were not very comfortable at their hotel; that it was not, as one of them said, "so private as those dear little English inns of yours." This last gentleman went on to say that unfortunately, as yet, perhaps, privacy was not quite so easily obtained in America as might be desired; still, he continued, you could generally get it by paying for it; in fact, you could get everything in America nowadays by paying for it. American life was certainly growing a great deal more private; it was growing very much like England. Everything at Newport, for instance, was thoroughly private; Lord Lambeth would probably be struck with that. It was also represented to the strangers that it mattered very little whether their hotel was agreeable, as every one would want them to make visits; they would stay with other people, and, in any case, they would be a great deal at Mrs. Westgate's. They would find that very charming; it was the pleasantest house in Newport. It was a pity Mr. Westgate was always away; he was a man of the highest ability—very acute, very acute. He worked like a horse, and he left his wife—well, to do about as she liked. He liked her to enjoy herself, and she seemed to know how. She was extremely brilliant, and a splendid talker. Some people preferred her sister, but Miss Alden was very different; she was in a different style altogether. Some people even thought her prettier, and, certainly, she was not so sharp. She was more in the Boston style; she had lived a great deal in Boston, and she was very highly educated. Boston girls, it was propounded, were more like English young ladies.

Lord Lambeth had presently a chance to test the truth of this proposition, for on the company rising in compliance with a suggestion from their hostess that they should walk down to the rocks and look at the sea, the young Englishman again found himself, as they strolled across the grass, in proximity to Mrs. Westgate's sister. Though she was but a girl of twenty, she appeared to feel the obligation to exert an active hospitality; and this was, perhaps, the more to be noticed as she seemed by nature a reserved and retiring person, and had little of her sister's fraternizing quality. She was, perhaps, rather too thin, and she was a little pale; but as she moved slowly over the grass, with her arms hanging at her sides, looking gravely for a moment at the sea and then brightly, for all her gravity, at him, Lord Lambeth thought her at least as pretty as Mrs. Westgate, and reflected that if this was the Boston style the Boston style was very charming. He thought she looked very clever; he could imagine that she was highly educated; but at the same time she seemed gentle and graceful. For all her cleverness, however, he felt that she had to think a little what to say; she didn't say the first thing that came into her head; he had come from a different part of the world and from a different society, and she was trying to adapt her conversation. The others were scattering themselves near the rocks; Mrs. Westgate had charge of Percy Beaumont.

"Very jolly place, isn't it?" said Lord Lambeth. "It's a very jolly place to sit."

"Very charming," said the young girl. "I often sit here; there are all kinds of cosey corners—as if they had been made on purpose."

"Ah, I suppose you have had some of them made," said the young man.

Miss Alden looked at him a moment. "Oh no, we have had nothing made. It's pure nature."

"I should think you would have a few little benches—rustic seats, and that sort of thing. It might be so jolly to sit here, you know," Lord Lambeth went on.

"I am afraid we haven't so many of those things as you," said the young girl, thoughtfully.

"I dare say you go in for pure nature, as you were saying. Nature over here must be so grand, you know." And Lord Lambeth looked about him.

The little coast-line hereabouts was very pretty, but it was not at all grand, and Miss Alden appeared to rise to a perception of this fact. "I am afraid it seems to you very rough," she said. "It's not like the coast scenery in Kingsley's novels."

"Ah, the novels always overdo it, you know," Lord Lambeth rejoined. "You must not go by the novels."

They were wandering about a little on the rocks, and they stopped and looked down into a narrow chasm where the rising tide made a curious bellowing sound. It was loud enough to prevent their hearing each other, and they stood there for some moments in silence. The young girl looked at her companion, observing him attentively, but covertly, as women, even when very young, know how to do. Lord Lambeth repaid observation; tall, straight, and strong, he was handsome as certain young Englishmen, and certain young Englishmen, almost alone, are handsome, with a perfect finish of feature and a look of intellectual repose and gentle good-temper which seemed somehow to be consequent upon his well-cut nose and chin. And to speak of Lord Lambeth's expression of intellectual repose is not simply a civil way of saying that he looked stupid. He was evidently not a young man of an irritable imagination; he was not, as he would himself have said, tremendously clever; but though there was a kind of appealing dulness in his eye, he looked thoroughly reasonable and competent, and his appearance proclaimed that to be a nobleman, an athlete, and an excellent fellow was a sufficiently brilliant combination of qualities. The young girl beside him, it may be attested without further delay, thought him the handsomest young man she had ever seen; and Bessie Alden's imagination, unlike that of her companion, was irritable. He, however, was also making up his mind that she was uncommonly pretty.

"I dare say it's very gay here—that you have lots of balls and parties," he said; for, if he was not tremendously clever, he rather prided himself on having, with women, a sufficiency of conversation.

"Oh yes, there is a great deal going on," Bessie Alden replied. "There are not so many balls, but there are a good many other things. You will see for yourself; we live rather in the midst of it."

"It's very kind of you to say that. But I thought you Americans were always dancing."

"I suppose we dance a good deal; but I have never seen much of it. We don't do it much, at any rate, in summer. And I am sure," said Bessie Alden, "that we don't have so many balls as you have in England."

"Really!" exclaimed Lord Lambeth. "Ah, in England it all depends, you know."

"You will not think much of our gayeties," said the young girl, looking at him with a little mixture of interrogation and decision which was peculiar to her. The interrogation seemed earnest and the decision seemed arch; but the mixture, at any rate, was charming. "Those things, with us, are much less splendid than in England."

"I fancy that you don't mean that," said Lord Lambeth, laughing.

"I assure you I mean everything I say," the young girl declared. "Certainly, from what I have read about English society, it is very different."

"Ah well, you know," said her companion, "those things are often described by fellows who know nothing about them. You mustn't mind what you read."

"Oh, I *shall* mind what I read!" Bessie Alden rejoined. "When I read Thackeray and George Eliot, how can I help minding them?"

"Ah, well, Thackeray and George Eliot," said the young nobleman; "I haven't read much of them."

"Don't you suppose they know about society?" asked Bessie Alden.

"Oh, I dare say they know; they were so clever. But these fashionable novels," said Lord Lambeth, "they are awful rot, you know."

His companion looked at him a moment with her dark blue eyes, and then she looked down in the chasm where the water was tumbling about. "Do you mean Mrs. Gore, for instance?" she said, presently, raising her eyes.

"I am afraid I haven't read that, either," was the young man's rejoinder, laughing a little and blushing. "I am afraid you'll think I am not very intellectual."

"Reading Mrs. Gore is no proof of intellect. But I like reading everything about English life—even poor books. I am so curious about it."

"Aren't ladies always curious?" asked the young man, jestingly.

But Bessie Alden appeared to desire to answer his question seriously. "I don't think so—I don't think we are enough so—that we care about many things. So it's all the more of a compliment," she added, "that I should want to know so much about England."

The logic here seemed a little close; but Lord Lambeth, made conscious of a compliment, found his natural modesty just at hand. "I am sure you know a great deal more than I do."

"I really think I know a great deal—for a person who has never been there."

"Have you really never been there?" cried Lord Lambeth. "Fancy!"

"Never—except in imagination," said the young girl.

"Fancy!" repeated her companion. "But I dare say you'll go soon, won't you?"

"It's the dream of my life!" said Bessie Alden, smiling.

"But your sister seems to know a tremendous lot about London," Lord Lambeth went on.

The young girl was silent a moment. "My sister and I are two very different persons," she presently said. "She has been a great deal in Europe. She has been in England several times. She has known a great many English people."

"But you must have known some, too," said Lord Lambeth.

"I don't think that I have ever spoken to one before. You are the first Englishman that—to my knowledge—I have ever talked with."

Bessie Alden made this statement with a certain gravity—almost, as it seemed to Lord Lambeth, an impressiveness. Attempts at impressiveness always made him feel awkward, and he now began to laugh and swing his stick. "Ah, you would have been sure to know!" he said. And then he added, after an instant, "I'm sorry I am not a better specimen."

The young girl looked away; but she smiled, laying aside her impressiveness. "You must remember that you are only a beginning," she said. Then she retraced her steps, leading the way back to the lawn, where they saw Mrs. Westgate come towards them with Percy Beaumont still at her side. "Perhaps I shall go to England next year," Miss Alden continued; "I want to, immensely. My sister is going to Europe, and she has asked me to go with her. If we go, I shall make her stay as long as possible in London."

"Ah, you must come in July," said Lord Lambeth. "That's the time when there is most going on."

"I don't think I can wait till July," the young girl rejoined. "By the first of May I shall be very impatient." They had gone farther, and Mrs. Westgate and her companion were near them. "Kitty," said Miss Alden, "I have given out that we are going to London next May. So please to conduct yourself accordingly."

Percy Beaumont wore a somewhat animated—even a slightly irritated—air. He was by no means so handsome a man as his cousin, although in his cousin's absence he might have passed for a striking specimen of the tall, muscular, fair-bearded, clear-eyed Englishman. Just now Beaumont's clear eyes, which were small and of a pale gray color, had a rather troubled light, and, after glancing at Bessie Alden while she spoke, he rested them upon his kinsman. Mrs. Westgate meanwhile, with her superfluously pretty gaze, looked at every one alike.

"You had better wait till the time comes," she said to her sister. "Perhaps next May you won't care so much about London. Mr. Beaumont and I," she went on, smiling at her companion, "have had a tremendous discussion. We don't agree about anything. It's perfectly delightful."

"Oh, I say, Percy!" exclaimed Lord Lambeth.

"I disagree," said Beaumont, stroking down his back hair, "even to the point of not thinking it delightful."

"Oh, I say!" cried Lord Lambeth again.

"I don't see anything delightful in my disagreeing with Mrs. Westgate," said Percy Beaumont.

"Well, I do!" Mrs. Westgate declared; and she turned to her sister. "You know you have to go to town. The phaeton is there. You had better take Lord Lambeth."

At this point Percy Beaumont certainly looked straight at his kinsman; he tried to catch his eye. But Lord Lambeth would not look at him; his own eyes were better occupied. "I shall be very happy," cried Bessie Alden. "I am only going to some shops. But I will drive you about and show you the place."

"An American woman who respects herself," said Mrs. Westgate, turning to Beaumont with her bright expository air, "must buy something every day of her life. If she cannot do it herself, she must send out some member of her family for the purpose. So Bessie goes forth to fulfil my mission."

The young girl had walked away, with Lord Lambeth by her side, to whom she was talking still; and Percy Beaumont watched them as they passed towards the house. "She fulfills her own mission," he presently said; "that of being a very attractive young lady."

"I don't know that I should say very attractive," Mrs. Westgate rejoined. "She is not so much that as she is charming, when you really know her. She is very shy."

"Oh, indeed!" said Percy Beaumont.

"Extremely shy," Mrs. Westgate repeated. "But she is a dear, good girl; she is a charming species of a girl. She is not in the least a flirt; that isn't at all her line; she doesn't know the alphabet of that sort of thing. She is very simple, very serious. She has lived a great deal in Boston, with another sister of mine—the eldest of us—who married a Bostonian. She is very cultivated—not at all like me; I am not in the least cultivated. She has studied immensely and read everything; she is what they call in Boston 'thoughtful.'"

"A rum sort of girl for Lambeth to get hold of!" his lordship's kinsman privately reflected.

"I really believe," Mrs. Westgate continued, "that the most charming girl in the world is a Boston superstructure upon a New York *fonds*; or perhaps a New York superstructure upon a Boston *fonds*. At any rate, it's the mixture," said Mrs. Westgate, who continued to give Percy Beaumont a great deal of information.

Lord Lambeth got into a little basket phaeton with Bessie Alden, and she drove him down the long avenue, whose extent he had measured on foot a couple of hours before, into the ancient town, as it was called in that part of the world, of Newport. The ancient town was a curious affair—a collection of fresh-looking little wooden houses, painted white, scattered over a hill-side and clustered about a long, straight street, paved with enormous cobblestones. There were plenty of shops, a large proportion of which appeared to be those of fruit venders, with piles of huge watermelons and pumpkins stacked in front of them; and, drawn up before the shops, or bumping about on the cobble-stones, were innumerable other basket-phaetons freighted with ladies of high fashion, who greeted each other from vehicle to vehicle, and conversed on the edge of the pavement in a manner that struck Lord Lambeth as demonstrative, with a great many "Oh, my dears," and little, quick exclamations and caresses. His companion went into seventeen shops—he amused himself with counting them—and accumulated at the bottom of the phaeton a pile of bundles that hardly left the young Englishman a place for his feet. As she had no groom nor footman, he sat in the phaeton to hold the ponies, where, although he was not a particularly acute observer, he saw much to entertain him—especially the ladies just mentioned, who wandered up and down with the appearance of a kind of aimless intentness, as if they were looking for something to buy, and who, tripping in and out of their vehicles, displayed remarkably pretty feet. It all seemed to Lord Lambeth very odd and bright and gay. Of course, before they got back to the villa, he had had a great deal of desultory conversation with Bessie Alden.

The young Englishmen spent the whole of that day and the whole of many successive days in what the French call the *intimité* of their new friends. They agreed that it was extremely jolly, that they had never known anything more agreeable. It is not proposed to narrate minutely the incidents of their sojourn on this charming shore; though if it were convenient I might present a record of impressions none the less delectable that they were not exhaustively analyzed. Many of them still linger in the minds of our travellers, attended by a train of harmonious images—images of brilliant mornings on lawns and piazzas that overlooked the sea; of innumerable pretty girls; of infinite lounging and talking and laughing and flirting and lunching and dining; of universal friendliness and frankness; of occasions on which they knew every one and everything, and had an extraordinary sense of ease; of drives and rides in the late afternoon over gleaming beaches, on long sea-roads beneath a sky lighted up by marvellous sunsets; of suppers, on the return, informal, irregular, agreeable; of evenings at open windows or on the perpetual verandas, in the summer starlight, above the warm Atlantic. The young Englishmen were introduced to everybody, entertained by everybody, intimate with everybody. At the end of three days they had removed their luggage from the hotel, and gone to stay with Mrs. Westgate —a step to which Percy Beaumont at first offered some conscientious opposition. I call his opposition conscientious, because it was founded upon some talk that he had had, on the second day, with Bessie Alden. He had indeed had a good deal of talk with her, for she was not literally always in conversation with Lord Lambeth. He had meditated upon Mrs. Westgate's account of her sister, and he discovered for himself that the young lady was clever, and appeared to have read a great deal. She seemed very nice, though he could not make out that, as Mrs. Westgate had said, she was shy. If she was shy, she carried it off very well.

"Mr. Beaumont," she had said, "please tell me something about Lord Lambeth's family. How would you say it in England—his position?"

"His position?" Percy Beaumont repeated.

"His rank, or whatever you call it. Unfortunately, we haven't got a 'peerage,' like the people in Thackeray."

"That's a great pity," said Beaumont. "You would find it all set forth there so much better than I can do it."

"He is a peer, then?"

"Oh yes, he is a peer."

"And has he any other title than Lord Lambeth?"

"His title is the Marquis of Lambeth," said Beaumont; and then he was silent. Bessie Alden appeared to be looking at him with interest. "He is the son of the Duke of Bayswater," he added, presently.

"The eldest son?"

"The only son."

"And are his parents living?"

"Oh yes; if his father were not living he would be a duke."

"So that when his father dies," pursued Bessie Alden, with more simplicity than might have been expected in a clever girl, "he will become Duke of Bayswater?"

"Of course," said Percy Beaumont. "But his father is in excellent health."

"And his mother?"

Beaumont smiled a little. "The duchess is uncommonly robust."

"And has he any sisters?"

"Yes, there are two."

"And what are they called?"

"One of them is married. She is the Countess of Pimlico."

"And the other?"

"The other is unmarried; she is plain Lady Julia."

Bessie Alden looked at him a moment. "Is she very plain?"

Beaumont began to laugh again. "You would not find her so handsome as her brother," he said; and it was after this that he attempted to dissuade the heir of the Duke of Bayswater from accepting Mrs. Westgate's invitation. "Depend upon it," he said, "that girl means to try for you."

"It seems to me you are doing your best to make a fool of me," the modest young nobleman answered.

"She has been asking me," said Beaumont, "all about your people and your possessions."

"I am sure it is very good of her!" Lord Lambeth rejoined.

"Well, then," observed his companion, "if you go, you go with your eyes open."

"D—n my eyes!" exclaimed Lord Lambeth. "If one is to be a dozen times a day at the house, it is a great deal more convenient to sleep there. I am sick of travelling up and down this beastly avenue."

Since he had determined to go, Percy Beaumont would, of course, have been very sorry to allow him to go alone; he was a man of conscience, and he remembered his promise to the duchess. It was obviously the memory of this promise that made him say to his companion a couple of days later that he rather wondered he should be so fond of that girl.

"In the first place, how do you know how fond I am of her?" asked Lord Lambeth. "And, in the second place, why shouldn't I be fond of her?"

"I shouldn't think she would be in your line."

"What do you call my 'line'? You don't set her down as 'fast'?"

"Exactly so. Mrs. Westgate tells me that there is no such thing as the 'fast girl' in America; that it's an English invention, and that the term has no meaning here."

"All the better. It's an animal I detest."

"You prefer a blue-stocking."

"Is that what you call Miss Alden?"

"Her sister tells me," said Percy Beaumont, "that she is tremendously literary."

"I don't know anything about that. She is certainly very clever."

"Well," said Beaumont, "I should have supposed you would have found that sort of thing awfully slow."

"In point of fact," Lord Lambeth rejoined, "I find it uncommonly lively."

After this Percy Beaumont held his tongue; but on August 10th he wrote to the Duchess of Bayswater. He was, as I have said, a man of conscience, and he had a strong, incorruptible sense of the proprieties of life. His kinsman, meanwhile, was having a great deal of talk with Bessie Alden—on the red sea-rocks beyond the lawn; in the course of long island rides, with a slow return in the glowing twilight; on the deep veranda late in the evening. Lord Lambeth, who had stayed at many houses, had never stayed at a house in which it was possible for a young man to converse so frequently with a young lady. This young lady no longer applied to Percy Beaumont for information concerning his lordship. She addressed herself directly to the young nobleman. She asked him a great many questions, some of which bored him a little; for he took no pleasure in talking about himself.

"Lord Lambeth," said Bessie Alden, "are you a hereditary legislator?"

"Oh, I say!" cried Lord Lambeth, "don't make me call myself such names as that."

"But you are a member of Parliament," said the young girl.

"I don't like the sound of that either."

"Don't you sit in the House of Lords?" Bessie Alden went on.

"Very seldom," said Lord Lambeth.

"Is it an important position?" she asked.

"Oh dear no," said Lord Lambeth.

"I should think it would be very grand," said Bessie Alden, "to possess, simply by an accident of birth, the right to make laws for a great nation."

"Ah, but one doesn't make laws. It's a great humbug."

"I don't believe that," the young girl declared. "It must be a great privilege, and I should think that if one thought of it in the right way—from a high point of view—it would be very inspiring."

"The less one thinks of it the better," Lord Lambeth affirmed.

"I think it's tremendous," said Bessie Alden; and on another occasion she asked him if he had any tenantry. Hereupon it was that, as I have said, he was a little bored.

"Do you want to buy up their leases?" he asked.

"Well, have you got any livings?" she demanded.

"Oh, I say!" he cried. "Have you got a clergyman that is looking out?" But she made him tell her that he had a castle; he confessed to but one. It was the place in which he had been born and brought up, and, as he had an old-time liking for it, he was beguiled into describing it a little, and saying it was really very jolly. Bessie Alden listened with great interest, and declared that she would give the world to see such a place. Whereupon—"It would be awfully kind of you to come and stay there," said Lord Lambeth. He took a vague satisfaction in the circumstance that Percy Beaumont had not heard him make the remark I have just recorded.

Mr. Westgate all this time had not, as they said at Newport, "come on." His wife more than once announced that she expected him on the morrow; but on the morrow she wandered about a little, with a telegram in her jewelled fingers, declaring it was very tiresome that his business detained him in New York; that he could only hope the Englishmen were having a good time. "I must say," said Mrs. Westgate, "that it is no thanks to him if you are." And she went on to explain, while she continued that slow-paced promenade which enabled her well-adjusted skirts to display themselves so advantageously, that unfortunately in America there was no leisure class. It was Lord Lambeth's theory, freely propounded when the young men were together, that Percy Beaumont was having a very good time with Mrs. Westgate, and that, under the pretext of meeting for the purpose of animated discussion, they were indulging in practices that imparted a shade of hypocrisy to the lady's regret for her husband's absence.

"I assure you we are always discussing and differing," said Percy Beaumont. "She is awfully argumentative. American ladies certainly don't mind contradicting you. Upon my word, I don't think I was ever treated so by a woman before. She's so devilish positive."

Mrs. Westgate's positive quality, however, evidently had its attractions, for Beaumont was constantly at his hostess's side. He detached himself one day to the extent of going to New York to talk over the Tennessee Central with Mr. Westgate; but he was absent only forty-eight hours, during which, with Mr. Westgate's assistance, he completely settled this piece of business. "They certainly do things quickly in New York," he observed to his cousin; and he added that Mr. Westgate had seemed very uneasy lest his wife should miss her visitor— he had been in such an awful hurry to send him back to her. "I'm afraid you'll never come up to an American husband, if that's what the wives expect," he said to Lord Lambeth.

Mrs. Westgate, however, was not to enjoy much longer the entertainment with which an indulgent husband had desired to keep her provided. On August 21st Lord Lambeth received a telegram from his mother, requesting him to return immediately to England; his father had been taken ill, and it was his filial duty to come to him.

The young Englishman was visibly annoyed. "What the deuce does it mean?" he asked of his kinsman. "What am I to do?"

Percy Beaumont was annoyed as well; he had deemed it

his duty, as I have narrated, to write to the duchess, but he had not expected that this distinguished woman would act so promptly upon his hint. "It means," he said, "that your father is laid up. I don't suppose it's anything serious; but you have no option. Take the first steamer; but don't be alarmed."

Lord Lambeth made his farewells; but the few last words that he exchanged with Bessie Alden are the only ones that have a place in our record. "Of course I needn't assure you," he said, "that if you should come to England next year, I expect to be the first person that you inform of it."

Bessie Alden looked at him a little and she smiled. "Oh, if we come to London," she answered, "I should think you would hear of it."

Percy Beaumont returned with his cousin, and his sense of duty compelled him, one windless afternoon, in mid-Atlantic, to say to Lord Lambeth that he suspected that the duchess's telegram was in part the result of something he himself had written to her. "I wrote to her—as I explicitly notified you I had promised to do—that you were extremely interested in a little American girl."

Lord Lambeth was extremely angry, and he indulged for some moments in the simple language of indignation. But I have said that he was a reasonable young man, and I can give no better proof of it than the fact that he remarked to his companion at the end of half an hour, "You were quite right, after all. I am very much interested in her. Only, to be fair," he added, "you should have told my mother also that she is not—seriously—interested in me."

Percy Beaumont gave a little laugh. "There is nothing so charming as modesty in a young man in your position. That speech is a capital proof that you are sweet on her."

"She is not interested—she is not!" Lord Lambeth repeated.

"My dear fellow," said his companion, "you are very far gone."

PART II

IN POINT of fact, as Percy Beaumont would have said, Mrs. Westgate disembarked on May 18th on the British coast. She was accompanied by her sister, but she was not attended by any other member of her family. To the deprivation of her husband's society Mrs. Westgate was, however, habituated; she had made half a dozen journeys to Europe without him, and she now accounted for his absence, to interrogative friends on this side of the Atlantic, by allusion to the regrettable but conspicuous fact that in America there was no leisure class. The two ladies came up to London and alighted at Jones's Hotel, where Mrs. Westgate, who had made on former occasions the most agreeable impression at this establishment, received an obsequious greeting. Bessie Alden had felt much excited about coming to England; she had expected the "associations" would be very charming, that it would be an infinite pleasure to rest her eyes upon the things she had read about in the poets and historians. She was very fond of the poets and historians, of the picturesque, of the past, of retrospect, of mementos and reverberations of greatness; so that on coming into the great English world, where strangeness and familiarity would go hand in hand, she was prepared for a multitude of fresh emotions. They began very promptly— these tender, fluttering sensations; they began with the sight of the beautiful English landscape, whose dark richness was quickened and brightened by the season; with the carpeted fields and flowering hedge-rows, as she looked at them from the window of the train; with the spires of rural churches peeping above the rook-haunted tree-tops; with the oak-studded parks, the ancient homes, the cloudy light, the speech, the manners, the thousand differences. Mrs. Westgate's impressions had, of course, much less novelty and keenness, and she gave but a wandering attention to her sister's ejaculations and rhapsodies.

"You know my enjoyment of England is not so intellectual as Bessie's," she said to several of her friends in the course of her visit to this country. "And yet if it is not intellectual, I can't say it is physical. I don't think I can quite say what it is—my enjoyment of England." When once it was settled that the two ladies should come abroad and should spend a few weeks in England on their way to the Continent, they of course exchanged a good many allusions to their London acquaintance.

"It will certainly be much nicer having friends there," Bessie Alden had said one day, as she sat on the sunny deck of the steamer at her sister's feet, on a large blue rug.

"Whom do you mean by friends?" Mrs. Westgate asked.

"All those English gentlemen whom you have known and entertained. Captain Littledale, for instance. And Lord Lambeth and Mr. Beaumont," added Bessie Alden.

"Do you expect them to give us a very grand reception?"

Bessie reflected a moment; she was addicted, as we know, to reflection. "Well, yes."

"My poor, sweet child!" murmured her sister.

"What have I said that is so silly?" asked Bessie.

"You are a little too simple; just a little. It is very be-coming, but it pleases people at your expense."

"I am certainly too simple to understand you," said Bessie.

"Shall I tell you a story?" asked her sister.

"If you would be so good. That is what they do to amuse simple people."

Mrs. Westgate consulted her memory, while her companion sat gazing at the shining sea. "Did you ever hear of the Duke of Green-Erin?"

"I think not," said Bessie.

"Well, it's no matter," her sister went on.

"It's a proof of my simplicity."

"My story is meant to illustrate that of some other peo-ple," said Mrs. Westgate. "The Duke of Green-Erin is what they call in England a great swell, and some five years ago he came to America. He spent most of his time in New York, and in New York he spent his days and his nights at the Butterworths'. You have heard, at least, of the Butterworths. *Bien.* They did everything in the world for him—they turned themselves inside out. They gave him a dozen din-ner-parties and balls, and were the means of his being in-vited to fifty more. At first he used to come into Mrs. Butter-worth's box at the opera in a tweed travelling suit; but some one stopped that. At any rate, he had a beautiful time, and they parted the best of friends in the world. Two years elapse, and the Butterworths come abroad and go to London. The first thing they see in all the papers—in England those things are in the most prominent place—is that the Duke of Green-Erin has arrived in town for the season. They wait a little, and then Mr. Butterworth—as polite as ever—goes and leaves a card. They wait a little more; the visit is not re-turned; they wait three weeks—*silence de mort*—the duke gives no sign. The Butterworths see a lot of other people, put down the Duke of Green-Erin as a rude, ungrateful man, and forget all about him. One fine day they go to the Ascot races, and there they meet him face to face. He stares a moment, and then comes up to Mr. Butterworth, taking some-thing from his pocket-book—something which proves to be bank-note. 'I'm glad to see you, Mr. Butterworth,' he says, so that I can pay you that £10 I lost to you in New York. I saw the other day you remembered our bet; here are the £10, Mr. Butterworth. Good-bye, Mr. Butterworth.' And off he goes, and that's the last they see of the Duke of Green-Erin."

"Is that your story?" asked Bessie Alden.

"Don't you think it's interesting?" her sister replied.

"I don't believe it."

"Ah," cried Mrs. Westgate, "you are not so simple, after all! Believe it or not, as you please; there is no smoke without fire."

"Is that the way," asked Bessie, after a moment, "that you expect your friends to treat you?"

"I defy them to treat me very ill, because I shall not give them the opportunity. With the best will in the world, in that case they can't be very offensive."

Bessie Alden was silent a moment. "I don't see what makes you talk that way," she said. "The English are a great people."

"Exactly; and that is just the way they have grown great—by dropping you when you have ceased to be useful. People say they are not clever; but I think they are very clever."

"You know you have liked them—all the Englishmen you have seen," said Bessie.

"They have liked me," her sister rejoined; "it would be more correct to say that. And, of course, one likes that."

Bessie Alden resumed for some moments her studies in sea-green. "Well," she said, "whether they like me or not, I mean to like them. And, happily," she added, "Lord Lambeth does not owe me £10."

During the first few days after their arrival at Jones's Hotel our charming Americans were much occupied with what they would have called looking about them. They found occasion to make a large number of purchases, and their opportunities for conversation were such only as were offered by the deferential London shopmen. Bessie Alden, even in driving from the station, took an immense fancy to the British metropolis, and at the risk of exhibiting her as a young woman of vulgar tastes, it must be recorded that for a considerable period she desired no higher pleasure than to drive about the crowded streets in a hansome cab. To her attentive eyes they were full of a strange, picturesque life, and it is at least beneath the dignity of our historic muse to enumerate the trivial objects and incidents which this simple young lady from Boston found so entertaining. It may be freely mentioned, however, that whenever, after a round of visits in Bond Street and Regent Street, she was about to return with her sister to Jones's Hotel, she made an earnest re-

quest that they should be driven home by way of West-
minster Abbey. She had begun by asking whether it would not
be possible to take in the Tower on the way to their lodgings;
but it happened that at a more primitive stage of her culture Mrs. Westgate had paid a visit to this venerable monument, which she spoke of ever afterwards vaguely as a dreadful disappointment; so that she expressed the liveliest disap-
proval of any attempt to combine historical researches with
the purchase of hair-brushes and notepaper. The most she
would consent to do in this line was to spend half an hour
at Madame Tussaud's, where she saw several dusty wax ef-
figies of members of the royal family. She told Bessie that if
she wished to go to the Tower she must get some one else
to take her. Bessie expressed hereupon an earnest disposition
to go alone; but upon this proposal as well, Mrs. Westgate
sprinkled cold water.

"Remember," she said, "that you are not in your innocent
little Boston. It is not a question of walking up and down
Beacon Street." Then she went on to explain that there were
two classes of American girls in Europe—those that walked
about alone and those that did not. "You happen to belong,
my dear," she said to her sister, "to the class that does
not."

"It is only," answered Bessie, laughing, "because you happen to prevent me." And she devoted much private medita-
tion to this question of effecting a visit to the Tower of London.

Suddenly it seemed as if the problem might be solved;
the two ladies at Jones's Hotel received a visit from Willie
Woodley. Such was the social appellation of a young American who had sailed from New York a few days after their
own departure, and who, having the privilege of intimacy with
them in that city had lost no time, on his arrival in London,
in coming to pay them his respects. He had, in fact, gone to
see them directly after going to see his tailor, than which
there can be no greater exhibition of promptitude on the
part of a young American who had just alighted at the
Charing Cross Hotel. He was a slim, pale youth, of the most
amiable disposition, famous for the skill with which he led
the "German" in New York. Indeed, by the young ladies who
habitually figured in this Terpsichorean revel he was believed
to be "the best dancer in the world"; it was in these terms
that he was always spoken of, and that his identity was indicated. He was the gentlest, softest young man it was possible to meet; he was beautifully dressed—"in the English

style"—and he knew an immense deal about London. He
had been at Newport during the previous summer, at the time
of our young Englishmen's visit, and he took extreme pleasure in the society of Bessie Alden, whom he always addressed as "Miss Bessie." She immediately arranged with
him, in the presence of her sister, that he should conduct her
to the scene of Anne Boleyn's execution.

"You may do as you please," said Mrs. Westgate. "Only
—if you desire the information—it is not the custom here for
young ladies to knock about London with young men."

"Miss Bessie has waltzed with me so often," observed
Willie Woodley; "she can surely go out with me in a han-
som!"

"I consider waltzing," said Mrs. Westgate, "the most innocent pleasure of our time."

"It's a compliment to our time!" exclaimed the young man,
with a little laugh in spite of himself.

"I don't see why I should regard what is done here," said
Bessie Alden. "Why should I suffer the restrictions of a society of which I enjoy none of the privileges?"

"That's very good—very good," murmured Willie Woodley.

"Oh, go to the Tower, and feel the axe, if you like," said
Mrs. Westgate. "I consent to your going with Mr. Woodley; but I should not let you go with an Englishman."

"Miss Bessie wouldn't care to go with an Englishman!" Mr.
Woodley declared, with a faint asperity that was, perhaps, not
unnatural in a young man, who, dressing in the manner that
I have indicated, and knowing a great deal, as I have said,
about London, saw no reason for drawing these sharp distinctions. He agreed upon a day with Miss Bessie—a day of
that same week.

An ingenious mind might, perhaps, trace a connection
between the young girl's allusion to her destitution of social
privileges and a question she asked on the morrow, as she
sat with her sister at lunch.

"Don't you mean to write to—to any one?" said Bessie.

"I wrote this morning to Captain Littledale," Mrs. Westgate
replied.

"But Mr. Woodley said that Captain Littledale had gone to
India."

"He said he thought he had heard so; he knew nothing
about it."

For a moment Bessie Alden said nothing more; then, at

last, "And don't you intend to write to—to Mr. Beaumont?" she inquired.

"You mean to Lord Lambeth," said her sister.

"I said Mr. Beaumont, because he was so good a friend of yours."

Mrs. Westgate looked at the young girl with sisterly candor. "I don't care two straws for Mr. Beaumont."

"You were certainly very nice to him."

"I am nice to every one," said Mrs. Westgate, simply.

"To every one but me," rejoined Bessie smiling.

Her sister continued to look at her; then, at last, "Are you in love with Lord Lambeth?" she asked.

The young girl stared a moment, and the question was apparently too humorous even to make her blush. "Not that I know of," she answered.

"Because, if you are," Mrs. Westgate went on, "I shall certainly not send for him."

"That proves what I said," declared Bessie, smiling—"that you are not nice to me."

"It would be a poor service, my dear child," said her sister.

"In what sense? There is nothing against Lord Lambeth that I know of."

Mrs. Westgate was silent a moment. "You *are* in love with him, then?"

Bessie stared again; but this time she blushed a little. "Ah! if you won't be serious," she answered, "we will not mention him again."

For some moments Lord Lambeth was not mentioned again, and it was Mrs. Westgate who, at the end of this period, reverted to him. "Of course I will let him know we are here, because I think he would be hurt—justly enough—if we should go away without seeing him. It is fair to give him a chance to come and thank me for the kindness we showed him. But I don't want to seem eager."

"Neither do I," said Bessie, with a little laugh.

"Though I confess," added her sister, "that I am curious to see how he will behave."

"He behaved very well at Newport."

"Newport is not London. At Newport he could do as he liked; but here it is another affair. He has to have an eye to consequences."

"If he had more freedom, then, at Newport," argued Bessie, "it is the more to his credit that he behaved well; and if he has to be so careful here, it is possible he will behave even better."

"Better—better," repeated her sister. "My dear child, what is your point of view?"

"How do you mean—my point of view?"

"Don't you care for Lord Lambeth—a little?"

This time Bessie Alden was displeased; she slowly got up from the table, turning her face away from her sister. "You will oblige me by not talking so," she said.

Mrs. Westgate sat watching her for some moments as she moved slowly about the room and went and stood at the window. "I will write to him this afternoon," she said at last.

"Do as you please!" Bessie answered; and presently she turned round. "I am not afraid to say that I like Lord Lambeth. I like him very much."

"He is not clever," Mrs. Westgate declared.

"Well, there have been clever people whom I have disliked," said Bessie Alden; "so that I suppose I may like a stupid one. Besides, Lord Lambeth is not stupid."

"Not so stupid as he looks!" exclaimed her sister, smiling.

"If I were in love with Lord Lambeth, as you said just now, it would be bad policy on your part to abuse him."

"My dear child, don't give me lessons in policy!" cried Mrs. Westgate. "The policy I mean to follow is very deep."

The young girl began to walk about the room again; then she stopped before her sister. "I have never heard in the course of five minutes," she said, "so many hints and innuendoes. I wish you would tell me in plain English what you mean."

"I mean that you may be much annoyed."

"That is still only a hint," said Bessie.

Her sister looked at her, hesitating an instant. "It will be said of you that you have come after Lord Lambeth—that you followed him."

Bessie Alden threw back her pretty head like a startled hind, and a look flashed into her face that made Mrs. Westgate rise from her chair. "Who says such things as that?" she demanded.

"People here."

"I don't believe it," said Bessie.

"You have a very convenient faculty of doubt. But my policy will be, as I say, very deep. I shall leave you to find out this kind of thing for yourself."

Bessie fixed her eyes upon her sister, and Mrs. Westgate thought for a moment there were tears in them. "Do they talk that way here?" she asked.

"You will see. I shall leave you alone."

"Don't leave me alone," said Bessie Alden. "Take me away."

"No; I want to see what you make of it," her sister continued.

"I don't understand."

"You will understand after Lord Lambeth has come," said Mrs. Westgate, with a little laugh.

The two ladies had arranged that on this afternoon Willie Woodley should go with them to Hyde Park, where Bessie Alden expected to derive much entertainment from sitting on a little green chair, under the great trees, beside Rotten Row. The want of a suitable escort had hitherto rendered this pleasure inaccessible; but no escort now, for such an expedition, could have been more suitable than their devoted young countryman, whose mission in life, it might almost be said, was to find chairs for ladies, and who appeared on the stroke of half past five with a white camellia in his buttonhole.

"I have written to Lord Lambeth, my dear," said Mrs. Westgate to her sister, on coming into the room where Bessie Alden, drawing on her long gray gloves, was entertaining their visitor.

Bessie said nothing, but Willie Woodley exclaimed that his lordship was in town; he had seen his name in the *Morning Post*.

"Do you read the *Morning Post?*" asked Mrs. Westgate.

"Oh yes; it's great fun," Willie Woodley affirmed.

"I want so to see it," said Bessie; "there is so much about it in Thackeray."

"I will send it to you every morning," said Willie Woodley.

He found them what Bessie Alden thought excellent places, under the great trees, beside the famous avenue whose humors had been made familiar to the young girl's childhood by the pictures in *Punch*. The day was bright and warm, and the crowd of riders and spectators, and the great procession of carriages, were proportionately dense and brilliant. The scene bore the stamp of the London Season at its height, and Bessie Alden found more entertainment in it than she was able to express to her companions. She sat silent, under her parasol, and her imagination, according to its wont, let itself loose into the great changing assemblage of striking and suggestive figures. They stirred up a host of old impressions and preconceptions, and she found herself fitting a history to this person and a theory to that, and making a place for them all in her little private museum of types. But if she said little, her sister on one side and Willie Woodley on the other expressed themselves in lively alternation.

"Look at that green dress with blue flounces," said Mrs. Westgate. *"Quelle toilette!"*

"That's the Marquis of Blackborough," said the young man—"the one in the white coat. I heard him speak the other night in the House of Lords; it was something about ramrods; he called them *wamwods*. He's an awful swell."

"Did you ever see anything like the way they are pinned back?" Mrs. Westgate resumed. "They never know where to stop."

"They do nothing but stop," said Willie Woodley. "It prevents them from walking. Here comes a great celebrity, Lady Beatrice Bellevue. She's awfully fast; see what little steps she takes."

"Well, my dear," Mrs. Westgate pursued, "I hope you are getting some ideas for your *couturière?*"

"I am getting plenty of ideas," said Bessie, "but I don't know that my *couturière* would appreciate them."

Willie Woodley presently perceived a friend on horseback, who drove up beside the barrier of the Row and beckoned to him. He went forward, and the crowd of pedestrians closed about him, so that for some ten minutes he was hidden from sight. At last he reappeared, bringing a gentleman with him—a gentleman whom Bessie at first supposed to be his friend dismounted. But at a second glance she found herself looking at Lord Lambeth, who was shaking hands with her sister.

"I found him over there," said Willie Woodley, "and I told him you were here."

And then Lord Lambeth, touching his hat a little, shook hands with Bessie. "Fancy your being here!" he said. He was blushing and smiling; he looked very handsome, and he had a kind of splendor that he had not had in America. Bessie Alden's imagination, as we know, was just then in exercise; so that the tall young Englishman, as he stood there looking down at her, had the benefit of it. "He is handsomer and more splendid than anything I have ever seen," she said to herself. And then she remembered that he was a marquis, and she thought he looked like a marquis.

"I say, you know," he cried, "you ought to have let a man know you were here!"

"I wrote to you an hour ago," said Mrs. Westgate.

"Doesn't all the world know it?" asked Bessie, smiling.

"I assure you I didn't know it!" cried Lord Lambeth. "Upon my honor, I hadn't heard of it. Ask Woodley, now; had I, Woodley?"

"Well, I think you are rather a humbug," said Willie Woodley.

"You don't believe that—do you, Miss Alden?" asked his lordship. "You don't believe I'm a humbug, eh?"

"No," said Bessie, "I don't."

"You are too tall to stand up, Lord Lambeth," Mrs. Westgate observed. "You are only tolerable when you sit down. Be so good as to get a chair."

He found a chair and placed it sidewise, close to the two ladies. "If I hadn't met Woodley I should never have found you," he went on. "Should I, Woodley?"

"Well, I guess not," said the young American.

"Not even with my letter?" asked Mrs. Westgate.

"Ah, well, I haven't got your letter yet; I suppose I shall get it this evening. It was awfully kind of you to write."

"So I said to Bessie," observed Mrs. Westgate.

"Did she say so, Miss Alden?" Lord Lambeth inquired. "I dare say you have been here a month."

"We have been here three," said Mrs. Westgate.

"Have you been here three months?" the young man asked again of Bessie.

"It seems a long time," Bessie answered.

"I say, after that you had better not call me a humbug!" cried Lord Lambeth. "I have only been in town three weeks; but you must have been hiding away; I haven't seen you anywhere."

"Where should you have seen us—where should we have gone?" asked Mrs. Westgate.

"You should have gone to Hurlingham," said Woodley.

"No; let Lord Lambeth tell us," Mrs. Westgate insisted.

"There are plenty of places to go to," said Lord Lambeth; "each one stupider than the other. I mean people's houses; they send you cards."

"No one has sent us cards," said Bessie.

"We are very quiet," her sister declared. "We are here as travellers."

"We have been to Madame Tussaud's," Bessie pursued.

"Oh, I say!" cried Lord Lambeth.

"We thought we should find your image there," said Mrs. Westgate—"yours and Mr. Beaumont's."

"In the Chamber of Horrors?" laughed the young man.

"It did duty very well for a party," said Mrs. Westgate.

"All the women were *décolletées,* and many of the figures looked as if they could speak if they tried."

"Upon my word," Lord Lambeth rejoined, "you see people at London parties that look as if they couldn't speak if they tried."

"Do you think Mr. Woodley could find us Mr. Beaumont?" asked Mrs. Westgate.

Lord Lambeth stared and looked round him. "I dare say he could. Beaumont often comes here. Don't you think you could find him, Woodley? Make a dive into the crowd."

"Thank you; I have had enough diving," said Willie Woodley. "I will wait till Mr. Beaumont comes to the surface."

"I will bring him to see you," said Lord Lambeth; "where are you staying?"

"You will find the address in my letter—Jones's Hotel."

"Oh, one of those places just out of Piccadilly? Beastly hole, isn't it?" Lord Lambeth inquired.

"I believe it's the best hotel in London," said Mrs. Westgate.

"But they give you awful rubbish to eat, don't they?" his lordship went on.

"Yes," said Mrs. Westgate.

"I always feel so sorry for the people that come up to town and go to live in those places," continued the young man. "They eat nothing but filth."

"Oh, I say!" cried Willie Woodley.

"Well, how do you like London, Miss Alden?" Lord Lambeth asked, unperturbed by this ejaculation.

"I think it's grand," said Bessie Alden.

"My sister likes it, in spite of the 'filth!' " Mrs. Westgate exclaimed.

"I hope you are going to stay a long time."

"As long as I can," said Bessie.

"And where is Mr. Westgate?" asked Lord Lambeth of this gentleman's wife.

"He's where he always is—in that tiresome New York."

"He must be tremendously clever," said the young man.

"I suppose he is," said Mrs. Westgate.

Lord Lambeth sat for nearly an hour with his American friends; but it is not our purpose to relate their conversation in full. He addressed a great many remarks to Bessie Alden, and finally turned towards her altogether, while Willie Woodley entertained Mrs. Westgate. Bessie herself said very little; she was on her guard, thinking of what her sister had said to her at lunch. Little by little, however, she interested herself

in Lord Lambeth again, as she had done at Newport; only it
seemed to her that here he might become more interesting.
He would be an unconscious part of the antiquity, the impressiveness, the picturesqueness, of England; and poor Bessie Alden, like many a Yankee maiden, was terribly at the
mercy of picturesqueness.

"I have often wished I were at Newport again," said the
young man. "Those days I spent at your sister's were awfully jolly."

"We enjoyed them very much; I hope your father is better."

"Oh dear, yes. When I got to England he was out grouse-
shooting. It was what you call in America a gigantic fraud.
My mother had got nervous. My three weeks at Newport
seemed like a happy dream."

"America certainly is very different from England," said
Bessie.

"I hope you like England better, eh?" Lord Lambeth rejoined, almost persuasively.

"No Englishman can ask that seriously of a person of
another country."

Her companion looked at her for a moment. "You mean
it's a matter of course?"

"If I were English," said Bessie, "it would certainly seem
to me a matter of course that every one should be a good
patriot."

"Oh dear, yes, patriotism is everything," said Lord Lambeth, not quite following, but very contented. "Now, what are
you going to do here?"

"On Thursday I am going to the Tower."

"The Tower?"

"The Tower of London. Did you never hear of it?"

"Oh yes, I have been there," said Lord Lambeth. "I was
taken there by my governess when I was six years old. It's
a rum idea, your going there."

"Do give me a few more rum ideas," said Bessie. "I want
to see everything of that sort. I am going to Hampton Court,
and to Windsor, and to the Dulwich Gallery."

Lord Lambeth seemed greatly amused. "I wonder you
don't go to the Rosherville Gardens."

"Are they interesting?" asked Bessie.

"Oh, wonderful!"

"Are they very old? That's all I care for," said Bessie.

"They are tremendously old; they are falling to ruins."

"I think there is nothing so charming as an old ruinous

garden," said the young girl. "We must certainly go there."

Lord Lambeth broke into merriment. "I say, Woodley," he cried, "here's Miss Alden wants to go to the Rosherville Gardens!"

Willie Woodley looked a little blank; he was caught in the fact of ignorance of an apparently conspicuous feature of London life. But in a moment he turned it off. "Very well," he said, "I'll write for a permit."

Lord Lambeth's exhilaration increased. "Gad, I believe you Americans would go anywhere!" he cried.

"We wish to go to Parliament," said Bessie. "That's one of the first things."

"Oh, it would bore you to death!" cried the young man.

"We wish to hear you speak."

"I never speak—except to young ladies," said Lord Lambeth, smiling.

Bessie Alden looked at him a while, smiling, too, in the shadow of her parasol. "You are very strange," she murmured. "I don't think I approve of you."

"Ah, now, don't be severe, Miss Alden," said Lord Lambeth, smiling still more. "Please don't be severe. I want you to like me—awfully."

"To like you awfully? You must not laugh at me, then, when I make mistakes. I consider it my right, as a free-born American, to make as many mistakes as I choose."

"Upon my word I didn't laugh at you," said Lord Lambeth.

"And not only that," Bessie went on: "but I hold that all my mistakes shall be set down to my credit. You must think the better of me for them."

"I can't think better of you than I do," the young man declared.

Bessie Alden looked at him a moment. "You certainly speak very well to young ladies. But why don't you address the House?—isn't that what they call it?"

"Because I have nothing to say," said Lord Lambeth.

"Haven't you a great position?" asked Bessie Alden.

He looked a moment at the back of his glove. "I'll set that down," he said, "as one of your mistakes to your credit." And as if he disliked talking about his position, he changed the subject. "I wish you would let me go with you to the Tower, and to Hampton Court, and to all those other places."

"We shall be most happy," said Bessie.

"And of course I shall be delighted to show you the House of Lords—some day that suits you. There are a lot of things

I want to do for you. I want to make you have a good time. And I should like very much to present some of my friends to you, if it wouldn't bore you. Then it would be awfully kind of you to come down to Branches."

"We are much obliged to you, Lord Lambeth," said Bessie. "What is Branches?"

"It's a house in the country. I think you might like it."

Willie Woodley and Mrs. Westgate at this moment were sitting in silence, and the young man's ear caught these last words of Lord Lambeth's. "He's inviting Miss Bessie to one of his castles," he murmured to his companion.

Mrs. Westgate, foreseeing what she mentally called "complications," immediately got up; and the two ladies, taking leave of Lord Lambeth, returned, under Mr. Woodley's conduct, to Jones's Hotel.

Lord Lambeth came to see them on the morrow, bringing Percy Beaumont with him—the latter having instantly declared his intention of neglecting none of the usual offices of civility. This declaration, however, when his kinsman informed him of the advent of their American friends, had been preceded by another remark.

"Here they are, then, and you are in for it."

"What am I in for?" demanded Lord Lambeth.

"I will let your mother give it a name. With all respect to whom," added Percy Beaumont, "I must decline on this occasion to do any more police duty. Her Grace must look after you herself."

"I will give her a chance," said her Grace's son, a trifle grimly. "I shall make her go and see them."

"She won't do it, my boy."

"We'll see if she doesn't," said Lord Lambeth.

But if Percy Beaumont took a sombre view of the arrival of the two ladies at Jones's Hotel, he was sufficiently a man of the world to offer them a smiling countenance. He fell into animated conversation—conversation, at least, that was animated on her side—with Mrs. Westgate, while his companion made himself agreeable to the young lady. Mrs. Westgate began confessing and protesting, declaring and expounding.

"I must say London is a great deal brighter and prettier just now than when I was here last—in the month of November. There is evidently a great deal going on, and you seem to have a good many flowers. I have no doubt it is very charming for all you people, and that you amuse yourselves immensely. It is very good of you to let Bessie and me come and sit and look at you. I suppose you think I am satirical, but I must confess that that's the feeling I have in London."

"I am afraid I don't quite understand to what feeling you allude," said Percy Beaumont.

"The feeling that it's all very well for you English people. Everything is beautifully arranged for you."

"It seems to me it is very well for some Americans, sometimes," rejoined Beaumont.

"For some of them, yes—if they like to be patronized. But I must say I don't like to be patronized. I may be very eccentric and undisciplined and outrageous, but I confess I never was fond of patronage. I like to associate with people on the same terms as I do in my own country; that's a peculiar taste that I have. But here people seem to expect something else—Heaven knows what! I am afraid you will think I am very ungrateful, for I certainly have received a great deal of attention. The last time I was here, a lady sent me a message that I was at liberty to come and see her."

"Dear me! I hope you didn't go," observed Percy Beaumont.

"You are deliciously naïve, I must say that for you!" Mrs. Westgate exclaimed. "It must be a great advantage to you here in London. I suppose if I myself had a little more naïveté, I should enjoy it more. I should be content to sit on a chair in the park, and see the people pass, and be told that this is the Duchess of Suffolk, and that is the Lord Chamberlain, and that I must be thankful for the privilege of beholding them. I dare say it is very wicked and critical of me to ask for anything else. But I was always critical, and I freely confess to the sin of being fastidious. I am told there is some remarkably superior second-rate society provided here for strangers. *Merci!* I don't want any superior second-rate society. I want the society that I have been accustomed to."

"I hope you don't call Lambeth and me second-rate," Beaumont interposed.

"Oh, I am accustomed to you," said Mrs. Westgate. "Do you know that you English sometimes make the most wonderful speeches? The first time I came to London I went out to dine—as I told you, I have received a great deal of attention. After dinner, in the drawing-room I had some conversation with an old lady; I assure you I had. I forget what we talked about, but she presently said, in allusion to something we were discussing, 'Oh, you know, the aristocracy do so-and-so; but in one's own class of life it is very different.' In one's own class of life! What is a poor unprotected American woman to do in a country where she is liable to have that sort of thing said to her?"

"You seem to get hold of some very queer old ladies; I compliment you on your acquaintance!" Percy Beaumont exclaimed. "If you are trying to bring me to admit that London is an odious place; you'll not succeed. I'm extremely fond of it, and I think it the jolliest place in the world."

"*Pour vous autres*. I never said the contrary," Mrs. Westgate retorted. I make use of this expression, because both interlocutors had begun to raise their voices. Percy Beaumont naturally did not like to hear his country abused, and Mrs. Westgate, no less naturally, did not like a stubborn debater.

"Hallo!" said Lord Lambeth; "what are they up to now?" And he came away from the window, where he had been standing with Bessie Alden.

"I quite agree with a very clever countrywoman of mine," Mrs. Westgate continued, with charming ardor, though with imperfect relevancy. She smiled at the two gentlemen for a moment with terrible brightness, as if to toss at their feet—upon their native heath—the gauntlet of defiance. "For me there are only two social positions worth speaking of—that of an American lady, and that of the Emperor of Russia."

"And what do you do with the American gentlemen?" asked Lord Lambeth.

"She leaves them in America!" said Percy Beaumont.

On the departure of their visitors, Bessie Alden told her sister that Lord Lambeth would come the next day, to go with them to the Tower, and that he had kindly offered to bring his "trap," and drive them thither.

Mrs. Westgate listened in silence to this communication, and for some time afterwards she said nothing. But at last: "If you had not requested me the other day not to mention it," she began, "there is something I should venture to ask you." Bessie frowned a little; her dark blue eyes were more dark than blue. But her sister went on. "As it is, I will take the risk. You are not in love with Lord Lambeth: I believe it, perfectly. Very good. But is there, by chance, any danger of your becoming so? It's a very simple question; don't take offence. I have a particular reason," said Mrs. Westgate, "for wanting to know."

Bessie Alden for some moment said nothing; she only looked displeased. "No; there is no danger," she answered at last, curtly.

"Then I should like to frighten them," declared Mrs. Westgate, clasping her jewelled hands.

"To frighten whom?"

"All these people; Lord Lambeth's family and friends."

"How should you frighten them?" asked the young girl.

"It wouldn't be I—it would be you. It would frighten them to think that you should absorb his lordship's young affections."

Bessie Alden, with her clear eyes still overshadowed by her dark brows, continued to interrogate. "Why should that frighten them?"

Mrs. Westgate poised her answer with a smile before delivering it. "Because they think you are not good enough. You are a charming girl, beautiful and amiable, intelligent and clever, and as *bien-élevée* as it is possible to be; but you are not a fit match for Lord Lambeth."

Bessie Alden was decidedly disgusted. "Where do you get such extraordinary ideas?" she asked. "You have said some such strange things lately. My dear Kitty, where do you collect them?"

Kitty was evidently enamoured of her idea. "Yes, it would put them on pins and needles, and it wouldn't hurt you. Mr. Beaumont is already most uneasy; I could soon see that."

The young girl meditated a moment. "Do you mean that they spy upon him—that they interfere with him?"

"I don't know what power they have to interfere, but I know that a British mamma may worry her son's life out."

It has been intimated that, as regards certain disagreeable things, Bessie Alden had a fund of scepticism. She abstained on the present occasion from expressing disbelief, for she wished not to irritate her sister. But she said to herself that Kitty had been misinformed—that this was a traveller's tale. Though she was a girl of a lively imagination, there could in the nature of things be, to her sense, no reality in the idea of her belonging to vulgar category. What she said aloud was, "I must say that in that case I am very sorry for Lord Lambeth."

Mrs. Westgate, more and more exhilarated by her scheme, was smiling at her again. "If I could only believe it was safe!" she exclaimed. "When you begin to pity him, I, on my side, am afraid."

"Afraid of what?"

"Of your pitying him too much."

Bessie Alden turned away impatiently; but at the end of a

minute she turned back. "What if I should pity him too much?" she asked.

Mrs. Westgate hereupon turned away, but after a moment's reflection she also faced her sister again. "It would come, after all, to the same thing," she said.

Lord Lambeth came the next day with his trap, and the two ladies, attended by Willie Woodley, placed themselves under his guidance, and were conveyed eastward, through some of the dusker portions of the metropolis, to the great turreted donjon which overlooks the London shipping. They all descended from their vehicle and entered the famous enclosures; and they secured the services of a venerable beef-eater, who, though there were many other claimants for legendary information, made a fine exclusive party of them, and marched them through courts and corridors, through armories and prisons. He delivered his usual peripatetic discourse, and they stopped and stared, and peeped and stooped, according to the official admonitions. Bessie Alden asked the old man in the crimson doublet a great many questions; she thought it a most fascinating place. Lord Lambeth was in high good-humor; he was constantly laughing; he enjoyed what he would have called the lark. Willie Woodley kept looking at the ceilings and tapping the walls with the knuckle of a pearl-gray glove; and Mrs. Westgate, asking at frequent intervals to be allowed to sit down and wait till they came back, was as frequently informed that they would never come back. To a great many of Bessie's questions—chiefly on collateral points of English history—the ancient warder was naturally unable to reply; whereupon she always appealed to Lord Lambeth. But his lordship was very ignorant. He declared that he knew nothing about that sort of thing, and he seemed greatly diverted at being treated as an authority.

"You can't expect every one to know as much as you," he said.

"I should expect you to know a great deal more." declared Bessie Alden.

"Women always know more than men about names and dates, and that sort of thing," Lord Lambeth rejoined. "There was Lady Jane Grey we have just been hearing about, who went in for Latin and Greek, and all the learning of her age."

"*You* have no right to be ignorant, at all events," said Bessie.

"Why haven't I as good a right as any one else?"

"Because you have lived in the midst of all these things."

"What things do you mean? Axes, and blocks, and thumb-screws?"

"All these historical things. You belong to a historical family."

"Bessie is really too historical," said Mrs. Westgate, catching a word of this dialogue.

"Yes, you are too historical," said Lord Lambeth, laughing, but thankful for a formula. "Upon my honor, you are too historical!"

He went with the ladies a couple of days later to Hampton Court, Willie Woodley being also of the party. The afternoon was charming, the famous horse-chestnuts were in blossom, and Lord Lambeth, who quite entered into the spirit of the cockney excursionist, declared that it was a jolly old place. Bessie Alden was in ecstasies; she went about murmuring and exclaiming.

"It's too lovely," said the young girl; "it's too enchanting; it's too exactly what it ought to be!"

At Hampton Court the little flocks of visitors are not provided with an official bell-wether, but are left to browse at discretion upon the local antiquities. It happened in this manner that, in default of another informant, Bessie Alden, who on doubtful questions was able to suggest a great many alternatives, found herself again applying for intellectual assistance to Lord Lambeth. But he again assured her that he was utterly helpless in such matters—that his education had been sadly neglected.

"And I am sorry it makes you unhappy," he added, in a moment.

"You are very disappointing, Lord Lambeth," she said.

"Ah, now, don't say that!" he cried. "That's the worst thing you could possibly say."

"No," she rejoined, "it is not so bad as to say that I had expected nothing of you."

"I don't know. Give me a notion of the sort of thing you expected."

"Well," said Bessie Alden, "that you would be more what I should like to be—what I should try to be—in your place."

"Ah, my place!" exclaimed Lord Lambeth. "You are always talking about my place!"

The young girl looked at him; he thought she colored a little; and for a moment she made no rejoinder.

"Does it strike you that I am always talking about your place?" she asked.

"I am sure you do it a great honor," he said, fearing he had been uncivil.

"I have often thought about it," she went on, after a moment. "I have often thought about your being a hereditary legislator. A hereditary legislator ought to know a great many things."

"Not if he doesn't legislate."

"But you do legislate; it's absurd your saying you don't. You are very much looked up to here—I am assured of that."

"I don't know that I ever noticed it."

"It is because you are used to it, then. You ought to fill the place."

"How do you mean to fill it?" asked Lord Lambeth.

"You ought to be very clever and brilliant, and to know almost everything."

Lord Lambeth looked at her a moment. "Shall I tell you something?" he asked. "A young man in my position, as you call it——"

"I didn't invent the term," interposed Bessie Alden. "I have seen it in a great many books."

"Hang it! you are always at your books. A fellow in my position, then, does very well whatever he does. That's about what I mean to say."

"Well, if your own people are content with you," said Bessie Alden, laughing, "it is not for me to complain. But I shall always think that, properly, you should have been a great mind—a great character."

"Ah, that's very theoretic," Lord Lambeth declared. "Depend upon it, that's a Yankee prejudice."

"Happy the country," said Bessie Alden, "where even people's prejudices are so elevated!"

"Well, after all," observed Lord Lambeth, "I don't know that I am such a fool as you are trying to make me out."

"I said nothing so rude as that; but I must repeat that you are disappointing."

"My dear Miss Alden," exclaimed the young man, "I am the best fellow in the world!"

"Ah, if it were not for that!" said Bessie Alden, with a smile.

Mrs. Westgate had a good many more friends in London than she pretended, and before long she had renewed acquaintance with most of them. Their hospitality was extreme, so that, one thing leading to another, she began, as the phrase is, to go out. Bessie Alden, in this way, saw something of what she found it a great satisfaction to call to herself English society. She went to balls and danced, she went to dinners and talked, she went to concerts and listened (at concerts Bessie always listened), she went to exhibitions and wondered. Her enjoyment was keen and her curiosity insatiable, and, grateful in general for all her opportunities, she especially prized the privilege of meeting certain celebrated persons—authors and artists, philosophers and statesmen—of whose renown she had been a humble and distant beholder, and who now, as a part of the habitual furniture of London drawing-rooms, struck her as stars fallen from the firmament and become palpable—revealing also sometimes, on contact, qualities not to have been predicted of sidereal bodies.

Bessie, who knew so many of her contemporaries by reputation, had a good many personal disappointments; but, on the other hand, she had innumerable satisfactions' and enthusiasms, and she communicated the emotions of either class to a dear friend of her own sex in Boston, with whom she was in voluminous correspondence. Some of her reflections, indeed, she attempted to impart to Lord Lambeth, who came almost every day to Jones's Hotel, and whom Mrs. Westgate admitted to be really devoted. Captain Littledale, it appeared, had gone to India; and of several others of Mrs. Westgate's ex-pensioners—gentlemen who, as she said, had made, in New York, a clubhouse of her drawing-room—no tidings were to be obtained; but Lord Lambeth was certainly attentive enough to make up for the accidental absences, the short memories, all the other irregularities, of every one else. He drove them in the park, he took them to visit private collections of pictures, and, having a house of his own, invited them to dinner. Mrs. Westgate, following the fashion of many of her compatriots, caused herself and her sister to be presented at the English court by her diplomatic representative—for it was in this manner that she alluded to the American minister to England, inquiring what on earth he was put there for, if not to make the proper arrangement for one's going to a Drawing-room.

Lord Lambeth declared that he hated Drawing-rooms, but he participated in the ceremony on the day on which the two ladies at Jones's Hotel repaired to Buckingham Palace in a remarkable coach which his lordship had sent to fetch them. He had a gorgeous uniform, and Bessie Alden was particularly struck with his appearance, especially when on her asking him—rather foolishly, as she felt—if he were a loyal subject, he replied that he was a loyal subject to *her*. This

declaration was emphasized by his dancing with her at a
royal ball to which the two ladies afterwards went, and was
not impaired by the fact that she thought he danced very
ill. He seemed to her wonderfully kind; she asked herself, with
growing vivacity, why he should be so kind. It was his disposition—that seemed the natural answer. She had told her
sister that she liked him very much, and now that she liked
him more she wondered why. She liked him for his disposition; to this question as well that seemed the natural
answer. When once the impressions of London life began
to crowd thickly upon her she completely forgot her sister's
warning about the cynicism of public opinion. It had given
her great pain at the moment, but there was no particular
reason why she should remember it; it corresponded to little
with any sensible reality; and it was disagreeable to Bessie
to remember disagreeable things. So she was not haunted
with the sense of a vulgar imputation. She was not in love
with Lord Lambeth—she assured herself of that.

It will immediately be observed that when such assurances
become necessary the state of a young lady's affections is already ambiguous; and, indeed, Bessie Alden made no attempt to dissimulate—to herself, of course—a certain
tenderness that she felt for the young nobleman. She said to
herself that she liked the type to which he belonged—
the simple, candid, manly, healthy English temperament.
She spoke to herself of him as women speak of young men
they like—alluded to his bravery (which she had never in the
least seen tested), to his honesty and gentlemanliness, and
was not silent upon the subject of his good looks. She was
perfectly conscious, moreover, that she liked to think of his
more adventitious merits; that her imagination was excited
and gratified by the sight of a handsome young man endowed
with such large opportunities—opportunities she hardly knew
for what, but, as she supposed, for doing great things—for
setting an example, for exerting an influence, for conferring happiness, for encouraging the arts. She had a kind of
ideal of conduct for a young man who should find himself
in this magnificent position, and she tried to adapt it to Lord
Lambeth's deportment, as you might attempt to fit a silhouette in cut paper upon a shadow projected upon a wall.

But Bessie Alden's silhouette refused to coincide with his
lordship's image, and this want of harmony sometimes vexed
her more than she thought reasonable. When he was absent
it was, of course, less striking; then he seemed to her a sufficiently graceful combination of high responsibilities and

amiable qualities. But when he sat there within sight, laughing and talking with his customary good-humor and simplicity, she measured it more accurately, and she felt acutely that if Lord Lambeth's position was heroic, there was but little of the hero in the young man himself. Then her imagination wandered away from him—very far away; for it was an incontestable fact that at such moments he seemed distinctly dull. I am afraid that while Bessie's imagination was thus invidiously roaming, she cannot have been herself a very lively companion; but it may well have been that these occasional fits of indifference seemed to Lord Lambeth a part of the young girl's personal charm. It had been a part of this charm from the first that he felt that she judged him and measured him more freely and irresponsibly—more at her ease and her leisure, as it were—than several young ladies with whom he had been, on the whole, about as intimate. To feel this, and yet to feel that she also liked him, was very agreeable to Lord Lambeth. He fancied he had compassed that gratification so desirable to young men of title and fortune—being liked for himself. It is true that a cynical counsellor might have whispered to him, "Liked for yourself? Yes; but not so very much!" He had, at any rate, the constant hope of being liked more.

It may seem, perhaps, a trifle singular—but it is nevertheless true—that Bessie Alden, when he struck her as dull, devoted some time, on grounds of conscience, to trying to like him more. I say on grounds of conscience, because she felt that he had been extremely "nice" to her sister, and because she reflected that it was no more than fair that she should think as well of him as he thought of her. This effort was possibly sometimes not so successful as it might have been, for the result of it was occasionally a vague irritation, which expressed itself in hostile criticism of several British institutions. Bessie Alden went to some entertainments at which she met Lord Lambeth; but she went to others at which his lordship was neither actually nor potentially present; and it was chiefly on these latter occasions that she encountered those literary and artistic celebrities of whom mention has been made. After a while she reduced the matter to a principle. If Lord Lambeth should appear anywhere, it was a symbol that there would be no poets and philosophers; and in consequence—for it was almost a strict consequence—she used to enumerate to the young man these objects of her admiration.

"You seem to be awfully fond of those sort of people,"

said Lord Lambeth one day, as if the idea had just occurred to him.

"They are the people in England I am most curious to see," Bessie Alden replied.

"I suppose that's because you have read so much," said Lord Lambeth, gallantly.

"I have not read so much. It is because we think so much of them at home."

"Oh, I see," observed the young nobleman. "In Boston."

"Not only in Boston; everywhere," said Bessie. "We hold them in great honor; they go to the best dinner-parties."

"I dare say you are right. I can't say I know many of them."

"It's a pity you don't," Bessie Alden declared. "It would do you good."

"I dare say it would," said Lord Lambeth, very humbly. "But I must say I don't like the looks of some of them."

"Neither do I—of some of them. But there are all kinds, and many of them are charming."

"I have talked with two or three of them," the young man went on, "and I thought they had a kind of fawning manner."

"Why should they fawn?" Bessie Alden demanded.

"I'm sure I don't know. Why, indeed?"

"Perhaps you only thought so," said Bessie.

"Well, of course," rejoined her companion, "that's a kind of thing that can't be proved."

"In America they don't fawn," said Bessie.

"Ah, well, then, they must be better company."

Bessie was silent a moment. "That is one of the things I don't like about England," she said—"your keeping the distinguished people apart."

"How do you mean apart?"

"Why, letting them come only to certain places. You never see them."

Lord Lambeth looked at her a moment. "What people do you mean?"

"The eminent people—the authors and artists—the clever people."

"Oh, there are other eminent people besides those," said Lord Lambeth.

"Well, you certainly keep them apart," repeated the young girl.

"And there are other clever people," added Lord Lambeth, simply.

Bessie Alden looked at him, and she gave a light laugh. "Not many," she said.

On another occasion—just after a dinner-party—she told him that there was something else in England she did not like.

"Oh, I say!" he cried, "haven't you abused us enough?"

"I have never abused you at all," said Bessie; "but I don't like your *precedence*."

"It isn't my precedence!" Lord Lambeth declared, laughing.

"Yes, it is yours—just exactly yours; and I think it's odious," said Bessie.

"I never saw such a young lady for discussing things! Has some one had the impudence to go before you?" asked his lordship.

"It is not the going before me that I object to," said Bessie; "it is their thinking that they have a right to do it—*a right that I recognize.*"

"I never saw such a young lady as you are for not 'recognizing.' I have no doubt the thing is *beastly,* but it saves a lot of trouble."

"It makes a lot of trouble. It's horrid," said Bessie.

"But how would you have the first people go?" asked Lord Lambeth. "They can't go last."

"Whom do you mean by the first people?"

"Ah, if you mean to question first principles!" said Lord Lambeth.

"If those are your first principles, no wonder some of your arrangements are horrid," observed Bessie Alden, with a very pretty ferocity. "I am a young girl, so of course I go last; but imagine what Kitty must feel on being informed that she is not at liberty to budge until certain other ladies have passed out."

"Oh, I say she is not 'informed'!" cried Lord Lambeth. "No one would do such a thing as that."

"She is made to feel it," the young girl insisted—"as if they were afraid she would make a rush for the door. No; you have a lovely country," said Bessie Alden, "but your precedence is horrid."

"I certainly shouldn't think your sister would like it," rejoined Lord Lambeth, with even exaggerated gravity. But Bessie Alden could induce him to enter no formal protest against this repulsive custom, which he seemed to think an extreme convenience.

Percy Beaumont all this time had been a very much less frequent visitor at Jones's Hotel than his noble kinsman;

he had, in fact, called but twice upon the two American ladies. Lord Lambeth, who often saw him, reproached him with his neglect, and declared that, although Mrs. Westgate had said nothing about it, he was sure that she was secretly wounded by it. "She suffers too much to speak," said Lord Lambeth.

"That's all gammon," said Percy Beaumont; "there's a limit to what people can suffer!" And, though sending no apologies to Jones's Hotel, he undertook, in a manner, to explain his absence. "You are always there," he said, "and that's reason enough for my not going."

"I don't see why. There is enough for both of us."

"I don't care to be a witness of your—your reckless passion," said Percy Beaumont.

Lord Lambeth looked at him with a cold eye, and for a moment said nothing. "It's not so obvious as you might suppose," he rejoined, dryly, "considering what a demonstrative beggar I am."

"I don't want to know anything about it—nothing whatever," said Beaumont. "Your mother asks me every time she sees me whether I believe you are really lost—and Lady Pimlico does the same. I prefer to be able to answer that I know nothing about it—that I never go there. I stay away for consistency's sake. As I said the other day, they must look after you themselves."

"You are devilish considerate," said Lord Lambeth. "They never question me."

"They are afraid of you. They are afraid of irritating you and making you worse. So they go to work very cautiously, and, somewhere or other, they get their information. They know a great deal about you. They know that you have been with those ladies to the dome of St. Paul's and—where was the other place?—to the Thames Tunnel."

"If all their knowledge is as accurate as that, it must be very valuable," said Lord Lambeth.

"Well, at any rate, they know that you have been visiting the 'sights of the metropolis.' They think—very naturally, as it seems to me—that when you take to visiting the sights of the metropolis with a little American girl, there is serious cause for alarm." Lord Lambeth responded to this intimation by scornful laughter, and his companion continued, after a pause: "I said just now I didn't want to know anything about the affair; but I will confess that I am curious to learn whether you propose to marry Miss Bessie Alden."

On this point Lord Lambeth gave his interlocutor no immediate satisfaction; he was musing, with a frown. "By Jove," he said, "they go rather too far! They *shall* find me dangerous—I promise them."

Percy Beaumont began to laugh. "You don't redeem your promises. You said the other day you would make your mother call."

Lord Lambeth continued to meditate. "I asked her to call," he said, simply.

"And she declined?"

"Yes; but she shall do it yet."

"Upon my word," said Percy Beaumont, "if she gets much more frightened I believe she will." Lord Lambeth looked at him, and he went on. "She will go to the girl herself."

"How do you mean she will go to her?"

"She will beg her off, or she will bribe her. She will take strong measures."

Lord Lambeth turned away in silence, and his companion watched him take twenty steps and then slowly return. "I have invited Mrs. Westgate and Miss Alden to Branches," he said, "and this evening I shall name a day."

"And shall you invite your mother and your sisters to meet them?"

"Explicitly!"

"That will set the duchess off," said Percy Beaumont. "I suspect she will come."

"She may do as she pleases."

Beaumont looked at Lord Lambeth. "You do really propose to marry the little sister, then?"

"I like the way you talk about it!" cried the young man. "She won't gobble me down; don't be afraid."

"She won't leave you on your knees," said Percy Beaumont. "What *is* the inducement?"

"You talk about proposing: wait till I *have* proposed," Lord Lambeth went on.

"That's right, my dear fellow; think about it," said Percy Beaumont.

"She's a charming girl," pursued his lordship.

"Of course she's a charming girl. I don't know a girl more charming, intrinsically. But there are other charming girls nearer home."

"I like her spirit," observed Lord Lambeth, almost as if he were trying to torment his cousin.

"What's the peculiarity of her spirit?"

"She's not afraid, and she says things out, and she thinks

herself as good as any one. She is the only girl I have ever seen that was not dying to marry me."

"How do you know that, if you haven't asked her?"

"I don't know how; but I know it."

"I am sure she asked me questions enough about your property and your titles," said Beaumont.

"She has asked me questions, too; no end of them," Lord Lambeth admitted. "But she asked for information, don't you know."

"Information? Aye, I'll warrant she wanted it. Depend upon it that she is dying to marry you just as much and just as little as all the rest of them."

"I shouldn't like her to refuse me—I shouldn't like that."

"If the thing would be so disagreeable, then, both to you and to her, in Heaven's name leave it alone," said Percy Beaumont.

Mrs. Westgate, on her side, had plenty to say to her sister about the rarity of Mr. Beaumont's visits and the non-appearance of the Duchess of Bayswater. She professed, however, to derive more satisfaction from this latter circumstance than she could have done from the most lavish attentions on the part of this great lady. "It is most marked," she said—"most marked. It is a delicious proof that we have made them miserable. The day we dined with Lord Lambeth I was really sorry for the poor fellow." It will have been gathered that the entertainment offered by Lord Lambeth to his American friends had not been graced by the presence of his anxious mother. He had invited several choice spirits to meet them, but the ladies of his immediate family were to Mrs. Westgate's sense—a sense possibly morbidly acute—conspicuous by their absence.

"I don't want to express myself in a manner that you dislike," said Bessie Alden; "but I don't know why you should have so many theories about Lord Lambeth's poor mother. You know a great many young men in New York without knowing their mothers."

Mrs. Westgate looked at her sister, and then turned away. "My dear Bessie, you are superb!" she said.

"One thing is certain," the young girl continued. "If I believed I were a cause of annoyance—however unwitting—to Lord Lambeth's family, I should insist——"

"Insist upon my leaving England," said Mrs. Westgate.

"No, not that. I want to go to the National Gallery again; I want to see Stratford-on-Avon and Canterbury Cathedral. But I should insist upon his coming to see us no more."

"That would be very modest and very pretty of you; but you wouldn't do it now."

"Why do you say 'now'?" asked Bessie Alden. "Have I ceased to be modest?"

"You care for him too much. A month ago, when you said you didn't, I believe it was quite true. But at present, my dear child," said Mrs. Westgate, "you wouldn't find it quite so simple a matter never to see Lord Lambeth again. I have seen it coming on."

"You are mistaken," said Bessie. "You don't understand."

"My dear child, don't be perverse," rejoined her sister.

"I know him better, certainly, if you mean that," said Bessie. "And I like him very much. But I don't like him enough to make trouble for him with his family. However, I don't believe in that."

"I like the way you say 'however,'" Mrs. Westgate exclaimed. "Come; you would not marry him?"

"Oh no," said the young girl.

Mrs. Westgate for a moment seemed vexed. "Why not, pray?" she demanded.

"Because I don't care to," said Bessie Alden.

The morning after Lord Lambeth had had, with Percy Beaumont, that exchange of ideas which has just been narrated, the ladies at Jones's Hotel received from his lordship a written invitation to pay their projected visit to Branches Castle on the following Tuesday. "I think I have made up a very pleasant party," the young nobleman said. "Several people whom you know, and my mother and sisters, who have so long been regrettably prevented from making your acquaintance." Bessie Alden lost no time in calling her sister's attention to the injustice she had done the Duchess of Bayswater, whose hostility was now proved to be a vain illusion.

"Wait till you see if she comes," said Mrs. Westgate. "And if she is to meet us at her son's house, the obligation was all the greater for her to call upon us."

Bessie had not to wait long, and it appeared that Lord Lambeth's mother now accepted Mrs. Westgate's view of her duties. On the morrow, early in the afternoon, two cards were brought to the apartment of the American ladies—one of them bearing the name of the Duchess of Bayswater, and the other that of the Countess of Pimlico. Mrs. Westgate glanced at the clock. "It is not yet four," she said; "they have come early; they wish to see us. We will receive them." And she gave orders that her visitors should be ad-

mitted. A few moments later they were introduced, and there
was a solemn exchange of amenities. The duchess was a
large lady, with a fine fresh color; the Countess of Pimlico
was very pretty and elegant.

The duchess looked about her as she sat down—looked
not especially at Mrs. Westgate. "I dare say my son has told
you that I have been wanting to come and see you," she observed.

"You are very kind," said Mrs. Westgate, vaguely—her
conscience not allowing her to assent to this proposition—
and, indeed, not permitting her to enunciate her own with
any appreciable emphasis.

"He says you were so kind to him in America," said the
duchess.

"We are very glad," Mrs. Westgate replied, "to have been
able to make him a little more—a little less—a little more
comfortable."

"I think that he stayed at your house," remarked the
Duchess of Bayswater, looking at Bessie Alden.

"A very short time," said Mrs. Westgate.

"Oh!" said the duchess; and she continued to look at
Bessie, who was engaged in conversation with her daughter.

"Do you like London?" Lady Pimlico had asked of Bessie,
after looking at her a good deal—at her face and her hands,
her dress and her hair.

"Very much indeed," said Bessie.

"Do you like this hotel?"

"It is very comfortable," said Bessie.

"Do you like stopping at hotels?" inquired Lady Pimlico, after a pause.

"I am very fond of travelling," Bessie answered, "and I
suppose hotels are a necessary part of it. But they are not the
part I am fondest of."

"Oh, I hate travelling," said the Countess of Pimlico, and
transferred her attention to Mrs. Westgate.

"My son tells me you are going to Branches," the duchess
said, presently.

"Lord Lambeth has been so good as to ask us," said Mrs.
Westgate, who perceived that her visitor had now begun to
look at her, and who had her customary happy consciousness of a distinguished appearance. The only mitigation of
her felicity on this point was that, having inspected her
visitor's own costume, she said to herself, "She won't know
how well I am dressed!"

"He has asked me to go, but I am not sure I shall be able," murmured the duchess.

"He had offered us the p— the prospect of meeting you," said Mrs. Westgate.

"I hate the country at this season," responded the duchess.

Mrs. Westgate gave a little shrug. "I think it is pleasanter than London."

But the duchess's eyes were absent again; she was looking fixedly at Bessie. In a moment she slowly rose, walked to a chair that stood empty at the young girl's right hand, and silently seated herself. As she was a majestic, voluminous woman, this little transaction had, inevitably, an air of somewhat impressive attention. It diffused a certain awkwardness, which Lady Pimlico, as a sympathetic daughter, perhaps desired to rectify in turning to Mrs. Westgate.

"I dare say you go out a great deal," she observed.

"No, very little. We are strangers, and we didn't come here for society."

"I see," said Lady Pimlico. "It's rather nice in town just now."

"It's charming," said Mrs. Westgate. "But we only go to see a few people—whom we like."

"Of course one can't like everyone," said Lady Pimlico.

"It depends upon one's society," Mrs. Westgate rejoined.

The duchess meanwhile had addressed herself to Bessie. "My son tells me the young ladies in America are so clever."

"I am glad they made so good an impression on him," said Bessie, smiling.

The duchess was not smiling; her large, fresh face was very tranquil. "He is very susceptible," she said. "He thinks every one clever, and sometimes they are."

"Sometimes," Bessie assented, smiling still.

The duchess looked at her a little, and then went on: "Lambeth is very susceptible, but he is very volatile, too."

"Volatile?" asked Bessie.

"He is very inconstant. It won't do to depend on him."

"Ah," said Bessie, "I don't recognize that description. We have depended on him greatly—my sister and I—and he has never disappointed us."

"He will disappoint you yet," said the duchess.

Bessie gave a little laugh, as if she were amused at the duchess's persistency. "I suppose it will depend on what we expect of him."

"The less you expect the better," Lord Lambeth's mother declared.

"Well," said Bessie, "we expect nothing unreasonable."

The duchess for a moment was silent, though she appeared to have more to say. "Lambeth says he has seen so much of you," she presently began.

"He has been to see us very often; he has been very kind," said Bessie Alden.

"I dare say you are used to that. I am told there is a great deal of that in America."

"A great deal of kindness?" the young girl inquired, smiling.

"Is that what you call it? I know you have different expressions."

"We certainly don't always understand each other," said Mrs. Westgate, the termination of whose interview with Lady Pimlico allowed her to give attention to their elder visitor.

"I am speaking of the young men calling so much upon the young ladies," the duchess explained.

"But surely in England," said Mrs. Westgate, "the young ladies don't call upon the young men?"

"Some of them do—almost!" Lady Pimlico declared. "When the young men are a great *parti*."

"Bessie, you must make a note of that," said Mrs. Westgate. "My sister," she added, "is a model traveller. She writes down all the curious facts she hears in a little book she keeps for the purpose."

The duchess was a little flushed; she looked all about the room, while her daughter turned to Bessie. "My brother told us you were wonderfully clever," said Lady Pimlico.

"He should have said my sister," Bessie answered—"when she says such things as that."

"Shall you be long at Branches?" the duchess asked, abruptly, of the young girl.

"Lord Lambeth has asked us for three days," said Bessie.

"I shall go," the duchess declared, "and my daughter, too."

"That will be charming!" Bessie rejoined.

"Delightful!" murmured Mrs. Westgate.

"I shall expect to see a great deal of you," the duchess continued. "When I go to Branches I monopolize my son's guests."

"They must be most happy," said Mrs. Westgate, very graciously.

"I want immensely to see it—to see the castle," said Bessie to the duchess. "I have never seen one—in England, at least; and you know we have none in America."

"Ah, you are fond of castles?" inquired her Grace.

"Immensely!" replied the young girl. "It has been the dream of my life to live in one."

The duchess looked at her a moment, as if she hardly knew how to take this assurance, which, from her Grace's point of view, was either very artless or very audacious. "Well," she said, rising, "I will show you Branches myself." And upon this the two great ladies took their departure.

"What did they mean by it?" asked Mrs. Westgate, when they were gone.

"They meant to be polite," said Bessie, "because we are going to meet them."

"It is too late to be polite," Mrs. Westgate replied, almost grimly. "They meant to overawe us by their fine manners and their grandeur, and to make you *lâcher prise*."

"*Lâcher prise?* What strange things you say!" murmured Bessie Alden.

"They meant to snub us, so that we shouldn't dare to go to Branches," Mrs. Westgate continued.

"On the contrary," said Bessie, "the duchess offered to show me the place herself."

"Yes, you may depend upon it she won't let you out of her sight. She will show you the place from morning till night."

"You have a theory for everything," said Bessie.

"And you apparently have none for anything."

"I saw no attempt to 'overawe' us," said the young girl. "Their manners were not fine."

"They were not even good!" Mrs. Westgate declared.

Bessie was silent a while, but in a few moments she observed that she had a very good theory. "They came to look at me," she said, as if this had been a very ingenious hypothesis. Mrs. Westgate did it justice; she greeted it with a smile, and pronounced it most brilliant, while, in reality, she felt that the young girl's scepticism, or her charity, or, as she had sometimes called it appropriately, her idealism, was proof against irony. Bessie, however, remained meditative all the rest of the day and well on into the morrow.

On the morrow, before lunch, Mrs. Westgate had occasion to go out for an hour, and left her sister writing a letter. When she came back she met Lord Lambeth at the door of the hotel, coming away. She thought he looked slightly embarrassed; he was certainly very grave. "I am sorry to have missed you. Won't you come back?" she asked.

"No," said the young man, "I can't. I have seen your sister. I can never come back." Then he looked at her a moment, and took her hand. "Good-bye, Mrs. Westgate," he said. "You have been very kind to me." And with what she thought a strange, sad look in his handsome young face, he turned away.

She went in, and she found Bessie still writing her letter—that is, Mrs. Westgate perceived she was sitting at the table with the pen in her hand and not writing. "Lord Lambeth has been here," said the elder lady at last.

Then Bessie got up and showed her a pale, serious face. She bent this face upon her sister for some time, confessing silently and a little pleading. "I told him," she said at last, "that we could not go to Branches."

Mrs. Westgate displayed just a spark of irritation. "He might have waited," she said, with a smile, "till one had seen the castle." Later, an hour afterwards, she said, "Dear Bessie, I wish you might have accepted him."

"I couldn't," said Bessie, gently.

"He is an excellent fellow," said Mrs. Westgate.

"I couldn't," Bessie repeated.

"If it is only," her sister added, "because those women will think that they succeeded—that they paralyzed us!"

Bessie Alden turned away; but presently she added, "They were interesting; I should have liked to see them again."

"So should I!" cried Mrs. Westgate, significantly.

"And I should have liked to see the castle," said Bessie. "But now we must leave England," she added.

Her sister looked at her. "You will not wait to go to the National Gallery?"

"Not now."

"Nor to Canterbury Cathedral?"

Bessie reflected a moment. "We can stop there on our way to Paris," she said.

Lord Lambeth did not tell Percy Beaumont that the contingency he was not prepared at all to like had occurred; but Percy Beaumont, on hearing that the two ladies had left London, wondered with some intensity what had happened—wondered, that is, until the Duchess of Bayswater came a little to his assistance. The two ladies went to Paris, and Mrs. Westgate beguiled the journey to that city by repeating several times: "That's what I regret; they will think they petrified us." But Bessie Alden seemed to regret nothing.

STEPHEN CRANE

The Blue Hotel

I

THE PALACE HOTEL at Fort Romper was painted a light blue, a shade that is on the legs of a kind of heron, causing the bird to declare its position against any background. The Palace Hotel, then, was always screaming and howling in a way that made the dazzling winter landscape of Nebraska seem only a gray, swampish hush. It stood alone on the prairie, and when the snow was falling, the town two hundred yards away was not visible. But when the traveler alighted at the railway station, he was obliged to pass the Palace Hotel before he could come upon the company of low, clapboard houses which composed Fort Romper, and it was not to be thought that any traveler could pass the Palace Hotel without looking at it. Pat Scully, the proprietor, had proved himself a master of strategy when he chose his paints. It is true that on clear days, when the great transcontinental expresses, long lines of swaying Pullmans, swept through Fort Romper, passengers were overcome at the sight, and the cult that knows the brown-reds and the subdivisions of the dark greens of the East expressed shame, pity, horror, in a laugh. But to the citizens of this prairie town and to the people who would naturally stop there, Pat Scully had performed a feat. With this opulence and splendor, these creeds, classes, egotisms that streamed through Romper on the rails day after day, they had no color in common.

As if the displayed delights of such a blue hotel were not sufficiently enticing, it was Scully's habit to go every morning and evening to meet the leisurely trains that stopped at Romper and work his seductions upon any man that he might see wavering, gripsack in hand.

One morning, when a snow-crusted engine dragged its long

121

string of freight cars and its one passenger coach to the station, Scully performed the marvel of catching three men. One was a shaky and quick-eyed Swede, with a great, shining, cheap valise; one was a tall, bronzed cowboy, who was on his way to a ranch near the Dakota line; one was a little, silent man from the East, who didn't look it, and didn't announce it. Scully practically made them prisoners. He was so nimble and merry and kindly that each probably felt it would be the height of brutality to try to escape. They trudged off over the creaking board sidewalks in the wake of the eager little Irishman. He wore a heavy fur cap squeezed tightly down on his head. It caused his two red ears to stick out stiffly, as if they were made of tin.

At last, Scully, elaborately, with boisterous hospitality, conducted them through the portals of the blue hotel. The room which they entered was small. It seemed to be merely a proper temple for an enormous stove, which, in the center, was humming with godlike violence. At various points on its surface the iron had become luminous and glowed yellow from the heat. Beside the stove, Scully's son Johnnie was playing high-five with an old farmer who had whiskers both gray and sandy. They were quarreling. Frequently the old farmer turned his face toward a box of sawdust—colored brown from tobacco juice—that was behind the stove, and spat with an air of great impatience and irritation. With a loud flourish of words, Scully destroyed the game of cards, and bustled his son upstairs with part of the baggage of the new guests. He himself conducted them to three basins of the coldest water in the world. The cowboy and the Eastern burnished themselves fiery red with this water, until it seemed to be some kind of metal polish. The Swede, however, merely dipped his fingers gingerly and with trepidation. It was notable that throughout this series of small ceremonies, the three travelers were made to feel that Scully was very benevolent. He was conferring great favors upon them. He handed the towel from one to another with an air of philanthropic impulse.

Afterward they went to the first room, and sitting about the stove, listened to Scully's officious clamor at his daughters, who were preparing the midday meal. They reflected in the silence of experienced men who tread carefully amid new people. Nevertheless, the old farmer, stationary, invincible in his chair near the warmest part of the stove, turned his face from the sawdust box frequently and addressed a glowing commonplace to the strangers. Usually he was answered in short but adequate sentences by either the cowboy or the Easterner. The Swede said nothing. He seemed to be occupied in making furtive estimates of each man in the room. One might have thought that he had the sense of silly suspicion which comes to guilt. He resembled a badly frightened man.

Later, at dinner, he spoke a little, addressing his conversation entirely to Scully. He volunteered that he had come from New York, where for ten years he had worked as a tailor. These facts seemed to strike Scully as fascinating, and afterward he volunteered that he had lived at Romper for fourteen years. The Swede asked about the crops and the price of labor. He seemed barely to listen to Scully's extended replies. His eyes continued to rove from man to man.

Finally, with a laugh and a wink, he said that some of these Western communities were very dangerous; and after his statement, he straightened his legs under the table, tilted his head, and laughed again, loudly. It was plain that the demonstration had no meaning to the others. They looked at him wondering and in silence.

II

As the men trooped heavily back into the front room, the two little windows presented views of a turmoiling sea of snow. The huge arms of the wind were making attempts—mighty, circular, futile—to embrace the flakes as they sped. A gatepost like a still man with a blanched face stood aghast amid this profligate fury. In a hearty voice Scully announced the presence of a blizzard. The guests of the blue hotel, lighting their pipes, assented with grunts of lazy, masculine contentment. No island of the sea could be exempt in the degree of this little room with its humming stove. Johnnie, son of Scully, in a tone which defined his opinion of his ability as a card-player, challenged the old farmer of both gray and sandy whiskers to a game of high-five. The farmer agreed with a contemptuous and bitter scoff. They sat close to the stove, and squared their knees under a wide board. The cowboy and the Easterner watched the game with interest. The Swede remained near the window, aloof, but with a countenance that showed signs of an inexplicable excitement.

The play of Johnnie and the graybeard was suddenly ended by another quarrel. The old man arose while casting a look of heated scorn at his adversary. He slowly buttoned his coat, and then stalked with fabulous dignity from the room. In the discreet silence of all the other men, the Swede laughed. His laughter rang somehow childish. Men by this time had begun to look at him askance, as if they wished to inquire what ailed him.

A new game was formed jocosely. The cowboy volunteered to become the partner of Johnnie, and they all then turned to ask the Swede to throw in his lot with the little Easterner. He asked some questions about the game, and learning that it wore many names, and that he had played it when it was under an alias, he accepted the invitation. He strode toward the men nervously, as if he expected to be assaulted. Finally, seated, he gazed from face to face and laughed shrilly. This laugh was so strange that the Easterner looked up quickly, the cowboy sat intent and with his mouth open, and Johnnie paused, holding the cards with still fingers.

Afterward there was a short silence. Then Johnnie said, "Well, let's get at it. Come on now!" They pulled their chairs forward until their knees were bunched under the board. They began to play, and their interest in the game caused the others to forget the manner of the Swede.

The cowboy was a board-whacker. Each time that he held superior cards, he whanged them, one by one, with exceeding force, down upon the improvised table, and took the tricks with a glowing air of prowess and pride that sent thrills of indignation into the hearts of his opponents. A game with a board-whacker in it is sure to become intense. The countenances of the Easterner and the Swede were miserable whenever the cowboy thundered down his aces and kings, while Johnnie, his eyes gleaming with joy, chuckled and chuckled.

Because of the absorbing play, none considered the strange ways of the Swede. They paid strict heed to the game. Finally, during a lull caused by a new deal, the Swede suddenly addressed Johnnie: "I suppose there have been a good many men killed in this room." The jaws of the others dropped and they looked at him.

"What in hell are you talking about?" said Johnnie.

The Swede laughed again his blatant laugh, full of a kind of false courage and defiance. "Oh, you know what I mean, all right," he answered.

"I'm a liar if I do!" Johnnie protested. The card was halted, and the men stared at the Swede. Johnnie evidently felt that as the son of the proprietor he should make a direct inquiry. "Now what might you be drivin' at, mister?" he asked. The Swede winked at him. It was a wink full of cunning. His fingers shook on the edge of the board. "Oh, maybe you think I have been to nowheres. Maybe you think I'm a tenderfoot?"

"I don't know nothin' about you," answered Johnnie, "and I don't give a damn where you've been. All I got to say is that I don't know what you're driving at. There hain't never been nobody killed in this room."

The cowboy, who had been steadily gazing at the Swede, then spoke: "What's wrong with you, mister?"

Apparently it seemed to the Swede that he was formidably menaced. He shivered and turned white near the corners of his mouth. He sent an appealing glance in the direction of the little Easterner. During these moments, he did not forget to wear his air of advanced pot valor. "They say they don't know what I mean," he remarked mockingly to the Easterner.

The latter answered after prolonged and cautious reflection. "I don't understand you," he said impassively.

The Swede made a movement then which announced that he thought he had encountered treachery from the only quarter where he had expected sympathy, if not help. "Oh, I see you are all against me. I see—"

The cowboy was in a state of deep stupefaction. "Say," he cried, as he tumbled the deck violently down upon the board. "Say, what are you gittin' at, hey?"

The Swede sprang up with the celerity of a man escaping from a snake on the floor. "I don't want to fight!" he shouted. "I don't want to fight!"

The cowboy stretched his long legs indolently and deliberately. His hands were in his pockets. He spat into the sawdust box. "Well, who the hell thought you did?" he inquired.

The Swede backed rapidly toward a corner of the room. His hands were out protectingly in front of his chest, but he was making an obvious struggle to control his fright. "Gentlemen," he quavered, "I suppose I am going to be killed before I can leave this house! I suppose I am going to be killed before I can leave this house!" In his eyes was the dying-swan look. Through the windows could be seen the snow turning blue in the shadow of dusk. The wind tore at the house, and some loose thing beat regularly against the clapboards like a spirit tapping.

A door opened, and Scully himself entered. He paused in surprise as he noted the tragic attitude of the Swede. Then he said, "What's the matter here?"

The Swede answered him swiftly and eagerly: "These men are going to kill me."

"Kill you!" ejaculated Scully. "Kill you! What are you talkin'?"

The Swede made the gesture of a martyr.

Scully wheeled sternly upon his son. "What is this, Johnnie?"

The lad had grown sullen. "Damned if I know," he answered. "I can't make no sense to it." He began to shuffle the cards, fluttering them together with an angry snap. "He says a good many men have been killed in this room, or something like that. And he says he's goin' to be killed here, too. I don't know what ails him. He's crazy, I shouldn't wonder."

Scully then looked for explanation to the cowboy, but the cowboy simply shrugged his shoulders.

"Kill you?" said Scully again to the Swede. "Kill you? Man, you're off your nut."

"Oh, I know," burst out the Swede. "I know what will happen. Yes, I'm crazy—yes. Yes, of course, I'm crazy—yes. But I know one thing—" There was a sort of sweat of misery and terror upon his face. "I know I won't get out of here alive."

The cowboy drew a deep breath, as if his mind was passing into the last stages of dissolution. "Well, I'm doggoned," he whispered to himself.

Scully wheeled suddenly and faced his son. "You've been troublin' this man!"

Johnnie's voice was loud with its burden of grievance. "Why, good Gawd, I ain't done nothin' to 'im."

The Swede broke in. "Gentlemen, do not disturb yourselves. I will leave this house. I will go away, because"—he accused them dramatically with his glance—"because I do not want to be killed."

Scully was furious with his son. "Will you tell me what is the matter, you young divil? What's the matter, anyhow? Speak out!"

"Blame it!" cried Johnnie in despair. "Don't I tell you I don't know? He—he says we want to kill him, and that's all I know. I can't tell what ails him."

The Swede continued to repeat, "Never mind, Mr. Scully; never mind. I will leave this house. I will go away, because I do not wish to be killed. Yes, of course, I am crazy—yes. But I know one thing! I will go away. I will leave this house. Never mind, Mr. Scully; never mind. I will go away."

"You will not go 'way," said Scully. "You will not go 'way until I hear the reason of this business. If anybody has troubled you, I will take care of him. This is my house. You are under my roof, and I will not allow any peaceable man to be troubled here." He cast a terrible eye upon Johnnie, the cowboy, and the Easterner.

"Never mind, Mr. Scully; never mind. I will go away. I do not wish to be killed." The Swede moved toward the door which opened upon the stairs. It was evidently his intention to go at once for his baggage.

"No, no," shouted Scully peremptorily; but the white-faced man slid by him and disappeared. "Now," said Scully severely, "what does this mane?"

Johnnie and the cowboy cried together, "Why, we didn't do nothin' to 'im!"

Scully's eyes were cold. "No," he said, "you didn't?"

Johnnie swore a deep oath. "Why, this is the wildest loon I ever see. We didn't do nothin' at all. We were jest sittin' here playin' cards, and he—"

The father suddenly spoke to the Easterner. "Mr. Blanc," he asked, "what has these boys been doin'?"

The Easterner reflected again. "I didn't see anything wrong at all," he said at last, slowly.

Scully began to howl. "But what does it mane?" He stared ferociously at his son. "I have a mind to lather you for this, me boy."

Johnnie was frantic. "Well, what have I done?" he bawled at his father.

III

"I think you are tongue-tied," said Scully finally to his son, the cowboy, and the Easterner; and at the end of his scornful sentence, he left the room.

Upstairs the Swede was swiftly fastening the straps of his great valise. Once his back happened to be half turned toward the door, and hearing a noise there, he wheeled and sprang up, uttering a loud cry. Scully's wrinkled visage showed grimly in the light of the small lamp he carried. This yellow effulgence, streaming upward, colored only his prominent features, and left his eyes, for instance, in mysterious shadow. He resembled a murderer.

"Man! Man!" he exclaimed. "Have you gone daffy?"

"Oh, no! Oh, no!" rejoined the other. "There are people

in this world who know pretty nearly as much as you do—understand?"

For a moment they stood gazing at each other. Upon the Swede's deathly pale cheeks were two spots brightly crimson and sharply edged, as if they had been carefully painted. Scully placed the light on the table and sat himself on the edge of the bed. He spoke ruminatively. "By cracky, I never heard of such a thing in my life. It's a complete muddle. I can't, for the soul of me, think how you ever got this idea into your head." Presently he lifted his eyes and asked, "And did you sure think they were going to kill you?"

The Swede scanned the old man as if he wished to see into his mind. "I did," he said at last. He obviously suspected that this answer might precipitate an outbreak. As he pulled on a strap, his whole arm shook, the elbow wavering like a bit of paper.

Scully banged his hand impressively on the footboard of the bed. "Why, man, we're goin' to have a line of ilictric streetcars in this town next spring."

"'A line of electric streetcars,'" repeated the Swede stupidly.

"And," said Scully, "there's a new railroad goin' to be built down from Broken Arm to here. Not to mintion the four churches and the smashin'-big brick schoolhouse. Then there's the big factory, too. Why, in two years, Romper'll be a met-tro-*pol*-is."

Having finished the preparation of his baggage, the Swede straightened himself. "Mr. Scully," he said, with sudden hardihood, "how much do I owe you?"

"You don't owe me anythin'," said the old man angrily.

"Yes, I do," retorted the Swede. He took seventy-five cents from his pocket and tendered it to Scully; but the latter snapped his fingers in disdainful refusal. However, it happened that they both stood gazing in a strange fashion at three silver pieces on the Swede's open palm.

"I'll not take your money," said Scully at last. "Not after what's been goin' on here." Then a plan seemed to strike him. "Here," he cried, picking up his lamp and moving toward the door. "Here! Come with me a minute."

"No," said the Swede, in overwhelming alarm.

"Yes," urged the old man. "Come on! I want you to come and see a picter—just across the hall—in my room."

The Swede must have concluded that his hour was come. His jaw dropped and his teeth showed like a dead man's. He ultimately followed Scully across the corridor, but he had the step of one hung in chains.

Scully flashed the light high on the wall of his own chamber. There was revealed a ridiculous photograph of a little girl. She was leaning against a balustrade of gorgeous decoration, and the formidable bang to her hair was prominent. The figure was as graceful as an upright sled stake, and, witha', it was of the hue of lead. "There," said Scully tender'y, "that's the picter of my little girl that died. Her name v as Carrie. She had the purtiest hair you ever saw! I was that fond of her, she—"

Turning then, he saw that the Swede was not contemplating the picture at all, but instead, was keeping keen watch on the gloom in the rear.

"Look, man!" cried Scully heartily. "That's the picter of my little gal that died. Her name was Carrie. And then here's the picter of my oldest boy, Michael. He's a lawyer in Lincoln, an' doin' well. I gave that boy a grand eddication, and I'm glad for it now. He's a fine boy. Look at 'im now. Ain't he bold as blazes, him there in Lincoln, an honored an' respicted gintleman! An honored and respicted gintleman," concluded Scully with a flourish. And so saying, he smote the Swede jovially on the back.

The Swede faintly smiled.

"Now," said the old man, "there's only one more thing." He dropped suddenly to the floor and thrust his head beneath the bed. The Swede could hear his muffled voice. "I'd keep it under me piller if it wasn't for that boy Johnnie. Then there's the old woman— Where is it now? I never put it twice in the same place. Ah, now come out with you!"

Presently he backed clumsily from under the bed, dragging with him an old coat rolled into a bundle. "I've fetched him," he muttered. Kneeling on the floor, he unrolled the coat and extracted from its heart a large, yellow-brown whisky bottle.

His first maneuver was to hold the bottle up to the light. Reassured, apparently, that nobody had been tampering with it, he thrust it with a generous movement toward the Swede.

The weak-kneed Swede was about to eagerly clutch this element of strength, but he suddenly jerked his hand away and cast a look of horror upon Scully.

"Drink," said the old man affectionately. He had risen to his feet, and now stood facing the Swede.

There was a silence. Then again Scully said, "Drink!"

The Swede laughed wildly. He grabbed the bottle, put it

to his mouth; and as his lips curled absurdly around the opening and his throat worked, he kept his glance, burning with hatred, upon the old man's face.

IV

After the departure of Scully, the three men, with the cardboard still upon their knees, preserved for a long time an astounded silence. Then Johnnie said, "That's the dod-dangedest Swede I ever see."

"He ain't no Swede," said the cowboy scornfully.

"Well, what is he, then?" cried Johnnie. "What is he then?"

"It's my opinion," replied the cowboy deliberately, "he's some kind of a Dutchman." It was a venerable custom of the country to entitle as Swedes all light-haired men who spoke with a heavy tongue. In consequence, the idea of the cowboy was not without its daring. "Yes, sir," he repeated. "It's my opinion this feller is some kind of a Dutchman."

"Well, he says he's a Swede, anyhow," muttered Johnnie sulkily. He turned to the Easterner: "What do you think, Mr. Blanc?"

"Oh, I don't know," replied the Easterner.

"Well, what do you think makes him act that way?" asked the cowboy.

"Why, he's frightened." The Easterner knocked his pipe against a rim of the stove. "He's clear frightened out of his boots."

"What at?" cried Johnnie and the cowboy together.

The Easterner reflected over his answer.

"What at?" cried the others again.

"Oh, I don't know, but it seems to me this man has been reading dime novels, and he thinks he's right out in the middle of it—the shootin' and stabbin' and all."

"But," said the cowboy, deeply scandalized, "this ain't Wyoming, ner none of them places. This is Nebrasker."

"Yes," added Johnnie, "an' why don't he wait till he gits *out West?*"

The traveled Easterner laughed. "It isn't different there even—not in these days. But he thinks he's right in the middle of hell."

Johnnie and the cowboy mused long.

"It's awful funny," remarked Johnnie at last.

"Yes," said the cowboy. "This is a queer game. I hope we don't git snowed in, because then we'd have to stand this here man bein' around with us all the time. That wouldn't be no good."

"I wish Pop would throw him out," said Johnnie.

Presently they heard a loud stamping on the stairs, accompanied by ringing jokes in the voice of old Scully, and laughter, evidently from the Swede. The men around the stove stared vacantly at each other. "Gosh!" said the cowboy. The door flew open, and old Scully, flushed and anecdotal, came into the room. He was jabbering at the Swede, who followed him, laughing bravely. It was the entry of two roisterers from a banquet hall.

"Come now," said Scully sharply to the three seated men, "move up and give us a chance at the stove." The cowboy and the Easterner obediently sidled their chairs to make room for the newcomers. Johnnie, however, simply arranged himself in a more indolent attitude, and then remained motionless.

"Come! Git over, there," said Scully.

"Plenty of room on the other side of the stove," said Johnnie.

"Do you think we want to sit in the draught?" roared the father.

But the Swede here interposed with a grandeur of confidence. "No, no. Let the boy sit where he likes," he cried in a bullying voice to the father.

"All right! All right!" said Scully deferentially. The cowboy and the Easterner exchanged glances of wonder.

The five chairs were formed in a crescent about one side of the stove. The Swede began to talk; he talked arrogantly, profanely, angrily. Johnnie, the cowboy, and the Easterner maintained a morose silence, while old Scully appeared to be receptive and eager, breaking in constantly with sympathetic ejaculations.

Finally the Swede announced that he was thirsty. He moved in his chair, and said that he would go for a drink of water.

"I'll git it for you," cried Scully at once.

"No," said the Swede contemptuously. "I'll get it for myself." He arose and stalked with the air of an owner off into the executive parts of the hotel.

As soon as the Swede was out of hearing, Scully sprang to his feet and whispered intensely to the others, "Upstairs he thought I was tryin' to poison 'im."

"Say," said Johnnie, "this makes me sick. Why don't you throw 'im out in the snow?"

"Why, he's all right now," declared Scully. "It was only that he was from the East, and he thought this was a tough place. That's all. He's all right now."

The cowboy looked with admiration upon the Easterner. "You were straight," he said. "You were on to that there Dutchman."

"Well," said Johnnie to his father, "he may be all right now, but I don't see it. Other time he was scared, but now he's too fresh."

Scully's speech was always a combination of Irish brogue and idiom, Western twang and idiom, and scraps of curiously formal diction taken from the storybooks and newspapers. He now hurled a strange mass of language at the head of his son. "What do I keep? What do I keep? What do I keep?" he demanded in a voice of thunder. He slapped his knee impressively, to indicate that he himself was going to make reply, and that all should heed. "I keep a hotel," he shouted. "A hotel, do you mind? A guest under my roof has sacred privileges. He is to be intimidated by none. Not one word shall he hear that would prijudice him in favor of goin' away. I'll not have it. There's no place in this here town where they can say they iver took in a guest of mine because he was afraid to stay here." He wheeled suddenly upon the cowboy and the Easterner. "Am I right?"

"Yes, Mr. Scully," said the cowboy. "I think you're right."

"Yes, Mr. Scully," said the Easterner, "I think you're right."

v

At six-o'clock supper, the Swede fizzed like a fire wheel. He sometimes seemed on the point of bursting into riotous song, and in all his madness he was encouraged by old Scully. The Easterner was encased in reserve; the cowboy sat in wide-mouthed amazement, forgetting to eat, while Johnnie wrathily demolished great plates of food. The daughters of the house, when they were obliged to replenish the biscuits, approached as warily as Indians, and having succeeded in their purpose, fled with ill-concealed trepidation. The Swede domineered the whole feast, and he gave it the appearance of a cruel bacchanal. He seemed to have grown suddenly taller; he gazed, brutally disdainful, into every face. His voice rang through the room. Once when he jabbed out harpoon-fashion with his fork to pinion a biscuit, the weapon nearly impaled the hand of the Easterner, which had been stretched quietly out for the same biscuit.

After supper, as the men filed toward the other room, the Swede smote Scully ruthlessly on the shoulder. "Well, old boy, that was a good, square meal." Johnnie looked hopefully at his father; he knew that shoulder was tender from an old fall; and indeed, it appeared for a moment as if Scully was going to flame out over the matter, but in the end he smiled a sickly smile and remained silent. The others understood from his manner that he was admitting his responsibility for the Swede's new viewpoint.

Johnnie, however, addressed his parent in an aside. "Why don't you license somebody to kick you downstairs?" Scully scowled darkly by way of reply.

When they were gathered about the stove, the Swede insisted on another game of high-five. Scully gently deprecated the plan at first, but the Swede turned a wolfish glare upon him. The old man subsided, and the Swede canvassed the others. In his tone there was always a great threat. The cowboy and the Easterner both remarked indifferently that they would play. Scully said that he would presently have to go to meet the six fifty-eight train, and so the Swede turned menacingly upon Johnnie. For a moment their glances crossed like blades, and then Johnnie smiled and said, "Yes, I'll play."

They formed a square, with the little board on their knees. The Easterner and the Swede were again partners. As the play went on, it was noticeable that the cowboy was not board-whacking as usual. Meanwhile Scully, near the lamp, had put on his spectacles, and with an appearance curiously like an old priest, was reading a newspaper. In time he went out to meet the six fifty-eight train, and despite his precautions, a gust of polar wind whirled into the room as he opened the door. Besides scattering the cards, it chilled the players to the marrow. The Swede cursed frightfully. When Scully returned, his entrance disturbed a cosy and friendly scene. The Swede again cursed. But presently they were once more intent, their heads bent forward and their hands moving swiftly. The Swede had adopted the fashion of board-whacking.

Scully took up his paper and for a long time remained immersed in matters which were extraordinarily remote from him. The lamp burned badly, and once he stopped to adjust the wick. The newspaper, as he turned from page to page, rustled with a slow and comfortable sound. Then suddenly he heard three terrible words: "You are cheatin'!"

Such scenes often prove that there can be little of dramatic import in environment. Any room can present a tragic front; any room can be comic. This little den was now hideous as a torture chamber. The new faces of the men themselves had changed it upon the instant. The Swede held a huge fist in front of Johnnie's face, while the latter looked steadily over it into the blazing orbs of his accuser. The Easterner had grown pallid; the cowboy's jaw had dropped in that expression of bovine amazement which was one of his important mannerisms. After the three words, the first sound in the room was made by Scully's paper as it floated forgotten to his feet. His spectacles had also fallen from his nose, but by a clutch he had saved them in air. His hand, grasping the spectacles, now remained poised awkwardly and near his shoulder. He stared at the card-players.

Probably the silence was while a second elapsed. Then, if the floor had been suddenly twitched out from under the men, they could not have moved quicker. The five had projected themselves headlong toward a common point. It happened that Johnnie, in rising to hurl himself upon the Swede, had stumbled slightly because of his curiously instinctive care for the cards and the board. The loss of the moment allowed time for the arrival of Scully, and also allowed the cowboy time to give the Swede a great push which sent him staggering back. The men found tongue together, and hoarse shouts of rage, appeal, or fear burst from every throat. The cowboy pushed and jostled feverishly at the Swede, and the Easterner and Scully clung wildly to Johnnie; but through the smoky air, above the swaying bodies of the peace-compellers, the eyes of the two warriors ever sought each other in glances of challenge that were at once hot and steely.

Of course the board had been overturned, and now the whole company of cards was scattered over the floor, where the boots of the men trampled the fat and painted kings and queens as they gazed with their silly eyes at the war that was waging above them.

Scully's voice was dominating the yells. "Stop, now! Stop, I say! Stop, now—"

Johnnie, as he struggled to burst through the rank formed by Scully and the Easterner, was crying, "Well, he says I cheated! He says I cheated! I won't allow no man to say I cheated! If he says I cheated, he's a ——— ———!"

The cowboy was telling the Swede, "Quit, now! Quit, d'ye hear—"

The screams of the Swede never ceased: "He did cheat! I saw him! I saw him—"

As for the Easterner, he was importuning in a voice that was not heeded: "Wait a moment, can't you? Oh, wait a moment. What's the good of a fight over a game of cards? Wait a moment—"

In this tumult, no complete sentences were clear. "Cheat" —"Quit"—"He says"—these fragments pierced the uproar and rang out sharply. It was remarkable that, whereas Scully undoubtedly made the most noise, he was the least heard of any of the riotous band.

Then suddenly there was a great cessation. It was as if each man had paused for breath; and although the room was still lighted with the anger of men, it could be seen that there was no danger of immediate conflict, and at once Johnnie, shouldering his way forward, almost succeeded in confronting the Swede. "What did you say I cheated for? What did you say I cheated for? I don't cheat, and I won't let no man say I do!"

The Swede said, "I saw you! I saw you!"

"Well," cried Johnnie, "I'll fight any man what says I cheat!"

"No, you won't," said the cowboy. "Not here."

"Ah, be still, can't you?" said Scully, coming between them.

The quiet was sufficient to allow the Easterner's voice to be heard. He was repeating, "Oh, wait a moment, can't you? What's the good of a fight over a game of cards? Wait a moment!"

Johnnie, his red face appearing above his father's shoulder, hailed the Swede again. "Did you say I cheated?"

The Swede showed his teeth. "Yes."

"Then," said Johnnie, "we must fight."

"Yes, fight," roared the Swede. He was like a demoniac. "Yes, fight! I'll show you what kind of a man I am! I'll show you who you want to fight! Maybe you think I can't fight! Maybe you think I can't! I'll show you, you skin, you cardsharp! Yes, you cheated! You cheated! You cheated!"

"Well, let's go at it, then, mister," said Johnnie coolly.

The cowboy's brow was beaded with sweat from his efforts in intercepting all sorts of raids. He turned in despair to Scully. "What are you goin' to do now?"

A change had come over the Celtic visage of the old man. He now seemed all eagerness; his eyes glowed.

"We'll let them fight," he answered stalwartly. "I can't put up with it any longer. I've stood this damned Swede till I'm sick. We'll let them fight."

VI

The men prepared to go out of doors. The Easterner was so nervous that he had great difficulty in getting his arms into the sleeves of his new leather coat. As the cowboy drew his fur cap down over his ears, his hands trembled. In fact, Johnnie and old Scully were the only ones who displayed no agitation. These preliminaries were conducted without words.

Scully threw open the door. "Well, come on," he said. Instantly a terrific wind caused the flame of the lamp to struggle at its wick, while a puff of black smoke sprang from the chimney top. The stove was in midcurrent of the blast, and its voice swelled to equal the roar of the storm. Some of the scarred and bedabbled cards were caught up from the floor and dashed helplessly against the farther wall. The men lowered their heads and plunged into the tempest as into a sea.

No snow was falling, but great whirls and clouds of flakes, swept up from the ground by the frantic winds, were streaming southward with the speed of bullets. The covered land was blue with the sheen of an unearthly satin, and there was no other hue save where, at the low, black railway station—which seemed incredibly distant—one light gleamed like a tiny jewel. As the men floundered into a thigh-deep drift, it was known that the Swede was bawling out something. Scully went to him, put a hand on his shoulder, and projected an ear. "What's that you say?" he shouted.

"I say," bawled the Swede again, "I won't stand much show against this gang. I know you'll all pitch on me."

Scully smote him reproachfully on the arm. "Tut, man!" he yelled. The wind tore the words from Scully's lips and scattered them far alee.

"You are all a gang of—" boomed the Swede, but the storm also seized the remainder of this sentence.

Immediately turning their backs upon the wind, the men had swung around a corner to the sheltered side of the hotel. It was the function of the little house to preserve here, amid this great devastation of snow, an irregular V-shape of heavily encrusted grass, which crackled beneath the feet. One could imagine the great drifts piled against the windward side. When the party reached the comparative peace of this spot, it was found that the Swede was still bellowing.

"Oh, I know what kind of a thing this is! I know you'll all pitch on me. I can't lick you all!"

Scully turned upon him panther-fashion. "You'll not have to whip all of us. You'll have to whip my son Johnnie. An' the man what troubles you durin' that time will have me to dale with."

The arrangements were swiftly made. The two men faced each other, obedient to the harsh commands of Scully, whose face, in the subtly luminous gloom, could be seen set in the austere, impersonal lines that are pictured on the countenances of the Roman veterans. The Easterner's teeth were chattering, and he was hopping up and down like a mechanical toy. The cowboy stood rocklike.

The contestants had not stripped off any clothing. Each was in his ordinary attire. Their fists were up, and they eyed each other in a calm that had the elements of leonine cruelty in it.

During this pause, the Easterner's mind, like a film, took lasting impressions of three men—the iron-nerved master of the ceremony; the Swede, pale, motionless, terrible; and Johnnie, serene yet ferocious, brutish yet heroic. The entire prelude had in it a tragedy greater than the tragedy of action, and this aspect was accentuated by the long, mellow cry of the blizzard, as it sped the tumbling and wailing flakes into the black abyss of the south.

"Now!" said Scully.

The two combatants leaped forward and crashed together like bullocks. There was heard the cushioned sound of blows, and of a curse squeezing out from between the tight teeth of one.

As for the spectators, the Easterner's pent-up breath exploded from him with a pop of relief, absolute relief from the tension of the preliminaries. The cowboy bounded into the air with a yowl. Scully was immovable as from supreme amazement and fear at the fury at the fight which he himself had permitted and arranged.

For a time the encounter in the darkness was such a perplexity of flying arms that it presented no more detail than would a swiftly revolving wheel. Occasionally a face, as if illumined by a flash of light, would shine out, ghastly and marked with pink spots. A moment later, the men might have been known as shadows, if it were not for the involuntary utterance of oaths that came from them in whispers.

Suddenly a holocaust of warlike desire caught the cowboy, and he bolted forward with the speed of a bronco. "Go it, Johnnie! Go it! Kill him! Kill him!"

Scully confronted him. "Kape back," he said; and by his glance the cowboy could tell that this man was Johnnie's father.

To the Easterner there was a monotony of unchangeable fighting that was an abomination. This confused mingling was eternal to his sense, which was concentrated in a longing for the end, the priceless end. Once the fighters lurched near him, and as he scrambled hastily backward, he heard them breathe like men on the rack.

"Kill him, Johnnie! Kill him! Kill him! Kill him!" The cowboy's face was contorted like one of those agony masks in museums.

"Keep still," said Scully icily.

Then there was a sudden loud grunt, incomplete, cut short, and Johnnie's body swung away from the Swede and fell with sickening heaviness to the grass. The cowboy was barely in time to prevent the mad Swede from flinging himself upon his prone adversary. "No, you don't," said the cowboy, interposing an arm. "Wait a second."

Scully was at his son's side. "Johnnie! Johnnie, me boy!" His voice had a quality of melancholy tenderness. "Johnnie! Can you go on with it?" He looked anxiously down into the bloody, pulpy face of his son.

There was a moment of silence, and then Johnnie answered in his ordinary voice, "Yes, I—it—yes."

Assisted by his father, he struggled to his feet. "Wait a bit now till you git your wind," said the old man.

A few paces away, the cowboy was lecturing the Swede. "No, you don't! Wait a second!"

The Easterner was plucking at Scully's sleeve. "Oh, this is enough," he pleaded. "This is enough! Let it go as it stands. This is enough!"

"Bill," said Scully, "git out of the road." The cowboy stepped aside. "Now." The combatants were actuated by a new caution as they advanced toward collision. They'd glared at each other, and then the Swede aimed a lightning blow that carried with it his entire weight. Johnnie was evidently half stupid from weakness, but he miraculously dodged, and his fist sent the overbalanced Swede sprawling.

The cowboy, Scully, and the Easterner burst into a cheer

that was like a chorus of triumphant soldiery, but before its conclusion the Swede had scuffled agilely to his feet and come in berserk abandon at his foe. There was another perplexity of flying arms, and Johnnie's body again swung away and fell, even as a bundle might fall from a roof. The Swede instantly staggered to a little wind-waved tree and leaned upon it, breathing like an engine, while his savage and flame-lit eyes roamed from face to face as the men bent over Johnnie. There was a splendor of isolation in his situation at this time which the Easterner felt once when, lifting his eyes from the man on the ground, he beheld that mysterious and lonely figure, waiting.

"Are you any good yet, Johnnie?" asked Scully in a broken voice.

The son gasped and opened his eyes languidly. After a moment, he answered, "No—I ain't—any good—any—more." Then, from shame and bodily ill, he began to weep, the tears furrowing down through the bloodstains on his face. "He was too—too—too heavy for me."

Scully straightened and addressed the waiting figure. "Stranger," he said evenly, "it's all up with our side." Then his voice changed into that vibrant huskiness which is commonly the tone of the most simple and deadly announcements. "Johnnie is whipped."

Without replying, the victor moved off on the route to the front door of the hotel.

The cowboy was formulating new and unspellable blasphemies. The Easterner was startled to find that they were out in a wind that seemed to come direct from the shadowed Arctic floes. He heard again the wail of the snow as it was flung to its grave in the south. He knew now that all this time the cold had been sinking into him deeper and deeper, and he wondered that he had not perished. He felt indifferent to the condition of the vanquished man.

"Johnnie, can you walk?" asked Scully.

"Did I hurt—hurt him any?" asked the son.

"Can you walk, boy? Can you walk?"

Johnnie's voice was suddenly strong. There was a robust impatience in it. "I asked you whether I hurt him any!"

"Yes, yes, Johnnie," answered the cowboy consolingly, "he's hurt a good deal."

They raised him from the ground, and as soon as he was on his feet, he went tottering off, rebuffing all attempts at assistance. When the party rounded the corner, they were fairly blinded by the pelting of the snow. It burned their faces like fire. The cowboy carried Johnnie through the drift to the door. As they entered, some cards again rose from the floor and beat against the wall.

The Easterner rushed to the stove. He was so profoundly chilled that he almost dared to embrace the glowing iron. The Swede was not in the room. Johnnie sank into a chair, and folding his arms on his knees, buried his face in them. Scully, warming one foot and then the other at a rim of the stove, muttered to himself with Celtic mournfulness. The cowboy had removed his fur cap, and with a dazed and rueful air, he was running one hand through his tousled locks. From overhead they could hear the creaking of boards, as the Swede tramped here and there in his room.

The sad quiet was broken by the sudden flinging open of a door that led toward the kitchen. It was instantly followed by an inrush of women. They precipitated themselves upon Johnnie amid a chorus of lamentation. Before they carried their prey off to the kitchen, there to be bathed and harangued with that mixture of sympathy and abuse which is a feat of their sex, the mother straightened herself and fixed old Scully with an eye of stern reproach. "Shame be upon you, Patrick Scully!" she cried. "Your own son, too. Shame be upon you!"

"There now! Be quiet now!" said the old man weakly.

"Shame be upon you, Patrick Scully!" The girls, rallying to this slogan, sniffed disdainfully in the direction of those trembling accomplices, the cowboy and the Easterner. Presently they bore Johnnie away, and left the three men to dismal reflection.

VII

"I'd like to fight this here Dutchman myself," said the cowboy, breaking a long silence.

Scully wagged his head sadly. "No, that wouldn't do. It wouldn't be right. It wouldn't be right."

"Well, why wouldn't it?" argued the cowboy. "I don't see no harm in it."

"No," answered Scully with mournful heroism. "It wouldn't be right. It was Johnnie's fight, and now we mustn't whip the man just because he whipped Johnnie."

"Yes, that's true enough," said the cowboy, "but—he better not get fresh with me, because I couldn't stand no more of it."

"You'll not say a word to him," commanded Scully, and

even then they heard the tread of the Swede on the stairs. His entrance was made theatric. He swept the door back with a bang and swaggered to the middle of the room. No one looked at him. "Well," he cried insolently at Scully, "I s'pose you'll tell me now how much I owe you?"

The old man remained stolid. "You don't owe me nothin'."

"Huh!" said the Swede. "Huh! Don't owe 'im nothin'."

The cowboy addressed the Swede. "Stranger, I don't see how you come to be so gay around here."

Old Scully was instantly alert. "Stop!" he shouted, holding his hand forth, fingers upward. "Bill, you shut up!"

The cowboy spat carelessly into the sawdust box. "I didn't say a word, did I?" he asked.

"Mr. Scully," called the Swede, "how much do I owe you?" It was seen that he was attired for departure, and that he had his valise in his hand.

"You don't owe me nothin'," repeated Scully in the same imperturbable way.

"Huh!" said the Swede. "I guess you're right. I guess if it was any way at all, you'd owe me somethin'. That's what I guess." He turned to the cowboy. " 'Kill him! Kill him! Kill him!' " he mimicked, and then guffawed victoriously. " 'Kill him!' " He was convulsed with ironical humor.

But he might have been jeering the dead. The three men were immovable and silent, staring with glassy eyes at the stove.

The Swede opened the door and passed into the storm, giving one derisive glance backward at the still group.

As soon as the door was closed, Scully and the cowboy leaped to their feet and began to curse. They trampled to and fro, waving their arms and smashing into the air with their fists. "Oh, but that was a hard minute!" wailed Scully. "That was a hard minute! Him there leerin' and scoffin'! One bang at his nose was worth forty dollars to me that minute! How did you stand it, Bill?"

"How did I stand it?" cried the cowboy in a quivering voice. "How did I stand it? Oh!"

The old man burst into sudden brogue. "I'd loike to take that Swede," he wailed, "and hould 'im down on a shtone flure and bate 'im to a jelly wid a shtick!"

The cowboy groaned in sympathy. "I'd like to git him by the neck and ha-ammer him"—he brought his hand down on a chair with a noise like a pistol shot—"hammer that there Dutchman until he couldn't tell himself from a dead coyote!"

"I'd bate 'im until he—"

"I'd show *him* some things—"

And then together they raised a yearning, fanatic cry: "Oh-o-oh! if we only could—"

"Yes!"

"Yes!"

"And then I'd—"

"O-o-oh!"

VIII

The Swede, tightly gripping his valise, tacked across the face of the storm as if he carried sails. He was following a line of little naked, gasping trees which, he knew, must mark the way of the road. His face, fresh from the pounding of Johnnie's fists, felt more pleasure than pain in the wind and the driving snow. A number of square shapes loomed upon him finally, and he knew them as the houses of the main body of the town. He found a street and made travel along it, leaning heavily upon the wind whenever, at a corner, a terrific blast caught him.

He might have been in a deserted village. We picture the world as thick with conquering and elate humanity, but here, with the bugles of the tempest pealing, it was hard to imagine a peopled earth. One viewed the existence of man then as a marvel, and conceded a glamour of wonder to these lice which were caused to cling to a whirling, fire-smitten, ice-locked, disease-stricken, space-lost bulb. The conceit of man was explained by this storm to be the very engine of life. One was a coxcomb not to die in it. However, the Swede found a saloon.

In front of it an indomitable red light was burning, and the snowflakes were made blood color as they flew through the circumscribed territory of the lamp's shining. The Swede pushed open the door of the saloon and entered. A sanded expanse was before him, and at the end of it four men sat about a table drinking. Down one side of the room extended a radiant bar, and its guardian was leaning upon his elbows listening to the talk of the men at the table. The Swede dropped his valise upon the floor, and smiling fraternally upon the barkeeper, said, "Gimme some whisky, will you?" The man placed a bottle, a whisky glass, and a glass of ice-thick water upon the bar. The Swede poured himself an abnormal portion of whisky and drank it in three gulps. "Pretty bad night," remarked the bartender indifferently. He was making the pretension of blindness which is usually a distinction of his class; but it could have been seen that he was furtively studying the half-erased bloodstains on the face of the Swede. "Bad night," he said again.

"Oh, it's good enough for me," replied the Swede hardily, as he poured himself some more whisky. The barkeeper took his coin and maneuvered it through its reception by the highly nickeled cash machine. A bell rang; a card labeled "20 cts." had appeared.

"No," continued the Swede, "this isn't too bad weather. It's good enough for me."

"So?" murmured the barkeeper languidly.

The copious drams made the Swede's eyes swim, and he breathed a trifle heavier. "Yes, I like this weather. I like it. It suits me." It was apparently his design to impart a deep significance to these words.

"So?" murmured the bartender again. He turned to gaze dreamily at the scroll-like birds and birdlike scrolls which had been drawn with soap upon the mirrors in back of the bar.

"Well, I guess I'll take another drink," said the Swede presently. "Have something?"

"No, thanks; I'm not drinkin'," answered the bartender. Afterward he asked, "How did you hurt your face?"

The Swede immediately began to boast loudly. "Why, in a fight. I thumped the soul out of a man down here at Scully's hotel."

The interest of the four men at the table was at last aroused.

"Who was it?" said one.

"Johnnie Scully," blustered the Swede. "Son of the man what runs it. He will be pretty near dead for some weeks, I can tell you. I made a nice thing of him, I did. He couldn't get up. They carried him in the house. Have a drink?"

Instantly the men in some subtle way encased themselves in reserve. "No, thanks," said one. The group was of curious formation. Two were prominent local businessmen; one was the district attorney; and one was a professional gambler of the kind known as "square." But a scrutiny of the group would not have enabled an observer to pick the gambler from the men of more reputable pursuits. He was, in fact, a man so delicate in manner, when among people of fair class, and so judicious in his choice of victims, that in the strictly masculine part of the town's life he had come to be explicitly trusted and admired. People called him a thoroughbred.

The fear and contempt with which his craft was regarded were undoubtedly the reason why his quiet dignity shone conspicuous above the quiet dignity of men who might be merely hatters, billiard-markers, or grocery clerks. Beyond an occasional unwary traveler who came by rail, this gambler was supposed to prey solely upon reckless and senile farmers, who, when flush with good crops, drove into town in all the pride and confidence of an absolutely invulnerable stupidity. Hearing at times in circuitous fashion of the despoilment of such a farmer, the important men of Romper invariably laughed in contempt of the victim, and if they thought of the wolf at all, it was with a kind of pride at the knowledge that he would never dare think of attacking their wisdom and courage. Besides, it was popular that this gambler had a real wife and two real children in a neat cottage in a suburb, where he led an exemplary home life; and when anyone even suggested a discrepancy in his character, the crowd immediately vociferated descriptions of this virtuous family circle. Then men who led exemplary home lives, and men who did not lead exemplary home lives, all subsided in a bunch, remarking that there was nothing more to be said.

However, when a restriction was placed upon him—as, for instance, when a strong clique of members of the new Pollywog Club refused to permit him, even as a spectator, to appear in the rooms of the organization—the candor and gentleness with which he accepted the judgment disarmed many of his foes and made his friends more desperately partisan. He invariably distinguished between himself and a respectable Romper man so quickly and frankly that his manner actually appeared to be a continual broadcast compliment.

And one must not forget to declare the fundamental fact of his entire position in Romper. It is irrefutable that in all affairs outside his business, in all matters that occur eternally and commonly between man and man, this thieving card-player was so generous, so just, so moral, that in a contest, he could have put to flight the consciences of nine-tenths of the citizens of Romper.

And so it happened that he was seated in this saloon with the two prominent local merchants and the district attorney.

The Swede continued to drink raw whisky, meanwhile babbling at the barkeeper and trying to induce him to indulge in potations. "Come on. Have a drink. Come on. What—no? Well, have a little one, then. By gawd, I've whipped a man tonight, and I want to celebrate. I whipped him good, too.

Gentlemen," the Swede cried to the men at the table, "have a drink?"

"Ssh!" said the barkeeper.

The group at the table, although furtively attentive, had been pretending to be deep in talk, but now a man lifted his eyes toward the Swede and said, shortly, "Thanks. We don't want any more."

At this reply, the Swede ruffled out his chest like a rooster. "Well," he exploded, "it seems I can't get anybody to drink with me in this town. Seems so, don't it? Well!"

"Ssh!" said the barkeeper.

"Say," snarled the Swede, "don't you try to shut me up. I won't have it. I'm a gentleman, and I want people to drink with me. And I want 'em to drink with me now. *Now*—do you understand?" He rapped the bar with his knuckles.

Years of experience had calloused the bartender. He merely grew sulky. "I hear you," he answered.

"Well," cried the Swede, "listen hard then. See those men over there? Well, they're going to drink with me, and don't you forget it. Now you watch."

"Hi!" yelled the barkeeper. "This won't do!"

"Why won't it?" demanded the Swede. He stalked over to the table, and by chance laid his hand upon the shoulder of the gambler. "How about this?" he asked wrathfully. "I asked you to drink with me."

The gambler simply twisted his head and spoke over his shoulder. "My friend, I don't know you."

"Oh, hell!" answered the Swede, "come and have a drink."

"Now, my boy," advised the gambler kindly, "take your hand off my shoulder and go 'way and mind your own business." He was a little, slim man, and it seemed strange to hear him use this tone of heroic patronage to the burly Swede. The other men at the table said nothing.

"What! You won't drink with me, you little dude? I'll make you, then! I'll make you!" The Swede had grasped the gambler frenziedly at the throat, and was dragging him from his chair. The other men sprang up. The barkeeper dashed around the corner of his bar. There was a great tumult, and then was seen a long blade in the hand of the gambler. It shot forward, and a human body, this citadel of virtue, wisdom, power, was pierced as easily as if it had been a melon. The Swede fell with a cry of supreme astonishment.

The prominent merchants and the district attorney must have at once tumbled out of the place backward. The bartender found himself hanging limply to the arm of a chair and gazing into the eyes of a murderer.

"Henry," said the latter, as he wiped his knife on one of the towels that hung beneath the bar rail, "you tell 'em where to find me. I'll be home, waiting for 'em." Then he vanished. A moment afterward the barkeeper was in the street dinning through the storm for help and, moreover, companionship.

The corpse of the Swede, alone in the saloon, had its eyes fixed upon a dreadful legend that dwelt atop of the cash machine: "This registers the amount of your purchase."

IX

Months later, the cowboy was frying pork over the stove of a little ranch near the Dakota line, when there was a quick thud of hoofs outside, and presently the Easterner entered with the letters and the papers.

"Well," said the Easterner at once, "the chap that killed the Swede has got three years. Wasn't much, was it?"

"He has? Three years?" The cowboy poised his pan of pork, while he ruminated upon the news. "Three years. That ain't much."

"No. It was a light sentence," replied the Easterner as he unbuckled his spurs. "Seems there was a good deal of sympathy for him in Romper."

"If the bartender had been any good," observed the cowboy thoughtfully, "he would have gone in and cracked that there Dutchman on the head with a bottle in the beginnin' of it and stopped all this here murderin'."

"Yes, a thousand things might have happened," said the Easterner tartly.

The cowboy returned his pan of pork to the fire, but his philosophy continued. "It's funny, ain't it? If he hadn't said Johnnie was cheatin' he'd be alive this minute. He was an awful fool. Game played for fun, too. Not for money. I believe he was crazy."

"I feel sorry for that gambler," said the Easterner.

"Oh, so do I," said the cowboy. "He don't deserve none of it for killin' who he did."

"The Swede might not have been killed if everything had been square."

"Might not have been killed?" exclaimed the cowboy. "Everythin' square? Why, when he said that Johnnie was cheatin' and acted like such a jackass? And then in the saloon he fairly walked up to git hurt?" With these arguments the cowboy browbeat the Easterner and reduced him to rage.

"You're a fool!" cried the Eastern viciously. "You're a bigger jackass than the Swede by a million majority. Now let me tell you one thing. Let me tell you something. Listen. Johnnie *was* cheating!"

" 'Johnnie,' " said the cowboy blankly. There was a minute of silence, and then he said robustly. "Why, no. The game was only for fun."

"Fun or not," said the Easterner, "Johnnie was cheating. I saw him. I know it. I saw him. And I refused to stand up and be a man. I let the Swede fight it out alone. And you— you were simply puffing around the place and wanting to fight. And then old Scully himself! We are all in it! This poor gambler isn't even a noun. He is kind of an adverb. Every sin is the result of a collaboration. We, five of us, have collaborated in the murder of this Swede. Usually there are from a dozen to forty women really involved in every murder, but in this case it seems to be only five men—you, I, Johnnie, old Scully; and that fool of an unfortunate gambler came merely as a culmination, the apex of a human movement, and gets all the punishment."

The cowboy, injured and rebellious, cried out blindly into this fog of mysterious theory: "Well, I didn't do anythin', did I?"

EDITH WHARTON

False Dawn

I

HAY, verbena and mignonette scented the languid July day. Large strawberries, crimsoning through sprigs of mint, floated in a bowl of pale yellow cup on the verandah table: an old Georgian bowl, with complex reflections on polygonal flanks, engraved with the Raycie arms between lions' heads. Now and again the gentlemen, warned by a menacing hum, slapped their cheeks, their brows or their bald crowns; but they did so as furtively as possible, for Mr. Halston Raycie, on whose verandah they sat, would not admit that there were mosquitoes at High Point.

The strawberries came from Mr. Raycie's kitchen garden; the Georgian bowl came from his great-grandfather (father of the Signer); the verandah was that of his country-house, which stood on a height above the Sound, at a convenient driving distance from his town house in Canal Street.

"Another glass, Commodore," said Mr. Raycie, shaking out a cambric handkerchief the size of a table-cloth, and applying a corner of it to his steaming brow.

Mr. Jameson Ledgely smiled and took another glass. He was known as "the Commodore" among his intimates because of having been in the Navy in his youth, and having taken part, as a midshipman under Admiral Porter, in the war of 1812. This jolly sunburnt bachelor, whose face resembled that of one of the bronze idols he might have brought back with him, had kept his naval air, though long retired from the service; and his white duck trousers, his gold-braided cap and shining teeth, still made him look as if he might be in command of a frigate. Instead of that, he had just sailed over a party of friends from his own place on the

Long Island shore; and his trim white sloop was now lying in the bay below the point.

The Halston Raycie house overlooked a lawn sloping to the Sound. The lawn was Mr. Raycie's pride: it was mown with a scythe once a fortnight, and rolled in the spring by an old white horse specially shod for the purpose. Below the verandah the turf was broken by three round beds of rose-geranium, heliotrope and Bengal roses, which Mrs. Raycie tended in gauntlet gloves, under a small hinged sunshade that folded back on its carved ivory handle. The house, re-modelled and enlarged by Mr. Raycie on his marriage, had played a part in the Revolutionary war as the settler's cot-tage where Benedict Arnold had had his headquarters. A contemporary print of it hung in Mr. Raycie's study; but no one could have detected the humble outline of the old house in the majestic stone-coloured dwelling built of tongued-and-grooved boards, with an angle tower, tall nar-row windows, and a verandah on chamfered posts, that fig-ured so confidently as a "Tuscan Villa" in Downing's "Land-scape Gardening in America." There was the same difference between the rude lithograph of the earlier house and the fine steel engraving of its successor (with a "specimen" weeping beech on the lawn) as between the buildings themselves. Mr. Raycie had reason to think well of his architect.

He thought well of most things related to himself by ties of blood or interest. No one had ever been quite sure that he made Mrs. Raycie happy, but he was known to have the highest opinion of her. So it was with his daughters, Sarah Anne and Mary Adeline, fresher replicas of the lymphatic Mrs. Raycie; no one would have sworn that they were quite at ease with their genial parent, yet every one knew how loud he was in their praises. But the most remarkable object with-in the range of Mr. Raycie's self-approval was his son Lewis. And yet, as Jameson Ledgely, who was given to speaking his mind, had once observed, you wouldn't have supposed young Lewis was exactly the kind of craft Halston would have turned out if he'd had the designing of his son and heir.

Mr. Raycie was a monumental man. His extent in height, width and thickness was so nearly the same that which-ever way he was turned one had an almost equally broad view of him; and every inch of that mighty circumference was so exquisitely cared for that to a farmer's eye he might have suggested a great agricultural estate of which not an acre is untilled. Even his baldness, which was in proportion to the rest, looked as if it received a special daily polish;

and on a hot day his whole person was like some wonderful example of the costliest irrigation. There was so much of him, and he had so many planes, that it was fascinating to watch each runnel of moisture follow its own particular watershed. Even on his large fresh-looking hands the drops divided, trickling in different ways from the ridges of the fingers; and as for his forehead and temples, and the raised cushion of cheek beneath each of his lower lids, every one of these slopes had its own particular stream, its hollow pools and sudden cataracts; and the sight was never unpleasant, because his whole vast bubbling surface was of such a clean and hearty pink, and the exuding moisture so perceptibly flavoured with expensive eau de Cologne and the best French soap.

Mrs. Raycie, though built on a less heroic scale, had a pale amplitude which, when she put on her best watered silk (the kind that stood alone), and framed her countenance in the innumerable blonde lace ruffles and clustered purple grapes of her newest Paris cap, almost balanced her husband's bulk. Yet from this full-rigged pair, as the Commodore would have put it, had issued the lean little runt of a Lewis, a shrimp of a baby, a shaver of a boy, and now a youth as scant as an ordinary man's midday shadow.

All these things, Lewis himself mused, dangling his legs from the verandah rail, were undoubtedly passing through the minds of the four gentlemen grouped about his father's bowl of cup.

Mr. Robert Huzzard, the banker, a tall broad man, who looked big in any company but Mr. Raycie's, leaned back, lifted his glass, and bowed to Lewis.

"Here's to the Grand Tour!"

"Don't perch on that rail like a sparrow, my boy," Mr. Raycie said reprovingly; and Lewis dropped to his feet, and returned Mr. Huzzard's bow.

"I wasn't thinking," he stammered. It was his too frequent excuse.

Mr. Ambrose Huzzard, the banker's younger brother, Mr. Ledgely and Mr. Donaldson Kent, all raised their glasses and cheerily echoed: "The Grand Tour!"

Lewis bowed again, and put his lips to the glass he had forgotten. In reality, he had eyes only for Mr. Donaldson Kent, his father's cousin, a silent man with a lean hawk-like profile, who looked like a retired Revolutionary hero, and lived in daily fear of the most trifling risk or responsibility.

To this prudent and circumspect citizen had come, some years earlier, the unexpected and altogether inexcusable demand that he should look after the daughter of his only brother, Julius Kent. Julius had died in Italy—well, that was his own business, if he chose to live there. But to let his wife die before him, and to leave a minor daughter, and a will entrusting her to the guardianship of his esteemed elder brother, Donaldson Kent Esquire, of Kent's Point, Long Island, and Great Jones Street, New York—well, as Mr. Kent himself said, and as his wife said for him, there had never been anything, anything whatever, in Mr. Kent's attitude or behaviour, to justify the ungrateful Julius (whose debts he had more than once paid) in laying on him this final burden.

The girl came. She was fourteen, she was considered plain, she was small and black and skinny. Her name was Beatrice, which was bad enough, and made worse by the fact that it had been shortened by ignorant foreigners to Treeshy. But she was eager, serviceable and good-tempered, and as Mr. and Mrs. Kent's friends pointed out, her plainness made everything easy. There were two Kent boys growing up, Bill and Donald; and if this penniless cousin had been compounded of cream and roses—well, she would have taken more watching, and might have rewarded the kindness of her uncle and aunt by some act of wicked ingratitude. But this risk being obviated by her appearance, they could be good-natured to her without afterthought, and to be good-natured was natural to them. So, as the years passed, she gradually became the guardian of her guardians; since it was equally natural to Mr. and Mrs. Kent to throw themselves in helpless reliance on every one whom they did not nervously fear or mistrust.

"Yes, he's off on Monday," Mr. Raycie said, nodding sharply at Lewis, who had set down his glass after one sip. "Empty it, you shirk!" the nod commanded; and Lewis, throwing back his head, gulped down the draught, though it almost stuck in his lean throat. He had already had to take two glasses, and even this scant conviviality was too much for him, and likely to result in a mood of excited volubility, followed by a morose evening and a head the next morning. And he wanted to keep his mind clear that day, and to think steadily and lucidly of Treeshy Kent.

Of course he couldn't marry her—yet. He was twenty-one that very day, and still entirely dependent on his father. And he wasn't altogether sorry to be going first on this Grand Tour. It was what he had always dreamed of, pined for,

from the moment when his infant eyes had first been drawn
to the prints of European cities in the long upper passage
that smelt of matting. And all that Treeshy had told him
about Italy had confirmed and intensified the longing. Oh,
to have been going there with her—with her as his guide, his
Beatrice! (For she had given him a little Dante of her father's, with a steel-engraved frontispiece of Beatrice; and
his sister Mary Adeline, who had been taught Italian by one
of the romantic Milanese exiles, had helped her brother out
with the grammar.)

The thought of going to Italy with Treeshy was only a
dream; but later, as man and wife, they would return there,
and by that time, perhaps, it was Lewis who would be her
guide, and reveal to her the historic marvels of her birth-
place, of which after all she knew so little, except in minor
domestic ways that were quaint but unimportant.

The prospect swelled her suitor's bosom, and reconciled
him to the idea of their separation. After all, he secretly felt
himself to be still a boy, and it was as a man that he would
return: he meant to tell her that when they met the next
day. When he came back his character would be formed,
his knowledge of life (which he already thought considerable)
would be complete; and then no one could keep them apart.
He smiled in advance to think how little his father's shouting
and booming would impress a man on his return from the
Grand Tour. . . .

The gentlemen were telling anecdotes about their own early
experiences in Europe. None of them—not even Mr. Raycie—
had travelled as extensively as it was intended that Lewis
should; but the two Huzzards had been twice to England
on banking matters, and Commodore Ledgely, a bold man,
to France and Belgium as well—not to speak of his early
experiences in the Far East. All three had kept a vivid and
amused recollection, slightly tinged with disapprobation, of
what they had seen—"Oh, those French wenches," the Commodore chuckled through his white teeth—but poor Mr. Kent,
who had gone abroad on his honeymoon, had been caught in
Paris by the revolution of 1830, had had the fever in Florence,
and had nearly been arrested as a spy in Vienna; and the only
satisfactory episode in 'this disastrous, and never repeated,
adventure. had been the fact of his having been mistaken
for the Duke of Wellington (as he was trying to slip out of a
Viennese hotel in his courier's blue surtout) by a crowd who
had been—"Well, very gratifying in their enthusiasm," Mr.
Kent admitted.

"How my poor brother Julius could have lived in Europe! Well, look at the consequences—" he used to say, as if poor Treeshy's plainness gave an awful point to his moral.

"There's one thing in Paris, my boy, that you must be warned against: those gambling-hells in the Pally Royle," Mr. Kent insisted. "I never set foot in the places myself; but a glance at the outside was enough."

"I knew a feller that was fleeced of a fortune there," Mr. Henry Huzzard confirmed; while the Commodore, at his tenth glass, chuckled with moist eyes: "The trollops, oh, the trollops—"

"As for Vienna—" said Mr. Kent.

"Even in London," said Mr. Ambrose Huzzard, "a young man must be on his look-out against gamblers. Every form of swindling is practised, and the touts are always on the look-out for greenhorns; a term," he added apologetically, "which they apply to any traveller new to the country."

"In Paris," said Mr. Kent, "I was once within an ace of being challenged to fight a duel." He fetched a sigh of horror and relief, and glanced reassuredly down the Sound in the direction of his own peaceful roof-tree.

"Oh, a duel," laughed the Commodore. "A man can fight duels here. I fought a dozen when I was a young feller in New Erleens." The Commodore's mother had been a southern lady, and after his father's death had spent some years with her parents in Louisiana, so that her son's varied experiences had begun early. " 'Bout women," he smiled confidentially, holding out his empty glass to Mr. Raycie.

"The ladies—!" exclaimed Mr. Kent in a voice of warning.

The gentlemen rose to their feet, the Commodore quite as promptly and steadily as the others. The drawing-room window opened, and from it emerged Mrs. Raycie, in a ruffled sarsenet dress and Point de Paris cap, followed by her two daughters in starched organdy with pink spencers. Mr. Raycie looked with proud approval at his womenkind.

"Gentlemen," said Mrs. Raycie, in a perfectly even voice, "supper is on the table, and if you will do Mr. Raycie and myself the favour—"

"The favour, ma'am," said Mr. Ambrose Huzzard, "is on your side, in so amiably inviting us."

Mrs. Raycie curtsied, the gentlemen bowed, and Mr. Raycie said: "Your arm to Mrs. Raycie, Huzzard. This little farewell party is a family affair, and the other gentlemen must content themselves with my two daughters. Sarah Anne, Mary Adeline—"

The Commodore and Mr. John Huzzard advanced cere-
moniously toward the two girls, and Mr. Kent, being a cousin,
closed the procession between Mr. Raycie and Lewis.

Oh, that supper-table! The vision of it used sometimes to
rise before Lewis Raycie's eyes in outlandish foreign places;
for though not a large or fastidious eater when he was at
home, he was afterward, in lands of chestnut-flour and garlic
and queer bearded sea-things, to suffer many pangs of hunger
at the thought of that opulent board. In the centre stood the
Raycie *épergne* of pierced silver, holding aloft a bunch
of June roses surrounded by dangling baskets of sugared
almonds and striped peppermints; and grouped about this
decorative "motif" were Lowestoft platters heavy with piles
of raspberries, strawberries and the first Delaware peaches.
An outer flanking of heaped-up cookies, crullers, strawberry
shortcake, piping hot corn-bread and deep golden butter in
moist blocks still bedewed from the muslin swathings of the
dairy, led the eye to the Virginia ham in front of Mr. Raycie,
and the twin dishes of scrambled eggs on toast and broiled
blue-fish over which his wife presided. Lewis could never
afterward fit into this intricate pattern the "side-dishes" of
devilled turkey legs and creamed chicken hash, the sliced
cucumbers and tomatoes, the heavy silver jugs of butter-
coloured cream, the floating-island, "slips" and lemon jellies
that were somehow interwoven with the solider elements of
the design; but they were all there, either together or succes-
sively, and so were the towering piles of waffles reeling on
their foundations, and the slender silver jugs of maple syrup
perpetually escorting them about the table as black Dinah
replenished the supply.

They ate—oh, how they all ate!—though the ladies were
supposed only to nibble; but the good things on Lewis's plate
remained untouched until, ever and again, an admonishing
glance from Mr. Raycie, or an entreating one from Mary
Adeline, made him insert a languid fork into the heap.

And all the while Mr. Raycie continued to hold forth.

"A young man, in my opinion, before setting up for himself, must see the world; form his taste; fortify his judgment.
He must study the most famous monuments, examine the
organization of foreign societies, and the habits and customs
of those older civilizations whose yoke it has been our glory
to cast off. Though he may see in them much to deplore
and to reprove—" ("Some of the gals, though," Commodore
Ledgely was heard to interject)—"much that will make him
give thanks for the privilege of having been born and

brought up under our own Free Institutions, yet I believe he
will also"—Mr. Raycie conceded it with magnanimity—"be
able to learn much."

"The Sundays, though," Mr. Kent hazarded warningly;
and Mrs. Raycie breathed across to her son: "Ah, that's what
I say!"

Mr. Raycie did not like interruption; and he met it by growing visibly larger. His huge bulk hung a moment, like an
avalanche, above the silence which followed Mr. Kent's in-
terjection and Mrs. Raycie's murmur; then he crashed down
on both.

"The Sundays—the Sundays? Well, what of the Sundays?
What is there to frighten a good Episcopalian in what we call
the Continental Sunday? I presume that we're all Church-
men here, eh? No puling Methodists or atheistical Unitarians
at my table tonight, that I'm aware of? Nor will I offend
the ladies of my household by assuming that they have
secretly lent an ear to the Baptist ranter in the chapel at
the foot of our lane. No? I thought not! Well, then, I say,
what's all this flutter about the Papists? Far be it from me
to approve of their heathenish doctrines—but, damn it, they
go to church, don't they? And they have a real service, as we
do, don't they? And real clergy, and not a lot of nondescripts
dressed like layman, and damned badly at that, who chat
familiarly with the Almighty in their own vulgar lingo? No,
sir"—he swung about on the shrinking Mr. Kent—"it's not
the Church I'm afraid of in foreign countries, it's the sewers,
sir!"

Mrs. Raycie had grown very pale: Lewis knew that she too
was deeply perturbed about the sewers. "And the night air,"
she scarce-audibly sighed.

But Mr. Raycie had taken up his main theme again. "In my
opinion, if a young man travels at all, he must travel as
extensively as his—er—means permit; must see as much of
the world as he can. Those are my son's sailing orders,
Commodore; and here's to his carrying them out to the best
of his powers!"

Black Dinah, removing the Virginia ham, or rather such of
its bony structure as alone remained on the dish, had managed to make room for a bowl of punch from which Mr.
Raycie poured deep ladlefuls of perfumed fire into the glasses
ranged before him on a silver tray. The gentlemen rose, the
ladies smiled and wept, and Lewis's health and the success of
the Grand Tour were toasted with an eloquence which caused
Mrs. Raycie, with a hasty nod to her daughters, and a cover-

ing rustle of starched flounces, to shepherd them softly from
the room.

"After all," Lewis heard her murmur to them on the threshold, "your father's using such language shows that he's in the
best of humor with dear Lewis."

II

In spite of his enforced potations, Lewis Raycie was up the
next morning before sunrise.

Unlatching his shutters without noise, he looked forth over
the wet lawn merged in a blur of shrubberies, and the waters
of the Sound dimly seen beneath a sky full of stars. His head
ached but his heart glowed; what was before him was thril-
ling enough to clear a heavier brain than his.

He dressed quickly and completely (save for his shoes),
and then, stripping the flowered quilt from his high mahogany
bed, rolled it in a tight bundle under his arm. Thus enigma-
tically equipped he was feeling his way, shoes in hand,
through the darkness of the upper story to the slippery oak
stairs, when he was startled by a candle-gleam in the pitch-
blackness of the hall below. He held his breath, and leaning
over the stair-rail saw with amazement his sister Mary Adeline come forth, cloaked and bonneted, but also in stocking-
feet, from the passage leading to the pantry. She too carried a
double burden: her shoes and the candle in one hand, in
the other a large covered basket that weighed down her bare
arm.

Brother and sister stopped and stared at each other in
the blue dusk: the upward slant of the candle-light distorted
Mary Adeline's mild features, twisting them into a frightened
grin as Lewis stole down to join her.

"Oh—" she whispered. "What in the world are you doing
here? I was just getting together a few things for that poor
young Mrs. Poe down the lane, who's so ill—before mother
goes to the store room. You won't tell, will you?"

Lewis signalled his complicity, and cautiously slid open the
bolt of the front door. They durst not say more till they were
out of earshot. On the doorstep they sat down to put on their
shoes; then they hastened on without a word through the
ghostly shrubberies till they reached the gate into the lane.

"But you, Lewis?" the sister suddenly questioned, with
an astonished stare at the rolled-up quilt under her brother's
arm.

"Oh, I—. Look here, Addy—" he broke off and began to

grope in his pocket—"I haven't much about me . . . the old gentleman keeps me as close as ever . . . but here's a dollar, if you think that poor Mrs. Poe could use it . . . I'd be too happy . . . consider it a privilege . . ."

"Oh, Lewis, Lewis, how noble, how generous of you! Of course I can buy a few extra things with it . . . they never see meat unless I can bring them a bit, you know . . . and I fear she's dying of a decline . . . and she and her mother are so fiery-proud . . ." She wept with gratitude, and Lewis drew a breath of relief. He had diverted her attention from the bed-quilt.

"Ah, there's the breeze," he murmured, sniffing the suddenly chilled air.

"Yes; I must be off; I must be back before the sun is up," said Mary Adeline anxiously, "and it would never do if mother knew—"

"She doesn't know of your visits to Mrs. Poe?"

A look of childish guile sharpened Mary Adeline's undeveloped face. "She *does*, of course; but yet she doesn't . . . we've arranged it so. You see, Mr. Poe's an Atheist; and so father—"

"I see," Lewis nodded. "Well, we part here; I'm off for a swim," he said glibly. But abruptly he turned back and caught his sister's arm. "Sister, tell Mrs. Poe, please, that I heard her husband give a reading from his poems in New York two nights ago—"

("Oh, Lewis—*you*? But father says he's a blasphemer!")

"—And that he's a great poet—a Great Poet. Tell her that from me, will you, please, Mary Adeline?"

"Oh, brother, I couldn't . . . we never speak of him," the startled girl faltered, hurrying away.

In the cove where the Commodore's sloop had ridden a few hours earlier a biggish rowing-boat took the waking ripples. Young Raycie paddled out to her, fastened his skiff to the moorings, and hastily clambered into the boat.

From various recesses of his pockets he produced rope, string, a carpet-layer's needle, and other unexpected and incongruous tackle; then, lashing one of the oars across the top of the other, and jamming the latter upright between the forward thwart and the bow, he rigged the flowered bed-quilt on this mast, knotted a rope to the free end of the quilt, and sat down in the stern, one hand on the rudder, the other on his improvised sheet.

Venus, brooding silverly above a line of pale green sky,

made a pool of glory in the sea as the dawn-breeze plumped the lover's sail. . . .

On the shelving pebbles of another cove, two or three miles down the Sound, Lewis Raycie lowered his queer sail and beached his boat. A clump of willows on the shingle-edge mysteriously stirred and parted, and Treeshy Kent was in his arms.

The sun was just pushing above a belt of low clouds in the east, spattering them with liquid gold, and Venus blanched as the light spread upward. But under the willows it was still dusk, a watery green dusk in which the secret murmurs of the night were caught.

"Treeshy—Treeshy!" the young man cried, kneeling beside her—and then, a moment later: "My angel, are you sure that no one guesses—?"

The girl gave a faint laugh which screwed up her funny nose. She leaned her head on his shoulder, her round forehead and rough braids pressed against his cheek, her hands in his, breathing quickly and joyfully.

"I thought I should never get here," Lewis grumbled, "with that ridiculous bed-quilt—and it'll be broad day soon! To think that I was of age yesterday, and must come to you in a boat rigged like a child's toy on a duck-pond! If you knew how it humiliates me—"

"What does it matter, dear, since you're of age now, and your own master?"

"But am I, though? He says so—but it's only on his own terms; only while I do what he wants! You'll see . . . I've a credit of ten thousand dollars . . . ten . . . thou . . . sand . . . d'you hear? . . . placed to my name in a London bank; and not a penny here to bless myself with meanwhile . . . Why, Treeshy darling, why, what's the matter?"

She flung her arms about his neck, and through their innocent kisses he could taste her tears. "What *is* it, Treeshy?" he implored her.

"I . . . oh, I'd forgotten it was to be our last day together till you spoke of London—cruel, cruel!" she reproached him; and through the green twilight of the willows her eyes blazed on him like two stormy stars. No other eyes he knew could express such elemental rage as Treeshy's.

"You little spitfire, you!" he laughed back somewhat chokingly. "Yes, it's our last day—but not for long; at our age two years are not so very long, after all, are they? And when I come back to you I'll come as my own master, independent, free—come to claim you in face of everything and everybody! Think of that, darling, and be brave for my sake . . . brave and patient . . . as I mean to be!" he declared heroically.

"Oh, but you—you'll see other girls; heaps and heaps of them; in those wicked old countries where they're so lovely. My uncle Kent says the European countries are all wicked, even my own poor Italy . . ."

"But *you*, Treeshy; you'll be seeing cousins Bill and Donald meanwhile—seeing them all day long and every day. And you know you've a weakness for that great hulk of a Bill. Ah, if only I stood six-foot-one in my stockings I'd go with an easier heart, you fickle child!" he tried to banter her.

"Fickle? Fickle? *Me*—oh, Lewis!"

He felt the premonitory sweep of sobs, and his untried courage failed him. It was delicious, in theory, to hold weeping beauty to one's breast, but terribly alarming, he found, in practice. There came a responsive twitching in his throat.

"No, no; firm as adamant, true as steel; that's what we both mean to be, isn't it, *cara*?"

"*Caro*, yes," she sighed, appeased.

"And you'll write to me regularly, Treeshy—long long letters? I may count on that, mayn't I, wherever I am? And they must all be numbered, every one of them, so that I shall know at once if I've missed one; remember!"

"And, Lewis, you'll wear them here?" (She touched his breast.) "Oh, not *all*," she added, laughing, "for they'd make such a big bundle that you'd soon have a hump in front like Pulcinella—but always at least the last one, just the last one. Promise!"

"Always, I promise—as long as they're kind," he said, still struggling to take a spirited line.

"Oh, Lewis, they will be, as long as yours are—and long long afterward . . ."

Venus failed and vanished in the sun's uprising.

III

The crucial moment, Lewis had always known, would be not that of his farewell to Treeshy, but of his final interview with his father.

On that everything hung: his immediate future as well as his more distant prospects. As he stole home in the early sunlight, over the dew-drenched grass, he glanced up apprehensively at Mr. Raycie's windows, and thanked his stars that they were still tightly shuttered.

There was no doubt, as Mrs. Raycie said, that her husband's "using language" before ladies showed him to be in high good humor, relaxed and slippered, as it were—a state his family so seldom saw him in that Lewis had sometimes impertinently wondered to what awful descent from the clouds he and his two sisters owed their timorous being.

It was all very well to tell himself, as he often did, that the bulk of the money was his mother's, and that he could turn her round his little finger. What difference did that make? Mr. Raycie, the day after his marriage, had quietly taken over the management of his wife's property, and deducted, from the very moderate allowance he accorded her, all her little personal expenses, even to the postage-stamps she used, and the dollar she put in the plate every Sunday. He called the allowance her "pin-money," since, as he often reminded her, he paid all the household bills himself, so that Mrs. Raycie's quarterly pittance could be entirely devoted, if she chose, to frills and feathers.

"And will be, if you respect my wishes, my dear," he always added. "I like to see a handsome figure well set-off, and not to have our friends imagine, when they come to dine, that Mrs. Raycie is sick above-stairs, and I've replaced her by a poor relation in *alla-pacca*." In compliance with which Mrs. Raycie, at once flattered and terrified, spent her last penny in adorning herself and her daughters, and had to stint their bedroom fires, and the servants' meals, in order to find a penny for any private necessity.

Mr. Raycie had long since convinced his wife that this method of dealing with her, if not lavish, was suitable, and in fact "handsome"; when she spoke of the subject to her relations it was with tears of gratitude for her husband's kindness in assuming the management of her property. As he managed it exceedingly well, her hard-headed brothers (glad to have the responsibility off their hands, and convinced that, if left to herself, she would have muddled her money away in ill-advised charities) were disposed to share her approval of Mr. Raycie; though her old mother sometimes said helplessly: "When I think that Lucy Ann can't as much as have a drop of gruel brought up to her without his weighing the oatmeal . . ." But even that was only whispered, lest Mr. Raycie's mysterious faculty of hearing what was said behind his back should bring sudden reprisals on the venerable lady to whom he always alluded, with a tremor in his genial voice, as "my dear mother-in-law—unless indeed she will allow me to call her, more briefly but more truly, my dear mother."

To Lewis, hitherto, Mr. Raycie had meted the same measure as to the females of the household. He had dressed him well, educated him expensively, lauded him to the skies—and counted every penny of his allowance. Yet there was a difference; and Lewis was as well aware of it as any one.

The dream, the ambition, the passion of Mr. Raycie's life, was (as his son knew) to found a Family; and he had only Lewis to found it with. He believed in primogeniture, in heirlooms, in entailed estates, in all the ritual of the English "landed" tradition. No one was louder than he in praise of the democratic institutions under which he lived; but he never thought of them as affecting that more private but more important institution, the Family; and to the Family all his care and all his thoughts were given. The result, as Lewis dimly guessed, was, that upon his own shrinking and inadequate head was centred all the passion contained in the vast expanse of Mr. Raycie's breast. Lewis was his very own, and Lewis represented what was most dear to him; and for both these reasons Mr. Raycie set an inordinate value on the boy (a quite different thing, Lewis thought, from loving him).

Mr. Raycie was particularly proud of his son's taste for letters. Himself not a wholly unread man, he admired intensely what he called the "cultivated gentleman"—and that was what Lewis was evidently going to be. Could he have combined with this tendency a manlier frame, and an interest in the few forms of sport then popular among gentlemen, Mr. Raycie's satisfaction would have been complete; but whose is, in this disappointing world? Meanwhile he flattered himself that, Lewis being still young and malleable, and his health certainly mending, two years of travel and adventure might send him back a very different figure, physically as well as mentally. Mr. Raycie had himself travelled in his youth, and was persuaded that the experience was formative; he secretly hoped for the return of a bronzed and broadened Lewis, seasoned by independence and adventure, and having discreetly sown his wild oats in foreign pastures, where they would not contaminate the home crop.

All this Lewis guessed; and he guessed as well that these two wander-years were intended by Mr. Raycie to lead up to a marriage and an establishment after Mr. Raycie's own heart, but in which Lewis's was not to have even a consulting voice.

"He's going to give me all the advantages—for his own purpose," the young man summed it up as he went down to join the family at the breakfast table.

Mr. Raycie was never more resplendent than at that moment of the day and season. His spotless white duck trousers, strapped under kid boots, his thin kerseymere coat, and drab *piqué* waistcoat crossed below a snowy stock, made him look as fresh as the morning and as appetizing as the peaches and cream banked before him.

Oppposite sat Mrs. Raycie, immaculate also, but paler than usual, as became a mother about to part from her only son; and between the two was Sarah Anne, unusually pink, and apparently occupied in trying to screen her sister's empty seat. Lewis greeted them, and seated himself at his mother's right.

Mr. Raycie drew out his *guillochée* repeating watch, and detaching it from its heavy gold chain laid it on the table beside him.

"Mary Adeline is late again. It is a somewhat unusual thing for a sister to be late at the last meal she is to take —for two years—with her only brother."

"Oh, Mr. Raycie!" Mrs. Raycie faltered.

"I say, the idea is peculiar. Perhaps," said Mr. Raycie sarcastically, "I am going to be blessed with a *peculiar* daughter."

"I'm afraid Mary Adeline is beginning a sick headache, sir. She tried to get up, but really could not," said Sarah Anne in a rush.

Mr. Raycie's only reply was to arch ironic eyebrows, and Lewis hastily intervened: "I'm sorry, sir; but it may be my fault—"

Mrs. Raycie paled, Sarah Anne, purpled, and Mr. Raycie echoed with punctilious incredulity: "Your—fault?"

"In being the occasion, sir, of last night's too-sumptuous festivity—"

"Ha—ha—ha!" Mr. Raycie laughed, his thunders instantly dispelled.

He pushed back his chair and nodded to his son with a smile; and the two, leaving the ladies to wash up the teacups (as was still the habit in genteel families) betook themselves to Mr. Raycie's study.

What Mr. Raycie studied in this apartment—except the accounts, and ways of making himself unpleasant to his family—Lewis had never been able to discover. It was a small bare formidable room; and the young man, who never crossed the threshold but with a sinking of his heart, felt it sink lower than ever. *"Now!"* he thought.

Mr. Raycie took the only easy-chair, and began.

"My dear fellow, our time is short, but long enough for what I have to say. In a few hours you will be setting out on your great journey: an important event in the life of any young man. Your talents and character—combined with your means of improving the opportunity—make me hope that in your case it will be decisive. I expect you to come home from this trip a man—"

So far, it was all to order, so to speak; Lewis could have recited it beforehand. He bent his head in acquiescence.

"A man," Mr. Raycie repeated, "prepared to play a part, a considerable part, in the social life of the community. I expect you to be a figure in New York; and I shall give you the means to be so." He cleared his throat. "But means are not enough—though you must never forget that they are essential. Education, polish, experience of the world; these are what so many of our men of standing lack. What do they know of Art or Letters? We have had little time here to produce either as yet—you spoke?" Mr. Raycie broke off with a crushing courtesy.

"I—oh, no," his son stammered.

"Ah; I thought you might be about to allude to certain blasphemous penny-a-liners whose poetic ravings are said to have given them a kind of pothouse notoriety."

Lewis reddened at the allusion but was silent, and his father went on:

"Where is our Byron—our Scott—our Shakespeare? And in painting it is the same. Where are our Old Masters? We are not without contemporary talent; but for works of genius we must still look to the past; we must in most cases, content ourselves with copies . . . Ah, here, I know, my dear boy, I touch a responsive chord! Your love of the arts has not passed unperceived; and I mean, I desire, to do all I can to encourage it. Your future position in the world—your duties and obligations as a gentleman and a man of fortune—will not permit you to become, yourself, an eminent painter or a famous sculptor; but I shall raise no objection to your dabbling in these arts as an amateur—at least while you are travelling abroad. It will form your taste, strengthen your judgment, and give you, I hope, the discernment necessary to select for me a few masterpieces which shall *not* be copies. Copies," Mr. Raycie pursued with a deepening emphasis, "are for the less discriminating, or for those less blessed with this world's goods. Yes, my dear Lewis, I wish to create a gallery: a gallery of Heirlooms. Your mother participates in this ambition—she desires to see on our walls a few original specimens of the Italian genius. Raphael, I fear, we can hardly aspire to; but a Domenichino, an Albano, a Carlo Dolci, a Guercino, a Carlo Maratta—one or two of Salvator Rosa's noble landscapes . . . you see my idea? There shall be a Raycie Gallery; and it shall be your mission to get together its nucleus." Mr. Raycie paused, and mopped his flowing forehead. "I believe I could have given my son no task more to his liking."

"Oh, no, sir, none indeed!" Lewis cried, flushing and paling. He had in fact never suspected this part of his father's plan, and his heart swelled with the honour of so unforeseen a mission. Nothing, in truth, could have made him prouder or happier. For a moment he forgot love, forgot Treeshy, forgot everything but the rapture of moving among the masterpieces of which he had so long dreamed, moving not as a mere hungry spectator but as one whose privilege it should at least be to single out and carry away some of the lesser treasures. He could hardly take in what had happened, and the shock of the announcement left him, as usual, inarticulate.

He heard his father booming on, developing the plan, explaining with his usual pompous precision that one of the partners of the London bank in which Lewis's funds were deposited was himself a noted collector, and had agreed to provide the young traveller with letters of introduction to other connoisseurs, both in France and Italy, so that Lewis's acquisitions might be made under the most enlightened guidance.

"It is," Mr. Raycie concluded, "in order to put you on a footing of equality with the best collectors that I have placed such a large sum at your disposal. I reckon that for ten thousand dollars you can travel for two years in the very best style; and I mean to place another five thousand to your credit"—he paused, and let the syllables drop slowly into his son's brain: "five thousand dollars for the purchase of works of art, which eventually—remember—will be yours; and will be handed on, I trust, to your sons' sons as long as the name of Raycie survives"—a length of time, Mr. Raycie's tone seemed to imply, hardly to be measured in periods less extensive than those of the Egyptian dynasties.

Lewis heard him with a whirling brain. *Five thousand dollars!* The sum seemed so enormous, even in dollars, and so incalculably larger when translated into any continental currency, that he wondered why his father, in advance, had given up all hope of a Raphael . . . "If I travel economically," he said to himself, "and deny myself unnecessary luxuries, I may yet be able to surprise him by bringing one back. And my mother—how magnanimous, how splendid! Now I see why she has consented to all the little economies that sometimes seemed so paltry and so humiliating . . ."

The young man's eyes filled with tears, but he was still silent, though he longed as never before to express his gratitude and admiration to his father. He had entered the study expecting a parting sermon on the subject of thrift, coupled with the prospective announcement of a "suitable establishment" (he could even guess the particular Huzzard girl his father had in view); and instead he had been told to spend his princely allowance in a princely manner, and to return home with a gallery of masterpieces. "At least," he murmured to himself, "it shall contain a Correggio."

"Well, sir?" Mr. Raycie boomed.

"Oh, sir—" his son cried, and flung himself on the vast slope of the parental waistcoat.

Amid all these accumulated joys there murmured deep down in him the thought that nothing had been said or done to interfere with his secret plans about Treeshy. It seemed almost as if his father had tacitly accepted the idea of their unmentioned engagement; and Lewis felt half guilty at not confessing to it then and there. But the gods are formidable even when they unbend; never more so, perhaps, than at such moments . . .

PART II

IV

Lewis Raycie stood on a projecting rock and surveyed the sublime spectacle of Mont Blanc.

It was a brilliant August day, and the air, at that height, was already so sharp that he had had to put on his fur-lined pelisse. Behind him, at a respectful distance, was the travelling servant who, at a signal, had brought it up to him; below, in the bend of the mountain road, stood the light and elegant carriage which had carried him thus far on his travels.

Scarcely more than a year had passed since he had waved a farewell to New York from the deck of the packet-ship headed down the bay; yet, to the young man confidently facing Mont Blanc, nothing seemed left in him of that fluid and insubstantial being, the former Lewis Raycie, save a lurking and abeyant fear of Mr. Raycie senior. Even that, however, was so attenuated by distance and time, so far sunk below the horizon, and anchored on the far side of the globe, that it stirred in its sleep only when a handsomely folded and wafered letter in his parent's writing was handed out across the desk of some continental counting-house. Mr. Raycie senior did not write often, and when he did it was in a bland and stilted strain. He felt at a disadvantage on paper, and his natural sarcasm was swamped in the rolling periods which it cost him hours of labour to bring forth; so that the dreaded quality lurked for his son only in the curve of certain letters, and in a positively awful way of writing out, at full length, the word *Esquire*.

It was not that Lewis had broken with all the memories of his past of a year ago. Many still lingered in him, or rather had been transferred to the new man he had become—as for instance his tenderness for Treeshy Kent, which, somewhat to his surprise, had obstinately resisted all the assaults of English keepsake beauties and almond-eyed houris of the East. It startled him, at times, to find Treeshy's short dusky face, with its round forehead, the widely spaced eyes and the high cheek-bones, starting out at him suddenly in the street of some legendary town, or in a landscape of languid beauty, just as he had now and again been arrested in an exotic garden by the very scent of the verbena under the verandah at home. His travels had confirmed rather than weakened the family view of Treeshy's plainness; she could not be made to fit into any of the patterns of female beauty so far submitted to him; yet there she was, ensconced in his new heart and mind as deeply as in the old, though her kisses seemed less vivid, and the peculiar rough notes of her voice hardly reached him. Sometimes, half irritably, he said to himself that with an effort he could disperse her once for all; yet she lived on in him, unseen yet ineffaceable, like the image on a daguerreotype plate, no less there because so often invisible.

To the new Lewis, however, the whole business was less important than he had once thought it. His suddenly acquired maturity made Treeshy seem a petted child rather than the guide, the Beatrice, he had once considered her;

and he promised himself, with an elderly smile, that as soon as he got to Italy he would write her the long letter for which he was now considerably in her debt.

His travels had first carried him to England. There he spent some weeks in collecting letters and recommendations for his tour, in purchasing his travelling-carriage and its numerous appurtenances, and in driving in it from cathedral town to storied castle, omitting nothing, from Abbotsford to Kenilworth, which deserved the attention of a cultivated mind. From England he crossed to Calais, moving slowly southward to the Mediterranean; and there, taking ship for the Piræus, he plunged into pure romance, and the tourist became a Giaour.

It was the East which had made him into a new Lewis Raycie; the East, so squalid and splendid, so pestilent and so poetic, so full of knavery and romance and fleas and nightingales, and so different, alike in its glories and its dirt, from what his studious youth had dreamed. After Smyrna and the bazaars, after Damascus and Palmyra, the Acropolis, Mytilene and Sunium, what could be left in his mind of Canal Street and the lawn above the Sound? Even the mosquitoes, which seemed at first the only connecting link, were different, because he fought with them in scenes so different; and a young gentleman who had journeyed across the desert in Arabian dress, slept under goats'-hair tents, been attacked by robbers in the Peloponnesus and despoiled by his own escort at Baalbek, and by customs' officials everywhere, could not but look with a smile on the terrors that walk New York and the Hudson river. Encased in security and monotony, that other Lewis Raycie, when his little figure bobbed up to the surface, seemed like a new-born babe preserved in alcohol. Even Mr. Raycie senior's thunders were now no more than the far-off murmur of summer lightning on a perfect evening. Had Mr. Raycie ever really frightened Lewis? Why, now he was not even frightened by Mont Blanc!

He was still gazing with a sense of easy equality at its awful pinnacles when another travelling-carriage paused near his own, and a young man, eagerly jumping from it, and also followed by a servant with a cloak, began to mount the slope. Lewis at once recognized the carriage, and the light springing figure of the young man, his blue coat and swelling stock, and the scar slightly distorting his handsome and eloquent mouth. It was the Englishman who had arrived at the Montanvert inn the night before with a valet, a guide, and such a cargo of books, maps and sketching-materials as threatened to overshadow ever Lewis's outfit.

Lewis, at first, had not been greatly drawn to the new-comer, who, seated aloof in the dining-room, seemed not to see his fellow-traveller. The truth was that Lewis was dying for a little conversation. His astonishing experiences were so tightly packed in him (with no outlet save the meagre trickle of his nightly diary) that he felt they would soon melt into the vague blur of other people's travels unless he could give them fresh reality by talking them over. And the stranger with the deep-blue eyes that matched his coat, the scarred cheek and eloquent lip, seemed to Lewis a worthy listener. The Englishman appeared to think other-wise. He preserved an air of moody abstraction, which Lewis's vanity imagined him to have put on as the gods becloud themselves for their secret errands; and the curtness of his goodnight was (Lewis flattered himself) surpassed only by the young New Yorker's.

But today all was different. The stranger advanced affably, raised his hat from his tossed statue-like hair, and enquired with a smile: "Are you by any chance interested in the forms of cirrus clouds?"

His voice was as sweet as his smile, and the two were reinforced by a glance so winning that it made the odd ques-tion seem not only pertinent but natural. Lewis, though sur-prised, was not disconcerted. He merely coloured with the unwonted sense of his ignorance, and replied ingenuously: "I believe, sir, I am interested in everything."

"A noble answer!" cried the other, and held out his hand.

"But I must add," Lewis continued with courageous hon-esty, "that I have never as yet had occasion to occupy my-self particularly with the forms of cirrus clouds."

His companion looked at him merrily. "That," said he, "is no reason why you shouldn't begin to do so now!" To which Lewis as merrily agreed. "For in order to be inter-ested in things," the other continued more gravely, "it is only necessary to see them; and I believe I am not wrong in saying that you are one of the privileged beings to whom the seeing eye has been given."

Lewis blushed his agreement, and his interlocutor contin-ued: "You are one of those who have been on the road to Damascus."

"On the road? I've been to the place itself!" the wanderer exclaimed, bursting with the particulars of his travels; and then blushed more deeply at the perception that the other's use of the name had of course been figurative.

The young Englishman's face lit up. "You've been to Damascus—literally been there yourself? But that may be almost as interesting, in its quite different way, as the formation of clouds or lichens. For the present," he continued with a gesture toward the mountain, "I must devote myself to the extremely inadequate rendering of some of these delicate *aiguilles*; a bit of drudgery not likely to interest you in the face of so sublime a scene. But perhaps this evening— if, as I think, we are staying in the same inn—you will give me a few minutes of your society, and tell me something of your travels. My father," he added with his engaging smile, "has had packed with my paint-brushes a few bottles of a wholly trustworthy Madeira; and if you will favour me with your company at dinner . . ."

He signed to his servant to undo the sketching materials, spread his cloak on the rock, and was already lost in his task as Lewis descended to the carriage.

The Madeira proved as trustworthy as his host had promised. Perhaps it was its exceptional quality which threw such a golden lustre over the dinner; unless it were rather the conversation of the blue-eyed Englishman which made Lewis Raycie, always a small drinker, feel that in his company every drop was nectar.

When Lewis joined his host it had been with the secret hope of at last being able to talk; but when the evening was over (and they kept it up to the small hours) he perceived that he had chiefly listened. Yet there had been no sense of suppression, of thwarted volubility; he had been given all the openings he wanted. Only, whenever he produced a little fact it was instantly overflowed by the other's imagination till it burned like a dull pebble tossed into a rushing stream. For whatever Lewis said was seen by his companion from a new angle, and suggested a new train of thought; each commonplace item of experience became a many-faceted crystal flashing with unexpected fires. The young Englishman's mind moved in a world of associations and references far more richly peopled than Lewis's; but his eager communicativeness, his directness of speech and manner, instantly opened its gates to the simpler youth. It was certainly not the Madeira which sped the hours and flooded them with magic; but the magic gave the Madeira—excellent, and reputed of its kind, as Lewis afterward learned—a taste no other vintage was to have for him.

"Oh, but we must meet again in Italy—there are many things there that I could perhaps help you to see," the young Englishman declared as they swore eternal friendship on the stairs of the sleeping inn.

V

It was in a tiny Venetian church, no more than a chapel, that Lewis Raycie's eyes had been unsealed—in a dull-looking little church not even mentioned in the guide-books. But for his chance encounter with the young Englishman in the shadow of Mont Blanc, Lewis would never have heard of the place; but then what else that was worth knowing would he ever have heard of, he wondered?

He had stood a long time looking at the frescoes, put off at first—he could admit it now—by a certain stiffness in the attitudes of the people, by the childish elaboration of their dress (so different from the noble draperies which Sir Joshua's Discourses on Art had taught him to admire in the great painters), and by the innocent inexpressive look in their young faces—for even the gray-beards seemed young. And then suddenly his gaze had lit on one of these faces in particular: that of a girl with round cheeks, high cheek-bones and widely set eyes under an intricate head-dress of pearl-woven braids. Why, it was Treeshy—Treeshy Kent to the life! And so far from being thought "plain," the young lady was no other than the peerless princess about whom the tale revolved. And what a fairy-land she lived in—full of lithe youths and round-faced pouting maidens, rosy old men and burnished blackamoors, pretty birds and cats and nibbling rabbits—and all involved and enclosed in golden balustrades, in colonnades of pink and blue, laurel-garlands festooned from ivory balconies, and domes and minarets against summer seas! Lewis's imagination lost itself in the scene; he forgot to regret the noble draperies, the exalted sentiments, the fuliginous backgrounds, of the artists he had come to Italy to admire—forgot Sassoferrato, Guido Reni, Carlo Dolce, Lo Spagnoletto, the Carracci, and even the Transfiguration of Raphael, though he knew it to be the greatest picture in the world.

After that he had seen almost everything else that Italian art had to offer; had been to Florence, Naples, Rome; to Bologna to study the Eclectic School, to Parma to examine

the Correggios and the Giulio Romanos. But that first vision
had laid a magic seed between his lips; the seed that makes
you hear what the birds say and the grasses whisper. Even
if his English friend had not continued at his side, pointing
out, explaining, inspiring, Lewis Raycie flattered himself that
the round face of the little Saint Ursula would have led him
safely and confidently past all her rivals. She had become
his touchstone, his star: how insipid seemed to him all the
sheep-faced Virgins draped in red and blue paint after he
had looked into her wondering girlish eyes and traced the
elaborate pattern of her brocades! He could remember now,
quite distinctly, the day when he had given up even Beatrice
Cenci . . . and as for that fat naked Magdalen of Carlo
Dolce's, lolling over the book she was not reading, and ogling
the spectator in the good old way . . . faugh! Saint Ursula
did not need to rescue him from *her* . . .

His eyes had been opened to a new world of art. And this
world it was his mission to reveal to others—he, the insignificant and ignorant Lewis Raycie, as "but for the grace of
God," and that chance encounter on Mont Blanc, he might
have gone on being to the end! He shuddered to think of
the army of Neapolitan beggar-boys, bituminous monks,
whirling prophets, languishing Madonnas and pink-rumped
amorini who might have been travelling home with him in
the hold of the fast new steampacket.

His excitement had something of the apostle's ecstasy. He
was not only, in a few hours, to embrace Treeshy, and be
reunited to his honoured parents; he was also to go forth
and preach the new gospel to them that sat in the darkness
of Salvator Rosa and Lo Spagnoletto. . .

The first thing that struck Lewis was the smallness of the
house on the Sound, and the largeness of Mr. Raycie.

He had expected to receive the opposite impression. In
his recollection the varnished Tuscan villa had retained something of its impressiveness, even when compared to its supposed originals. Perhaps the very contrast between their
draughty distances and naked floors, and the expensive
carpets and bright fires of High Point, magnified his memory
of the latter—there were moments when the thought of its
groaning board certainly added to the effect. But the image
of Mr. Raycie had meanwhile dwindled. Everything about
him, as his son looked back, seemed narrow, juvenile, almost
childish. His bluster about Edgar Poe, for instance—true poet
still to Lewis, though he had since heard richer notes; his
fussy tyranny of his womenkind; his unconscious but total

ignorance of most of the things, books, people, ideas, that
now filled his son's mind; above all, the arrogance and in-
competence of his artistic judgments. Beyond a narrow range
of reading—mostly, Lewis suspected, culled in drowsy after-
dinner snatches from Knight's "Half-hours with the Best
Authors"—Mr. Raycie made no pretence to book-learning;
left *that*, as he handsomely said, "to the professors." But
on matters of art he was dogmatic and explicit, prepared to
justify his opinions by the citing of eminent authorities and
of market-prices, and quite clear, as his farewell talk with his
son had shown, as to which Old Masters should be privileged
to figure in the Raycie collection.

The young man felt no impatience of these judgments.
America was a long way from Europe, and it was many
years since Mr. Raycie had travelled. He could hardly be
blamed for not knowing that the things he admired were no
longer admirable, still less for not knowing why. The pictures before which Lewis had knelt in spirit had been virtually undiscovered, even by art-students and critics, in his father's youth. How was an American gentleman, filled with his
own self-importance, and paying his courier the highest
salary to show him the accredited "Masterpieces"—how was
he to guess that whenever he stood rapt before a Sassoferrato or a Carlo Dolce one of those unknown treasures lurked
near by under dust and cobwebs?

No; Lewis felt only tolerance and understanding. Such a
view was not one to magnify the paternal image; but when
the young man entered the study where Mr. Raycie sat im-
mobilized by gout, the swathed leg stretched along his sofa
seemed only another reason for indulgence . . .

Perhaps, Lewis thought afterward, it was his father's prone
position, the way his great bulk billowed over the sofa, and
the lame leg reached out like a mountain-ridge, that made
him suddenly seem to fill the room; or else the sound of his
voice booming irritably across the threshold, and scattering
Mrs. Raycie and the girls with a fierce: "And now, ladies, if
the hugging and kissing are over, I should be glad of a moment with my son." But it was odd that, after mother and
daughters had withdrawn with all their hoops and flounces,
the study seemed to grow even smaller, and Lewis himself
to feel more like a David without the pebble.

"Well, my boy," his father cried, crimson and puffing,
"here you are at home again, with many adventures to relate,
no doubt; and a few masterpieces to show me, as I gathered
from the drafts on my exchequer."

"Oh, as to the masterpieces, sir, certainly," Lewis simpered, wondering why his voice sounded so fluty, and his smile was produced with such a conscious muscular effort.

"Good—good," Mr. Raycie approved, waving a violet hand which seemed to be ripening for a bandage. "Reedy carried out my orders, I presume? Saw to it that the paintings were deposited with the bulk of your luggage in Canal Street?"

"Oh, yes, sir: Mr. Reedy was on the dock with precise instructions. You know he always carries out your orders," Lewis ventured with a faint irony.

Mr. Raycie stared. "Mr. Reedy," he said, "does what I tell him, if that's what you mean; otherwise he would hardly have been in my employ for over thirty years."

Lewis was silent, and his father examined him critically. "You appear to have filled out; your health is satisfactory? Well . . . well . . . Mr. Robert Huzzard and his daughters are dining here this evening, by the way, and will no doubt be expecting to see the latest French novelties in stocks and waistcoats. Malvina has become a very elegant figure, your sisters tell me." Mr. Raycie chuckled, and Lewis thought: "I *knew* it was the oldest Huzzard girl!" while a slight chill ran down his spine.

"As to the pictures," Mr. Raycie pursued with growing animation, "I am laid low, as you see, by this cursèd affliction, and till the doctors get me up again, here must I lie and try to imagine how your treasures will look in the new gallery. And meanwhile, my dear boy, I need hardly say that no one is to be admitted to see them till they have been inspected by me and suitably hung. Reedy shall begin unpacking at once; and when we move to town next month Mrs. Raycie, God willing, shall give the handsomest evening party New York has yet seen, to show my son's collection, and perhaps . . . eh, well? . . . to celebrate another interesting event in his history."

Lewis met this with a faint but respectful gurgle, and before his blurred eyes rose the wistful face of Treeshy Kent.

"Ah, well, I shall see her tomorrow," he thought, taking heart again as soon as he was out of his father's presence.

VI

Mr. Raycie stood silent for a long time after making the round of the room in the Canal Street house where the unpacked pictures had been set out.

He had driven to town alone with Lewis, sternly rebuffing
his daughters' timid hints, and Mrs. Raycie's mute but
visible yearning to accompany him. Though the gout was
over he was still weak and irritable, and Mrs. Raycie, flut-
tered at the thought of "crossing him," had swept the girls
away at his first frown.

Lewis's hopes rose as he followed his parent's limping
progress. The pictures, though standing on chairs and tables
and set clumsily askew to catch the light, bloomed out of
the half-dusk of the empty house with a new and persuasive
beauty. Ah, how right he had been—how inevitable that his
father should own it!

Mr. Raycie halted in the middle of the room. He was still
silent, and his face, so quick to frown and glare, wore the
calm, almost expressionless look known to Lewis as the mask
of inward perplexity. "Oh, of course it will take a little
time," the son thought, tingling with the eagerness of youth.

At last, Mr. Raycie woke the echoes by clearing his throat;
but the voice which issued from it was as inexpressive as his
face. "It is singular," he said, "how little the best copies of the
Old Masters resemble the originals. For these *are* Originals?"
he questioned, suddenly swinging about on Lewis.

"Oh, absolutely, sir! Besides—" The young man was about
to add: "No one would ever have taken the trouble to copy
them"—but hastily checked himself.

"Besides——?"

"I meant, I had the most competent advice obtainable."

"So I assume; since it was the express condition on which
I authorized your purchases."

Lewis felt himself shrinking and his father expanding; but
he sent a glance along the wall, and beauty shed her reviving
beam on him.

Mr. Raycie's brows projected ominously; but his face remained smooth and dubious. Once more he cast a slow glance
about him.

"Let us," he said pleasantly, "begin with the Raphael." And
it was evident that he did not know which way to turn.

"Oh, sir, a Raphael nowadays—I warned you it would be
far beyond my budget."

Mr. Raycie's face fell slightly. "I had hoped nevertheless
. . . for an inferior specimen. . . ." Then, with an effort: "The
Sassoferrato, then."

Lewis felt more at his ease; he even ventured a respectful
smile. "Sassoferrato is *all* inferior, isn't he? The fact is, he no
longer stands . . . quite as he used to. . . ."

Mr. Raycie stood motionless: his eyes were vacuously fixed on the nearest picture.

"Sassoferrato . . . no longer . . . ?"

"Well, sir, *no;* not for a collection of this quality."

Lewis saw that he had at last struck the right note. Something large and uncomfortable appeared to struggle in Mr. Raycie's throat; then he gave a cough which might almost have been said to cast out Sassoferrato.

There was another pause before he pointed with his stick to a small picture representing a snub-nosed young woman with a high forehead and jewelled coif, against a background of delicately interwoven columbines. "Is *that*," he questioned, "your Carlo Dolce? The style is much the same, I see; but it seems to me lacking in his peculiar sentiment."

"Oh, but it's not a Carlo Dolce: it's a Piero della Francesca, sir!" burst in triumph from the trembling Lewis.

His father sternly faced him. "It's a *copy*, you mean? I thought so!"

"No, no; not a copy; it's by a great painter . . . a much greater . . ."

Mr. Raycie had reddened sharply at his mistake. To conceal his natural annoyance he assumed a still more silken manner. "In that case," he said, "I think I should like to see the inferior painters first. Where *is* the Carlo Dolce?"

"There *is* no Carlo Dolce," said Lewis, white to the lips.

The young man's next distinct recollection was of standing, he knew not how long afterward, before the armchair in which his father had sunk down, almost as white and shaken as himself.

"This," stammered Mr. Raycie, "this is going to bring back my gout. . . ." But when Lewis entreated: "Oh, sir, do let us drive back quietly to the country, and give me a chance later to explain . . . to put my case" . . . the old gentleman had struck through the pleading with a furious wave of his stick.

"Explain later? Put your case later? It's just what I insist upon your doing here and now!" And Mr. Raycie added hoarsely, and as if in actual physical anguish: "I understand that young John Huzzard returned from Rome last week with a Raphael."

After that, Lewis heard himself—as if with the icy detachment of a spectator—marshalling his arguments, pleading the cause he hoped his pictures would have pleaded for him, dethroning the old Powers and Principalities, and setting up these new names in their place. It was first of all the

names that stuck in Mr. Raycie's throat: after spending a
life-time in committing to memory the correct pronunciation
of words like Lo Spagnoletto and Giulio Romano, it was bad
enough, his wrathful eyes seemed to say, to have to begin a
new set of verbal gymnastics before you could be sure of
saying to a friend with careless accuracy: "And *this* is my
Giotto da Bondone."

But that was only the first shock, soon forgotten in the rush
of greater tribulation. For one might conceivably learn
how to pronounce Giotto da Bondone, and even enjoy doing
so, provided the friend in question recognized the name
and bowed to its authority. But to have your effort received
by a blank stare, and the playful request: "You'll have to say
that over again, please"—to know that, in going the round of
the gallery (the Raycie Gallery!) the same stare and the
same request were likely to be repeated before each picture;
the bitterness of this was so great that Mr. Raycie, without ex-
aggeration, might have likened his case to that of Agag.

"God! God! God! Carpatcher, you say this other fellow's
called? Kept him back till the last because it's the gem of the
collection, did you? Carpatcher—well, he'd have done better
to stick to his trade. Something to do with those new
European steam-cars, I suppose, eh?" Mr. Raycie was so incensed that his irony was less subtle than usual. "And Angelico you say did that kind of Noah's Ark soldier in pink
armour on gold-leaf? Well, *there* I've caught you tripping, my
boy. Not Angelico, Angelica; Angelica Kauffman was a lady.
And the damned swindler who foisted that barbarous daub
on you as a picture of hers deserves to be drawn and quart-
ered—and shall be, sir, by God, if the law can reach him!
He shall disgorge every penny he's rooked you out of, or my
name's not Halston Raycie! A bargain . . . you say the thing
was a *bargain*? Why, the price of a clean postage stamp would
be too dear for it! God—my son; do you realize you had a
trust to carry out?"

"Yes, sir, yes; and it's just because—"

"You might have written; you might at least have placed
your views before me . . ."

How could Lewis say: "If I had, I knew you'd have
refused to let me buy the pictures?" He could only stammer:
"I *did* allude to the revolution in taste . . . new names coming up . . . you may remember . . ."

"Revolution! New names! Who says so? I had a letter last
week from the London dealers to whom I especially rec-

ommended you, telling me that an undoubted Guido Reni was coming into the market this summer."

"Oh, the dealers—*they* don't know!"

"The dealers . . . don't? . . . Who does . . . except yourself?" Mr. Raycie pronounced in a white sneer.

Lewis, as white, still held his ground. "I wrote you, sir, about my friends; in Italy, and afterward in England."

"Well, God damn it, I never heard of one of *their* names before, either; no more'n of these painters of yours here. I supplied you with the names of all the advisers you needed, and all the painters, too; I all but made the collection for you myself, before you started. . . . I was explicit enough, in all conscience, wasn't I?"

Lewis smiled faintly. "That's what I hoped the pictures would be . . ."

"What? Be what? What'd you mean?"

"Be explicit . . . Speak for themselves . . . make you see that their painters are already superseding some of the better-known . . ."

Mr. Raycie gave an awful laugh. "They are, are they? In whose estimation? Your friends', I suppose. What's the name, again, of that fellow you met in Italy, who picked 'em out for you?"

"Ruskin—John Ruskin," said Lewis.

Mr. Raycie's laugh, prolonged, gathered up into itself a fresh shower of expletives. "Ruskin—Ruskin—just plain John Ruskin, eh? And who *is* this great John Ruskin, who sets God A'mighty right in his judgments? Who'd you say John Ruskin's father was, now?"

"A respected wine-merchant in London, sir."

Mr. Raycie ceased to laugh: he looked at his son with an expression of unutterable disgust.

"Retail?"

"I . . . believe so . . ."

"Faugh!" said Mr. Raycie.

"It wasn't only Ruskin, father. . . . I told you of those other friends in London, whom I met on the way home. They inspected the pictures, and all of them agreed that . . . that the collection would some day be very valuable."

"*Some day*—did they give you a date . . . the month and the year? Ah, those other friends; yes. You said there was a Mr. Brown and a Mr. Hunt and a Mr. Rossiter, was it? Well, I never heard of any of those names, either—except perhaps in a trades' directory."

"It's not Rossiter, father: Dante Rossetti."

"Excuse me: Rossetti. And what does Mr. Dante Rossetti's father do? Sell macaroni, I presume?"

Lewis was silent, and Mr. Raycie went on, speaking now with a deadly steadiness: "The friends I sent you to were judges of art, sir; men who know what a picture's worth; not one of 'em but could pick out a genuine Raphael. Couldn't you find 'em when you got to England? Or hadn't they the time to spare for you? You'd better not," Mr. Raycie added, "tell me *that,* for I know how they'd have received your father's son."

"Oh, most kindly . . . they did indeed, sir . . ."

"Ay; but that didn't suit you. You didn't *want* to be advised. You wanted to show off before a lot of ignoramuses like yourself. You wanted—how'd I know what you wanted? It's as if I'd never given you an instruction or laid a charge on you! And the money—God! Where'd it go to? Buying *this*? Nonsense—." Mr. Raycie raised himself heavily on his stick and fixed his angry eyes on his son. "Own up, Lewis; tell me they got it out of you at cards. Professional gamblers the lot, I make no doubt; your Ruskin and your Brown and your Rossiter. Make a business to pick up young American greenhorns on their travels, I daresay . . . No? Not that, you say? Then—women? . . . God A'mighty, Lewis," gasped Mr. Raycie, tottering toward his son with outstretched stick, "I'm no bluenosed Puritan, sir, and I'd a damn sight rather you told me you'd spent it on a woman, every penny of it, than let yourself be fleeced like a simpleton, buying these things that look more like cuts out o' Foxe's Book of Martyrs than Originals of the Old Masters for a Gentleman's Gallery . . . Youth's youth . . . Gad, sir, I've been young myself . . . a fellow's got to go through his apprenticeship . . . Own up now: women?"

"Oh, not women——"

"Not even!" Mr. Raycie groaned. "All in pictures, then? Well, say no more to me now . . . I'll get home, I'll get home . . ." He cast a last apoplectic glance about the room. "The Raycie Gallery! That pack of bones and mummers' finery! . . . Why, let alone the rest, there's not a full-bodied female among 'em . . . Do you know what those Madonnas of yours are like, my son? Why, there ain't one of 'em that don't remind me of a bad likeness of poor Treeshy Kent . . . I should say you'd hired half the sign-painters of Europe to do her portrait for you—if I could imagine your wanting it . . . No, sir! I don't need your arm," Mr. Raycie snarled, heaving his great bulk painfully across the hall. He withered

Lewis with a last look from the doorstep. "And to buy *that* you overdrew your account?—No, I'll drive home alone."

VII

Mr. Raycie did not die till nearly a year later; but New York agreed it was the affair of the pictures that had killed him.

The day after his first and only sight of them he sent for his lawyer, and it became known that he had made a new will. Then he took to his bed with a return of the gout, and grew so rapidly worse that it was thought "only proper" to postpone the party Mrs. Raycie was to have given that autumn to inaugurate the gallery. This enabled the family to pass over in silence the question of the works of art themselves; but outside of the Raycie house, where they were never mentioned, they formed, that winter, a frequent and fruitful topic of discussion.

Only two persons besides Mr. Raycie were known to have seen them. One was Mr. Donaldson Kent, who owed the privilege to the fact of having once been to Italy; the other, Mr. Reedy, the agent, who had unpacked the pictures. Mr. Reedy, beset by Raycie cousins and old family friends, had replied with genuine humility: "Why, the truth is, I never was taught to see any difference between one picture and another, except as regards the size of them; and these struck me as smallish . . . on the small side, I would say . . ."

Mr. Kent was known to have unbosomed himself to Mr. Raycie with considerable frankness—he went so far, it was rumored, as to declare that he had never seen any pictures in Italy like those brought back by Lewis, and begged to doubt if they really came from there. But in public he maintained that noncommittal attitude which passed for prudence, but proceeded only from timidity; no one ever got anything from him but the guarded statement: "The subjects are wholly inoffensive."

It was believed that Mr. Raycie dared not consult the Huzzards. Young John Huzzard had just brought home a Raphael; it would have been hard not to avoid comparisons which would have been too galling. Neither to them, nor to any one else, did Mr. Raycie ever again allude to the Raycie Gallery. But when his will was opened it was found that he had bequeathed the pictures to his son. The rest of his property was left absolutely to his two daughters. The bulk of the estate was Mrs. Raycie's; but it was known that Mrs. Raycie had had her instructions, and among them, perhaps,

was the order to fade away in her turn after six months of
widowhood. When she had been laid beside her husband in
Trinity churchyard her will (made in the same week as Mr.
Raycie's, and obviously at his dictation) was found to allow
five thousand dollars a year to Lewis during his life-time; the
residue of the fortune, which Mr. Raycie's thrift and good
management had made into one of the largest in New York,
was divided between the daughters. Of these, the one
promptly married a Kent and the other a Huzzard; and the
latter, Sarah Anne (who had never been Lewis's favourite),
was wont to say in later years: "Oh, no, I never grudged
my poor brother those funny old pictures. You see, we have
a Raphael."

The house stood on the corner of Third Avenue and Tenth
Street. It had lately come to Lewis Raycie as his share in
the property of a distant cousin, who had made an "old New
York will" under which all his kin benefited in proportion to
their consanguinity. The neighbourhood was unfashionable,
and the house in bad repair; but Mr. and Mrs. Lewis Raycie,
who, since their marriage, had been living in retirement at
Tarrytown, immediately moved into it.

Their arrival excited small attention. Within a year of his
father's death, Lewis had married Treeshy Kent. The al-
liance had not been encouraged by Mr. and Mrs. Kent, who
went so far as to say that their niece might have done better;
but as that one of their sons who was still unmarried had
always shown a lively sympathy for Treeshy, they yielded to
the prudent thought, that, after all, it was better than
having her entangle Bill.

The Lewis Raycies had been four years married, and during that time had dropped out of the memory of New York
as completely as if their exile had covered half a century.
Neither of them had ever cut a great figure there. Treeshy
had been nothing but the Kents' Cinderella, and Lewis's
ephemeral importance, as heir to the Raycie millions,
had been effaced by the painful episode which resulted in
his being deprived of them.

So secluded was their way of living, and so much had it
come to be a habit, that when Lewis announced that he
had inherited Uncle Ebenezers' house his wife hardly looked
up from the baby-blanket she was embroidering.

"Uncle Ebenezer's house in New York?"

He drew a deep breath. "Now I shall be able to show the
pictures."

"Oh, Lewis—" She dropped the blanket. "Are we going to live there?"

"Certainly. But the house is so large that I shall turn the two corner rooms on the ground floor into a gallery. They are very suitably lighted. It was there that Cousin Ebenezer was laid out."

"Oh, Lewis——"

If anything could have made Lewis Raycie believe in his own strength of will it was his wife's attitude. Merely to hear that unquestioning murmur of submission was to feel something of his father's tyrannous strength arise in him; but with the wish to use it more humanely.

"You'll like that, Treeshy? It's been dull for you here, I know."

She flushed up. "Dull? With *you*, darling? Besides, I like the country. But I shall like Tenth Street too. Only—you said there were repairs?"

He nodded sternly. "I shall borrow money to make them. If necessary—" he lowered his voice—"I shall mortgage the pictures."

He saw her eyes fill. "Oh, but it won't be! There are so many ways still in which I can economize."

He laid his hand on hers and turned his profile toward her, because he knew it was so much stronger than his full face. He did not feel sure that she quite grasped his intention about the pictures; was not even certain that he wished her to. He went in to New York every week now, occupying himself mysteriously and importantly with plans, specifications and other business transactions with long names; while Treeshy, through the hot summer months, sat in Tarrytown and waited for the baby.

A little girl was born at the end of the summer and christened Louisa; and when she was a few weeks old the Lewis Raycies left the country for New York.

"Now!" thought Lewis, as they bumped over the cobblestones of Tenth Street in the direction of Cousin Ebenezer's house.

The carriage stopped, he handed out his wife, the nurse followed with the baby, and they all stood and looked up at the house-front.

"Oh, Lewis—" Treeshy gasped; and even little Louisa set up a sympathetic wail.

Over the door—over Cousin Ebenezer's respectable, conservative and intensely private front-door—hung a large signboard bearing, in gold letters on a black ground, the inscription:

GALLERY OF CHRISTIAN ART
OPEN ON WEEK-DAYS FROM 2 TO 4
ADMISSION 25 CENTS.   CHILDREN 10 CENTS

Lewis saw his wife turn pale, and pressed her arm in his. "Believe me, it's the only way to make the pictures known. And they *must* be made known," he said with a thrill of his old ardour.

"Yes, dear, of course. But . . . to every one? Publicly?"

"If we showed them only to our friends, of what use would it be? Their opinion is already formed."

She sighed her acknowledgment. "But the . . . the entrance fee . . ."

"If we can afford it later, the gallery will be free. But meanwhile——"

"Oh, Lewis, I quite understand!" And clinging to him, the still-protesting baby in her wake, she passed with a dauntless step under the awful signboard.

"At last I shall see the pictures properly lighted!" she exclaimed, and turned in the hall to fling her arms about her husband.

"It's all they need . . . to be appreciated," he answered, aglow with her encouragement.

Since his withdrawal from the world it had been a part of Lewis's system never to read the daily papers. His wife eagerly conformed to his example, and they lived in a little air-tight circle of aloofness, as if the cottage at Tarrytown had been situated in another and happier planet.

Lewis, nevertheless, the day after the opening of the Gallery of Christian Art, deemed it his duty to derogate from this attitude, and sallied forth secretly to buy the principal journals. When he reentered his house he went straight up to the nursery where he knew that, at that hour, Treeshy would be giving the little girl her bath. But it was later than he supposed. The rite was over, the baby lay asleep in its modest cot, and the mother sat crouched by the fire, her face hidden in her hands. Lewis instantly guessed that she too had seen the papers.

"Treeshy—you mustn't . . . consider this of any consequence. . . ," he stammered.

She lifted a tear-stained face. "Oh, my darling! I thought you never read the papers."

"Not usually. But I thought it my duty——"

"Yes; I see. But, as you say, what earthly conse-quence——?"

"None whatever; we must just be patient and persist."

She hesitated, and then, her arms about him, her head on his breast: "Only, dearest, I've been counting up again, ever so carefully; and even if we give up fires everywhere but in the nursery, I'm afraid the wages of the door-keeper and the guardian . . . especially if the gallery's open to the public every day . . ."

"I've thought of that already, too; and I myself shall here-after act as door-keeper and guardian."

He kept his eyes on hers as he spoke. "This is the test," he thought. Her face paled under its brown glow, and the eyes dilated in her effort to check her tears. Then she said gaily: "That will be . . . very interesting, won't it, Lewis? Hearing what the people say . . . Because, as they begin to know the pictures better, and to understand them, they can't fail to say very interesting things . . . can they?" She turned and caught up the sleeping Louisa. "Can they . . . oh, you darling—darling?"

Lewis turned away too. Not another woman in New York would have been capable of that. He could hear all the town echoing with this new scandal of his showing the pic-tures himself—and she, so much more sensitive to ridicule, so much less carried away by apostolic ardour, how much louder must that mocking echo ring in her ears! But his pang was only momentary. The one thought that possessed him for any length of time was that of vindicating himself by making the pictures known; he could no longer fix his atten-tion on lesser matters. The derision of illiterate journalists was not a thing to wince at; once let the pictures be seen by educated and intelligent people, and they would speak for themselves—especially if he were at hand to interpret them.

VIII

For a week or two a great many people came to the gallery; but, even with Lewis as interpreter, the pictures failed to make themselves heard. During the first days, indeed, owing to the unprecedented idea of holding a paying exhibition in a private house, and to the mockery of the newspapers, the Gallery of Christian Art was thronged with noisy curiosity-seekers; once the astonished metropolitan police had to be invited in to calm their comments and control their movements. But the name of "Christian Art" soon chilled this class of sightseer, and before long they were replaced by a dumb and respectable throng, who roamed vacantly through the rooms and out again, grumbling that it wasn't worth the money. Then these too diminished; and once the tide had turned, the ebb was rapid. Every day from two to four Lewis still sat shivering among his treasures, or patiently measured the length of the deserted gallery: as long as there was a chance of any one coming he would not admit that he was beaten. For the next visitor might always be the one who understood.

One snowy February day he had thus paced the rooms in unbroken solitude for above an hour when carriage-wheels stopped at the door. He hastened to open it, and in a great noise of silks his sister Sarah Anne Huzzard entered.

Lewis felt for a moment as he used to under his father's glance. Marriage and millions had given the moon-faced Sarah something of the Raycie awfulness; but her brother looked into her empty eyes, and his own kept their level.

"Well, Lewis," said Mrs. Huzzard with a simpering sternness, and caught her breath.

"Well, Sarah Anne—I'm happy that you've come to take a look at my pictures."

"I've come to see you and your wife." She gave another nervous gasp, shook out her flounces, and added in a rush: "And to ask you how much longer this . . . this spectacle is to continue. . . ."

"The exhibition?" Lewis smiled. She signed a flushed assent.

"Well, there has been a considerable falling-off lately in the number of visitors——"

"Thank heaven!" she interjected.

"But as long as I feel that any one wishes to come . . . I shall be here . . . to open the door, as you see."

She sent a shuddering glance about her. "Lewis—I wonder if you realize . . . ?"

"Oh, fully."

"Then *why* do you go on? Isn't it enough—aren't you satisfied?"

"With the effect they have produced?"

"With the effect *you* have produced—on your family and on the whole of New York. With the slur on poor Papa's memory."

"Papa left me the pictures, Sarah Anne."

"Yes. But not to make yourself a mountebank about them."

Lewis considered this impartially. "Are you sure? Perhaps, on the contrary, he did it for that very reason."

"Oh, don't heap more insults on our father's memory! Things are bad enough without that. How your wife can allow it I can't see. Do you ever consider the humiliation to *her*?"

Lewis gave another dry smile. "She's used to being humiliated. The Kents accustomed her to that."

Sarah Anne reddened. "I don't know why I should stay to be spoken to in this way. But I came with my husband's approval."

"Do you need that to come and see your brother?"

"I need it to—to make the offer I am about to make; and which he authorizes."

Lewis looked at her in surprise, and she purpled up to the lace ruffles inside her satin bonnet.

"Have you come to make an offer for my collection?" he asked her, humorously.

"You seem to take pleasure in insinuating preposterous things. But anything is better than this public slight on our name." Again she ran a shuddering glance over the pictures. "John and I," she announced, "are prepared to double the allowance mother left you on condition that this . . . this ends . . . for good. That that horrible sign is taken down tonight."

Lewis seemed mildly to weigh the proposal. "Thank you very much, Sarah Anne," he said at length. "I'm touched . . . touched and . . . and surprised . . . that you and John should have made this offer. But perhaps, before I decline it, you will accept *mine*: simply to show you my pictures. When once you've looked at them I think you'll understand——"

Mrs. Huzzard drew back hastily, her air of majesty collapsing. "Look at the pictures? Oh, thank you . . . but I can see them very well from here. And besides, I don't pretend to be a judge . . ."

"Then come up and see Treeshy and the baby," said Lewis quietly.

She stared at him, embarrassed. "Oh, thank you," she stammered again; and as she prepared to follow him: "Then it's *no*, really no, Lewis? Do consider, my dear! You say yourself that hardly any one comes. What harm can there be in closing the place?"

"What—when tomorrow the man may come who understands?"

Mrs. Huzzard tossed her plumes despairingly and followed him in silence.

"What—Mary Adeline?" she exclaimed, pausing abruptly
on the threshold of the nursery. Treeshy, as usual, sat holding her baby by the fire; and from a low seat opposite her
rose a lady as richly furred and feathered as Mrs. Huzzard,
but with far less assurance to carry off her furbelows. Mrs.
Kent ran to Lewis and laid her plump cheek against his,
while Treeshy greeted Sarah Anne.

"I had no idea you were here, Mary Adeline," Mrs. Huzzard murmured. It was clear that she had not imparted her
philanthropic project to her sister, and was disturbed at the
idea that Lewis might be about to do so. "I just dropped in
for a minute," she continued, "to see that darling little pet
of an angel child—" and she enveloped the astonished baby
in her ample rustlings and flutterings.

"I'm very glad to see you here, Sarah Anne," Mary Adeline answered with simplicity.

"Ah, it's not for want of wishing that I haven't come before! Treeshy knows that, I hope. But the cares of a household like mine . . ."

"Yes; and it's been so difficult to get about in the bad
weather," Treeshy suggested sympathetically.

Mrs. Huzzard lifted the Raycie eyebrows. "Has it really?
With two pairs of horses one hardly notices the weather. . .
Oh, the pretty, pretty, *pretty* baby! . . . Mary Adeline,"
Sarah Anne continued, turning severely to her sister, "I shall
be happy to offer you a seat in my carriage if you're thinking
of leaving."

But Mary Adeline was a married woman too. She raised
her mild head and her glance crossed her sister's quietly. "My
own carriage is at the door, thank you kindly, Sarah Anne,"
she said; and the baffled Sarah Anne withdrew on Lewis's arm.
But a moment later the old habit of subordination reasserted
itself. Mary Adeline's gentle countenance grew as timorous
as a child's, and she gathered up her cloak in haste.

"Perhaps I was too quick . . . I'm sure she meant it kindly,"
she exclaimed, overtaking Lewis as he turned to come up
the stairs; and with a smile he stood watching his two sisters drive off together in the Huzzard coach.

He returned to the nursery, where Treeshy was still croon-
ing over her daughter.

"Well, my dear," he said, "what do you suppose Sarah

Anne came for?" And, in reply to her wondering gaze: "To buy me off from showing the pictures!"

His wife's indignation took just the form he could have wished. She simply went on with her rich cooing laugh and hugged the baby tighter. But Lewis felt the perverse desire to lay a still greater strain upon her loyalty.

"Offered to double my allowance, she and John, if only I'll take down the sign!"

"No one shall touch the sign!" Treeshy flamed.

"Not till I do," said her husband grimly.

She turned about and scanned him with anxious eyes. "Lewis . . . *you?*"

"Oh, my dear . . . they're right. . . It can't go on forever . . ." He went up to her, and put his arm about her and the child. "You've been braver than an army of heroes; but it won't do. The expenses have been a good deal heavier than I was led to expect. And I . . . I can't raise a mortgage on the pictures. Nobody will touch them."

She met this quickly. "No; I know. That was what Mary Adeline came about."

The blood rushed angrily to Lewis's temples. "Mary Adeline—how the devil did *she* hear of it?"

"Through Mr. Reedy, I suppose. But you must not be angry. She was kindness itself: she doesn't want you to close the gallery, Lewis . . . that is, not as long as you really continue to believe in it. . . She and Donald Kent will lend us enough to go on with for a year longer. That is what she came to say."

For the first time since the struggle had begun, Lewis Raycie's throat was choked with tears. His faithful Mary Adeline! He had a sudden vision of her, stealing out of the house at High Point before daylight to carry a basket of scraps to the poor Mrs. Edgar Poe who was dying of a decline down the lane. . . He laughed aloud in his joy.

"Dear old Mary Adeline! How magnificent of her! Enough to give me a whole year more . . ." He pressed his wet cheek against his wife's in a long silence. "Well, dear," he said at length, "it's for you to say—do we accept?"

He held her off, questioningly, at arm's length, and her wan little smile met his own and mingled with it.

"Of course we accept!"

IX

Of the Raycie family, which prevailed so powerfully in

the New York of the 'forties, only one of the names sur-
vived in my boyhood, half a century later. Like so many of
the descendants of the proud little Colonial society, the
Raycies had totally vanished, forgotten by everyone but a
few old ladies, one or two genealogists and the sexton of
Trinity Church, who kept the record of their graves.

The Raycie blood was of course still to be traced in various
allied families: Kents, Huzzards, Cosbys and many others,
proud to claim cousinship with a "Signer," but already indifferent or incurious as to the fate of his progeny. These old
New Yorkers, who lived so well and spent their money so
liberally, vanished like a pinch of dust when they disappeared
from their pews and their dinner-tables.

If I happen to have been familiar with the name since my
youth, it is chiefly because its one survivor was a distant
cousin of my mother's, whom she sometimes took me to
see on days when she thought I was likely to be good because I had been promised a treat for the morrow.

Old Miss Alethea Raycie lived in a house I had always
heard spoken of as "Cousin Ebenezer's." It had evidently, in
its day, been an admired specimen of domestic architecture;
but was now regarded as the hideous though venerable relic
of a bygone age. Miss Raycie, being crippled by rheumatism,
sat above stairs in a large cold room, meagerly furnished with
beadwork tables, rosewood étagères and portraits of pale
sad-looking people in odd clothes. She herself was large and
saturnine, with a battlemented black lace cap, and so deaf
that she seemed a survival of forgotten days, a Rosetta
Stone to which the clue was lost. Even to my mother, nursed
in that vanished tradition, and knowing instinctively to whom
Miss Raycie alluded when she spoke of Mary Adeline, Sarah
Anne or Uncle Doctor, intercourse with her was difficult
and languishing, and my juvenile interruptions were oftener
encouraged than reproved.

In the course of one of these visits my eye, listlessly roaming, singled out among the pallid portraits a three-crayon
drawing of a little girl with a large forehead and dark eyes,
dressed in a plaid frock and embroidered pantalettes, and
sitting on a grass-bank. I pulled my mother's sleeve to ask
who she was, and my mother answered: "Ah, that was poor
little Louisa Raycie, who died of a decline. How old was
little Louisa when she died, Cousin Alethea?"

To batter this simple question into Cousin Alethea's brain
was the affair of ten laborious minutes; and when the job
was done, and Miss Raycie, with an air of mysterious dis-

pleasure, had dropped a deep "Eleven," my mother was too exhausted to continue. So she turned to me to add, with one of the private smiles we kept for each other: "It was the poor child who would have inherited the Raycie Gallery." But to a little boy of my age this item of information lacked interest, nor did I understand my mother's surreptitious amusement.

This far-off scene suddenly came back to me last year, when, on one of my infrequent visits to New York, I went to dine with my old friend, the banker, John Selwyn, and came to an astonished stand before the mantelpiece in his new library.

"Hal*lo!*" I said, looking up at the picture above the chimney.

My host squared his shoulders, thrust his hands into his pockets, and affected the air of modesty which people think it proper to assume when their possessions are admired. "The Macrino d'Alba? Y—yes . . . it was the only thing I managed to capture out of the Raycie collection."

"The only thing? Well——"

"Ah, but you should have seen the Mantegna; *and* the Giotto; *and* the Piero della Francesca—hang it, one of the most beautiful Piero della Francescas in the world. . . A girl in profile, with her hair in a pearl net, against a background of columbines; *that* went back to Europe—the National Gallery, I believe. And the Carpaccio, the most exquisite little St. George . . . that went to California . . . *Lord!*" He sat down with the sigh of a hungry man turned away from a groaning board. "Well, it nearly broke me buying *this!*" he murmured, as if at least that fact were some consolation.

I was turning over my early memories in quest of a clue to what he spoke of as the Raycie collection, in a tone which implied that he was alluding to objects familiar to all art-lovers.

Suddenly: "They weren't poor little Louisa's pictures, by any chance?" I asked, remembering my mother's cryptic smile.

Selwyn looked at me perplexedly. "Who the deuce is poor little Louisa?" And, without waiting for my answer, he went on: "They were that fool Netta Cosby's until a year ago—and she never even knew it."

We looked at each other interrogatively, my friend perplexed at my ignorance, and I now absorbed in trying to run down the genealogy of Netta Cosby. I did so finally.

"Netta Cosby—you don't mean Netta Kent, the one who married Jim Cosby?"

"That's it. They were cousins of the Raycies', and she inherited the pictures."

I continued to ponder. "I wanted awfully to marry her, the year I left Harvard," I said presently, more to myself than to my hearer.

"Well, if you had you'd have annexed a prize fool; *and* one of the most beautiful collections of Italian Primitives in the world."

"In the world?"

"Well—you wait till you see them; if you haven't already. And I seem to make out that you haven't—that you can't have. How long have you been in Japan? Four years? I thought so. Well, it was only last winter that Netta found out."

"Found out what?"

"What there was in old Alethea Raycie's attic. You must remember the old Miss Raycie who lived in that hideous house in Tenth Street when we were children. She was a cousin of your mother's, wasn't she? Well, the old fool lived there for nearly half a century, with five millions' worth of pictures shut up in the attic over her head. It seems they'd been there ever since the death of a poor young Raycie who collected them in Italy years and years ago. I don't know much about the story; I never was strong on genealogy, and the Raycies have always been rather dim to me. They were everybody's cousins, of course; but as far as one can make out that seems to have been their principal if not their only function. Oh—and I suppose the Raycie Building was called after them; only *they* didn't build it!

"But there was this one young fellow—I wish I could find out more about him. All that Netta seems to know (or to care, for that matter) is that when he was very young—barely out of college—he was sent to Italy by his father to buy Old Masters—in the 'forties, it must have been—and came back with this extraordinary, this unbelievable collection . . . a boy of that age! . . . and was disinherited by the old gentleman for bringing home such rubbish. The young fellow and his wife died ever so many years ago, both of them. It seems he was so laughed at for buying such pictures that they went away and lived like hermits in the depths of the country. There were some funny spectral portraits of them that old Alethea had up in her bedroom. Netta showed me one of them that last time I went to see her: a pathetic drawing of the only child, an anæmic little girl with a big forehead. Jove, but that must have been your little Louisa!"

I nodded. "In a plaid frock and embroidered pantalettes?"

"Yes, something of the sort. Well, when Louisa and her parents died, I suppose the pictures went to old Miss Raycie. At any rate, at some time or other—and it must have been longer ago than you or I can remember—the old lady inherited them with the Tenth Street house; and when *she* died, three or four years ago, her relations found she'd never even been upstairs to look at them."

"Well——?"

"Well, she died intestate, and Netta Kent—Netta Cosby—turned out to be the next of kin. There wasn't much to be got out of the estate (or so they thought) and, as the Cosbys are always hard up, the house in Tenth Street had to be sold, and the pictures were very nearly sent off to the auction room with all the rest of the stuff. But nobody supposed they would bring anything, and the auctioneer said that if you tried to sell pictures with carpets and bedding and kitchen furniture it always depreciated the whole thing; and so, as the Cosbys had some bare walls to cover, they sent for the lot—there were about thirty—and decided to have them cleaned and hang them up. 'After all,' Netta said, 'as well as I can make out through the cobwebs, some of them look like rather jolly copies of early Italian things.' But as she was short of cash she decided to clean them at home instead of sending them to an expert; and one day, while she was operating on this very one before you, with her sleeves rolled up, the man called who always *does* call on such occasions; the man who knows. In the given case, it was a quiet fellow connected with the Louvre, who'd brought her a letter from Paris, and whom she'd invited to one of her stupid dinners. He was announced, and she thought it would be a joke to let him see what she was doing; she has pretty arms, you may remember. So he was asked into the dining-room, where he found her with a pail of hot water and soap-suds, and *this* laid out on the table; and the first thing he did was to grab her pretty arm so tight that it was black and blue, while he shouted out: 'God in heaven! Not *hot* water!'"

My friend leaned back with a sigh of mingled resentment and satisfaction, and we sat silently looking up at the lovely "Adoration" above the mantelpiece.

"That's how I got it a little cheaper—most of the old varnish was gone for good. But luckily for her it was the first

picture she had attacked; and as for the others—you must
see them, that's all I can say. . . . Wait; I've got the catalogue
somewhere about . . ."

He began to rummage for it, and I asked, remembering
how nearly I had married Netta Kent: "Do you mean to
say she didn't keep a single one of them?"

"Oh, yes—in the shape of pearls and Rolls-Royces. And
you've seen their new house in Fifth Avenue?" He ended
with a grin of irony: "The best of the joke is that Jim was
just thinking of divorcing her when the pictures were discovered."

"Poor little Louisa!" I sighed.

SHERWOOD ANDERSON

The Man Who Became A Woman

MY FATHER was a retail druggist in our town, out in Nebraska, which was so much like a thousand other towns I've been in since that there's no use fooling around and taking up your time and mine trying to describe it.

Anyway I became a drug clerk and after father's death the store was sold and mother took the money and went west, to her sister in California, giving me four hundred dollars with which to make my start in the world. I was only nineteen years old then.

I came to Chicago, where I worked as a drug clerk for a time, and then, as my health suddenly went back on me, perhaps because I was so sick of my lonely life in the city and of the sight and smell of the drug store, I decided to set out on what seemed to me then the great adventure and became for a time a tramp, working now and then, when I had no money, but spending all the time I could loafing around out of doors or riding up and down the land on freight trains and trying to see the world. I even did some stealing in lonely towns at night—once a pretty good suit of clothes that someone had left hanging out on a clothesline, and once some shoes out of a box in a freight car—but I was in constant terror of being caught and put into jail so realized that success as a thief was not for me.

The most delightful experience of that period of my life was when I once worked as a groom, or swipe, with race horses and it was during that time I met a young fellow of about my own age who has since become a writer of some prominence.

The young man of whom I now speak had gone into race track work as a groom, to bring a kind of flourish, a high spot, he used to say, into his life.

He was then unmarried and had not been successful as a writer. What I mean is he was free and I guess, with him as with me, there was something he liked about the people who hang about a race track, the touts, swipes, drivers, niggers and

193

gamblers. You know what a gaudy undependable lot they are
—if you've ever been around the tracks much—about the best
liars I've ever seen, and not saving money or thinking about
morals, like most druggists, dry-goods merchants and the
others who used to be my father's friends in our Nebraska
town—and not bending the knee much either, or kowtowing
to people, they thought must be grander or richer or more
powerful than themselves.

What I mean is, they were an independent, go-to-the-devil,
come-have-a-drink-of-whisky, kind of a crew and when one of
them won a bet, "knocked 'em off," we called it, his money
was just dirt to him while it lasted. No king or president or
soap manufacturer—gone on a trip with his family to Europe
—could throw on more dog than one of them, with his big
diamond rings and the diamond horse-shoe stuck in his neck-
ties and all.

I liked the whole blamed lot pretty well and he did too.
He was groom temporarily for a pacing gelding named
Lumpy Joe owned by a tall black-mustached man named
Alfred Kreymborg and trying the best he could to make the
bluff to himself he was a real one. It happened that we were on
the same circuit, doing the West Pennsylvania county fairs
all that fall, and on fine evenings we spent a good deal of
time walking and talking together.

Let us suppose it to be a Monday or Tuesday evening
and our horses had been put away for the night. The racing
didn't start until later in the week, maybe Wednesday,
usually. There was always a little place called a dining-hall,
run mostly by the Woman's Christian Temperance Associations of the towns, and we would go there to eat where we
could get a pretty good meal for twenty-five cents. At least
then we thought it pretty good.

I would manage it so that I sat beside this fellow, whose
name was Tom Means and when we had got through eating
we would go look at our two horses again and when we got
there Lumpy Joe would be eating his hay in his box stall
and Alfred Kreymborg would be standing there, pulling his
mustache and looking as sad as a sick crane.

But he wasn't really sad. "You two boys want to go down
town to see the girls. I'm an old duffer and way past that
myself. You go on along. I'll be setting here anyway, and I'll
keep an eye on both the horses for you," he would say.

So we would set off, going, not into the town to try to
get in with some of the town girls, who might have taken
up with us because we were strangers and race track fellows,

but out into the country. Sometimes we got into a hilly country and there was a moon. The leaves were falling off the trees and lay in the road so that we kicked them up with the dust as we went along.

To tell the truth I suppose I got to love Tom Means, who was five years older than me, although I wouldn't have dared say so, then. Americans are shy and timid about saying things like that and a man here don't dare own up he loves another man, I've found out, and they are afraid to admit such feelings to themselves even. I guess they're afraid it may be taken to mean something it don't need to at all.

Anyway we walked along and some of the trees were already bare and looked like people standing solemnly beside the road and listening to what we had to say. Only I didn't say much. Tom Means did most of the talking.

Sometimes we came back to the race track and it was late and the moon had gone down and it was dark. Then we often walked round and round the track, sometimes a dozen times, before we crawled into the hay to go to bed.

Tom talked always on two subjects, writing and race horses, but mostly about race horses. The quiet sounds about the race tracks and the smells of horses, and the things that go with horses, seemed to get him all excited. "Oh, hell, Herman Dudley," he would burst out suddenly, "don't go talking to me. I know what I think. I've been around more than you have and I've seen a world of people. There isn't any man or woman, not even a fellow's own mother, as fine as a horse, that is to say a thoroughbred horse."

Sometimes he would go on like that a long time, speaking of people he had seen and their characteristics. He wanted to be a writer later and what he said was that when he came to be one he wanted to write the way a well bred horse runs or trots or paces. Whether he ever did it or not I can't say. He has written a lot, but I'm not too good a judge of such things. Anyway I don't think he has.

But when he got on the subject of horses he certainly was a darby. I would never have felt the way I finally got to feel about horses or enjoyed my stay among them half so much if it hadn't been for him. Often he would go on talking for an hour maybe, speaking of horses' bodies and of their minds and wills as though they were human beings. "Lord help us, Herman," he would say, grabbing hold of my arm, "don't it get you up in the throat? I say now, when a good one, like that Lumpy Joe I'm swiping, flattens himself at the head of the stretch and he's coming, and you know he's coming, and you know his heart's sound, and he's game, and you know he isn't going to let himself get licked— don't it get you Herman, don't it get you like the old Harry?"

That's the way he would talk, and then later, sometimes, he'd talk about writing and get himself all het up about that too. He had some notions about writing I've never got myself around to thinking much about but just the same maybe his talk, working in me, has led me to want to begin to write this story myself.

There was one experience of that time on the tracks that I am forced, by some feeling inside myself, to tell.

Well, I don't know why but I've just got to. It will be kind of like confession is, I suppose, to a good Catholic, or maybe, better yet, like cleaning up the room you live in, if you are a bachelor, like I was for so long. The room gets pretty mussy and the bed not made some days and clothes and things thrown on the closet floor and maybe under the bed. And then you clean all up and put on new sheets, and then you take off all your clothes and get down on your hands and knees, and scrub the floor so clean you could eat bread off it, and then take a walk and come home after a while and your room smells sweet and you feel sweetened-up and better inside yourself too.

What I mean is, this story has been on my chest, and I've often dreamed about the happenings in it, even after I married Jessie and was happy. Sometimes I even screamed out at night and so I said to myself, "I'll write the dang story," and here goes.

Fall had come on and in the mornings now when we crept out of our blankets, spread out on the hay in the tiny lofts above the horse stalls, and put our heads out to look around, there was a white rime of frost on the ground. When we woke the horses woke too. You know how it is at the tracks—the little barn-like stalls with the tiny lofts above are all set along in a row and there are two doors to each stall, one coming up to a horse's breast and then a top one, that is only closed at night and in bad weather.

In the mornings the upper door is swung open and fastened back and the horses put their heads out. There is the white rime on the grass over inside the grey oval the track makes. Usually there is some outfit that has six, ten or even twelve horses, and perhaps they have a negro cook who does his cooking at an open fire in the clear space before the row of stalls and he is at work now and the horses with their big fine eyes are looking about and whinnying, and a stallion looks out at the door of one of the stalls and sees a sweet-eyed mare looking at him and sends up his trumpet-call, and a man's voice laughs, and there are no women anywhere in sight or no sign of one anywhere, and everyone feels like laughing and usually does.

It's pretty fine but I didn't know how fine it was until I got to know Tom Means and heard him talk about it all.

At the time the thing happened of which I am trying to tell now Tom was no longer with me. A week before his owner, Alfred Kreymborg, had taken his horse Lumpy Joe over into the Ohio Fair Circuit and I saw no more of Tom at the tracks.

There was a story going about the stalls that Lumpy Joe, a big rangy brown gelding, wasn't really named Lumpy Joe at all, that he was a ringer who had made a fast record out in Iowa and up through the northwest country the year before, and that Kreymborg had picked him up and had kept him under wraps all winter and had brought him over into the Pennsylvania country under this new name and made a clean-up in the books.

I know nothing about that and never talked to Tom about it but anyway he, Lumpy Joe and Kreymborg were all gone now.

I suppose I'll always remember those days, and Tom's talk at night, and before that in the early September evenings how we sat around in front of the stalls, and Kreymborg sitting on an upturned feed box and pulling at his long black mustache and some times humming a little ditty one couldn't catch the words of. It was something about a deep well and a little grey squirrel crawling up the sides of it, and he never laughed or smiled much but there was something in his solemn grey eyes, not quite a twinkle, something more delicate than that.

The others talked in low tones and Tom and I sat in silence. He never did his best talking except when he and I were alone.

For his sake—if he ever sees my story—I should mention that at the only big track we ever visited, at Readville, Pennsylvania, we saw old Pop Geers, the great racing driver, himself. His horses were at a place far away across the tracks from where we were stabled. I suppose a man like him was likely to get the choice of all the good places for his horses.

We went over there one evening and stood about and

there was Geers himself, sitting before one of the stalls on a box tapping the ground with a riding whip. They called him, around the tracks, "The silent man from Tennessee" and he was silent—that night anyway. All we did was to stand and look at him for maybe a half hour and then we went away and that night Tom talked better than I had ever heard him. He said that the ambition of his life was to wait until Pop Geers died and then write a book about him, and to show in the book that there was at least one American who never went nutty about getting rich or owning a big factory or being any other kind of a hell of a fellow. "He's satisfied I think to sit around like that and wait until the big moments of his life come, when he heads a fast one into the stretch and then, darn his soul, he can give all of himself to the thing right in front of him," Tom said, and then he was so worked up he began to blubber. We were walking along the fence on the inside of the tracks and it was dusk and, in some trees nearby, some birds, just sparrows maybe, were making a chirping sound, and you could hear insects singing and, where there was a little light, off to the west between some trees, motes were dancing in the air. Tom said that about Pop Geers, although I think he was thinking most about something he wanted to be himself and wasn't, and then he went and stood by the fence and sort of blubbered and I began to blubber too, although I didn't know what about.

But perhaps I did know, after all. I suppose Tom wanted to feel, when he became a writer, like he thought old Pop must feel when his horse swung around the upper turn, and there lay the stretch before him, and if he was going to get his horse home in front he had to do it right then. What Tom said was that any man had something in him that understands about a thing like that but that no woman ever did except up in her brain. He often got off things like that about women but I notice he later married one of them just the same.

But to get back to my knitting. After Tom had left, the stable I was with kept drifting along through nice little Pennsylvania county seat towns. My owner, a strange excitable kind of a man from over in Ohio, who had lost a lot of money on horses but was always thinking he would maybe get it all back in some big killing, had been playing in pretty good luck that year. The horse I had, a tough little gelding, a five year old, had been getting home in front pretty regular and so he took some of his winnings and bought a three years old black pacing stallion named "O, My Man." My gelding was called "Pick-it-boy" because

when he was in a race and had got into the stretch my owner
always got half wild with excitement and shouted so you
could hear him a mile and a half. "Go, pick it boy, pick it
boy, pick it boy," he kept shouting and so when he had got
hold of this good little gelding he had named him that.

The gelding was a fast one, all right. As the boys at the
tracks used to say, he "picked 'em up sharp and set 'em down
clean," and he was what we called a natural race horse,
right up to all the speed he had, and didn't require much
training. "All you got to do is to drop him down on the
track and he'll go," was what my owner was always saying to
other men, when he was bragging about his horse.

And so you see, after Tom left, I hadn't much to do evenings and then the new stallion, the three year old, came on
with a negro swipe named Burt.

I liked him fine and he liked me but not the same as Tom
and me. We got to be friends all right and I suppose Burt
would have done things for me, and maybe me for him, that
Tom and me wouldn't have done for each other.

But with a negro you couldn't be close friends like you
can with another white man. There's some reason you can't
understand but it's true. There's been too much talk about
the difference between whites and blacks and you're both
shy, and anyway no use trying and I suppose Burt and I both
knew it and so I was pretty lonesome.

Something happened to me that happened several times,
when I was a young fellow, that I have never exactly understood. Sometimes now I think it was all because I had got to
be almost a man and had never been with a woman. I don't
know what's the matter with me. I can't ask a woman. I've
tried it a good many times in my life but every time I've
tried the same thing happened.

Of course, with Jessie now, it's different, but at the time
of which I'm speaking Jessie was a long ways off and a good
many things were to happen to me before I got to her.

Around a race track, as you may suppose, the fellows
who are swipes and drivers and strangers in the towns do
not go without women. They don't have to. In any town there
are always some fly girls will come around a place like that. I
suppose they think they are fooling with men who lead romantic lives. Such girls will come along by the front of the
stalls where the race horses are and, if you look all right to
them, they will stop and make a fuss over your horse. They
rub their little hands over the horse's nose and then is the
time for you—if you aren't a fellow like me who can't get up

the nerve—then is the time for you to smile and say, "Hello, kid," and make a date with one of them for that evening up town after supper. I couldn't do that, although the Lord knows I tried hard enough, often enough. A girl would come along alone, and she would be a little thing and give me the eye, and I would try and try but couldn't say anything. Both Tom, and Burt afterwards, used to laugh at me about it sometimes but what I think is that, had I been able to speak up to one of them and had managed to make a date with her, nothing would have come of it. We would probably have walked around the town and got off together in the dark somewhere, where the town came to an end, and then she would have had to knock me over with a club before it got any further.

And so there I was, having got used to Tom and our talks together, and Burt of course had his own friends among the black men. I got lazy and mopey and had a hard time doing my work.

It was like this. Sometimes I would be sitting, perhaps under a tree in the late afternoon when the races were over for the day and the crowds had gone away. There were always a lot of other men and boys who hadn't any horses in the races that day and they would be standing or sitting about in front of the stalls and talking.

I would listen for a time to their talk and then their voices would seem to go far away. The things I was looking at would go far away too. Perhaps there would be a tree, not more than a hundred yards away, and it would just come out of the ground and float away like a thistle. It would get smaller and smaller, away off there in the sky, and then suddenly—bang, it would be back where it belonged, in the ground, and I would begin hearing the voices of the men talking again.

When Tom was with me that summer the nights were splendid. We usually walked about and talked until pretty late and then I crawled up into my hole and went to sleep. Always out of Tom's talk I got something that stayed in my mind, after I was off by myself, curled up in my blanket. I suppose he had a way of making pictures as he talked and the pictures stayed by me as Burt was always saying pork chops did by him. "Give me the old pork chops, they stick to the ribs," Burt was always saying and with the imagination it was always that way about Tom's talks. He started something inside you that went on and on, and your mind played with it like walking about in a strange town and seeing the sights, and you slipped off to sleep and had splendid dreams and woke up in the morning feeling fine.

And then he was gone and it wasn't that way any more and I got into the fix I have described. At night I kept seeing women's bodies and women's lips and things in my dreams, and woke up in the morning feeling like the old Harry.

Burt was pretty good to me. He always helped me cool Pick-it-boy out after a race and he did the things himself that take the most skill and quickness, like getting the bandages on a horse's leg smooth, and seeing that every strap is setting just right, and every buckle drawn up to just the right hole, before your horse goes out on the track for a heat.

Burt knew there was something wrong with me and put himself out not to let the boss know. When the boss was around he was always bragging about me. "The brightest kid I've ever worked with around the tracks," he would say and grin, and that at a time when I wasn't worth my salt.

When you go out with the horses there is one job that always takes a lot of time. In the late afternoon, after your horse has been in a race and after you have washed him and rubbed him out, he has to be walked slowly, sometimes for hours and hours, so he'll cool out slowly and won't get muscle-bound. I got so I did that job for both our horses and Burt did the more important things. It left him free to go talk or shoot dice with the other niggers and I didn't mind. I rather liked it and after a hard race even the stallion, O My Man, was tame enough, even when there were mares about.

You walk and walk and walk, around a little circle, and your horse's head is right by your shoulder, and all around you the life of the place you are in is going on, and in a queer way you get so you aren't really a part of it at all. Perhaps no one ever gets as I was then, except boys that aren't quite men yet and who like me have never been with girls or women—to really be with them, up to the hilt, I mean. I used to wonder if young girls got that way too before they married or did what we used to call "go on the town."

If I remember it right though, I didn't do much thinking then. Often I would have forgotten supper if Burt hadn't shouted at me and reminded me, and sometimes he forgot and went off to town with one of the other niggers and I did forget.

There I was with the horse, going slow slow slow, around a circle that way. The people were leaving the fair grounds now, some afoot, some driving away to the farms in wagons and fords. Clouds of dust floated in the air and over to the west, where the town was, maybe the sun was going down, a red ball of fire through the dust. Only a few hours before the crowd had been all filled with excitement and everyone shouting. Let us suppose my horse had been in a race that afternoon and I had stood in front of the grandstand with my horse blanket over my shoulder, alongside of Burt perhaps, and when they came into the stretch my owner began to call, in that queer high voice of his that seemed to float over the top of all the shouting up in the grandstand. And his voice was saying over and over, "Go, pick it boy, pick it boy, pick it boy," the way he always did, and my heart was thumping so I could hardly breathe, and Burt was leaning over and snapping his fingers and muttering, "Come, little sweet. Come on home. Your Mama wants you. Come get your 'lasses and bread, little Pick-it-boy."

Well, all that was over now and the voices of the people left around were all low. And Pick-it-boy—I was leading him slowly around the little ring, to cool him slowly, as I've said,—he was different too. Maybe he had pretty nearly broken his heart trying to get down to the wire in front, or getting down there in front, and now everything inside him was quiet and tired, as it was nearly all the time those days in me, except in me tired but not quiet.

You remember I've told you we always walked in a circle, round and round and round. I guess something inside me got to going round and round and round too. The sun did sometimes and the trees and the clouds of dust. I had to think sometimes about putting down my feet so they went down in the right place and I didn't get to staggering like a drunken man.

And a funny feeling came that it is going to be hard to describe. It had something to do with the life in the horse and in me. Sometimes, these late years, I've thought maybe negroes would understand what I'm trying to talk about now better than any white man ever will. I mean something about men and animals, something between them, something that can perhaps only happen to a white man when he has slipped off his base a little, as I suppose I had then. I think maybe a lot of horsey people feel it sometimes though. It's something like this, maybe—do you suppose it could be that something we whites have got, and think such a lot of, and are so proud about, isn't much of any good after all?

It's something in us that wants to be big and grand and important maybe and won't let us just be, like a horse or a dog or a bird can. Let's say Pick-it-boy had won his race that day. He did that pretty often that summer. Well, he was neither proud, like I would have been in his place, or mean in one part of the inside of him either. He was just himself, doing something with a kind of simplicity. That's what Pick-it-boy was like and I got to feeling it in him as I walked with him slowly in the gathering darkness. I got inside him in some way I can't explain and he got inside me. Often we would stop walking for no cause and he would put his nose up against my face.

I wished he was a girl sometimes or that I was a girl and he was a man. It's an odd thing to say but it's a fact. Being with him that way, so long, and in such a quiet way, cured something in me a little. Often after an evening like that I slept all right and did not have the kind of dreams I've spoken about.

But I wasn't cured for very long and couldn't get cured. My body seemed all right and just as good as ever but there wasn't no pep in me.

Then the fall got later and later and we came to the last town we were going to make before my owner laid his horses up for the winter, in his home town over across the State line in Ohio, and the track was up on a hill, or rather in a kind of high plain above the town.

It wasn't much of a place and the sheds were rather rickety and the track bad, especially at the turns. As soon as we got to the place and got stabled it began to rain and kept it up all week so the fair had to be put off.

As the purses weren't very large a lot of the owners shipped right out but our owner stayed. The fair owners guaranteed expenses, whether the races were held the next week or not.

And all week there wasn't much of anything for Burt and me to do but clean manure out of the stalls in the morning, watch for a chance when the rain let up a little to jog the horses around the track in the mud and then clean them off, blanket them and stick them back in their stalls.

It was the hardest time of all for me. Burt wasn't so bad off as there were a dozen or two blacks around and in the evening they went off to town, got liquored up a little and came home late, singing and talking, even in the cold rain.

And then one night I got mixed up in the thing I'm trying to tell you about.

It was a Saturday evening and when I look back at it now

it seems to me everyone had left the tracks but just me. In the early evening swipe after swipe came over to my stall and asked me if I was going to stick around. When I said I was he would ask me to keep an eye out for him, that nothing happened to his horse. "Just take a stroll down that way now and then, eh, kid," one of them would say, "I just want to run up to town for an hour or two."

I would say "yes" to be sure, and so pretty soon it was dark as pitch up there in that little ruined fairground and nothing living anywhere around but the horses and me.

I stood it as long as I could, walking here and there in the mud and rain, and thinking all the time I wished I was someone else and not myself. "If I were someone else," I thought, "I wouldn't be here but down there in town with the others." I saw myself going into saloons and having drinks and later going off to a house maybe and getting myself a woman.

I got to thinking so much that, as I went stumbling around up there in the darkness, it was as though what was in my mind was actually happening.

Only I wasn't with some cheap woman, such as I would have found had I had the nerve to do what I wanted but with such a woman as I thought then I should never find in this world. She was slender and like a flower and with something in her like a race horse too, something in her like Pick-it-boy in the stretch, I guess.

And I thought about her and thought about her until I couldn't stand thinking any more. "I'll do something anyway," I said to myself.

So, although I had told all the swipes I would stay and watch their horses, I went out of the fair grounds and down the hill a ways. I went down until I came to a little low saloon, not in the main part of the town itself but half way up the hillside. The saloon had once been a residence, a farmhouse perhaps, but if it was ever a farmhouse I'm sure the farmer who lived there and worked the land on that hillside hadn't made out very well. The country didn't look like a farming country, such as one sees all about the other county-seat towns we had been visiting all through the late summer and fall. Everywhere you looked there were stones sticking out of the ground and the trees mostly of the stubby, stunted kind. It looked wild and untidy and ragged, that's what I mean. On the flat plain, up above, where the fairground was, there were a few fields and pastures, and there were some sheep raised and in the field right next to the tracks, on the furtherest side from town, on the back stretch side, there had once been a slaughter-house, the ruins of which were still standing. It hadn't been used for quite some time but there were bones of animals lying all about in the field, and there was a smell coming out of the old building that would curl your hair.

The horses hated the place, just as we swipes did, and in the morning when we were jogging them around the track in the mud, to keep them in racing condition, Pick-it-boy and O My Man both raised old Ned every time we headed them up the back stretch and got near to where the old slaughter-house stood. They would rear and fight at the bit, and go off their stride and run until they got clear of the rotten smells, and neither Burt nor I could make them stop it. "It's a hell of a town down there and this is a hell of a track for racing," Burt kept saying. "If they ever have their danged old fair someone's going to get spilled and maybe killed back here." Whether they did or not I don't know as I didn't stay for the fair, for reasons I'll tell you pretty soon, but Burt was speaking sense all right. A race horse isn't like a human being. He won't stand for it to have to do his work in any rotten ugly kind of a dump the way a man will, and he won't stand for the smells a man will either.

But to get back to my story again. There I was, going down the hillside in the darkness and the cold soaking rain and breaking my word to all the others about staying up above and watching the horses. When I got to the little saloon I decided to stop and have a drink or two. I'd found out long before that about two drinks upset me so I was two-thirds piped and couldn't walk straight, but on that night I didn't care a tinker's dam.

So I went up a kind of path, out of the road, toward the front door of the saloon. It was in what must have been the parlor of the place when it was a farmhouse and there was a little front porch.

I stopped before I opened the door and looked about a little. From where I stood I could look right down into the main street of the town, like being in a big city, like New York or Chicago, and looking down out of the fifteenth floor of an office building into the street.

The hillside was mighty steep and the road up had to wind and wind or no one could ever have come up out of the town to their plagued old fair at all.

It wasn't much of a town I saw—a main street with a lot

of saloons and a few stores, one or two dinky moving-picture places, a few fords, hardly any women or girls in sight and a raft of men. I tried to think of the girl I had been dreaming about, as I walked around in the mud and darkness up at the fair ground, living in the place but I couldn't make it. It was like trying to think of Pick-it-boy getting himself worked up to the state I was in then, and going into the ugly dump I was going into. It couldn't be done.

All the same I knew the town wasn't all right there in sight. There must have been a good many of the kinds of houses Pennsylvania miners live in back in the hills, or around a turn in the valley in which the main street stood.

What I suppose is that, it being Saturday night and raining, the women and kids had all stayed at home and only the men were out, intending to get themselves liquored up. I've been in some other mining towns since and if I was a miner and had to live in one of them, or in one of the houses they live in with their women and kids, I'd get out and liquor myself up too.

So there I stood looking, and as sick as a dog inside myself, and as wet and cold as a rat in a sewer pipe. I could see the mass of dark figures moving about down below, and beyond the main street there was a river that made a sound you could hear distinctly, even up where I was, and over beyond the river were some railroad tracks with switch engines going up and down. I suppose they had something to do with the mines in which the men of the town worked. Anyway, as I stood watching and listening there was, now and then, a sound like thunder rolling down the sky, and I suppose that was a lot of coal, maybe a whole carload, being let down plunk into a coal car.

And then besides there was, on the side of a hill far away, a long row of coke ovens. They had little doors, through which the light from the fire within leaked out and as they were set closely, side by side, they looked like the teeth of some big man-eating giant lying and waiting over there in the hills.

The sight of it all, even the sight of the kind of hell-holes men are satisfied to go on living in, gave me the fantods and the shivers right down in my liver, and on that night I guess I had in me a kind of contempt for all men, including myself, that I've never had so thoroughly since. Come right down to it, I suppose women aren't so much to blame as men. They aren't running the show.

Then I pushed open the door and went into the saloon. There were about a dozen men, miners I suppose, playing cards at tables in a little long dirty room, with a bar at one side of it, and with a big red-faced man with a mustache standing back of the bar.

The place smelled, as such places do where men hang around who have worked and sweated in their clothes and perhaps slept in them too, and have never had them washed but have just kept on wearing them. I guess you know what I mean if you've ever been in a city. You smell that smell in a city, in street cars on rainy nights when a lot of factory hands get on. I got pretty used to that smell when I was a tramp and pretty sick of it too.

And so I was in the place now, with a glass of whisky in my hand, and I thought all the miners were staring at me, which they weren't at all, but I thought they were and so I felt just the same as though they had been. And then I looked up and saw my own face in the old cracked looking-glass back of the bar. If the miners had been staring, or laughing at me, I wouldn't have wondered when I saw what I looked like.

It—I mean my own face—was white and pasty-looking, and for some reason, I can't tell exactly why, it wasn't my own face at all. It's a funny business I'm trying to tell you about and I know what you may be thinking of me as well as you do, so you needn't suppose I'm innocent or ashamed. I'm only wondering. I've thought about it a lot since and I can't make it out. I know I was never that way before that night and I know I've never been that way since. Maybe it was lonesomeness, just lonesomeness, gone on in me too long. I've often wondered if women generally are lonesomer than men.

The point is that the face I saw in the looking-glass back of that bar, when I looked up from my glass of whisky that evening, wasn't my own face at all but the face of a woman. It was a girl's face, that's what I mean. That's what it was. It was a girl's face, and a lonesome and scared girl too. She was just a kid at that.

When I saw that the glass of whisky came pretty near falling out of my hand but I gulped it down, put a dollar on the bar, and called for another. "I've got to be careful here— I'm up against something new," I said to myself. "If any of these men in here get on to me there's going to be trouble." When I had got the second drink in me I called for a third and I thought, "When I get this third drink down I'll get out of here and back up the hill to the fair ground before I make a fool of myself and begin to get drunk."

And then, while I was thinking and drinking my third glass of whisky, the men in the room began to laugh and of course I thought they were laughing at me. But they weren't. No one in the place had really paid any attention to me.

What they were laughing at was a man who had just come in at the door. I'd never seen such a fellow. He was a huge big man, with red hair, that stuck straight up like bristles out of his head, and he had a red-haired kid in his arms. The kid was just like himself, big, I mean, for his age, and with the same kind of stiff red hair.

He came and set the kid up on the bar, close beside me, and called for a glass of whisky for himself and all the men in the room began to shout and laugh at him and his kid. Only they didn't shout and laugh when he was looking, so he could tell which ones did it, but did all their shouting and laughing when his head was turned the other way. They kept calling him "cracked." "The crack is getting wider in the old tin pan," someone sang and then they all laughed.

I'm puzzled you see, just how to make you feel as I felt that night. I suppose, having undertaken to write this story, that's what I'm up against, trying to do that. I'm not claiming to be able to inform you or to do you any good. I'm just trying to make you understand some things about me, as I would like to understand some things about you, or anyone, if I had the chance. Anyway the whole blamed thing, the thing that went on I mean in that little saloon on that rainy Saturday night, wasn't like anything quite real. I've already told you how I had looked into the glass back of the bar and had seen there, not my own face but the face of a scared young girl. Well, the men, the miners, sitting at the tables in the half dark room, the red-faced bartender, the unholy looking big man who had come in and his queer-looking kid, now sitting on the bar—all of them were like characters in some play, not like real people at all.

There was myself, that wasn't myself—and I'm not any fairy. Anyone who has ever known me knows better than that.

And then there was the man who had come in. There was a feeling came out of him that wasn't like the feeling you get from a man at all. It was more like the feeling you get maybe from a horse, only his eyes weren't like a horse's eyes. Horses' eyes have a kind of calm something in them and his hadn't. If you've ever carried a lantern through a wood at night, going along a path, and then suddenly you felt something funny in the air and stopped, and there ahead of you somewhere were the eyes of some little animal, gleaming out at you from a dead wall of darkness—The eyes shine big and quiet but there is a point right in the centre of each, where there is something dancing and wavering. You aren't afraid the little animal will jump at you, you are afraid the little eyes will jump at you—that's what's the matter with you.

Only of course a horse, when you go into his stall at night, or a little animal you had disturbed in a wood that way, wouldn't be talking and the big man who had come in there with his kid was talking. He kept talking all the time, saying something under his breath, as they say, and I could only understand now and then a few words. It was his talking made him kind of terrible. His eyes said one thing and his lips another. They didn't seem to get together, as though they belonged to the same person.

For one thing the man was too big. There was about him an unnatural bigness. It was in his hands, his arms, his shoulders, his body, his head, a bigness like you might see in trees and bushes in a tropical country perhaps. I've never been in a tropical country but I've seen pictures. Only his eyes were small. In his big head they looked like the eyes of a bird. And I remember that his lips were thick, like negroes' lips.

He paid no attention to me or to the others in the room but kept on muttering to himself, or to the kid sitting on the bar—I couldn't tell to which.

First he had one drink and then, quick, another. I stood staring at him and thinking—a jumble of thoughts, I suppose.

What I must have been thinking was something like this. "Well he's one of the kind you are always seeing about towns," I thought. I meant he was one of the cracked kind. In almost any small town you go to you will find one, and sometimes two or three cracked people, walking around. They go through the street, muttering to themselves and people generally are cruel to them. Their own folks make a bluff at being kind, but they aren't really, and the others in the town, men and boys, like to tease them. They send such a fellow, the mild silly kind, on some fool errand after a round square or a dozen post-holes or tie cards on his back saying "Kick me," or something like that, and then carry on and laugh as though they had done something funny.

And so there was this cracked one in that saloon and I could see the men in there wanted to have some fun putting up some kind of horseplay on him, but they didn't quite dare. He wasn't one of the mild kind, that was a cinch. I kept looking at the man and at his kid, and then up at that strange unreal reflection of myself in the cracked looking-glass back of the bar. "Rats, rats, digging in the ground —miners are rats, little jack-rabbit," I heard him say to his solemn-faced kid. I guess, after all, maybe he wasn't so cracked.

The kid sitting on the bar kept blinking at his father, like an owl caught out in the daylight, and now the father was having another glass of whisky. He drank six glasses, one right after the other, and it was cheap ten-cent stuff. He must have had cast-iron insides all right.

Of the men in the room there were two or three (maybe they were really more scared than the others so had to put up a bluff of bravery by showing off) who kept laughing and making funny cracks about the big man and his kid and there was one fellow was the worst of the bunch. I'll never forget that fellow because of his looks and what happened to him afterwards.

He was one of the showing-off kind all right, and he was the one that had started the song about the crack getting bigger in the old tin pan. He sang it two or three times, and then he grew bolder and got up and began walking up and down the room singing it over and over. He was a showy kind of man with a fancy vest, on which there were brown tobacco spots, and he wore glasses. Every time he made some crack he thought was funny, he winked at the others as though to say, "You see me. I'm not afraid of this big fellow," and then the others laughed.

The proprietor of the place must have known what was going on, and the danger in it, because he kept leaning over the bar and saying, "Shush, now quit it," to the showy-off man, but it didn't do any good. The fellow kept prancing like a turkey-cock and he put his hat on one side of his head and stopped right back of the big man and sang that song about the crack in the old tin pan. He was one of the kind you can't shush until they get their blocks knocked off, and it didn't take him long to come to it that time anyhow.

Because the big fellow just kept on muttering to his kid and drinking his whisky, as though he hadn't heard anything, and then suddenly he turned and his big hand flashed out and he grabbed, not the fellow who had been showing off, but me. With just a sweep of his arm he brought me up against his big body. Then he shoved me over with my breast jammed against the bar and looking right into his kid's face and he said, "Now you watch him, and if you let him fall I'll kill you," in just quiet ordinary tones as though he was saying "good morning" to some neighbor.

Then the kid leaned over and threw his arms around my head, and in spite of that I did manage to screw my head around enough to see what happened.

It was a sight I'll never forget. The big fellow had whirled around, and he had the showy-off man by the shoulder now, and the fellow's face was a sight. The big man must have had some reputation as a bad man in the town, even though he was cracked for the man with the fancy vest had his mouth open now, and his hat had fallen off his head, and he was silent and scared. Once, when I was a tramp, I saw a kid killed by a train. The kid was walking on the rail and showing off before some other kids, by letting them see how close he could let an engine come to him before he got out of the way. And the engine was whistling and a woman, over on the porch of a house nearby, was jumping up and down and screaming, and the kid let the engine get nearer and nearer, wanting more and more to show off, and then he stumbled and fell. God, I'll never forget the look on his face, in just the second before he got hit and killed, and now, there in that saloon, was the same terrible look on another face.

I closed my eyes for a moment and was sick all through me and then, when I opened my eyes, the big man's fist was just coming down in the other man's face. The one blow knocked him cold and he fell down like a beast hit with an axe.

And then the most terrible thing of all happened. The big man had on heavy boots, and he raised one of them and brought it down on the other man's shoulder, as he lay white and groaning on the floor. I could hear the bones crunch and it made me so sick I could hardly stand up, but I had to stand up and hold on to that kid or I knew it would be my turn next.

Because the big fellow didn't seem excited or anything, but kept on muttering to himself as he had been doing when he was standing peacefully by the bar drinking his whisky, and now he had raised his foot again, and maybe this time he would bring it down in the other man's face and, "just eliminate his map for keeps," as sports and prize-fighters sometimes say. I trembled, like I was having a chill, but thank God at that moment the kid, who had his arms around me and one hand clinging to my nose, so that there were the marks of his finger-nails on it the next morning, at that moment the kid, thank God, began to howl, and his father didn't bother any more with the man on the floor but turned around, knocked me aside, and taking the kid in his arms tramped out of that place, muttering to himself as he had been doing ever since he came in.

I went out too but I didn't prance out with any dignity, I'll tell you that. I slunk out like a thief or a coward, which perhaps I am, partly anyhow.

And so there I was, outside there in the darkness, and it was as cold and wet and black and Godforsaken a night as any man ever saw. I was so sick at the thought of human beings that night I could have vomited to think of them at all. For a while I just stumbled along in the mud of the road, going up the hill, back to the fair ground, and then, almost before I knew where I was, I found myself in the stall with Pick-it-boy.

That was one of the best and sweetest feelings I've ever had in my whole life, being in that warm stall alone with that horse that night. I had told the other swipes that I would go up and down the row of stalls now and then and have an eye on the other horses, but I had altogether forgotten my promise now. I went and stood with my back against the side of the stall, thinking how mean and low and all balled-up and twisted-up human beings can become, and how the best of them are likely to get that way any time, just because they are human beings and not simple and clear in their minds, and inside themselves, as animals are, maybe.

Perhaps you know how a person feels at such a moment. There are things you think of, odd little things you had thought you had forgotten. Once, when you were a kid, you were with your father, and he was all dressed up, as for a funeral or Fourth of July, and was walking along a street holding your hand. And you were going past a railroad station, and there was a woman standing. She was a stranger in your town and was dressed as you had never seen a woman dressed before, and never thought you would see one, looking so nice. Long afterwards you knew that was because she had lovely taste in clothes, such as so few women have really, but then you thought she must be a queen. You had read about queens in fairy stories and the thoughts of them thrilled you. What lovely eyes the strange lady had and what beautiful rings she wore on her fingers.

Then your father came out, from being in the railroad station, maybe to set his watch by the station clock, and took you by the hand and he and the woman smiled at each other, in an embarrassed kind of way, and you kept looking longingly back at her, and when you were out of her hearing you asked your father if she really were a queen. And it may be that your father was one who wasn't so very hot on democracy and a free country and talked-up bunk about a free citizenry, and he said he hoped she was a queen, and maybe, for all he knew, she was.

Or maybe, when you get jammed up as I was that night, and can't get things clear about yourself or other people and why you are alive, or for that matter why anyone you can think about is alive, you think, not of people at all but of other things you have seen and felt—like walking along a road in the snow in the winter, perhaps out in Iowa, and hearing soft warm sounds in a barn close to the road, or of another time when you were on a hill and the sun was going down and the sky suddenly became a great soft-colored bowl, all glowing like a jewel-handled bowl, a great queen in some far away mighty kingdom might have put on a vast table out under the tree, once a year, when she invited all her loyal and loving subjects to come and dine with her.

I can't, of course, figure out what you try to think about when you are as desolate as I was that night. Maybe you are like me and inclined to think of women, and maybe you are like a man I met once, on the road, who told me that when he was up against it he never thought of anything but grub and a big nice clean warm bed to sleep in. "I don't care about anything else and I don't ever let myself think of anything else," he said. "If I was like you and went to thinking about women sometime I'd find myself hooked up to some skirt, and she'd have the old double cross on me, and the rest of my life maybe I'd be working in some factory for her and her kids."

As I say, there I was anyway, up there alone with that horse in that warm stall in that dark lonesome fair ground and I had that feeling about being sick at the thought of human beings and what they could be like.

Well, suddenly I got again the queer feeling I'd had about

him once or twice before, I mean the feeling about our understanding each other in some way I can't explain.

So having it again I went over to where he stood and
began running my hands all over his body, just because
I loved the feel of him and as sometimes, to tell the plain
truth, I've felt about touching with my hands the body of a
woman I've seen and who I thought was lovely too. I ran my
hands over his head and neck and then down over his hard
firm round body and then over his flanks and down his legs.
His flanks quivered a little I remember and once he turned
his head and stuck his cold nose down along my neck and
nipped my shoulder a little, in a soft playful way. It hurt a
little but I didn't care.

So then I crawled up through a hole into the loft above
thinking that night was over anyway and glad of it, but it
wasn't, not by a long sight.

As my clothes were all soaking wet and as we race track
swipes didn't own any such things as night-gowns or paja-
mas I had to go to bed naked, of course.

But we had plenty of horse blankets and so I tucked myself in between a pile of them and tried not to think any
more that night. The being with Pick-it-boy and having him
close right under me that way made me feel a little better.

Then I was sound asleep and dreaming and—bang like
being hit with a club by someone who has sneaked up behind you—I got another wallop.

What I suppose is that, being upset the way I was, I had
forgotten to bolt the door to Pick-it-boy's stall down below
and two negro men had come in there, thinking they were in
their own place, and had climbed up through the hole where
I was. They were half lit up but not what you might call
dead drunk, and I suppose they were up against something a
couple of white swipes, who had some money in their
pockets, wouldn't have been up against.

What I mean is that a couple of white swipes, having
liquored themselves up and being down there in the town on
a bat, if they wanted a woman or a couple of women would
have been able to find them. There is always a few women of
that kind can be found around any town I've ever seen or
heard of, and of course a bar tender would have given them
the tip where to go.

But a negro, up there in that country, where there aren't
any, or anyway mighty few negro women, wouldn't know
what to do when he felt that way and would be up against it.

It's so always. Burt and several other negroes I've known pretty well have talked to me about it, lots of times. You take now a young negro man—not a race track swipe or a tramp or any other low-down kind of a fellow—but, let us say, one who has been to college, and has behaved himself and tried to be a good man, the best he could, and be clean, as they say. He isn't any better off, is he? If he has made himself some money and wants to go sit in a swell restaurant, or go to hear some good music, or see a good play at the theatre, he gets what we used to call on the tracks, "the messy end of the dung fork," doesn't he?

And even in such a low-down place as what people call a "bad house" it's the same way. The white swipes and others can go into a place where they have negro women fast enough, and they do it too, but you let a negro swipe try it the other way around and see how he comes out.

You see, I can think this whole thing out fairly now, sitting here in my own house and writing, and with my wife Jessie in the kitchen making a pie or something, and I can show just how the two negro men who came into that loft, where I was asleep, were justified in what they did, and I can preach about how the negroes are up against it in this country, like a daisy, but I tell you what, I didn't think things out that way that night.

For, you understand, what they thought, they being half liquored-up, and when one of them had jerked the blankets off me, was that I was a woman. One of them carried a lantern but it was smoky and dirty and didn't give out much light. So they must have figured it out—my body being pretty white and slender then, like a young girl's body I suppose— that some white swipe had brought me up there. The kind of girl around a town that will come with a swipe to a race track on a rainy night aren't very fancy females but you'll find that kind in the towns all right. I've seen many a one in my day.

And so, I figure, these two big buck niggers, being piped that way, just made up their minds they would snatch me away from the white swipe who had brought me out there, and who had left me lying carelessly around.

"Jes' you lie still honey. We ain't gwine hurt you none," one of them said, with a little chuckling laugh that had something in it besides a laugh, too. It was the kind of laugh that gives you the shivers.

The devil of it was I couldn't say anything, not even a

word. Why I couldn't yell out and say "What the hell," and just kid them a little and shoo them out of there I don't know, but I couldn't. I tried and tried so that my throat hurt but I didn't say a word. I just lay there staring at them.

It was a mixed-up night. I've never gone through another night like it.

Was I scared? Lord Almighty, I'll tell you what, I was scared.

Because the two big black faces were leaning right over me now, and I could feel their liquored-up breaths on my cheeks, and their eyes were shining in the dim light from that smoky lantern, and right in the centre of their eyes was that dancing flickering light I've told you about your seeing in the eyes of wild animals, when you were carrying a lantern through the woods at night.

It was a puzzler! All my life, you see—me never having had any sisters, and at that time never having had a sweetheart either—I had been dreaming and thinking about women, and I suppose I'd always been dreaming about a pure innocent one, for myself, made for me by God, maybe. Men are that way. No matter how big they talk about "let the women go hang," they've always got that notion tucked away inside themselves, somewhere. It's a kind of chesty man's notion, I suppose, but they've got it and the kind of up-and-coming women we have nowdays who are always saying, "I'm as good as a man and will do what the men do," are on the wrong trail if they have really ever want to, what you might say "hog-tie" a fellow of their own.

So I had invented a kind of princess, with black hair and a slender willowy body to dream about. And I thought of her as being shy and afraid to ever tell anything she really felt to anyone but just me. I suppose I fancied that if I ever found such a woman in the flesh I would be the strong sure one and she the timid shrinking one.

And now I was that woman, or something like her, myself.

I gave a kind of wriggle, like a fish, you have just taken off the hook. What I did next wasn't a thought-out thing. I was caught and I squirmed, that's all.

The two niggers both jumped at me but somehow—the lantern having been kicked over and having gone out the first move they made—well in some way, when they both lunged at me they missed.

As good luck would have it my feet found the hole,

where you put hay down to the horse in the stall below, and through which we crawled up when it was time to go to bed in our blankets up in the hay, and down I slid, not bothering to try to find the ladder with my feet but just letting myself go.

In less than a second I was out of doors in the dark and the rain and the two blacks were down the hole and out the door of the stall after me.

How long or how far they really followed me I suppose I'll never know. It was black dark and raining hard now and a roaring wind had begun to blow. Of course, my body being white; it must have made some kind of a faint streak in the darkness as I ran, and anyway I thought they could see me and I knew I couldn't see them and that made my terror ten times worse. Every minute I thought they would grab me.

You know how it is when a person is all upset and full of terror as I was. I suppose maybe the two niggers followed me for a while, running across the muddy race track and into the grove of trees that grew in the oval inside the track, but likely enough, after just a few minutes, they gave up the chase and went back, found their own place and went to sleep. They were liquored-up, as I've said, and maybe partly funning too.

But I didn't know that, if they were. As I ran I kept hearing sounds, sounds made by the rain coming down through the dead old leaves left on the trees and by the wind blowing, and it may be that the sound that scared me most of all was my own bare feet stepping on a dead branch and breaking it or something like that.

There was something strange and scary, a steady sound, like a heavy man running and breathing hard, right at my shoulder. It may have been my own breath, coming quick and fast. And I thought I heard that chuckling laugh I'd heard up in the loft, the laugh that sent the shivers right down through me. Of course every tree I came close to looked like a man standing there, ready to grab me, and I kept dodging and going—bang—into other trees. My shoulders kept knocking against trees in that way and the skin was all knocked off, and every time it happened I thought a big black hand had come down and clutched at me and was tearing my flesh.

How long it went on I don't know, maybe an hour, maybe five minutes. But anyway the darkness didn't let up, and the terror didn't let up, and I couldn't, to save my life, scream or make any sound.

Just why I couldn't I don't know. Could it be because at the time I was a woman, while at the same time I wasn't a woman? It may be that I was too ashamed of having turned into a girl and being afraid of a man to make any sound. I don't know about that. It's over my head.

But anyway I couldn't make a sound. I tried and tried and my throat hurt from trying and no sound came.

And then, after a long time, or what seemed like a long time, I got out from among the trees inside the track and was on the track itself again. I thought the two black men were still after me, you understand, and I ran like a madman.

Of course, running along the track that way, it must have been up the back stretch, I came after a time to where the old slaughter-house stood, in that field, beside the track. I knew it by its ungodly smell, scared as I was. Then, in some way, I managed to get over the high old fairground fence and was in the field, where the slaughter-house was.

All the time I was trying to yell or scream, or be sensible and tell those two black men that I was a man and not a woman, but I couldn't make it. And then I heard a sound like a board cracking or breaking in the fence and thought they were still after me.

So I kept on running like a crazy man, in the field, and just then I stumbled and fell over something. I've told you how the old slaughter-house field was filled with bones, that had been lying there a long time and had all been washed white. There were heads of sheep and cows and all kinds of things.

And when I fell and pitched forward I fell right into the midst of something, still and cold and white.

It was probably the skeleton of a horse lying there. In small towns like that, they take an old worn-out horse, that has died, and haul him off to some field outside of town and skin him for the hide, that they can sell for a dollar or two. It doesn't make any difference what the horse has been, that's the way he usually ends up. Maybe even Pick-it-boy, or O My Man, or a lot of other good fast ones I've seen and known have ended that way by this time.

And so I think it was the bones of a horse lying there and he must have been lying on his back. The birds and wild animals had picked all his flesh away and the rain had washed his bones clean.

Anyway I fell and pitched forward and my side got cut pretty deep and my hands clutched at something. I had fallen right in between the ribs of the horse and they seemed to wrap themselves around me close. And my hands, clutching upwards, had got hold of the cheeks of that dead horse and the bones of his cheeks were cold as ice with the rain washing over them. White bones wrapped around me and white bones in my hands.

There was a new terror now that seemed to go down to the very bottom of me, to the bottom of the inside of me, I mean. It shook me like I have seen a rat in a barn shaken by a dog. It was a terror like a big wave that hits you when you are walking on a seashore, maybe. You see it coming and you try to run and get away but when you start to run inshore there is a stone cliff you can't climb. So the wave comes high as a mountain, and there it is, right in front of you and nothing in all this world can stop it. And now it had knocked you down and rolled and tumbled you over and over and washed you clean, clean, but dead maybe.

And that's the way I felt—I seemed to myself dead with blind terror. It was a feeling like the finger of God running down your back and burning you clean, I mean.

It burned all that silly nonsense about being a girl right out of me.

I screamed at last and the spell that was on me was broken. I'll bet the scream I let out of me could have been heard a mile and a half.

Right away I felt better and crawled out from among the pile of bones, and then I stood on my own feet again and I wasn't a woman, or a young girl any more but a man and my own self, and as far as I know I've been that way ever since. Even the black night seemed warm and alive now, like a mother might be to a kid in the dark.

Only I couldn't go back to the race track because I was blubbering and crying and was ashamed of myself and of what a fool I had made of myself. Someone might see me and I couldn't stand that, not at that moment.

So I went across the field, walking now, not running like a crazy man, and pretty soon I came to a fence and crawled over and got into another field, in which there was a straw stack, I just happened to find in the pitch darkness.

The straw stack had been there a long time and some sheep had nibbled away at it until they had made a pretty deep hole, like a cave, in the side of it. I found the hole and crawled in and there were some sheep in there, about a dozen of them.

When I came in, creeping on my hands and knees, they didn't make much fuss, just stirred around a little and then settled down.

So I settled down amongst them too. They were warm and gentle and kind, like Pick-it-boy, and being in there with them made me feel better than I would have felt being with any human person I knew at that time.

So I settled down and slept after a while, and when I woke up it was daylight and not very cold and the rain was over. The clouds were breaking away from the sky now and maybe there would be a fair the next week but if there was I knew I wouldn't be there to see it.

Because what I expected to happen did happen. I had to go back across the fields and the fairground to the place where my clothes were, right in the broad daylight, and me stark naked, and of course I knew someone would be up and would raise a shout, and every swipe and every driver would stick his head out and would whoop with laughter.

And there would be a thousand questions asked, and I would be too mad and too ashamed to answer, and would perhaps begin to blubber, and that would make me more ashamed than ever.

It all turned out just as I expected, except that when the noise and the shouts of laughter were going it the loudest, Burt came out of the stall where O My Man was kept, and when he saw me he didn't know what was the matter but he knew something was up that wasn't on the square and for which I wasn't to blame.

So he got so all-fired mad he couldn't speak for a minute, and then he grabbed a pitchfork and began prancing up and down before the other stalls, giving that gang of swipes and drivers such a royal old dressing-down as you never heard. You should have heard him sling language. It was grand to hear.

And while he was doing it I sneaked up into the loft, blubbering because I was so pleased and happy to hear him swear that way, and I got my wet clothes on quick and got down, and gave Pick-it-boy a good-bye kiss on the cheek and lit out.

The last I saw of all that part of my life was Burt, still going it, and yelling out for the man who had put up a trick on me to come out and get what was coming to him. He had the pitchfork in his hand and was swinging it around, and every now and then he would make a kind of lunge at a tree or something, he was so mad through, and there was no one else in sight at all. And Burt didn't even see me cutting out along the fence through a gate and down the hill and out of the race-horse and the tramp life for the rest of my days.

WILLIAM FAULKNER

Red Leaves

I

THE TWO INDIANS crossed the plantation toward the slave quarters. Neat with whitewash, of baked soft brick, the two rows of houses in which lived the slaves belonging to the clan, faced one another across the mild shade of the lane marked and scored with naked feet and with a few home-made toys mute in the dust. There was no sign of life.

"I know what we will find," the first Indian said.

"What we will not find," the second said. Although it was noon, the lane was vacant, the doors of the cabins empty and quiet; no cooking smoke rose from any of the chinked and plastered chimneys.

"Yes. It happened like this when the father of him who is now the Man died."

"You mean, of him who was the Man."

"Yao."

The first Indian's name was Three Basket. He was perhaps sixty. They were both squat men, a little solid, burgherlike; paunchy, with big heads, big, broad, dust-colored faces of a certain blurred serenity like carved heads on a ruined wall in Siam or Sumatra, looming out of a mist. The sun had done it, the violent sun, the violent shade. Their hair looked like sedge grass on burnt-over land. Clamped through one ear Three Basket wore an enameled snuffbox.

"I have said all the time that this is not the good way. In the old days there were no quarters, no Negroes. A man's time was his own then. He had time. Now he must spend most of it finding work for them who prefer sweating to do."

"They are like horses and dogs."

"They are like nothing in this sensible world. Nothing contents them save sweat. They are worse than the white people."

222

"It is not as though the Man himself had to find work for them to do."

"You said it. I do not like slavery. It is not the good way. In the old days, there was the good way. But not now."

"You do not remember the old way either."

"I have listened to them who do. And I have tried this way. Man was not made to sweat."

"That's so. See what it has done to their flesh."

"Yes. Black. It has a bitter taste, too."

"You have eaten of it?"

"Once. I was young then, and more hardy in the appetite than now. Now it is different with me."

"Yes. They are too valuable to eat now."

"There is a bitter taste to the flesh which I do not like."

"They are too valuable to eat, anyway, when the white men will give horses for them."

They entered the lane. The mute, meager toys—the fetish-shaped objects made of wood and rags and feathers—lay in the dust about the patinaed doorsteps, among bones and broken gourd dishes. But there was no sound from any cabin, no face in any door; had not been since yesterday, when Issetibbeha died. But they already knew what they would find.

It was in the central cabin, a house a little larger than the others, where at certain phases of the moon the Negroes would gather to begin their ceremonies before removing after nightfall to the creek bottom, where they kept the drums. In this room they kept the minor accessories, the cryptic ornaments, the ceremonial records which consisted of sticks daubed with red clay in symbols. It had a hearth in the center of the floor, beneath a hole in the roof, with a few cold wood ashes and a suspended iron pot. The window shutters were closed; when the two Indians entered, after the abashless sunlight they could distinguish nothing with the eyes save a movement, shadow, out of which eyeballs rolled, so that the place appeared to be full of Negroes. The two Indians stood in the door.

"Yao," Basket said. "I said this is not the good way."

"I don't think I want to be here," the second said.

"That is black man's fear which you smell. It does not smell as ours does."

"I don't think I want to be here."

"Your fear has an odor too."

"Maybe it is Issetibbeha which we smell."

"Yao. He knows. He knows what we will find here. He

knew when he died what we should find here today." Out
of the rank twilight of the room the eyes, the smell, of
Negroes rolled about them. "I am Three Basket, whom you
know," Basket said into the room. "We are come from the
Man. He whom we seek is gone?" The Negroes said nothing.
The smell of them, of their bodies, seemed to ebb and flux
in the still hot air. They seemed to be musing as one
upon something remote, inscrutable. They were like a single
octopus. They were like the roots of a huge tree uncovered,
the earth broken momentarily upon the writhen, thick, fetid
tangle of its lightless and outraged life. "Come," Basket said.
"You know our errand. Is he whom we seek gone?"

"They are thinking something," the second said. "I do not
want to be here."

"They are knowing something," Basket said.

"They are hiding him, you think?"

"No. He is gone. He has been gone since last night. It happened like this before, when the grandfather of him who is
now the Man died. It took us three days to catch him. For
three days Doom lay above the ground, saying, 'I see my
horse and my dog. But I do not see my slave. What have you
done with him that you will not permit me to lie quiet?' "

"They do not like to die."

"Yao. They cling. It makes trouble for us, always. A people
without honor and without decorum. Always a trouble."

"I do not like it here."

"Nor do I. But then, they are savages; they cannot be expected to regard usage. That is why I say that this way is a
bad way."

"Yao. They cling. They would even rather work in the
sun than to enter the earth with a chief. But he is gone."

The Negroes had said nothing, made no sound. The white
eyeballs rolled, wild, subdued; the smell was rank, violent.
"Yes, they fear," the second said. "What shall we do now?"

"Let us go and talk with the Man."

"Will Moketubbe listen?"

"What can he do? He will not like to. But he is the Man
now."

"Yao. He is the Man. He can wear the shoes with the red
heels all the time now." They turned and went out. There
was no door in the door frame. There were no doors in any
of the cabins.

"He did that anyway," Basket said.

"Behind Issetibbeha's back. But now they are his shoes,
since he is the Man."

"Yao. Issetibbeha did not like it. I have heard. I know that he said to Moketubbe: 'When you are the Man, the shoes will be yours. But until then, they are my shoes.' But now Moketubbe is the Man; he can wear them."

"Yao," the second said. "He is the Man now. He used to wear the shoes behind Issetibbeha's back, and it was not known if Issetibbeha knew this or not. And then Issetibbeha became dead, who was not old, and the shoes are Moketubbe's, since he is the Man now. What do you think of that?"

"I don't think about it," Basket said. "Do you?"

"No," the second said.

"Good," Basket said. "You are wise."

II

The house sat on a knoll, surrounded by oak trees. The front of it was one story in height, composed of the deck house of a steamboat which had gone ashore and which Doom, Issetibbeha's father, had dismantled with his slaves and hauled on cypress rollers twelve miles home overland. It took them five months. His house consisted at the time of one brick wall. He set the steamboat broadside on to the wall, where now the chipped and flaked gilding of the rococo cornices arched in faint splendor above the gilt lettering of the stateroom names above the jalousied doors.

Doom had been born merely a subchief, a Mingo, one of three children on the mother's side of the family. He made a journey—he was a young man then and New Orleans was a European city—from north Mississippi to New Orleans by keel boat, where he met the Chevalier Sœur Blonde de Vitry, a man whose social position, on its face, was as equivocal as Doom's own. In New Orleans, among the gamblers and cutthroats of the river front, Doom, under the tutelage of his patron, passed as the chief, the Man, the hereditary owner of that land which belonged to the male side of the family; it was the Chevalier de Vitry who spoke of him as *l'Homme* or *de l'Homme*, and hence Doom.

They were seen everywhere together—the Indian, the squat man with a bold, inscrutable, underbred face, and the Parisian, the expatriate, the friend, it was said, of Carondelet and the intimate of General Wilkinson. Then they disappeared, the two of them, vanishing from their old equivocal haunts and leaving behind them the legend of the sums which Doom was believed to have won, and some tale about a young woman, daughter of a fairly well-to-do West Indian family, the son and brother of whom sought Doom with a pistol about his old haunts for some time after his disappearance.

Six months later the young woman herself disappeared, boarding the Saint Louis packet, which put in one night at a wood landing on the north Mississippi side, where the woman, accompanied by a Negro maid, got off. Four Indians met her with a horse and wagon, and they traveled for three days, slowly, since she was already big with child, to the plantation, where she found that Doom was now chief. He never told her how he accomplished it, save that his uncle and his cousin had died suddenly. Before that time the house had consisted of a brick wall built by shiftless slaves, against which was propped a thatched lean-to divided into rooms and littered with bones and refuse, set in the center of ten thousand acres of matchless parklike forest where deer grazed like domestic cattle. Doom and the woman were married there a short time before Issetibbeha was born, by a combination itinerant minister and slave trader who arrived on a mule, to the saddle of which was lashed a cotton umbrella and a three-gallon demijohn of whiskey. After that, Doom began to acquire more slaves and to cultivate some of his land, as the white people did. But he never had enough for them to do. In utter idleness the majority of them led lives transplanted whole out of African jungles, save on the occasions when, entertaining guests, Doom coursed them with dogs.

When Doom died, Issetibbeha, his son, was nineteen. He became proprietor of the land and of the quintupled herd of blacks for which he had no use at all. Though the title of Man rested with him, there was a hierarchy of cousins and uncles who ruled the clan and who finally gathered in squatting conclave over the Negro question, squatting profoundly beneath the golden names above the doors of the steamboat.

"We cannot eat them," one said.

"Why not?"

"There are too many of them."

"That's true," a third said. "Once we started, we should have to eat them all. And that much flesh diet is not good for man."

"Perhaps they will be like deer flesh. That cannot hurt you."

"We might kill a few of them and not eat them," Issetibbeha said.

They looked at him for a while. "What for?" one said.

"That is true," a second said. "We cannot do that. They are too valuable; remember all the bother they have caused us, finding things for them to do. We must do as the white men do."

"How is that?" Issetibbeha said.

"Raise more Negroes by clearing more land to make corn to feed them, then sell them. We will clear the land and plant it with food and raise Negroes and sell them to the white men for money."

"But what will we do with this money?" a third said.

They thought for a while.

"We will see," the first said. They squatted, profound, grave.

"It means work," the third said.

"Let the Negroes do it," the first said.

"Yao. Let them. To sweat is bad. It is damp. It opens the pores."

"And then the night air enters."

"Yao. Let the Negroes do it. They appear to like sweating."

So they cleared the land with the Negroes and planted it in grain. Up to that time the slaves had lived in a huge pen with a lean-to roof over one corner, like a pen for pigs. But now they began to build quarters, cabins, putting the young Negroes in the cabins in pairs to mate; five years later Issetibbeha sold forty head to a Memphis trader, and he took the money and went abroad upon it, his maternal uncle from New Orleans conducting the trip. At that time the Chevalier Sœur Blonde de Vitry was an old man in Paris, in a toupee and a corset and a careful, toothless old face fixed in a grimace quizzical and profoundly tragic. He borrowed three hundred dollars from Issetibbeha and in return he introduced him into certain circles; a year later Issetibbeha returned home with a gilt bed, a pair of girandoles by whose light it was said that Pompadour arranged her hair while Louis smirked at his mirrored face across her powdered shoulder, and a pair of slippers with red heels. They were too small for him, since he had not worn shoes at all until he reached New Orleans on his way abroad.

He brought the slippers home in tissue paper and kept them in the remaining pocket of a pair of saddlebags filled with cedar shavings, save when he took them out on occasion for his son, Moketubbe, to play with. At three years of age Moketubbe had a broad, flat, Mongolian face that appeared to exist in a complete and unfathomable lethargy, until confronted by the slippers.

Moketubbe's mother was a comely girl whom Issetibbeha had seen one day working in her shift in a melon patch. He stopped and watched her for a while—the broad, solid thighs, the sound back, the serene face. He was on his way to the creek to fish that day, but he didn't go any farther; perhaps while he stood there watching the unaware girl he may have remembered his own mother, the city woman, the fugitive with her fans and laces and her Negro blood, and all the tawdry shabbiness of that sorry affair. Within the year Moketubbe was born; even at three he could not get his feet into the slippers. Watching him in the still, hot afternoons as he struggled with the slippers with a certain monstrous repudiation of fact, Issetibbeha laughed quietly to himself. He laughed at Moketubbe's antics with the shoes for several years, because Moketubbe did not give up trying to put them on until he was sixteen. Then he quit. Or Issetibbeha thought he had. But he had merely quit trying in Issetibbeha's presence. Issetibbeha's newest wife told him that Moketubbe had stolen and hidden the shoes. Issetibbeha quit laughing then, and he sent the woman away, so that he was alone. "Yao," he said. "I too like being alive, it seems." He sent for Moketubbe. "I give them to you," he said.

Moketubbe was twenty-five then, unmarried. Issetibbeha was not tall, but he was taller by six inches than his son and almost a hundred pounds lighter. Moketubbe was already diseased with flesh, with a pale, broad, inert face and dropsical hands and feet. "They are yours now," Issetibbeha said, watching him. Moketubbe had looked at him once when he entered, a glance brief, discreet, veiled.

"Thanks," he said.

Issetibbeha looked at him. He could never tell if Moketubbe saw anything, looked at anything. "Why will it not be the same if I give the slippers to you?"

"Thanks," Moketubbe said. Issetibbeha was using snuff at the time; a white man had shown him how to put the powder into his lip and scour it against his teeth with a twig of gum or of alphea.

"Well," he said, "a man cannot live forever." He looked at his son, then his gaze went blank in turn, unseeing, and he mused for an instant. You could not tell what he was thinking, save that he said half aloud: "Yao. But Doom's uncle had no shoes with red heels." He looked at his son again, fat, inert. "Beneath all that, a man might think of doing anything and it not be known until too late." He sat in a splint chair hammocked with deer thongs. "He cannot even get them on; he and I are both frustrated by the same gross meat which he wears. He cannot even get them on. But is that my fault?"

He lived for five years longer, then he died. He was sick one night, and though the doctor came in a skunkskin vest and burned sticks, Issetibbeha died before noon.

That was yesterday; the grave was dug, and for twelve hours now the People had been coming in wagons and carriages and on horseback and afoot, to eat the baked dog and the succotash and the yams cooked in ashes and to attend the funeral.

III

"It will be three days," Basket said, as he and the other Indian returned to the house. "It will be three days and the food will not be enough; I have seen it before."

The second Indian's name was Louis Berry. "He will smell too, in this weather."

"Yao. They are nothing but a trouble and a care."

"Maybe it will not take three days."

"They run far. Yao. We will smell this Man before he enters the earth. You watch and see if I am not right."

They approached the house.

"He can wear the shoes now," Berry said. "He can wear them now in man's sight."

"He cannot wear them for a while yet," Basket said. Berry looked at him. "He will lead the hunt."

"Moketubbe?" Berry said. "Do you think he will? A man to whom even talking is travail?"

"What else can he do? It is his own father who will soon begin to smell."

"That is true," Berry said. "There is even yet a price he must pay for the shoes. Yao. He has truly bought them. What do you think?"

"What do you think?"

"What do you think?"

"I think nothing."

"Nor do I. Issetibbeha will not need the shoes now. Let Moketubbe have them; Issetibbeha will not care."

"Yao. Man must die."

"Yao. Let him; there is still the Man."

The bark roof of the porch was supported by peeled

cypress poles, high above the texas of the steamboat, shading an unfloored banquette where on the trodden earth mules and horses were tethered in bad weather. On the forward end of the steamboat's deck sat an old man and two women. One of the women was dressing a fowl, the other was shelling corn. The old man was talking. He was barefoot, in a long linen frock coat and a beaver hat.

"This world is going to the dogs," he said. "It is being ruined by white men. We got along fine for years and years, before the white men foisted their Negroes upon us. In the old days the old men sat in the shade and ate stewed deer's flesh and corn and smoked tobacco and talked of honor and grave affairs; now what do we do? Even the old wear themselves into the grave taking care of them that like sweating." When Basket and Berry crossed the deck he ceased and looked up at them. His eyes were querulous, bleared; his face was myriad with tiny wrinkles. "He is fled also," he said.

"Yes," Berry said, "he is gone."

"I knew it. I told them so. It will take three weeks, like when Doom died. You watch and see."

"It was three days, not three weeks," Berry said.

"Were you there?"

"No," Berry said. "But I have heard."

"Well, I was there," the old man said. "For three whole weeks, through the swamps and the briers—" They went on and left him talking.

What had been the saloon of the steamboat was now a shell, rotting slowly; the polished mahogany, the carving glinting momentarily and fading through the mold in figures cabalistic and profound; the gutted windows were like cataracted eyes. It contained a few sacks of seed or grain, and the fore part of the running gear of a barouche, to the axle of which two C-springs rusted in graceful curves, supporting nothing. In one corner a fox cub ran steadily and soundlessly up and down a willow cage; three scrawny game-cocks moved in the dust, and the place was pocked and marked with their dried droppings.

They passed through the brick wall and entered a big room of chinked logs. It contained the hinder part of the barouche, and the dismantled body lying on its side, the window slatted over with willow withes, through which protruded the heads, the still, beady, outraged eyes and frayed combs of still more game chickens. It was floored with packed clay; in one corner leaned a crude plow and two hand-hewn boat paddles. From the ceiling, suspended by four deer thongs, hung the gilt bed which Issetibbeha had fetched from Paris. It had neither mattress nor springs, the frame criss-crossed now by a neat hammocking of thongs.

Issetibbeha had tried to have his newest wife, the young one, sleep in the bed. He was congenitally short of breath himself, and he passed the nights half reclining in his splint chair. He would see her to bed and, later, wakeful, sleeping as he did but three or four hours a night, he would sit in the darkness and simulate slumber and listen to her sneak infinitesimally from the gilt and ribboned bed, to lie on a quilt pallet on the floor until just before daylight. Then she would enter the bed quietly again and in turn simulate slumber, while in the darkness beside her Issetibbeha quietly laughed and laughed.

The girandoles were lashed by thongs to two sticks propped in a corner where a ten-gallon whiskey keg lay also. There was a clay hearth; facing it, in the splint chair, Moketubbe sat. He was maybe an inch better than five feet tall, and he weighed two hundred and fifty pounds. He wore a broadcloth coat and no shirt, his round, smooth copper balloon of belly swelling above the bottom piece of a suit of linen underwear. On his feet were the slippers with the red heels. Behind his chair stood a stripling with a punkah-like fan made of fringed paper. Moketubbe sat motionless, with his broad, yellow face with its closed eyes and flat nostrils, his flipper-like arms extended. On his face was an expression profound, tragic, and inert. He did not open his eyes when Basket and Berry came in.

"He has worn them since daylight?" Basket said.

"Since daylight," the stripling said. The fan did not cease. "You can see."

"Yao," Basket said. "We can see." Moketubbe did not move. He looked like an effigy, like a Malay god in frock coat, drawers, naked chest, the trivial scarlet-heeled shoes.

"I wouldn't disturb him, if I were you," the stripling said.

"Not if I were you," Basket said. He and Berry squatted. The stripling moved the fan steadily. "O Man," Basket said, "listen." Moketubbe did not move. "He is gone," Basket said.

"I told you so," the stripling said. "I knew he would flee. I told you."

"Yao," Basket said. "You are not the first to tell us afterward what we should have known before. Why is it that some of you wise men took no steps yesterday to prevent this?"

"He does not wish to die," Berry said.

"Why should he not wish it?" Basket said.

"Because he must die some day is no reason," the stripling said. "That would not convince me either, old man."

"Hold your tongue," Berry said.

"For twenty years," Basket said, "while others of his race sweat in the fields, he served the Man in the shade. Why should he not wish to die, since he did not wish to sweat?"

"And it will be quick," Berry said. "It will not take long."

"Catch him and tell him that," the stripling said.

"Hush," Berry said. They squatted, watching Moketubbe's face. He might have been dead himself. It was as though he were cased so in flesh that even breathing took place too deep within him to show.

"Listen, O Man," Basket said. "Issetibbeha is dead. He waits. His dog and his horse we have. But his slave has fled. The one who held the pot for him, who ate of his food, from his dish, is fled. Issetibbeha waits."

"Yao," Berry said.

"This is not the first time," Basket said. "This happened when Doom, thy grandfather, lay waiting at the door of the earth. He lay waiting three days, saying, 'Where is my Negro?' And Issetibbeha, thy father, answered, 'I will find him. Rest; I will bring him to you so that you may begin the journey.' "

"Yao," Berry said.

Moketubbe had not moved, had not opened his eyes.

"For three days Issetibbeha hunted in the bottom," Basket said. "He did not even return home for food, until the Negro was with him; then he said to Doom, his father, 'Here is thy dog, thy horse, thy Negro; rest.' Issetibbeha, who is dead since yesterday, said it. And now Issetibbeha's Negro is fled. His horse and his dog wait with him, but his Negro is fled."

"Yao," Berry said.

Moketubbe had not moved. His eyes were closed; upon his supine monstrous shape there was a colossal inertia, something profoundly immobile, beyond and impervious to flesh. They watched his face, squatting.

"When thy father was newly the Man, this happened," Basket said. "And it was Issetibbeha who brought back the slave to where his father waited to enter the earth."

Moketubbe's face had not moved, his eyes had not moved. After a while Basket said, "Remove the shoes."

The stripling removed the shoes. Moketubbe began to pant, his bare chest moving deep, as though he were rising from beyond his unfathomed flesh back into life, like up from the water, the sea. But his eyes had not opened yet.

Berry said, "He will lead the hunt."

"Yao," Basket said. "He is the Man. He will lead the hunt."

IV

All that day the Negro, Issetibbeha's body servant, hidden in the barn, watched Issetibbeha's dying. He was forty, a Guinea man. He had a flat nose, a close, small head; the inside corners of his eyes showed red a little, and his prominent gums were a pale bluish red above his square, broad teeth. He had been taken at fourteen by a trader off Kamerun, before his teeth had been filed. He had been Issetibbeha's body servant for twenty-three years.

On the day before, the day on which Issetibbeha lay sick, he returned to the quarters at dusk. In that unhurried hour the smoke of the cooking fires blew slowly across the street from door to door, carrying into the opposite one the smell of the identical meat and bread. The women tended them; the men were gathered at the head of the lane, watching him as he came down the slope from the house, putting his naked feet down carefully in a strange dusk. To the waiting men his eyeballs were a little luminous.

"Issetibbeha is not dead yet," the headman said.

"Not dead," the body servant said. "Who not dead?"

In the dusk they had faces like his, the different ages, the thoughts sealed inscrutable behind faces like the death masks of apes. The smell of the fires, the cooking, blew sharp and slow across the strange dusk, as from another world, above the lane and the pickaninnies naked in the dust.

"If he lives past sundown, he will live until daybreak," one said.

"Who says?"

"Talk says."

"Yao. Talk says. We know but one thing." They looked at the body servant as he stood among them, his eyeballs a little luminous. He was breathing slow and deep. His chest was bare; he was sweating a little. "He knows. He knows it."

"Let us let the drums talk."

"Yao. Let the drums tell it."

The drums began after dark. They kept them hidden in the creek bottom. They were made of hollowed cypress knees, and the Negroes kept them hidden; why, none knew. They were buried in the mud on the bank of a slough; a lad of fourteen guarded them. He was undersized, and a mute; he squatted in the mud there all day, clouded over with mosquitoes, naked save for the mud with which he coated himself against the mosquitoes, and about his neck a fiber bag containing a pig's rib to which black shreds of flesh still adhered, and two scaly barks on a wire. He slobbered onto his clutched knees, drooling; now and then Indians came noiselessly out of the bushes behind him and stood there and contemplated him for a while and went away, and he never knew it.

From the loft of the stable where he lay hidden until dark and after, the Negro could hear the drums. They were three miles away, but he could hear them as though they were in the barn itself below him, thudding and thudding. It was as though he could see the fire too, and the black limbs turning into and out of the flames in copper gleams. Only there would be no fire. There would be no more light there than where he lay in the dusty loft, with the whispering arpeggios of rat feet along the warm and immemorial ax-squared rafters. The only fire there would be the smudge against mosquitoes where the women were nursing children crouched, their heavy, sluggish breasts nippled full and smooth into the mouths of men children; contemplative, oblivious of the drumming, since a fire would signify life.

There was a fire in the steamboat, where Issetibbeha lay dying among his wives, beneath the lashed girandoles and the suspended bed. He could see the smoke, and just before sunset he saw the doctor come out, in a waistcoat made of skunk skins, and set fire to two clay-daubed sticks at the bows of the boat deck. "So he is not dead yet," the Negro said into the whispering gloom of the loft, answering himself; he could hear the two voices, himself and himself:

"Who not dead?"

"You are dead."

"Yao, I am dead," he said quietly. He wished to be where the drums were. He imagined himself springing out of the bushes, leaping among the drums on his bare, lean, greasy, invisible limbs. But he could not do that, because man leaped past life, into where death was; he dashed into death and did not die because when death took a man, it took him just this side of the end of living. It was when death over-

an him from behind, still in life. The thin whisper of rat
eet died in fainting gusts along the rafters. Once he had
aten rat. He was a boy then, but just come to America.
hey had lived ninety days in a three-foot-high 'tween deck
n tropic latitudes, hearing from topside the drunken New
England captain intoning aloud from a book which he did not
ecognize for ten years afterward to be the Bible. Squatting in
he stable so, he had watched the rat, civilized, by as-
ociation with man reft of its inherent cunning of limb and
ye; he had caught it without difficulty, with scarce a movement of his hand, and he ate it slowly, wondering how any
f the rats had escaped so long. At that time he was still
vearing the single white garment which the trader, a deacon
n the Unitarian church, had given him, and he spoke then
nly his native tongue.

He was naked now, save for a pair of dungaree pants
ought by Indians from white men, and an amulet slung on
 thong about his hips. The amulet consisted of one half
f a mother-of-pearl lorgnon which Issetibbeha had
rought back from Paris, and the skull of a cottonmouth moc-
asin. He had killed the snake himself and eaten it, save the
oison head. He lay in the loft, watching the house, the
teamboat, listening to the drums, thinking of himself among
he drums.

He lay there all night. The next morning he saw the doc-
or come out, in his skunk vest, and get on his mule and
ide away, and he became quite still and watched the final
ust from beneath the mule's delicate feet die away, and
hen he found that he was still breathing and it seemed
trange to him that he still breathed air, still needed air.
hen he lay and watched quietly, waiting to move, his eye-
alls a little luminous, but with a quiet light, and his breath-
ng light and regular, and saw Louis Berry come out and
ook at the sky. It was good light then, and already five In-
ians squatted in their Sunday clothes along the steamboat
eck; by noon there were twenty-five there. That afternoon
hey dug the trench in which the meat would be baked, and
he yams; by that time there were almost a hundred guests—
ecorous, quiet, patient in their stiff European finery—and he
atched Berry lead Issetibbeha's mare from the stable and
e her to a tree, and then he watched Berry emerge from the
ouse with the old hound which lay beside Issetibbeha's
hair. He tied the hound to the tree too, and it sat there,
ooking gravely about at the faces. Then it began to howl.
t was still howling at sundown, when the Negro climbed

down the back wall of the barn and entered the spring
branch, where it was already dusk. He began to run then. He
could hear the hound howling behind him, and near the
spring, already running, he passed another Negro. The two
men, the one motionless and the other running, looked for
an instant at each other as though across an actual boundary
between two different worlds. He ran on into full darkness,
mouth closed, fists doubled, his broad nostrils bellowing
steadily.

He ran on in the darkness. He knew the country well, because he had hunted it often with Issetibbeha, following
on his mule the course of the fox or the cat beside Issetibbeha's mare; he knew it as well as did the men who
would pursue him. He saw them for the first time shortly before sunset of the second day. He had run thirty miles
then, up the creek bottom, before doubling back; lying in
a pawpaw thicket he saw the pursuit for the first time. There
were two of them, in shirts and straw hats, carrying their
neatly rolled trousers under their arms, and they had no
weapons. They were middle-aged, paunchy, and they could
not have moved very fast anyway; it would be twelve hours
before they could return to where he lay watching them. "So
I will have until midnight to rest," he said. He was near
enough to the plantation to smell the cooking fires, and he
thought how he ought to be hungry, since he had not eaten
in thirty hours. "But it is more important to rest," he told
himself. He continued to tell himself that, lying in the
pawpaw thicket, because the effort of resting, the need and
the haste to rest, made his heart thud the same as the running had done. It was as though he had forgot how to rest,
as though the six hours were not long enough to do it in,
to remember again how to do it.

As soon as dark came he moved again. He had thought to
keep going steadily and quietly through the night, since there
was nowhere for him to go, but as soon as he moved he
began to run at top speed, breasting his panting chest, his
broad-flaring nostrils through the choked and whipping darkness. He ran for an hour, lost by then, without direction,
when suddenly he stopped, and after a time his thudding
heart unraveled from the sound of the drums. By the sound
they were not two miles away; he followed the sound until
he could smell the smudge fire and taste the acrid smoke.
When he stood among them the drums did not cease; only
the headman came to him where he stood in the drifting
smudge, panting, his nostrils flaring and pulsing, the hushed

glare of his ceaseless eyeballs in his mud-daubed face as though they were worked from lungs.

"We have expected thee," the headman said. "Go, now."

"Go?"

"Eat, and go. The dead may not consort with the living; thou knowest that."

"Yao. I know that." They did not look at one another. The drums had not ceased.

"Wilt thou eat?" the headman said.

"I am not hungry. I caught a rabbit this afternoon, and ate while I lay hidden."

"Take some cooked meat with thee, then."

He accepted the cooked meat, wrapped in leaves, and entered the creek bottom again; after a while the sound of the drums ceased. He walked steadily until daybreak. "I have twelve hours," he said. "Maybe more, since the trail was followed by night." He squatted and ate the meat and wiped his hands on his thighs. Then he rose and removed the dungaree pants and squatted again beside a slough and coated himself with mud—face, arms, body and legs—and squatted again, clasping his knees, his head bowed. When it was light enough to see, he moved back into the swamp and squatted again and went to sleep so. He did not dream at all. It was well that he moved, for, waking suddenly in broad daylight and the high sun, he saw the two Indians. They still carried their neatly rolled trousers; they stood opposite the place where he lay hidden, paunchy, thick, soft-looking, a little ludicrous in their straw hats and shirt tails.

"This is wearying work," one said.

"I'd rather be at home in the shade myself," the other said. "But there is the Man waiting at the door to the earth."

"Yao." They looked quietly about; stooping, one of them removed from his shirt tail a clot of cockleburs. "Damn that Negro," he said.

"Yao. When have they ever been anything but a trial and a care to us?"

In the early afternoon, from the top of a tree, the Negro looked down into the plantation. He could see Issetibbeha's body in a hammock between the two trees where the horse and the dog were tethered, and the concourse about the steamboat was filled with wagons and horses and mules, with carts and saddlehorses, while in bright clumps the women and the smaller children and the old men squatted about the long trench where the smoke from the barbecuing

meat blew slow and thick. The men and the big boys would
all be down there in the creek bottom behind him, on the
trail, their Sunday clothes rolled carefully up and wedged
into tree crotches. There was a clump of men near the door
to the house, to the saloon of the steamboat, though, and he
watched them, and after a while he saw them bring Moketubbe out in a litter made of buckskin and persimmon poles;
high hidden in his leafed nook the Negro, the quarry,
looked quietly down upon his irrevocable doom with an
expression as profound as Moketubbe's own. "Yao," he
said quietly. "He will go then. That man whose body has
been dead for fifteen years, he will go also."

In the middle of the afternoon he came face to face with
an Indian. They were both on a footlog across a slough—
the Negro gaunt, lean, hard, tireless and desperate; the Indian thick, soft-looking, the apparent embodiment of the
ultimate and the supreme reluctance and inertia. The Indian
made no move, no sound; he stood on the log and watched
the Negro plunge into the slough and swim ashore and crash
away into the undergrowth.

Just before sunset he lay behind a down log. Up the log
in slow procession moved a line of ants. He caught them
and ate them slowly, with a kind of detachment, like that of
a dinner guest eating salted nuts from a dish. They too had a
salt taste, engendering a salivary reaction out of all proportion. He ate them slowly, watching the unbroken line move
up the log and into oblivious doom with a steady and terrific undeviation. He had eaten nothing else all day; in
his caked mud mask his eyes rolled in reddened rims. At
sunset, creeping along the creek bank toward where he had
spotted a frog, a cottonmouth moccasin slashed him suddenly across the forearm with a thick, sluggish blow. It
struck clumsily, leaving two long slashes across his arm like
two razor slashes, and half sprawled with its own mo-
mentum and rage, it appeared for the moment utterly helpless with its own awkwardness and choleric anger. "Olé,
Grandfather," the Negro said. He touched its head and
watched it slash him again across his arm, and again, with
thick, raking, awkward blows. "It's that I do not wish to die,"
he said. Then he said it again—"It's that I do not wish to
die"—in a quiet tone, of slow and low amaze, as though it
were something that, until the words had said themselves,
he found that he had not known, or had not known the
depth and extent of his desire.

v

Moketubbe took the slippers with him. He could not wear
them very long while in motion, not even in the litter where
he was slung reclining, so they rested upon a square of
fawnskin upon his lap—the cracked, frail slippers a little
shapeless now, with their scaled patent-leather surface and
buckleless tongues and scarlet heels, lying upon the supine,
obese shape just barely alive, carried through swamp
and brier by swinging relays of men who bore steadily all
day long the crime and its object, on the business of the
slain. To Moketubbe it must have been as though, himself
immortal, he were being carried rapidly through hell by
doomed spirits which, alive, had contemplated his disaster,
and, dead, were oblivious partners to his damnation.

After resting for a while, the litter propped in the center
of the squatting circle and Moketubbe motionless in it, with
closed eyes and his face at once peaceful for the instant and
filled with inescapable foreknowledge, he could wear the
slippers for a while. The stripling put them on him, forcing
his big, tender, dropsical feet into them; whereupon into his
face came again that expression, tragic, passive, and profoundly attentive, which dyspeptics wear. Then they went
on. He made no move, no sound, inert in the rhythmic litter out of some reserve of inertia, or maybe of some kingly
virtue such as courage or fortitude. After a time they set
the litter down and looked at him, at the yellow face like
that of an idol, beaded over with sweat. Then Three Basket or
Louis Berry would say: "Take them off. Honor has been
served." They would remove the shoes. Moketubbe's face
would not alter, but only then would his breathing become
perceptible, going in and out of his pale lips with a faint ah-
ah-ah sound, and they would squat again while the couriers
and the runners came up.

"Not yet?"

"Not yet. He is going east. By sunset he will reach Mouth
of Tippah. Then he will turn back. We may take him tomorrow."

"Let us hope so. It will not be too soon."

"Yao. It has been three days now."

"When Doom died, it took only three days."

"But that was an old man. This one is young."

"Yao. A good race. If he is taken tomorrow, I will win
a horse."

"May you win it."

"Yao. This work is not pleasant."

That was the day on which the food gave out at the plantation. The guests returned home and came back the next day with more food, enough for a week longer. On that day Issetibbeha began to smell; they could smell him for a long way up and down the bottom when it got hot toward noon and the wind blew. But they didn't capture the Negro on that day, nor on the next. It was about dusk on the sixth day when the couriers came up to the litter; they had found blood. "He has injured himself."

"Not bad, I hope," Basket said. "We cannot send with Issetibbeha one who will be of no service to him."

"Nor whom Issetibbeha himself will have to nurse and care for," Berry said.

"We do not know," the courier said. "He has hidden himself. He has crept back into the swamp. We have left pickets."

They trotted with the litter now. The place where the Negro had crept into the swamp was an hour away. In the hurry and excitement they had forgotten that Moketubbe still wore the slippers; when they reached the place Moketubbe had fainted. They removed the slippers and brought him to.

With dark, they formed a circle about the swamp. They squatted, clouded over with gnats and mosquitoes; the evening star burned low and close down the west, and the constellations began to wheel overhead. "We will give him time," they said. "Tomorrow is just another name for today."

"Yao. Let him have time." Then they ceased, and gazed as one into the darkness where the swamp lay. After a while the noise ceased, and soon the courier came out of the darkness.

"He tried to break out."

"But you turned him back?"

"He turned back. We feared for a moment, the three of us. We could smell him creeping in the darkness, and we could smell something else, which we did not know. That was why we feared, until he told us. He said to slay him there, since it would be dark and he would not have to see the face when it came. But it was not that which we smelled; he told us what it was. A snake had struck him. That was two days ago. The arm swelled, and it smelled bad. But it was not that which we smelled then, because the swelling had gone down and his arm was no larger than that of a child. He showed us. We felt the arm, all of us did; it was no larger than that of a child. He said to give him a hatchet so he could chop the arm off. But tomorrow is today also."

"Yao. Tomorrow is today."

"We feared for a while. Then he went back into the swamp."

"That is good."

"Yao. We feared. Shall I tell the Man?"

"I will see," Basket said. He went away. The courier squatted, telling again about the Negro. Basket returned. "The Man says that it is good. Return to your post."

The courier crept away. They squatted about the litter; now and then they slept. Some time after midnight the Negro waked them. He began to shout and talk to himself, his voice coming sharp and sudden out of the darkness, then he fell silent. Dawn came; a white crane flapped slowly across the jonquil sky. Basket was awake. "Let us go now," he said. "It is today."

Two Indians entered the swamp, their movements noisy. Before they reached the Negro they stopped, because he began to sing. They could see him, naked and mud-caked, sitting on a log, singing. They squatted silently a short distance away, until he finished. He was chanting something in his own language, his face lifted to the rising sun. His voice was clear, full, with a quality wild and sad. "Let him have time," the Indians said, squatting, patient, waiting. He ceased and they approached. He looked back and up at them through the cracked mud mask. His eyes were bloodshot, his lips cracked upon his square short teeth. The mask of mud appeared to be loose on his face, as if he might have lost flesh since he put it there; he held his left arm close to his breast. From the elbow down it was caked and shapeless with black mud. They could smell him, a rank smell. He watched them quietly until one touched him on the arm. "Come," the Indian said. "You ran well. Do not be ashamed."

VI

As they neared the plantation in the tainted bright morning, the Negro's eyes began to roll a little, like those of a horse. The smoke from the cooking pit blew low along the earth and upon the squatting and waiting guests about the yard and upon the steamboat deck, in their bright, stiff, harsh finery; the women, the children, the old men. They had sent couriers along the bottom, and another on ahead, and Issetibbeha's body had already been removed to where the grave waited, along with the horse and the dog, though they could still smell him in death about the house where he had lived in life. The guests were beginning to move toward the grave when the bearers of Moketubbe's litter mounted the slope.

The Negro was the tallest there, his high, close, mud-caked head looming above them all. He was breathing hard, as though the desperate effort of the six suspended and desperate days had capitulated upon him at once; although they walked slowly, his naked scarred chest rose and fell above the close-clutched left arm. He looked this way and that continuously, as if he were not seeing, as though sight never quite caught up with the looking. His mouth was open a little upon his big white teeth; he began to pant. The already moving guests halted, pausing, looking back, some with pieces of meat in their hands, as the Negro looked about at their faces with his wild, restrained, unceasing eyes.

"Will you eat first?" Basket said. He had to say it twice.

"Yes," the Negro said. "That's it. I want to eat."

The throng had begun to press back toward the center; the word passed to the outermost: "He will eat first."

They reached the steamboat. "Sit down," Basket said. The Negro sat on the edge of the deck. He was still panting, his chest rising and falling, his head ceaseless with its white eyeballs, turning from side to side. It was as if the inability to see came from within, from hopelessness, not from absence of vision. They brought food and watched quietly as he tried to eat it. He put the food into his mouth and chewed it, but chewing, the half-masticated matter began to emerge from the corners of his mouth and to drool down his chin, onto his chest, and after a while he stopped chewing and sat there, naked, covered with dried mud, the plate on his knees, and his mouth filled with a mass of chewed food, open, his eyes wide and unceasing, panting and panting. They watched him, patient, implacable, waiting.

"Come," Basket said at last.

"It's water I want," the Negro said. "I want water."

The well was a little way down the slope toward the quarters. The slope lay dappled with the shadows of noon, of that peaceful hour when, Issetibbeha napping in his chair and waiting for the noon meal and the long afternoon to sleep in, the Negro, the body servant, would be free. He would sit in the kitchen door then, talking with the women that prepared the food. Beyond the kitchen the lane between the quarters would be quiet, peaceful, with the women talking to one another across the lane and the smoke of the dinner fires blowing upon the pickaninnies like ebony toys in the dust.

"Come," Basket said.

The Negro walked among them, taller than any. The guests were moving on toward where Issetibbeha and the horse and the dog waited. The Negro walked with his high ceaseless head, his panting chest. "Come," Basket said. "You wanted water."

"Yes," the Negro said. "Yes." He looked back at the house, then down to the quarters, where today no fire burned, no face showed in any door, no pickaninny in the dust, panting. "It struck me here, raking me across this arm; once, twice, three times. I said, 'Olé, Grandfather.' "

"Come now," Basket said. The Negro was still going through the motion of walking, his knee action high, his head high, as though he were on a treadmill. His eyeballs had a wild, restrained glare, like those of a horse. "You wanted water," Basket said. "Here it is."

There was a gourd in the well. They dipped it full and gave it to the Negro, and they watched him try to drink. His eyes had not ceased rolling as he tilted the gourd slowly against his caked face. They could watch his throat working and the bright water cascading from either side of the gourd, down his chin and breast. Then the water stopped. "Come," Basket said.

"Wait," the Negro said. He dipped the gourd again and tilted it against his face, beneath his ceaseless eyes. Again they watched his throat working and the unswallowed water sheathing broken and myriad down his chin, channeling his caked chest. They waited, patient, grave, decorous, implacable; clansman and guest and kin. Then the water ceased, though still the empty gourd tilted higher and higher, and still his black throat aped the vain motion of his frustrated swallowing. A piece of water-loosened mud carried away from his chest and broke at his muddy feet, and in the empty gourd they could hear his breath: ah-ah-ah.

"Come," Basket said, taking the gourd from the Negro and hanging it back in the well.

FLANNERY O'CONNOR

Wise Blood

AUTHOR'S NOTE

WISE BLOOD has reached the age of ten and is still alive. My critical powers are just sufficient to determine this, and I am gratified to be able to say it. The book was written with zest and, if possible, it should be read that way. It is a comic novel about a Christian *malgré lui*, and as such, very serious, for all comic novels that are any good must be about matters of life and death. *Wise Blood* was written by an author congenitally innocent of theory, but one with certain preoccupations. That belief in Christ is to some a matter of life and death has been a stumbling block for readers who would prefer to think it a matter of no great consequence. For them Hazel Motes' integrity lies in his trying with such vigor to get rid of the ragged figure who moves from tree to tree in the back of his mind. For the author Hazel's integrity lies in his not being able to. Does one's integrity ever lie in what he is not able to do? I think that usually it does, for free will does not mean one will, but many wills conflicting in one man. Freedom cannot be conceived simply. It is a mystery and one which a novel, even a comic novel, can only be asked to deepen.

—1962

FOR REGINA

I

HAZEL MOTES sat at a forward angle on the green plush train seat, looking one minute at the window as if he might want to jump out of it, and the next down the aisle at the other end of the car. The train was racing through tree tops that fell away at intervals and showed the sun standing, very red, on the edge of the farthest woods. Nearer, the plowed fields curved and faded and the few hogs nosing in the furrows looked like large spotted stones. Mrs. Wally Bee Hitchcock, who was facing Motes in the section, said that she thought the early evening like this was the prettiest time of day and she asked him if he didn't think so too. She was a fat woman with pink collars and cuffs and pear-shaped legs that slanted off the train seat and didn't reach the floor.

He looked at her a second and, without answering, leaned forward and stared down the length of the car again. She turned to see what was back there but all she saw was a child peering around one of the sections and, farther up at the end of the car, the porter opening the closet where the sheets were kept.

"I guess you're going home," she said, turning back to him again. He didn't look, to her, much over twenty, but he had a stiff black broad-brimmed hat on his lap, a hat that an elderly country preacher would wear. His suit was a glaring blue and the price tag was still stapled on the sleeve of it.

He didn't answer her or move his eyes from whatever he was looking at. The sack at his feet was an army duffel bag and she decided that he had been in the army and had been released and that now he was going home. She wanted to get close enough to see what the suit had cost him but she found herself squinting instead at his eyes, trying almost to look into them. They were the color of pecan shells and set in deep sockets. The outline of a skull under his skin was plain and insistent.

She felt irked and wrenched her attention loose and squinted at the price tag. The suit had cost him $11.98. She felt that that placed him and looked at his face again as if she were fortified against it now. He had a nose like a shrike's bill and a long vertical crease on either side of his mouth; his hair looked as if it had been permanently flattened under the heavy hat, but his eyes were what held her attention longest. Their settings were so deep that they seemed, to her, almost like passage leading somewhere and she leaned halfway across the space that separated the two seats, trying to see into them. He turned toward the window suddenly and then almost as quickly turned back again to where his stare had been fixed.

What he was looking at was the porter. When he had first got on the train, the porter had been standing between the two cars—a thick-figured man with a round yellow bald head. Haze had stopped and the porter's eyes had turned toward him and away, indicating which car he was to go into. When he didn't go, the porter said, "To the left," irritably, "to the left," and Haze had moved on.

"Well," Mrs. Hitchcock said, "there's no place like home."

He gave her a glance and saw the flat of her face, reddish under a cap of fox-colored hair. She had got on two stops back. He had never seen her before that. "I got to go see the porter," he said. He got up and went toward the end of the car where the porter had begun making up a berth. He stopped beside him and leaned on a seat arm, but the porter didn't look at him. He was pulling a wall of the section farther out.

"How long does it take you to make one up?"

"Seven minutes," the porter said, not looking at him.

Haze sat down on the seat arm. He said, "I'm from Eastrod."

"That isn't on this line," the porter said. "You on the wrong train."

"Going to the city," Haze said. "I said I was raised in Eastrod."

The porter didn't say anything.

"Eastrod," Haze said, louder.

The porter jerked the shade down. "You want your berth made up now, or what you standing there for?" he asked.

"Eastrod," Haze said. "Near Melsy."

The porter wrenched one side of the seat flat. "I'm from Chicago," he said. He wrenched the other side down. When he bent over, the back of his neck came out in three bulges.

"Yeah, I bet you are," Haze said with a leer.

"Your feet in the middle of the aisle. Somebody going to want to get by you," the porter said, turning suddenly and brushing past.

Haze got up and hung there a few seconds. He looked as if he were held by a rope caught in the middle of his back and attached to the train ceiling. He watched the porter move in a fine controlled lurch down the aisle and disappear at the other end of the car. He knew him to be a Parrum nigger from Eastrod. He went back to his section and folded into a slouched position and settled one foot on a pipe that ran under the window. Eastrod filled his head and then went out beyond and filled the space that stretched from the train across the empty darkening fields. He saw the two houses and the rust-colored road and the few Negro shacks and the one barn and the stall with the red and white CCC snuff ad peeling across the side of it.

"Are you going home?" Mrs. Hitchcock asked.

He looked at her sourly and gripped the black hat by the brim. "No, I ain't," he said in a sharp high nasal Tennessee voice.

Mrs. Hitchcock said neither was she. She told him she had been a Miss Weatherman before she married and that she was going to Florida to visit her married daughter, Sarah Lucile. She said it seemed like she had never had time to take a trip that far off. The way things happened, one thing after another, it seemed like time went by so fast you couldn't tell if you were young or old.

He thought he could tell her she was old if she asked him. He stopped listening to her after a while. The porter passed back up the aisle and didn't look at him. Mrs. Hitchcock lost her train of talk. "I guess you're on your way to visit somebody?" she asked.

"Going to Taulkinham," he said and ground himself into the seat and looked at the window. "Don't know nobody there, but I'm going to do some things.

"I'm going to do some things I never have done before," he said and gave her a sidelong glance and curled his mouth slightly.

She said she knew an Albert Sparks from Taulkinham. She said he was her sister-in-law's brother-in-law and that he . . .

"I ain't from Taulkinham," he said. "I said I'm going there, that's all." Mrs. Hitchcock began to talk again but he cut her short and said, "That porter was raised in the same place where I was raised but he says he's from Chicago."

Mrs. Hitchcock said she knew a man who lived in Chi . . .

"You might as well go one place as another," he said. "That's all I know."

Mrs. Hitchcock said well that time flies. She said she hadn't seen her sister's children in five years and she didn't know if she'd know them if she saw them. There were three of them, Roy, Bubber, and John Wesley. John Wesley was six years old and he had written her a letter, dear Mammadoll. They called her Mammadoll and her husband Papadoll . . .

"I reckon you think you been redeemed," he said.

Mrs. Hitchcock snatched at her collar.

"I reckon you think you been redeemed," he repeated.

She blushed. After a second she said yes, life was an inspiration and then she said she was hungry and asked him if he didn't want to go into the diner. He put on the fierce black hat and followed her out of the car.

The dining car was full and people were waiting to get in it. He and Mrs. Hitchcock stood in line for a half-hour, rocking in the narrow passageway and every few minutes flattening themselves against the side to let a trickle of people through. Mrs. Hitchcock talked to the woman on the side of her. Hazel Motes looked at the wall. Mrs. Hitchcock told the woman about her sister's husband who was with the City Water Works in Toolafalls, Alabama, and the lady told about a cousin who had cancer of the throat. Finally they got almost up to the entrance of the diner and could see inside it. There was a steward beckoning people to places and handing out menus. He was a white man with greased black hair and a greased black look to his suit. He moved like a crow, darting from table to table. He motioned for two people and the line moved up so that Haze and Mrs. Hitchcock and the lady she was talking to were ready to go next. In a minute two more people left. The steward beckoned and Mrs. Hitchcock and the woman walked in and Haze followed them. The man stopped him and said, "Only two," and pushed him back to the doorway.

Haze's face turned an ugly red. He tried to get behind the next person and then he tried to get through the line to go back to the car he had come from but there were too many people bunched in the opening. He had to stand there while everyone around looked at him. No one left for a while. Finally a woman at the far end of the car got up and the steward jerked his hand. Haze hesitated and saw the hand jerk again. He lurched up the aisle, falling against two tables on the way and getting his hand wet in somebody's coffee. The steward placed him with three youngish women dressed like parrots.

Their hands were resting on the table, red-speared at the tips. He sat down and wiped his hand on the tablecloth. He didn't take off his hat. The women had finished eating and were smoking cigarettes. They stopped talking when he sat down. He pointed to the first thing on the menu and the steward, standing over him, said, "Write it down, sonny," and winked at one of the women; she made a noise in her nose. He wrote it down and the steward went away with it. He sat and looked in front of him, glum and intense, at

the neck of the woman across from him. At intervals her
hand holding the cigarette would pass the spot on her neck;
it would go out of his sight and then it would pass again,
going back down to the table; in a second a straight line of
smoke would blow in his face. After it had blown at him
three or four times, he looked at her. She had a bold game-
hen expression and small eyes pointed directly on him.

"If you've been redeemed," he said, "I wouldn't want to
be." Then he turned his head to the window. He saw his pale
reflection with the dark empty space outside coming through
it. A boxcar roared past, chopping the empty space in two,
and one of the women laughed.

"Do you think I believe in Jesus?" he said, leaning toward
her and speaking almost as if he were breathless. "Well I
wouldn't even if He existed. Even if He was on this train."

"Who said you had to?" she asked in a poisonous Eastern
voice.

He drew back.

The waiter brought his dinner. He began eating slowly
at first, then faster as the women concentrated on watching
the muscles that stood out on his jaw when he chewed. He
was eating something spotted with eggs and livers. He finished that and drank his coffee and then pulled his money
out. The steward saw him but he wouldn't come total the
bill. Every time he passed the table, he would wink at the
women and stare at Haze. Mrs. Hitchcock and the lady had
already finished and gone. Finally the man came and added
up the bill. Haze shoved the money at him and then pushed
past him out of the car.

For a while he stood between two train cars where there
was fresh air of a sort and made a cigarette. Then the
porter passed between the two cars. "Hey you Parrum," he
called.

The porter didn't stop.

Haze followed him into the car. All the berths were made
up. The man in the station in Melsy had sold him a berth
because he said he would have to sit up all night in the
coaches; he had sold him an upper one. Haze went to it and
pulled his sack down and went into the men's room and got
ready for the night. He was too full and he wanted to hurry
and get in the berth and lie down. He thought he would lie
there and look out the window and watch how the country
went by a train at night. A sign said to get the porter to let
you into the uppers. He stuck his sack up into his berth
and then went to look for the porter. He didn't find him at

one end of the car and he started back to the other. Going around the corner he ran into something heavy and pink; it gasped and muttered, "Clumsy!" It was Mrs. Hitchcock in a pink wrapper, with her hair in knots around her head. She looked at him with her eyes squinted nearly shut. The knobs framed her face like dark toadstools. She tried to get past him and he tried to let her but they were both moving the same way each time. Her face became purplish except for little white marks over it that didn't heat up. She drew herself stiff and stopped and said, "What is the matter with you?" He slipped past her and dashed down the aisle and ran into the porter so that the porter fell down.

"You got to let me into the berth, Parrum," he said.

The porter picked himself up and went lurching down the aisle and after a minute he came lurching back again, stone-faced, with the ladder. Haze stood watching him while he put the ladder up; then he started up it. Halfway up, he turned and said, "I remember you. Your father was a nigger named Cash Parrum. You can't go back there neither, nor anybody else, not if they wanted to."

"I'm from Chicago," the porter said in an irritated voice. "My name is not Parrum."

"Cash is dead," Haze said. "He got the cholera from a pig."

The porter's mouth jerked down and he said, "My father was a railroad man."

Haze laughed. The porter jerked the ladder off suddenly with a wrench of his arm that sent the boy clutching at the blanket into the berth. He lay on his stomach for a few minutes and didn't move. After a while he turned and found the light and looked around him. There was no window. He was closed up in the thing except for a little space over the curtain. The top of the berth was low and curved over. He lay down and noticed that the curved top looked as if it were not quite closed; it looked as if it were closing. He lay there for a while, not moving. There was something in his throat like a sponge with an egg taste; he didn't want to turn over for fear it would move. He wanted the light off. He reached up without turning and felt for the button and snapped it and the darkness sank down on him and then faded a little with light from the aisle that came in through the foot of space not closed. He wanted it all dark, he didn't want it diluted. He heard the porter's footsteps coming down the aisle, soft into the rug, coming steadily down, brushing against the green curtains and fading up the other way out of hearing. Then after a while when he was almost asleep, he thought he heard them again coming back. His curtains stirred and the footsteps faded.

In his half-sleep he thought where he was lying was like a coffin. The first coffin he had seen with someone in it was his grandfather's. They had left it propped open with a stick of kindling the night it had sat in the house with the old man in it, and Haze had watched from a distance, thinking: he ain't going to let them shut it on him; when the time comes, his elbow is going to shoot into the crack. His grandfather had been a circuit preacher, a waspish old man who had ridden over three counties with Jesus hidden in his head like a stinger. When it was time to bury him, they shut the top of his box down and he didn't make a move.

Haze had had two younger brothers; one died in infancy and was put in a small box. The other fell in front of a mowing machine when he was seven. His box was about half the size of an ordinary one, and when they shut it, Haze ran and opened it up again. They said it was because he was heartbroken to part with his brother, but it was not; it was because he had thought, what if he had been in it and they had shut it on him.

He was asleep now and he dreamed he was at his father's burying again. He saw him humped over on his hands and knees in his coffin, being carried that way to the graveyard. "If I keep my can in the air," he heard the old man say, "nobody can shut nothing on me," but when they got his box to the hole, they let it drop down with a thud and his father flattened out like anybody else. The train jolted and stirred him half awake again and he thought, there must have been twenty-five people in Eastrod then, three Motes. Now there were no more Motes, no more Ashfields, no more Blasengames, Feys, Jacksons . . . or Parrums—even niggers wouldn't have it. Turning in the road, he saw in the dark the store boarded and the barn leaning and the smaller house half carted away, the porch gone and no floor in the hall.

It had not been that way when he was eighteen years old and had left it. Then there had been ten people there and he had not noticed that it had got smaller from his father's time. He had left it when he was eighteen years old because the army had called him. He had thought at first he would shoot his foot and not go. He was going to be a preacher like his grandfather and a preacher can always do without a foot. A preacher's power is in his neck and tongue and arm. His grandfather had traveled three counties in a Ford automobile. Every fourth Saturday he had driven into Eastrod as if he were just in time to save them all from Hell, and he was shouting before he had the car door open. People gathered around his Ford because he seemed to dare them to. He would climb up on the nose of it and preach from there and sometimes he would climb onto the top of it and shout down at them. They were like stones! he would shout. But Jesus had died to redeem them! Jesus was so soul-hungry that He had died, one death for all, but He would have died every soul's death for one! Did they understand that? Did they understand that for each stone soul, He would have died ten million deaths, had His arms and legs stretched on the cross and nailed ten million times for one of them? (The old man would point to his grandson, Haze. He had a particular disrespect for him because his own face was repeated almost exactly in the child's and seemed to mock him.) Did they know that even for that boy there, for that mean sinful unthinking boy standing there with his dirty hands clenching and unclenching at his sides, Jesus would die ten million deaths before He would let him lose his soul? He would chase him over the waters of sin! Did they doubt Jesus could walk on the waters of sin? That boy had been redeemed and Jesus wasn't going to leave him ever. Jesus would never let him forget he was redeemed. What did the sinner think there was to be gained? Jesus would have him in the end!

The boy didn't need to hear it. There was already a deep black wordless conviction in him that the way to avoid Jesus was to avoid sin. He knew by the time he was twelve years old that he was going to be a preacher. Later he saw Jesus move from tree to tree in the back of his mind, a wild ragged figure motioning him to turn around and come off into the dark where he was not sure of his footing, where he might be walking on the water and not know it and then suddenly know it and drown. Where he wanted to stay was in Eastrod with his two eyes open, and his hands always handling the familiar thing, his feet on the known track, and his tongue not too loose. When he was eighteen and the army called him, he saw the war as a trick to lead him into temptation, and he would have shot his foot except that he trusted himself to get back in a few months, uncorrupted. He had a strong confidence in his power to resist evil; it was something he had inherited, like his face, from his grandfather.

He thought that if the government wasn't through with him in four months, he would leave anyway. He had thought, then when he was eighteen years old, that he would give them exactly four months of his time. He was gone four years; he didn't get back, even for a visit.

The only things from Eastrod he took into the army with him were a black Bible and a pair of silver-rimmed spectacles that had belonged to his mother. He had gone to a country school where he had learned to read and write but that it was wiser not to; the Bible was the only book he read. He didn't read it often but when he did he wore his mother's glasses. They tired his eyes so that after a short time he was always obliged to stop. He meant to tell anyone in the army who invited him to sin that he was from Eastrod, Tennessee, and that he meant to get back there and stay back there, that he was going to be a preacher of the gospel and that he wasn't going to have his soul damned by the government or by any foreign place it sent him to.

After a few weeks in the camp, when he had some friends —they were not actually friends but he had to live with them—he was offered the chance he had been waiting for; the invitation. He took his mother's glasses out of his pocket and put them on. Then he told them he wouldn't go with them for a million dollars and a feather bed to lie on; he said he was from Eastrod, Tennessee, and that he was not going to have his soul damned by the government or any foreign place they . . . but his voice cracked and he didn't finish. He only stared at them, trying to steel his face. His friends told him that nobody was interested in his goddam soul unless it was the priest and he managed to answer that no priest taking orders from no pope was going to tamper with his soul. They told him he didn't have any soul and left for their brothel.

He took a long time to believe them because he wanted to believe them. All he wanted was to believe them and get rid of it once and for all, and he saw the opportunity here to get rid of it without corruption, to be converted to nothing instead of to evil. The army sent him halfway around the world and forgot him. He was wounded and they remembered him long enough to take the shrapnel out of his chest —they said they took it out but they never showed it to him and he felt it still in there, rusted, and poisoning him—and then they sent him to another desert and forgot him again. He had all the time he could want to study his soul in and assure himself that it was not there. When he was thoroughly

convinced, he saw that this was something that he had always
known. The misery he had was a longing for home; it had
nothing to do with Jesus. When the army finally let him go,
he was pleased to think that he was still uncorrupted. All
he wanted was to get back to Eastrod, Tennessee. The black
Bible and his mother's glasses were still in the bottom of
his duffel bag. He didn't read any book now but he kept the
Bible because it had come from home. He kept the glasses
in case his vision should ever become dim.

When the army had released him two days before in a
city about three hundred miles north of where he wanted
to be, he had gone immediately to the railroad station there
and bought a ticket to Melsy, the nearest railroad stop to
Eastrod. Then since he had to wait four hours for the train,
he went into a dark dry-goods store near the station. It was
a thin cardboard-smelling store that got darker as it got
deeper. He went deep into it and was sold a blue suit and
a dark hat. He had his army suit put in a paper sack and he
stuffed it into a trashbox on the corner. Once outside in the
light, the new suit turned glare-blue and the lines of the hat
seemed to stiffen fiercely.

He was in Melsy at five o'clock in the afternoon and he
caught a ride on a cotton-seed truck that took him more
than half the distance to Eastrod. He walked the rest of
the way and got there at nine o'clock at night, when it had
just got dark. The house was as dark as the night and open
to it and though he saw that the fence around it had partly
fallen and that weeds were growing through the porch floor,
he didn't realize all at once that it was only a shell, that
there was nothing here but the skeleton of a house. He
twisted an envelope and struck a match to it and went
through all the empty rooms, upstairs and down. When the
envelope burnt out, he lit another one and went through
them all again. That night he slept on the floor in the kitchen,
and a board fell on his head out of the roof and cut his face.

There was nothing left in the house but the chifforobe in
the kitchen. His mother had always slept in the kitchen and
had her walnut chifforobe in there. She had given thirty
dollars for it and hadn't bought herself anything else big
again. Whoever had got everything else, had left that. He
opened all the drawers. There were two lengths of wrapping
cord in the top one and nothing in the others. He was surprised nobody had come and stolen a chifforobe like that.
He took the wrapping cord and tied it around the legs and
through the floor boards and left a piece of paper in each of

the drawers: THIS SHIFFER-ROBE BELONGS TO HAZEL MOTES.
DO NOT STEAL IT OR YOU WILL BE HUNTED DOWN AND KILLED.

He thought about the chifforobe in his half-sleep and decided his mother would rest easier in her grave, knowing
it was guarded. If she came looking any time at night, she
would see. He wondered if she walked at night and came
there ever. She would come with that look on her face, un-
rested and looking; the same look he had seen through the
crack of her coffin. He had seen her face through the crack
when they were shutting the top on her. He was sixteen then.
He had seen the shadow that came down over her face and
pulled her mouth down as if she wasn't any more satisfied
dead than alive, as if she were going to spring up and
shove the lid back and fly out and satisfy herself: but they
shut it. She might have been going to fly out of there, she
might have been going to spring. He saw her in his sleep,
terrible, like a huge bat, dart from the closing, fly out of
there, but it was falling dark on top of her, closing down
all the time. From inside he saw it closing, coming closer
closer down and cutting off the light and the room. He
opened his eyes and saw it closing and he sprang up between
the crack and wedged his head and shoulders through it and
hung there, dizzy, with the dim light of the train slowly
showing the rug below. He hung there over the top of the
berth curtain and saw the porter at the other end of the car,
a white shape in the darkness, standing there watching him
and not moving.

"I'm sick!" he called. "I can't be closed up in this thing.
Get me out!"

The porter stood watching him and didn't move.

"Jesus," Haze said, "Jesus."

The porter didn't move. "Jesus been a long time gone," he
said in a sour triumphant voice.

II

He didn't get to the city until six the next evening. That
morning he had got off the train at a junction stop to get
some air and while he had been looking the other way, the
train had slid off. He had run after it but his hat had blown
away and he had had to run in the other direction to save
the hat. Fortunately, he had carried his duffel bag out with
him lest someone should steal something out of it. He had to
wait six hours at the junction stop until the right train came.
When he got to Taulkinham, as soon as he stepped off

the train, he began to see signs and lights. PEANUTS, WESTERN UNION, AJAX, TAXI, HOTEL, CANDY. Most of them were electric and moved up and down or blinked frantically. He walked very slowly, carrying his duffel bag by the neck. His head turned to one side and then the other, first toward one sign and then another. He walked the length of the station and then he walked back as if he might be going to get on the train again. His face was stern and determined under the heavy hat. No one observing him would have known that he had no place to go. He walked up and down the crowded waiting room two or three times, but he did not want to sit on the benches there. He wanted a private place to go to.

Finally he pushed open a door at one end of the station where a plain black and white sign said, MEN'S TOILET. WHITE. He went into a narrow room lined on one side with washbasins and on the other with a row of wooden stalls. The walls of this room had once been a bright cheerful yellow but now they were more nearly green and were decorated with handwriting and with various detailed drawings of the parts of the body of both men and women. Some of the stalls had doors on them and on one of the doors, written with what must have been a crayon, was the large word, WELCOME, followed by three exclamation points and something that looked like a snake. Haze entered this one.

He had been sitting in the narrow box for some time, studying the inscriptions on the sides and door, before he noticed one that was to the left over the toilet paper. It was written in a drunken-looking hand. It said,

> Mrs. Leora Watts!
> 60 Buckley Road
> The friendliest bed in town!
> Brother.

After a while he took a pencil out of his pocket and wrote down the address on the back of an envelope.

Outside he got in a yellow taxi and told the driver where he wanted to go. The driver was a small man with a big leather cap on his head and the tip of a cigar coming out from the center of his mouth. They had driven a few blocks before Haze noticed him squinting at him through the rear-view mirror. "You ain't no friend of hers, are you?" the driver asked.

"I never saw her before," Haze said.

"Where'd you hear about her? She don't usually have no preachers for company." He did not disturb the position of the cigar when he spoke; he was able to speak on either side of it.

"I ain't any preacher," Haze said, frowning. "I only seen her name in the toilet."

"You look like a preacher," the driver said. "That hat looks like a preacher's hat."

"It ain't," Haze said, and leaned forward and gripped the back of the front seat. "It's just a hat."

They stopped in front of a small one-story house between a filling station and a vacant lot. Haze got out and paid his fare through the window.

"It ain't only the hat," the driver said. "It's a look in your face somewheres."

"Listen," Haze said, tilting the hat over one eye, "I'm not a preacher."

"I understand," the driver said. "It ain't anybody perfect on this green earth of God's, preachers nor nobody else. And you can tell people better how terrible sin is if you know from your own personal experience."

Haze put his head in at the window, knocking the hat accidentally straight again. He seemed to have knocked his face straight too for it became completely expressionless. "Listen," he said, "get this: I don't believe in anything."

The driver took the stump of cigar out of his mouth. "Not in nothing at all?" he asked, leaving his mouth open after the question.

"I don't have to say it but once to nobody," Haze said.

The driver closed his mouth and after a second he returned the piece of cigar to it. "That's the trouble with you preachers," he said. "You've all got too good to believe in anything," and he drove off with a look of disgust and righteousness.

Haze turned and looked at the house he was going into. It was little more than a shack but there was a warm glow in one front window. He went up on the front porch and put his eye to a convenient crack in the shade, and found himself looking directly at a large white knee. After some time he moved away from the crack and tried the front door. It was not locked and he went into a small dark hall with a door on either side of it. The door to the left was cracked and let out a narrow shaft of light. He moved into the light and looked through the crack.

Mrs. Watts was sitting alone in a white iron bed, cut-

ting her toenails with a large pair of scissors. She was a big
woman with very yellow hair and white skin that glistened
with a greasy preparation. She had on a pink nightgown that
would better have fit a smaller figure.

Haze made a noise with the doorknob and she looked up
and observed him standing behind the crack. She had a bold
steady penetrating stare. After a minute, she turned it away
from him and began cutting her toenails again.

He went in and stood looking around him. There was
nothing much in the room but the bed and a bureau and
a rocking chair full of dirty clothes. He went to the bureau
and fingered a nail file and then an empty jelly glass while
he looked into the yellowish mirror and watched Mrs. Watts,
slightly distorted, grinning at him. His senses were stirred
to the limit. He turned quickly and went to her bed and sat
down on the far corner of it. He drew a long draught of air
through one side of his nose and began to run his hand carefully along the sheet.

The pink tip of Mrs. Watts's tongue appeared and
moistened her lower lip. She seemed just as glad to see him
as if he had been an old friend but she didn't say anything.

He picked up her foot, which was heavy but not cold,
and moved it about an inch to one side, and kept his hand
on it.

Mrs. Watts's mouth split in a wide full grin that showed
her teeth. They were small and pointed and speckled with
green and there was a wide space between each one. She
reached out and gripped Haze's arm just above the elbow.
"You huntin' something?" she drawled.

If she had not had him so firmly by the arm, he might
have leaped out the window. Involuntarily his lips formed
the words, "Yes, mam," but no sound came through them.

"Something on your mind?" Mrs. Watts asked, pulling his
rigid figure a little closer.

"Listen," he said, keeping his voice tightly under control,
"I come for the usual business."

Mrs. Watts's mouth became more round, as if she were
perplexed at this waste of words. "Make yourself at home,"
she said simply.

They stared at each other for almost a minute and neither
moved. Then he said in a voice that was higher than his usual
voice, "What I mean to have you know is: I'm no goddam
preacher."

Mrs. Watts eyed him steadily with only a slight smirk.
Then she put her other hand under his face and tickled

it in a motherly way. "That's okay, son," she said. "Momma don't mind if you ain't a preacher."

<hr>

III

His second night in Taulkinham, Hazel Motes walked along down town close to the store fronts but not looking in them. The black sky was underpinned with long silver streaks that looked like scaffolding and depth on depth behind it were thousands of stars that all seemed to be moving very slowly as if they were about some vast construction work that involved the whole order of the universe and would take all time to complete. No one was paying any attention to the sky. The stores in Taulkinham stayed open on Thursday nights so that people could have an extra opportunity to see what was for sale. Haze's shadow was now behind him and now before him and now and then broken up by other people's shadows, but when it was by itself, stretching behind him, it was a thin nervous shadow walking backwards. His neck was thrust forward as if he were trying to smell something that was always being drawn away. The glary light from the store windows made his blue suit look purple.

After a while he stopped where a lean-faced man had a card table set up in front of a department store and was demonstrating a potato peeler. The man had on a small canvas hat and a shirt patterned with bunches of upside-down pheasants and quail and bronze turkeys. He was pitching his voice under the street noises so that it reached every ear distinctly as if in a private conversation. A few people gathered around. There were two buckets on the card table, one empty and the other full of potatoes. Between the two buckets there was a pyramid of green cardboard boxes and, on top of the stack, one peeler was open for demonstration. The man stood in front of this altar, pointing over it at various people. "How about you?" he said, pointing at a damp-haired pimpled boy. "You ain't gonna let one of these go by?" He stuck a brown potato in one side of the open machine. The machine was a square tin box with a red handle, and as he turned the handle, the potato went into the box and then in a second, backed out the other side, white. "You ain't gonna let one of these go by!" he said.

The boy guffawed and looked at the other people gathered around. He had yellow hair and a fox-shaped face.

"What's yer name?" the peeler man asked.

"Name Enoch Emery," the boy said and snuffled.

"Boy with a pretty name like that ought to have one of these," the man said, rolling his eyes, trying to warm up the others. Nobody laughed but the boy. Then a man standing across from Hazel Motes laughed, not a pleasant laugh but one that had a sharp edge. He was a tall cadaverous man with a black suit and a black hat on. He had on dark glasses and his cheeks were streaked with lines that looked as if they had been painted on and had faded. They gave him the expression of a grinning mandrill. As soon as he laughed, he began to move forward in a deliberate way, jiggling a tin cup in one hand and tapping a white cane in front of him with the other. Just behind him there came a child, handing out leaflets. She had on a black dress and a black knitted cap pulled down low on her forehead; there was a fringe of brown hair sticking out from it on either side; she had a long face and a short sharp nose. The man selling peelers was irritated when he saw the people looking at this pair instead of him. "How about you, you there," he said, pointing at Haze. "You'll never be able to get a bargain like this in any store."

Haze was looking at the blind man and the child. "Hey!" Enoch Emery said, reaching across a woman and punching his arm. "He's talking to you! He's talking to you!" Enoch had to punch him again before he looked at the peeler man.

"Whyn't you take one of these home to yer wife?" the peeler man was saying.

"Don't have one," Haze muttered, looking back at the blind man again.

"Well, you got a dear old mother, ain't you?"

"No."

"Well pshaw," the man said, with his hand cupped to the people, "he needs one theseyer just to keep him company."

Enoch Emery thought that was so funny that he doubled over and slapped his knee, but Hazel Motes didn't look as if he had heard it yet. "I'm going to give away a half a dozen peeled potatoes to the first person purchasing one theseyer machines," the man said. "Who's gonna step up first? Only a dollar and a half for a machine'd cost you three dollars in any store!" Enoch Emery began fumbling in his pockets. "You'll thank the day you ever stopped here," the man said, "you'll never forget it. Ever' one of you people purchasing one theseyer machines'll never forget it!"

The blind man was moving forward slowly, saying in a kind of garbled mutter, "Help a blind preacher. If you won't repent, give up a nickel. I can use it as good as you. Help a blind unemployed preacher. Wouldn't you rather have me beg than preach? Come on and give a nickel if you won't repent."

There were not many people gathered around but the ones who were began to move off. When the machine-seller saw this, he leaned, glaring over the card table. "Hey you!" he yelled at the blind man. "What you think you doing? Who you think you are, running people off from here?" The blind man didn't pay any attention to him. He kept on rattling the cup and the child kept on handing out the pamphlets. He passed Enoch Emery and came on toward Haze, hitting the white cane out at an angle from his leg. Haze leaned forward and saw that the lines on his face were not painted on; they were scars.

"What the hell you think you doing?" the man selling peelers yelled. "I got these people together, how you think you can horn in?"

The child held one of the pamphlets out to Haze and he grabbed it. The words on the outside of it said, "Jesus Calls You."

"I'd like to know who the hell you think you are!" the man with the peelers was yelling. The child went back to where he was and handed him a tract. He looked at it for an instant with his lip curled and then he charged around the card table, upsetting the bucket of potatoes. "These damn Jesus fanatics," he yelled, glaring around, trying to find the blind man. New people gathered, hoping to see a disturbance. "These goddam Communist foreigners!" the peeler man screamed. "I got this crowd together!" He stopped, realizing there was a crowd.

"Listen folks," he said, "one at a time, there's plenty to go around, just don't push, a half a dozen peeled potatoes to the first person stepping up to buy." He got back behind the card table quietly and started holding up the peeler boxes. "Step on up, plenty to go around," he said, "no need to crowd."

Haze didn't open his tract. He looked at the outside of it and then he tore it across. He put the two pieces together and tore them across again. He kept re-stacking the pieces and tearing them again until he had a little handful of confetti. He turned his hand over and let the shredded leaflet sprinkle to the ground. Then he looked up and saw the blind man's child not three feet away, watching him. Her mouth was open and her eyes glittered on him like two chips of green bottle glass. She had a white gunny sack hung over her shoulder. Haze scowled and began rubbing his sticky hands on his pants.

"I seen you," she said. Then she moved quickly over to where the blind man was standing now, beside the card table, and turned her head and looked at Haze from there. Most of the people had moved off.

The peeler man leaned over the card table and said, "Hey!" to the blind man. "I reckon that showed you. Trying to horn in."

"Lookerhere," Enoch Emery said, "I ain't got but a dollar sixteen cent but I . . ."

"Yah," the man said, "I reckon that'll show you you can't muscle in on me. Sold eight peelers, sold . . ."

"Give me one of them," the blind man's child said, pointing to the peelers.

"Hanh," he said.

She was untying a handkerchief. She untied two fifty-cent pieces out of the knotted corner of it. "Give me one of them," she said, holding out the money.

The man eyed it with his mouth hiked to one side. "A buck fifty, sister," he said.

She pulled her hand in quickly and all at once glared at Hazel Motes as if he had made a noise at her. The blind man was moving on. She stood a second glaring at Haze, and then she turned and followed the blind man. Haze started.

"Listen," Enoch Emery said, "I ain't got but a dollar sixteen cent and I want me one of them . . ."

"You can keep it," the man said, taking the bucket off the card table. "This ain't no cut-rate joint."

Haze could see the blind man moving down the street some distance away. He stood staring after him, jerking his hands in and out of his pockets as if he were trying to move forward and backward at the same time. Then suddenly he thrust two dollars at the man selling peelers and snatched a box off the card table and started running down the street. In a second Enoch Emery was panting at his elbow. "My, I reckon you got a heap of money," Enoch Emery said.

Haze saw the child catch up with the blind man and take him by the elbow. They were about a block ahead of him. He slowed down some and saw Enoch Emery there. Enoch had on a yellowish white suit and a pinkish white shirt and his tie was the color of green peas. He was smiling. He looked like a friendly hound dog with light mange. "How long you been here?" he inquired.

"Two days," Haze muttered.

"I been here two months," Enoch said. "I work for the city. Where you work?"

"Not working," Haze said.

"That's too bad," Enoch said. "I work for the city." He skipped a step to get in line with Haze, then he said, "I'm eighteen year old and I ain't been here but two months and I already work for the city."

"That's fine," Haze said. He pulled his hat down farther on the side Enoch Emery was on and walked very fast. The blind man up ahead began to make mock bows to the right and left.

"I didn't ketch your name good," Enoch said.

Haze said his name.

"You look like you might be follerin' them hicks," Enoch remarked. "You go in for a lot of Jesus business?"

"No," Haze said.

"No, me neither, not much," Enoch agreed. "I went to thisyer Rodemill Boys' Bible Academy for four weeks. Thisyer woman that traded me from my daddy she sent me. She was a Welfare woman. Jesus, four weeks and I thought I was going to be sanctified crazy."

Haze walked to the end of the block and Enoch stayed at his elbow, panting and talking. When Haze started across the street, Enoch yelled, "Don't you see theter light! That means you got to wait!" A cop blew a whistle and a car blasted its horn and stopped short. Haze went on across, keeping his eyes on the blind man in the middle of the block. The policeman kept on blowing his whistle. He crossed the street to where Haze was and stopped him. He had a thin face and oval-shaped yellow eyes.

"You know what that little thing hanging up there is for?" he asked, pointing to the traffic light over the intersection.

"I didn't see it," Haze said.

The policeman looked at him without saying anything. A few people stopped. He rolled his eyes at them. "Maybe you thought the red ones was for white folks and the green ones for niggers," he said.

"Yeah I thought that," Haze said. "Take your hand off me."

The policeman took his hand off and put it on his hip. He backed one step away and said, "You tell all your friends about these lights. Red is to stop, green is to go—men and

women, white folks and niggers, all go on the same light
You tell all your friends so when they come to town, they'll
know." The people laughed.

"I'll look after him," Enoch Emery said, pushing in by
the policeman. "He ain't been here but only two days. I'll
look after him."

"How long you been here?" the cop asked.

"I was born and raised here," Enoch said. "This is my
ol' home town. I'll take care of him for you. Hey wait!" he
yelled at Haze. "Wait on me!" He pushed out of the crowd
and caught up with him. "I reckon I saved you that time,"
he said.

"I'm obliged," Haze said.

"It wasn't nothing," Enoch said. "Whyn't we go in Walgreen's and get us a soda? Ain't no night clubs open this
early."

"I don't like drug stores," Haze said. "Good-by."

"That's all right," Enoch said. "I reckon I'll go along
and keep you company for a while." He looked up ahead at
the blind man and the child and said, "I sho wouldn't want
to get messed up with no hicks this time of night, particularly
the Jesus kind. I done had enough of them myself. Thisyer
Welfare woman that traded me from my daddy didn't do
nothing but pray. Me and daddy we moved around with a
sawmill where we worked and it set up outside Boonville
one summer and here come thisyer woman." He caught hold
of Haze's coat. "Only objection I got to Taulkinham is
there's too many people on the streets," he said confidentially.
"Look like all they want to do is knock you down—well here
she come and I reckon she took a fancy to me. I was twelve
year old and I could sing some hymns good I learnt off a
nigger. So here she comes taking a fancy to me and traded
me off my daddy and took me to Boonville to live with her.
She had a brick house but it was Jesus all day long." A little
man lost in a pair of faded overalls jostled him. "Whyn't
you look wher you going?" Enoch growled.

The little man stopped and raised his arm in a vicious
gesture and a nasty-dog look came on his face. "Who you
tellin' what?" he snarled.

"You see," Enoch said, jumping to catch up with Haze,
"all they want to do is knock you down. I ain't never been
to such a unfriendly place before. Even with that woman
I stayed with her for two months in that house of hers," he
went on, "and then come fall she sent me to the Rodemill
Boys' Bible Academy and I thought that sho was going to

be some relief. This woman was hard to get along with—
she wasn't old, I reckon she was forty year old—but she
sho was ugly. She had theseyer brown glasses and her hair
was so thin it looked like ham gravy trickling over her skull.
I thought it was going to be some certain relief to get to
theter Academy. I had run away oncet on her and she got
me back and come to find out she had papers on me and
she could send me to the penitentiary if I didn't stay with
her so I sho was glad to get to theter Academy. You ever
been to a academy?"

Haze didn't seem to hear the question.

"Well, it won't no relief," Enoch said. "Good Jesus, it
won't no relief. I run away from there after four weeks and
durn if she didn't get me back and brought me to that house
of hers again. I got out though." He waited a minute. "You
want to know how?"

After a second he said, "I scared hell out of that woman,
that's how. I studied on it and studied on it. I even prayed.
I said, 'Jesus, show me the way to get out of here without
killing thisyer woman and getting sent to the penitentiary,'
and durn if He didn't. I got up one morning at just daylight and I went in her room without my pants on and
pulled the sheet off her and giver a heart attact. Then I
went back to my daddy and we ain't seen hide of her since."

"Your jaw just crawls," he observed, watching the side of
Haze's face. "You don't never laugh. I wouldn't be surprised
if you wasn't a real wealthy man."

Haze turned down a side street. The blind man and the
girl were on the corner a block ahead. "Well, I reckon we
going to ketch up with them after all," Enoch said. "You
know many people here?"

"No," Haze said.

"You ain't gonna know none neither. This is one more
hard place to make friends in. I been here two months and
I don't know nobody. Look like all they want to do is knock
you down. I reckon you got a right heap of money," he said.
"I ain't got none. Had, I'd sho know what to do with it."
The blind man and his child stopped on the corner and
turned up the left side of the street. "We ketchin' up," he
said. "I bet we'll be at some meeting singing hymns with
her and her daddy if we don't watch out."

Up in the next block there was a large building with columns and a dome. The blind man and the girl were going
toward it. There was a car parked in every space around the
building and on the other side of the street and up and

down the streets near it. "That ain't no picture show,"
Enoch said. The blind man and the girl turned up the steps
to the building. The steps went all the way across the front,
and on either side there were stone lions, sitting on pedestals.
"Ain't no church," Enoch said. Haze stopped at the steps.
He looked as if he were trying to settle his face into an expression. He pulled the black hat forward at a sharp angle
and started toward the two, who had sat down in the corner
by one of the lions. He came up to where the blind man
was without saying anything and stood leaning forward in
front of him as if he were trying to see through the black
glasses. The child stared at him.

The blind man's mouth thinned slightly. "I can smell the
sin on your breath," he said.

Haze drew back.

"What'd you follow me for?"

"I never followed you," Haze said.

"She said you were following," the blind man said, jerking
his thumb in the direction of the child.

"I ain't followed you," Haze said. He felt the peeler box
in his hand and looked at the girl. Her black knitted cap
made a straight line across her forehead. She grinned suddenly and then quickly drew her expression back together
as if she smelled something bad. "I ain't followed you nowhere," Haze said. "I followed her." He stuck the peeler out
at her.

At first she looked as if she were going to grab it, but she
didn't. "I don't want that thing," she said. "What you think
I want with that thing? Take it. It ain't mine. I don't want
it!"

"You take it," the blind man said. "You put it in your
sack and shut up before I hit you."

Haze thrust the peeler at her again.

"I won't have it," she muttered.

"You take it like I told you," the blind man said. "He
never followed you."

She took it and shoved it in the sack where the tracts
were. "It ain't mine," she said. "I got it but it ain't mine."

"I followed her to say I ain't beholden for none of her
fast eye like she gave me back there," Haze said, looking at
the blind man.

"What you mean?" she shouted. "I never looked at you
with no fast eye. I only watched you tearing up that tract.
He tore it up in little pieces," she said, pushing the blind

man's shoulder. "He tore it up and sprinkled it all over the ground like salt and wiped his hands on his pants."

"He followed me," the blind man said. "Nobody would follow you. I can hear the urge for Jesus in his voice."

"Jesus," Haze muttered. "My Jesus." He sat down by the girl's leg and set his hand on the step next to her foot. She had on sneakers and black cotton stockings.

"Listen at him cursing," she said in a low tone. "He never followed you, Papa."

The blind man gave his edgy laugh. "Listen boy," he said, "you can't run away from Jesus. Jesus is a fact."

"I know a whole heap about Jesus," Enoch said. "I attended thisyer Rodemill Boys' Bible Academy that a woman sent me to. If it's anything you want to know about Jesus, just ast me." He had got up on the lion's back and he was sitting there sideways, cross-legged.

"I come a long way," Haze said, "since I would believe anything. I come halfway around the world."

"Me too," Enoch Emery said.

"You ain't come so far that you could keep from following me," the blind man said. He reached out suddenly and his hands covered Haze's face. For a second Haze didn't move or make any sound. Then he knocked the hands off.

"Quit it," he said in a faint voice. "You don't know anything about me."

"My daddy looks just like Jesus," Enoch remarked from the lion's back. "His hair hangs to his shoulders. Only difference is he's got a scar acrost his chin. I ain't never seen who my mother is."

"Some preacher has left his mark on you," the blind man said with a kind of snicker. "Did you follow for me to take it off or give you another one?"

"Listen here, there's nothing for your pain but Jesus," the child said suddenly. She tapped Haze on the shoulder. He sat there with his black hat tilted forward over his face. "Listen," she said in a louder voice, "this here man and woman killed this little baby. It was her own child but it was ugly and she never give it any love. This child had Jesus and this woman didn't have nothing but good looks and a man she was living in sin with. She sent the child away and it come back and she sent it away again and it come back again and ever' time she sent it away, it come back to where her and this man was living in sin. They strangled it with a silk stocking and hung it up in the chimney. It didn't give her any peace after that, though. Everything she looked at was that child. Jesus made it beautiful to haunt her. She couldn't lie with that man without she saw it, staring through the chimney at her, shining through the brick in the middle of the night."

"My Jesus," Haze muttered.

"She didn't have nothing but good looks," she said in the loud fast voice. "That ain't enough. No sirree."

"I hear them scraping their feet inside there," the blind man said. "Get out the tracts, they're fixing to come out."

"It ain't enough," she repeated.

"What we gonna do?" Enoch asked. "What's inside theter building?"

"A program letting out," the blind man said. "My congregation."

The child took the tracts out of the gunny sack and gave him two bunches of them, tied with a string. "You and the other boy go over on that side and give out," he said to her. "Me and the one that followed me'll stay over here."

"He don't have no business touching them," she said. "He don't want to do anything but shred them up."

"Go like I told you," the blind man said.

She stood there a second, scowling. Then she said, "You come on if you're coming," to Enoch Emery and Enoch jumped off the lion and followed her over to the other side.

Haze ducked down a step but the blind man's hand shot out and clamped him around the arm. He said in a fast whisper, "Repent! Go to the head of the stairs and renounce your sins and distribute these tracts to the people!" and he thrust a stack of pamphlets into Haze's hand.

Haze jerked his arm away but he only pulled the blind man nearer. "Listen," he said, "I'm as clean as you are."

"Fornication and blasphemy and what else?" the blind man said.

"They ain't nothing but words," Haze said. "If I was in sin I was in it before I ever committed any. There's no change come in me." He was trying to pry the fingers off from around his arm but the blind man kept wrapping them tighter. "I don't believe in sin," Haze said, "take your hand off me."

"Jesus loves you," the blind man said in a flat mocking voice, "Jesus loves you, Jesus loves you . . ."

"Nothing matters but that Jesus don't exist," Haze said, pulling his arm free.

"Go to the head of the stairs and distribute these tracts and . . ."

"I'll take them up there and throw them over into the bushes!" Haze shouted. "You be watching and see can you see."

"I can see more than you!" the blind man yelled, laughing. "You got eyes and see not, ears and hear not, but you'll have to see some time."

"You be watching if you can see!" Haze said, and started running up the steps. A crowd of people were already coming out the auditorium doors and some were halfway down the steps. He pushed through them with his elbows out like sharp wings and when he got to the top, a new surge of them pushed him back almost to where he had started up. He fought through them again until somebody shouted, "Make room for this idiot!" and people got out of his way. He rushed to the top and pushed his way over to the side and stood there, glaring and panting.

"I never followed him," he said aloud. "I wouldn't follow a blind fool like that. My Jesus." He stood against the building, holding the stack of leaflets by the string. A fat man stopped near him to light a cigar and Haze pushed his shoulder. "Look down yonder," he said. "See that blind man down there? He's giving out tracts and begging. Jesus. You ought to see him and he's got this here ugly child dressed up in woman's clothes, giving them out too. My Jesus."

"There's always fanatics," the fat man said, moving on.

"My Jesus," Haze said. He leaned forward near an old woman with blue hair and a collar of red wooden beads. "You better get on the other side, lady," he said. "There's a fool down there giving out tracts." The crowd behind the old woman pushed her on, but she looked at him for an instant with two bright flea eyes. He started toward her through the people but she was already too far away and he pushed back to where he had been standing against the wall. "Sweet Jesus Christ Crucified," he said, "I want to tell you people something. Maybe you think you're not clean because you don't believe. Well you are clean, let me tell you that. Every one of you people are clean and let me tell you why if you think it's because of Jesus Christ Crucified you're wrong. I don't say he wasn't crucified but I say it wasn't for you. Listenhere, I'm a preacher myself and I preach the truth." The crowd was moving fast. It was like a large spread raveling and the separate threads disappeared down the dark streets. "Don't I know what exists and what don't?" he cried. "Don't I have eyes in my head? Am I a blind man? Listenhere," he called, "I'm going to preach a new church—the church of truth without Jesus Christ Crucified. It won't cost you nothing to join my church. It's not started yet but it's going to be." The few people who were left glanced at him once or twice. There were tracts scattered below over the sidewalk and out on the street. The blind man was sitting on the bottom step. Enoch Emery was on the other side, standing on the lion's head, trying to balance himself, and the child was standing near him, watching Haze. "I don't need Jesus," Haze said. "What do I need with Jesus? I got Leora Watts."

He went down the stairs quietly to where the blind man was and stopped. He stood there a second and the blind man laughed. Haze moved away, and started across the street. He was on the other side before the voice pierced after him. He turned and saw the blind man standing in the middle of the street, shouting, "Hawks, Hawks, my name is Asa Hawks when you try to follow me again!" A car had to swerve to the side to keep from hitting him. "Repent!" he shouted and laughed and ran forward a little way, pretending he was going to come after Haze and grab him.

Haze drew his head down nearer his hunched shoulders and went on quickly. He didn't look back until he heard other footsteps coming behind him.

"Now that we got shut of them," Enoch Emery panted, "whyn't we go somewhere and have us some fun?"

"Listen," Haze said roughly, "I got business of my own. I seen all of you I want." He began walking very fast.

Enoch kept skipping steps to keep up. "I been here two months," he said, "and I don't know nobody. People ain't friendly here. I got me a room and there ain't never nobody in it but me. My daddy said I had to come. I wouldn't never have come but he made me. I think I seen you sommers before. You ain't from Stockwell, are you?"

"No."

"Melsy?"

"No."

"Sawmill set up there oncet," Enoch said. "Look like you had a kind of familer face."

They walked on without saying anything until they got on the main street again. It was almost deserted. "Good-by," Haze said.

"I'm going thisaway too," Enoch said in a sullen voice. On the left there was a movie house where the electric bill was being changed. "We hadn't got tied up with them hicks we could have gone to a show," he muttered. He strode along

at Haze's elbow, talking in a half mumble, half whine. Once
he caught at his sleeve to slow him down and Haze jerked
it away. "My daddy made me come," he said in a cracked
voice. Haze looked at him and saw he was crying, his face
seamed and wet and a purple-pink color. "I ain't but eighteen
year old," he cried, "an' he made me come and I don't know
nobody, nobody here'll have nothing to do with nobody else.
They ain't friendly. He done gone off with a woman and
made me come but she ain't going to stay for long, he'll
beat hell out of her before she gets herself stuck to a chair.
You the first familer face I seen in two months. I seen you
sommers before. I know I seen you sommers before."

Haze looked straight ahead with his face set and Enoch
kept up the half mumble, half blubber. They passed a church
and a hotel and an antique shop and turned up Mrs. Watts's
street.

"If you want you a woman you don't have to be follering
nothing looked like that kid you give a peeler to," Enoch
said. "I heard about where there's a house where we could
have us some fun. I could pay you back next week."

"Look," Haze said, "I'm going where I'm going—two doors
from here. I got a woman. I got a woman, see? And that's
where I'm going—to visit her. I don't need to go with you."

"I could pay you back next week," Enoch said. "I work
at the city zoo. I guard a gate and I get paid ever' week."

"Get away from me," Haze said.

"People ain't friendly here. You ain't from here but you
ain't friendly neither."

Haze didn't answer him. He went on with his neck drawn
close to his shoulder blades as if he were cold.

"You don't know nobody neither," Enoch said. "You ain't
got no woman nor nothing to do. I knew when I first seen
you you didn't have nobody nor nothing but Jesus. I seen
you and I knew it."

"This is where I'm going in at," Haze said, and he turned
up the walk without looking back at Enoch.

Enoch stopped. "Yeah," he cried, "oh yeah," and he ran
his sleeve under his nose to stop the snivel. "Yeah," he
cried, "go on where you goin' but lookerhere." He slapped
at his pocket and ran up and caught Haze's sleeve and
rattled the peeler box at him. "She give me this. She give
it to me and there ain't nothing you can do about it. She
told me where they lived and ast me to visit them and bring
you—not you bring me, me bring you—and it was you follerin' them." His eyes glinted through his tears and his face

stretched in an evil crooked grin. "You act like you think
you got wiser blood than anybody else," he said, "but you
ain't! I'm the one has it. Not you. *Me*."

Haze didn't say anything. He stood there for an instant,
small in the middle of the steps, and then he raised his arm
and hurled the stack of tracts he had been carrying. It hit
Enoch in the chest and knocked his mouth open. He stood
looking, with his mouth hanging open, at where it had hit
his front, and then he turned and tore off down the street;
and Haze went into the house.

Since the night before was the first time he had slept with
any woman, he had not been very successful with Mrs. Watts.
When he finished, he was like something washed ashore
on her, and she had made obscene comments about him,
which he remembered off and on during the day. He was
uneasy in the thought of going to her again. He didn't know
what she would say when he opened the door and she saw
him there.

When he opened the door and she saw him there, she said,
"Ha ha."

The black hat sat on his head squarely. He came in with
it on and when it knocked the electric light bulb that hung
down from the middle of the ceiling, he took it off. Mrs.
Watts was in bed, applying a grease to her face. She rested
her chin on her hand and watched him. He began to move
around the room, examining this and that. His throat got
dryer and his heart began to grip him like a little ape clutching the bars of its cage. He sat down on the edge of her
bed, with his hat in his hand.

Mrs. Watts's grin was as curved and sharp as the blade
of a sickle. It was plain that she was so well-adjusted that
she didn't have to think any more. Her eyes took everything
in whole, like quicksand. "That Jesus-seeing hat!" she said.
She sat up and pulled her nightgown from under her and
took it off. She reached for his hat and put it on her head
and sat with her hands on her hips, walling her eyes in a
comical way. Haze stared for a minute, then he made three
quick noises that were laughs. He jumped for the electric
light cord and took off his clothes in the dark.

Once when he was small, his father took him to a carnival
that stopped in Melsy. There was one tent that cost more
money a little off to one side. A dried-up man with a horn
voice was barking it. He didn't say what was inside. He said
it was so SINsational that it would cost any man that wanted
to see it thirty-five cents, and it was so EXclusive, only

fifteen could get in at a time. His father sent him to a tent where two monkeys danced, and then he made for it, moving close to the walls of things like he moved. Haze left the monkeys and followed him, but he didn't have thirty-five cents. He asked the barker what was inside.

"Beat it," the man said. "There ain't no pop and there ain't no monkeys."

"I already seen them," he said.

"That's fine," the man said, "beat it."

"I got fifteen cents," he said. "Whyn't you lemme in and I could see half of it?" It's something about a privy, he was thinking. It's some men in a privy. Then he thought, maybe it's a man and a woman in a privy. She wouldn't want me in there. "I got fifteen cents," he said.

"It's more than half over," the man said, fanning with his straw hat. "You run along."

"That'll be fifteen cents worth then," Haze said.

"Scram," the man said.

"Is it a nigger?" Haze asked. "Are they doing something to a nigger?"

The man leaned off his platform and his dried-up face drew into a glare. "Where'd you get that idear?" he said.

"I don't know," Haze said.

"How old are you?" the man asked.

"Twelve," Haze said. He was ten.

"Gimme that fifteen cents," the man said, "and get in there."

He slid the money on the platform and scrambled to get in before it was over. He went through the flap of the tent and inside there was another tent and he went through that. All he could see were the backs of the men. He climbed up on a bench and looked over their heads. They were looking down into a lowered place where something white was lying, squirming a little, in a box lined with black cloth. For a second he thought it was a skinned animal and then he saw it was a woman. She was fat and she had a face like an ordinary woman except there was a mole on the corner of her lip, that moved when she grinned, and one on her side.

"Had one of themther built into ever' casket," his father, up toward the front, said, "be a heap ready to go sooner."

Haze recognized the voice without looking. He slid down off the bench and scrambled out of the tent. He crawled out under the side of the outside one because he didn't want to pass the barker. He got in the back of a truck and sat down in the far corner of it. The carnival was making a tin roar outside.

His mother was standing by the washpot in the yard, looking at him, when he got home. She wore black all the time and her dresses were longer than other women's. She was standing there straight, looking at him. He moved behind a tree and got out of her view, but in a few minutes, he could feel her watching him through the tree. He saw the lowered place and the casket again and a thin woman in the casket who was too long for it. Her head stuck up at one end and her knees were raised to make her fit. She had a cross-shaped face and hair pulled close to her head. He stood flat against the tree, waiting. She left the washpot and came toward him with a stick. She said, "What you seen?

"What you seen?" she said.

"What you seen," she said, using the same tone of voice all the time. She hit him across the legs with the stick, but he was like part of the tree. "Jesus died to redeem you," she said.

"I never ast him," he muttered.

She didn't hit him again but she stood looking at him, shut-mouthed, and he forgot the guilt of the tent for the nameless unplaced guilt that was in him. In a minute she threw the stick away from her and went back to the washpot, still shut-mouthed.

The next day he took his shoes in secret out into the woods. He didn't wear them except for revivals and in the winter. He took them out of the box and filled the bottoms of them with stones and small rocks and then he put them on. He laced them up tight and walked in them through the woods for what he knew to be a mile, until he came to a creek, and then he sat down and took them off and eased his feet in the wet sand. He thought, that ought to satisfy Him. Nothing happened. If a stone had fallen he would have taken it as a sign. After a while he drew his feet out of the sand and let them dry, and then he put the shoes on again with the rocks still in them and he walked a half-mile back before he took them off.

IV

He got out of Mrs. Watts's bed early in the morning before any light came in the room. When he woke up, her arm was flung across him. He leaned up and lifted it off and eased it down by her side, but he didn't look at her. There was only one thought in his mind: he was going to buy a car. The thought was full grown in his head when he woke up, and he didn't think of anything else. He had never thought before of buying a car; he had never even wanted one before. He had driven one only a little in his life and he didn't have any license. He had only fifty dollars but he thought he could buy a car for that. He got stealthily out the bed, without disturbing Mrs. Watts, and put his clothes on silently. By six-thirty, he was down town, looking for used-car lots.

Used-car lots were scattered among the blocks of old buildings that separated the business section from the railroad yards. He wandered around in a few of them before they were open. He could tell from the outside of the lot if it would have a fifty-dollar car in it. When they began to be open for business, he went through them quickly, paying no attention to anyone who tried to show him the stock. His black hat sat on his head with a careful, placed expression and his face had a fragile look as if it might have been broken and stuck together again, or like a gun no one knows is loaded.

It was a wet glary day. The sky was like a piece of thin polished silver with a dark sour-looking sun in one corner of it. By ten o'clock he had canvassed all the better lots and was nearing the railroad yards. Even here, the lots were full of cars that cost more than fifty dollars. Finally he came to one between two deserted warehouses. A sign over the entrance said: SLADE'S FOR THE LATEST.

There was a gravel road going down the middle of the lot and over to one side near the front, a tin shack with the word, OFFICE, painted on the door. The rest of the lot was full of old cars and broken machinery. A white boy was sitting on a gasoline can in front of the office. He had the look of being there to keep people out. He wore a black raincoat and his face was partly hidden under a leather cap. There was a cigarette hanging out of one corner of his mouth and the ash on it was about an inch long.

Haze started off toward the back of the lot where he saw a particular car. "Hey!" the boy yelled. "You don't just walk in here like that. I'll show you what I got to show," but Haze didn't pay any attention to him. He went on toward the back of the lot where he saw the car. The boy came huffing behind him, cursing. The car he saw was on the last row of cars. It was a high rat-colored machine with large thin wheels and bulging headlights. When he got up to it, he saw that one door was tied on with a rope and that it had an oval window in the back. This was the car he was going to buy.

"Lemme see Slade," he said.

"What you want to see him for?" the boy asked in a testy voice. He had a wide mouth and when he talked he used one side only of it.

"I want to see him about this car," Haze said.

"I'm him," the boy said. His face under the cap was like a thin picked eagle's. He sat down on the running board of a car across the gravel road and kept on cursing.

Haze walked around the car. Then he looked through the window at the inside of it. Inside it was a dull greenish dust-color. The back seat was missing but it had a two-by-four stretched across the seat frame to sit on. There were dark green fringed window shades on the two side-back windows. He looked through the two front windows and he saw the boy sitting on the running board of the car across the gravel road. He had one trouser leg hitched up and he was scratching his ankle that stuck up out of a pulp of yellow sock. He cursed far down in his throat as if he were trying to get up phlegm. The two window glasses made him a yellow color and distorted his shape. Haze moved quickly from the far side of the car and came around in front. "How much is it?" he asked.

"Jesus on the cross," the boy said, "Christ nailed."

"How much is it?" Haze growled, paling a little.

"How much do you think it's worth?" the boy said. "Give us a estimit."

"It ain't worth what it would take to cart it off. I wouldn't have it."

The boy gave all his attention to his ankle where there was a scab. Haze looked up and saw a man coming from between two cars over on the boy's side. As he came closer, he saw that the man looked exactly like the boy except that he was two heads taller and he had on a sweat-stained brown felt hat. He was coming up behind the boy, between a row of cars. When he got just behind him, he stopped and waited a second. Then he said in a sort of controlled roar, "Get your butt off that running board!"

The boy snarled and disappeared, scrambling between two cars.

The man stood looking at Haze. "What you want?" he asked.

"This car here," Haze said.

"Seventy-fi' dollars," the man said.

On either side of the lot there were two old buildings, reddish with black empty windows, and behind there was another without any windows. "I'm obliged," Haze said, and he started back toward the office.

When he got to the entrance, he glanced back and saw the man about four feet behind him. "We might argue it some," he said.

Haze followed him back to where the car was.

"You won't find a car like that ever' day," the man said. He sat down on the running board that the boy had been sitting on. Haze didn't see the boy but he was there, sitting up on the hood of a car two cars over. He was sitting huddled up as if he were freezing but his face had a sour composed look. "All new tires," the man said.

"They were new when it was built," Haze said.

"They was better cars built a few years ago," the man said. "They don't make no more good cars."

"What you want for it?" Haze asked again.

The man stared off, thinking. After a while he said, "I might could let you have it for sixty-fi'."

Haze leaned against the car and started to roll a cigarette but he couldn't get it rolled. He kept spilling the tobacco and then the papers.

"Well, what you want to pay for it?" the man asked. "I wouldn't trade me a Chrysler for a Essex like that. That car yonder ain't been built by a bunch of niggers.

"All the niggers are living in Detroit now, putting cars together," he said, making conversation. "I was up there a while myself and I seen. I come home."

"I wouldn't pay over thirty dollars for it," Haze said.

"They got one nigger up there," the man said, "is almost as light as you or me." He took off his hat and ran his finger around the sweat band inside it. He had a little bit of carrot-colored hair.

"We'll drive it around," the man said, "or would you like to get under and look up it?"

"No," Haze said.

The man gave him a half look. "You pay when you leave," he said easily. "You don't find what you looking for in one there's others for the same price obliged to have it." Two cars over the boy began to curse again. It was like a hacking cough. Haze turned suddenly and kicked his foot into the front tire. "I done tole you them tires won't bust," the man said.

"How much?" Haze said.

"I might could make it fifty dollar," the man offered.

Before Haze bought the car, the man put some gas in it and drove him around a few blocks to prove it would run. The boy sat hunched up in the back on the two-by-four, cursing. "Something's wrong with him howcome he curses so much," the man said. "Just don't listen at him." The car rode with a high growling noise. The man put on the brakes to show how well they worked and the boy was thrown off the two-by-four at their heads. "Goddam you," the man roared, "quit jumping at us thataway. Keep your butt on the board." The boy didn't say anything. He didn't even curse. Haze looked back and he was sitting huddled up in the black raincoat with the black leather cap pulled down almost to his eyes. The only thing different was that the ash had been knocked off his cigarette.

He bought the car for forty dollars and then he paid the man extra for five gallons of gasoline. The man had the boy go in the office and bring out a five-gallon can of gas to fill up the tank with. The boy came cursing and lugging the yellow gas can, bent over almost double. "Give it here," Haze said, "I'll do it myself." He was in a terrible hurry to get away in the car. The boy jerked the can away from him and straightened up. It was only half full but he held it over the tank until five gallons would have spilled out slowly. All the time he kept saying, "Sweet Jesus, sweet Jesus, sweet Jesus."

"Why don't he shut up?" Haze said suddenly. "What's he keep talking like that for?"

"I don't never know what ails him," the man said and shrugged.

When the car was ready the man and the boy stood by to watch him drive it off. He didn't want anybody watching him because he hadn't driven a car in four or five years. The man and the boy didn't say anything while he tried to start it. They only stood there, looking in at him. "I wanted this car mostly to be a house for me," he said to the man. "I ain't got any place to live."

"You ain't took the brake off yet," the man said.

He took off the brake and the car shot backward because the man had left it in reverse. In a second he got it going forward and he drove off crookedly, past the man and the boy still standing there watching. He kept going forward, thinking nothing and sweating. For a long time he stayed on the street he was on. He had a hard time holding the car in the road. He went past railroad yards for about a half-mile and then warehouses. When he tried to slow the car down, it stopped altogether and then he had to start it again. He went past long blocks of gray houses and then blocks of better, yellow houses. It began to drizzle rain and he turned on the windshield wipers; they made a great clatter like two idiots clapping in church. He went past blocks of white houses, each sitting with an ugly dog face on a square of grass. Finally he went over a viaduct and found the highway.

He began going very fast.

The highway was ragged with filling stations and trailer camps and roadhouses. After a while there were stretches where red gulleys dropped off on either side of the road and behind them there were patches of field buttoned together with 666 posts. The sky leaked over all of it and then it began to leak into the car. The head of a string of pigs appeared snout-up over the ditch and he had to screech to a stop and watch the rear of the last pig disappear shaking into the ditch on the other side. He started the car again and went on. He had the feeling that everything he saw was a broken-off piece of some giant blank thing that he had forgotten had happened to him. A black pick-up truck turned off a side road in front of him. On the back of it an iron bed and a chair and table were tied, and on top of them, a crate of barred-rock chickens. The truck went very slowly, with a rumbling sound, and in the middle of the road. Haze started pounding his horn and he had hit it three times before he realized it didn't make any sound. The crate was stuffed so full of wet barred-rock chickens that the ones facing him had their heads outside the bars. The truck didn't go any faster and he was forced to drive slowly. The fields stretched sodden on either side until they hit the scrub pines.

The road turned and went down hill and a high embankment appeared on one side with pines standing on it, facing a gray boulder that jutted out of the opposite gulley wall. White letters on the boulder said, WOE TO THE BLASPHEMER AND WHOREMONGER! WILL HELL SWALLOW YOU UP? The pick-up truck slowed even more as if it were reading the sign and Haze pounded his empty horn. He beat on it and beat on it but it didn't make any sound. The pick-up truck went on, bumping the glum barred-rock chickens over the edge of the next hill. Haze's car was stopped and his eyes were turned toward the two words at the bottom of the sign. They said in smaller letters, "Jesus Saves.'

He sat looking at the sign and he didn't hear the horn. An oil truck as long as a railroad car was behind him. In a second a red square face was at his car window. It watched the back of his neck and hat for a minute and then a hand came in and sat on his shoulder. "What you doing parked in the middle of the road?" the truck driver asked.

Haze turned his fragile placed-looking face toward him. "Take your hand off me," he said. "I'm reading the sign." The driver's expression and his hand stayed exactly the way they were, as if he didn't hear very well.

"There's no person a whoremonger, who wasn't something worse first," Haze said. "That's not the sin, nor blasphemy. The sin came before them."

The truck driver's face remained exactly the same.

"Jesus is a trick on niggers," Haze said.

The driver put both his hands on the window and gripped it. He looked as if he intended to pick up the car. "Will you get your goddam outhouse off the middle of the road?" he said.

"I don't have to run from anything because I don't believe in anything," Haze said. He and the driver looked at each other for about a minute. Haze's look was the more distant; another plan was forming in his mind. "Which direction is the zoo in?" he asked.

"Back around the other way," the driver said. "Did you exscape from there?"

"I got to see a boy that works in it," Haze said. He started the car up and left the driver standing there, in front of the letters painted on the boulder.

v

That morning Enoch Emery knew when he woke up that today the person he could show it to was going to come. He knew by his blood. He had wise blood like his daddy.

At two o'clock that afternoon, he greeted the second-shift gate guard. "You ain't but only fifteen minutes late," he said irritably. "But I stayed. I could of went on but I stayed." He wore a green uniform with yellow piping on the neck and sleeves and a yellow stripe down the outside of each leg. The second-shift guard, a boy with a jutting shale-textured face and a toothpick in his mouth, wore the same. The gate they were standing by was made of iron bars and the concrete arch that held it was fashioned to look like two trees; branches curved to form the top of it where twisted letters said, CITY FOREST PARK. The second-shift guard leaned against one of the trunks and began prodding between his teeth with the pick.

"Ever' day," Enoch complained; "look like ever' day I lose fifteen good minutes standing here waiting for you."

Every day when he got off duty, he went into the park, and every day when he went in, he did the same thing. He went first to the swimming pool. He was afraid of the water but he liked to sit up on the bank above it if there were any women in the pool, and watch them. There was one woman who came every Monday who wore a bathing suit that was split on each hip. At first he thought she didn't know it, and instead of watching openly on the bank, he had crawled into some bushes, snickering to himself, and had watched from there. There had been no one else in the pool —the crowds didn't come until four o'clock—to tell her about the splits and she had splashed around in the water and then lain up on the edge of the pool asleep for almost an hour, all the time without suspecting there was somebody in the bushes looking at her. Then on another day when he stayed a little later, he saw three women, all with their suits split, the pool full of people, and nobody paying them any mind. That was how the city was—always surprising him. He visited a whore when he felt like it but he was always being shocked by the looseness he saw in the open. He crawled into the bushes out of a sense of propriety. Very often the women would pull the suit straps down off their shoulders and lie stretched out.

The park was the heart of the city. He had come to the city and—with a knowing in his blood—he had established himself at the heart of it. Every day he looked at the heart of it; every day; and he was so stunned and awed and overwhelmed that just to think about it made him sweat. There was something, in the center of the park, that he had discovered. It was a mystery, although it was right there in a glass case for everybody to see and there was a typewritten card over it telling all about it. But there was something the card couldn't say and what it couldn't say was inside him, a terrible knowledge without any words to it, a terrible knowledge like a big nerve growing inside him. He could not show the mystery to just anybody; but he had to show it to somebody. Who he had to show it to was a special person. This person could not be from the city but he didn't know why. He knew he would know him when he saw him and he knew that he would have to see him soon or the nerve inside him would grow so big that he would be forced to steal a car or rob a bank or jump out of a dark alley onto a woman. His blood all morning had been saying the person would come today.

He left the second-shift guard and approached the pool from a discreet footpath that led behind the ladies' end of the bath house to a small clearing where the entire pool could be seen at once. There was nobody in it—the water was bottle-green and motionless—but he saw, coming up the other side and heading for the bath house, the woman with the two little boys. She came every other day or so and brought the two children. She would go in the water with them and swim down the pool and then she would lie up on the side in the sun. She had a stained white bathing suit that fit her like a sack, and Enoch had watched her with pleasure on several occasions. He moved from the clearing up a slope to some abelia bushes. There was a nice tunnel under them and he crawled into it until he came to a slightly wider place where he was accustomed to sit. He settled himself and adjusted the abelia so that he could see through it properly. His face was always very red in the bushes. Anyone who parted the abelia sprigs at just that place, would think he saw a devil and would fall down the slope and into the pool. The woman and the two little boys entered the bath house.

Enoch never went immediately to the dark secret center of the park. That was the peak of the afternoon. The other things he did built up to it. When he left the bushes, he would go to the FROSTY BOTTLE, a hotdog stand in the shape of an Orange Crush with frost painted in blue around the top of it. Here he would have a chocolate malted milkshake and would make some suggestive remarks to the waitress, whom he believed to be secretly in love with him. After that he would go to see the animals. They were in a long set of steel cages like Alcatraz Penitentiary in the movies. The cages were electrically heated in the winter and air-conditioned in the summer and there were six men hired to wait on the animals and feed them T-bone steaks. The animals didn't do anything but lie around. Enoch watched them every day, full of awe and hate. Then he went *there*.

The two little boys ran out the bath house and dived into the water, and simultaneously a grating noise issued from the driveway on the other side of the pool. Enoch's head pierced out of the bushes. He saw a high rat-colored car passing, which sounded as if its motor were dragging out of

the back. The car passed and he could hear it rattle
around the turn in the drive and on away. He listened carefully, trying to hear if it would stop. The noise receded and
then gradually grew louder. The car passed again. Enoch
saw this time that there was only one person in it, a man.
The sound of it died away again and then grew louder. The
car came around a third time and stopped almost directly
opposite Enoch across the pool. The man in the car looked
out the window and down the grass slope to the water where
the two little boys were splashing and screaming. Enoch's
head was as far out of the bushes as it would come and he
was squinting. The door by the man was tied on with a rope.
The man got out the other door and walked in front of the
car and came halfway down the slope to the pool. He stood
there a minute as if he were looking for somebody and then
he sat down stiffly on the grass. He had on a blue suit and
a black hat. He sat with his knees drawn up. "Well, I'll be
dog," Enoch said. "Well, I'll be dog."

He began crawling out of the bushes immediately, his heart
moving so fast it was like one of those motorcycles at
fairs that the fellow drives around the walls of a pit. He even
remembered the man's name—Mr. Hazel Motes. In a second
he appeared on all fours at the end of the abelia and looked
across the pool. The blue figure was still sitting there in the
same position. He had the look of being held there, as if by
an invisible hand, as if, if the hand lifted up, the figure
would spring across the pool in one leap without the expression on his face changing once.

The woman came out of the bath house and went to the
diving board. She spread her arms out and began to bounce,
making a big flapping sound with the board. Then suddenly
she swirled backward and disappeared below the water. Mr.
Hazel Motes's head turned very slowly, following her down
the pool.

Enoch got up and went down the path behind the bath
house. He came stealthily out on the other side and started
walking toward Haze. He stayed on the top of the slope,
moving softly in the grass just off the sidewalk, and making
no noise. When he was directly behind him, he sat down
on the edge of the sidewalk. If his arms had been ten feet
long, he could have put his hands on Haze's shoulders. He
studied him quietly.

The woman was climbing out of the pool, chinning herself
up on the side. First her face appeared, long and cadaverous, with a bandage-like bathing cap coming down almost

to her eyes, and sharp teeth protruding from her mouth. Then she rose on her hands until a large foot and leg came up from behind her and another on the other side and she was out, squatting there, panting. She stood up loosely and shook herself, and stamped in the water dripping off her. She was facing them and she grinned. Enoch could see part of Hazel Motes's face watching the woman. It didn't grin in return but it kept on watching her as she padded over to a spot of sun almost directly under where they were sitting. Enoch had to move a little closer to see.

The woman sat down in the spot of sun and took off her bathing cap. Her hair was short and matted and all colors, from deep rust to a greenish yellow. She shook her head and then she looked up at Hazel Motes again, grinning through her pointed teeth. She stretched herself out in the spot of sun, raising her knees and settling her backbone down against the concrete. The two little boys, at the other end of the water, were knocking each other's heads against the side of the pool. She settled herself until she was flat against the concrete and then she reached up and pulled the bathing suit straps off her shoulders.

"King Jesus!" Enoch whispered and before he could get his eyes off the woman, Hazel Motes had sprung up and was almost to his car. The woman was sitting straight up with the suit half off her in front, and Enoch was looking both ways at once.

He wrenched his attention loose from the woman and darted after Hazel Motes. "Wait on me!" he shouted and waved his arms in front of the car which was already rattling and starting to go. Hazel Motes cut off the motor. His face behind the windshield was sour and frog-like; it looked as if it had a shout closed up in it; it looked like one of those closet doors in gangster pictures where someone is tied to a chair behind it with a towel in his mouth.

"Well," Enoch said, "I declare if it ain't Hazel Motes. How are you, Hazel?"

"The guard said I'd find you at the swimming pool," Hazel Motes said. "He said you hid in the bushes and watched the swimming."

Enoch blushed. "I allus have admired swimming," he said. Then he stuck his head farther through the window. "You were looking for me?" he exclaimed.

"That blind man," Haze said, "that blind man named Hawks —did his child tell you where they lived?"

Enoch didn't seem to hear. "You came out here special to see me?" he said.

"Asa Hawks. His child gave you the peeler. Did she tell you where they lived?"

Enoch eased his head out of the car. He opened the door and climbed in beside Haze. For a minute he only looked at him, wetting his lips. Then he whispered, "I got to show you something."

"I'm looking for those people," Haze said. "I got to see that man. Did she tell you where they lived?"

"I got to show you this thing," Enoch said. "I got to show it to you, here, this afternoon. I got to." He gripped Hazel Motes's arm and Haze shook him off.

"Did she tell you where they live?" he said again.

Enoch kept wetting his lips. They were pale except for his fever blister, which was purple. "Cert'nly," he said. "Ain't she invited me to come to see her and bring my mouth organ? I got to show you this thing, then I'll tell you."

"What thing?" Haze muttered.

"This thing I got to show you," Enoch said. "Drive straight on ahead and I'll tell you where to stop."

"I don't want to see anything of yours," Haze Motes said. "I want that address."

Enoch didn't look at Hazel Motes. He looked out the window. "I won't be able to remember it unless you come," he said. In a minute the car started. Enoch's blood was beating fast. He knew he had to go to the FROSTY BOTTLE and the zoo before there, and he foresaw a terrible struggle with Hazel Motes. He would have to get him there, even if he had to hit him over the head with a rock and carry him on his back up to it.

Enoch's brain was divided into two parts. The part in communication with his blood did the figuring but it never said anything in words. The other part was stocked up with all kinds of words and phrases. While the first part was figuring how to get Hazel Motes through the FROSTY BOTTLE and the zoo, the second inquired, "Where'd you git thisyer fine car? You ought to paint you some signs on the outside it, like 'Step-in, baby'—I seen one with that on it, then I seen another, said . . ."

Hazel Motes's face might have been cut out of the side of a rock.

"My daddy once owned a yeller Ford automobile he won on a ticket," Enoch murmured. "It had a roll-top and two aerials and a squirrel tail all come with it. He swapped it off. Stop here! Stop here!" he yelled—they were passing the FROSTY BOTTLE.

"Where is it?" Hazel Motes said as soon as they were inside. They were in a dark room with a counter across the back of it and brown stools like toad stools in front of the counter. On the wall facing the door there was a large advertisement for ice cream, showing a cow dressed up like a housewife.

"It ain't here," Enoch said. "We have to stop here on the way and get something to eat. What you want?"

"Nothing," Haze said. He stood stiffly in the middle of the room with his hands in his pockets.

"Well, sit down," Enoch said. "I have to have a little drink."

Something stirred behind the counter and a woman with bobbed hair like a man's got up from a chair where she had been reading the newspaper, and came forward. She looked sourly at Enoch. She had on a once-white uniform clotted with brown stains. "What you want?" she said in a loud voice, leaning close to his ear. She had a man's face and big muscled arms.

"I want a chocolate malted milkshake, baby girl," Enoch said softly. "I want a lot of ice cream in it."

She turned fiercely from him and glared at Haze.

"He says he don't want nothing but to sit down and look at you for a while," Enoch said. "He ain't hungry but for just to see you."

Haze looked woodenly at the woman and she turned her back on him and began mixing the milkshake. He sat down on the last stool in the row and started cracking his knuckles.

Enoch watched him carefully. "I reckon you done changed some," he said after a few minutes.

Haze got up. "Give me those people's address. Right now," he said.

It came to Enoch in an instant—the police. His face was suddenly suffused with secret knowledge. "I reckon you ain't as uppity as you was last night," he said. "I reckon maybe," he said, "you ain't got so much cause now as you had then." Stole theter automobile, he thought.

Hazel Motes sat back down.

"Howcome you jumped up so fast down yonder by the pool?" Enoch asked. The woman turned around to him with the malted milk in her hand. "Of course," he said evilly, "I wouldn't have had no truck with a ugly dish like that neither."

The woman thumped the malted milk on the counter in front of him. "Fifteen cents," she roared.

"You're worth more than 'that, baby girl," Enoch said. He snickered and began gassing his malted milk through the straw.

The woman strode over to where Haze was. "What you come in here with a son of a bitch like that for?" she shouted. "A nice quiet boy like you to come in here with a son of a bitch. You ought to mind the company you keep." Her name was Maude and she drank whisky all day from a fruit jar under the counter. "Jesus," she said, wiping her hand under her nose. She sat down in a straight chair in front of Haze but facing Enoch, and folded her arms across her chest. "Ever' day," she said to Haze, looking at Enoch, "ever' day that son of a bitch comes in here."

Enoch was thinking about the animals. They had to go next to see the animals. He hated them; just thinking about them made his face turn a chocolate purple color as if the malted milk were rising in his head.

"You're a nice boy," she said. "I can see, you got a clean nose, well keep it clean, don't go messin' with a son a bitch like that yonder. I always know a clean boy when I see one." She was shouting at Enoch, but Enoch watched Hazel Motes. It was as if something inside Hazel Motes was winding up, although he didn't move on the outside. He only looked pressed down in that blue suit, as if inside it, the thing winding was getting tighter and tighter. Enoch's blood told him to hurry. He raced the milkshake up the straw.

"Yes sir," she said, "there ain't anything sweeter than a clean boy. God for my witness. And I know a clean one when I see him and I know a son a bitch when I see him and there's a heap of difference and that pus-marked bastard zlurping through that straw is a goddamned son a bitch and you a clean boy had better mind how you keep him company. I know a clean boy when I see one."

Enoch screeched in the bottom of his glass. He fished fifteen cents from his pocket and laid it on the counter and got up. But Hazel Motes was already up; he was leaning over the counter toward the woman. She didn't see him right away because she was looking at Enoch. He leaned on his hands over the counter until his face was just a foot from hers. She turned around and stared at him.

"Come on," Enoch started, "we don't have no time to be sassing around with her. I got to show you this right away,

I got . . ."

"I AM clean," Haze said.

It was not until he said it again that Enoch caught the words.

"I AM clean," he said again, without any expression on his face or in his voice, just looking at the woman as if he were looking at a wall. "If Jesus existed, I wouldn't be clean," he said.

She stared at him, startled and then outraged. "What do you think I care!" she yelled. "Why should I give a goddam what you are!"

"Come on," Enoch whined, "come on or I won't tell you where them people live." He caught Haze's arm and pulled him back from the counter and toward the door.

"You bastard!" the woman screamed, "what do you think I care about any of you filthy boys?"

Hazel Motes pushed the door open quickly and went out. He got back in his car and Enoch climbed in behind him. "Okay," Enoch said, "drive straight on ahead down this road."

"What you want for telling me?" Haze said. "I'm not staying here. I have to go. I can't stay here any longer."

Enoch shuddered. He began wetting his lips. "I got to show it to you," he said hoarsely. "I can't show it to nobody but you. I had a sign it was you when I seen you drive up at the pool. I knew all morning somebody was going to come and then when I saw you at the pool, I had thisyer sign."

"I don't care about your signs," Haze said.

"I go to see it ever' day," Enoch said. "I go ever' day but I ain't ever been able to take nobody else with me. I had to wait on the sign. I'll tell you them people's address just as soon as you see it. You got to see it," he said. "When you see it, something's going to happen."

"Nothing's going to happen," Haze said.

He started the car again and Enoch sat forward on the seat. "Them animals," he muttered. "We got to walk by them first. It won't take long for that. It won't take a minute." He saw the animals waiting evil-eyed for him, ready to throw him off time. He thought what if the police were screaming out here now with sirens and squad cars and they got Hazel Motes just before he showed it to him.

"I got to see those people," Haze said.

"Stop here! Stop here!" Enoch yelled.

There was a long shining row of steel cages over to the

left and behind the bars, black shapes were sitting or pacing. "Get out," Enoch said. "This won't take one second."

Haze got out. Then he stopped. "I got to see those people," he said.

"Okay, okay, come on," Enoch whined.

"I don't believe you know the address."

"I do! I do!" Enoch cried. "It begins with a three, now come on!" He pulled Haze toward the cages. Two black bears sat in the first one, facing each other like two matrons having tea, their faces polite and self-absorbed. "They don't do nothing but sit there all day and stink," Enoch said. "A man comes and washes them cages out ever' morning with a hose and it stinks just as much· as if he'd left it." He went past two more cages of bears, not looking at them, and then he stopped at the next cage where there were two yellow-eyed wolves nosing around the edges of the concrete. "Hyenas," he said. "I ain't got no use for hyenas." He leaned closer and spit into the cage, hitting one of the wolves on the leg. It shuttled to the side, giving him a slanted evil look. For a second he forgot Hazel Motes. Then he looked back quickly to make sure he was still there. He was right behind him. He was not looking at the animals. Thinking about them police, Enoch thought. He said, "Come on, we don't have time to look at all theseyer monkeys that come next." Usually he stopped at every cage and made an obscene comment aloud to himself, but today the animals were only a form he had to get through. He hurried past the cages of monkeys, looking back two or three times to make sure Hazel Motes was behind him. At the last of the monkey cages, he stopped as if he couldn't help himself.

"Look at that ape," he said, glaring. The animal had its back to him, gray except for a small pink seat. "If I had a ass like that," he said prudishly, "I'd sit on it. I wouldn't be exposing it to all these people come to this park. Come on, we don't have to look at theseyer birds that come next." He ran past the cages of birds and then he was at the end of the zoo. "Now we don't need the car," he said, going on ahead, "we'll go right down that hill yonder through them trees." Haze had stopped at the last cage for birds. "Oh Jesus," Enoch groaned. He stood and waved his arms wildly and shouted, "Come on!" but Haze didn't move from where he was looking into the cage.

Enoch ran back to him and grabbed him by the arm but Haze pushed him off and kept on looking in the cage. It was empty. Enoch stared. "It's empty!" he shouted. "What you have to look in that ole empty cage for? You come on!" He stood there, sweating and purple. "It's empty!" he shouted. And then he saw it wasn't empty. Over in one corner on the floor of the cage, there was an eye. The eye was in the middle of something that looked like a piece of mop sitting on an old rag. He squinted close to the wire and saw that the piece of mop was an owl with one eye open. It was looking directly at Hazel Motes. "That ain't nothing but a ole hoot owl," he moaned. "You seen them things before."

"I AM clean," Haze said to the eye. He said it just the way he said it to the woman in the FROSTY BOTTLE. The eye shut softly and the owl turned its face to the wall.

He's done murdered somebody, Enoch thought. "Oh sweet Jesus, come on!" he wailed. "I got to show you this right now." He pulled him away but a few feet from the cage, Haze stopped again, looking at something in the distance. Enoch's eyesight was very poor. He squinted and made out a figure far down the road behind them. There were two smaller figures jumping on either side of it.

Hazel Motes turned back to him suddenly and said, "Where's this thing? Let's see it right now and get it over with. Come on."

"Ain't that where I been trying to take you?" Enoch said. He felt the perspiration drying on him and stinging and his skin was pin-pointed, even in his scalp. "We got to cross this road and go down this hill. We got to go on foot," he said.

"Why?" Haze muttered.

"I don't know," Enoch said. He knew something was going to happen to him. His blood stopped beating. All the time it had been beating like drum noises and now it had stopped. They started down the hill. It was a steep hill, full of trees painted white from the ground up four feet. They looked as if they had on ankle-socks. He gripped Hazel Motes's arm. "It gets damp as you go down," he said, looking around vaguely. Hazel Motes shook him off. In a second, Enoch gripped his arm again and stopped him. He pointed down through the trees. "Muvseevum," he said. The strange word made him shiver. That was the first time he had ever said it aloud. A piece of gray building was showing where he pointed. It grew larger as they went down the hill, then as they came to the end of the wood and stepped out on the gravel driveway, it seemed to shrink suddenly. It was round and soot-colored. There were columns at the front of it and in between each column there was an eyeless stone woman holding a pot on her head. A concrete band was over the columns and the letters, M V S E V M, were cut into it. Enoch was afraid to pronounce the word again.

"We got to go up the steps and through the front door," he whispered. There were ten steps up to the porch. The door was wide and black. Enoch pushed it in cautiously and inserted his head in the crack. In a minute he brought it out again and said, "All right, go on in and walk easy. I don't want to wake up theter ole guard. He ain't very friendly with me." They went into a dark hall. It was heavy with the odor of linoleum and creosote and another odor behind these two. The third one was an undersmell and Enoch couldn't name it as anything he had ever smelled before. There was nothing in the hall but two urns and an old man asleep in a straight chair against the wall. He had on the same kind of uniform as Enoch and he looked like a dried-up spider stuck there. Enoch looked at Hazel Motes to see if he was smelling the undersmell. He looked as if he were. Enoch's blood began to beat again, urging him forward. He gripped Haze's arm and tiptoed through the hall to another black door at the end of it. He cracked it a little and inserted his head in the crack. Then in a second he drew it out and crooked his finger in a gesture for Haze to follow him. They went into another hall, like the last one, but running crosswise. "It's in that first door yonder," Enoch said in a small voice. They went into a dark room full of glass cases. The glass cases covered the walls and there were three coffin-like ones in the middle of the floor. The ones on the walls were full of birds tilted on varnished sticks and looking down with dried piquant expressions.

"Come on," Enoch whispered. He went past the two cases in the middle of the floor and toward the third one. He went to the farthest end of it and stopped. He stood looking down with his neck thrust forward and his hands clutched together; Hazel Motes moved up beside him.

The two of them stood there, Enoch rigid and Hazel Motes bent slightly forward. There were three bowls and a row of blunt weapons and a man in the case. It was the man Enoch was looking at. He was about three feet long. He was naked and a dried yellow color and his eyes were drawn almost shut as if a giant block of steel were falling down on top of him.

"See theter notice," Enoch said in a church whisper, pointing to a typewritten card at the man's foot, "it says he was

once as tall as you or me. Some A-rabs did it to him in
six months." He turned his head cautiously to see Hazel
Motes.

All he could tell was that Hazel Motes's eyes were on
the shrunken man. He was bent forward so that his face
was reflected on the glass top of the case. The reflection
was pale and the eyes were like two clean bullet holes.
Enoch waited, rigid. He heard footsteps in the hall. Oh
Jesus Jesus, he prayed, let him hurry up and do whatever
he's going to do! The woman with the two little boys
came in the door. She had one by each hand, and she was
grinning. Hazel Motes had not raised his eyes once from
the shrunken man. The woman came toward them. She
stopped on the other side of the case and looked down into
it and the reflection of her face appeared grinning on the
glass, over Hazel Motes's.

She snickered and put two fingers in front of her teeth.
The little boys' faces were like pans set on either side to
catch the grins that overflowed from her. When Haze saw
her face on the glass, his neck jerked back and he made a
noise. It might have come from the man inside the case.
In a second Enoch knew it had. "Wait!" he screamed, and
tore out of the room after Hazel Motes.

He overtook him halfway up the hill. He caught him by
the arm and swung him around and then he stood there,
suddenly weak and light as a balloon, and stared. Hazel
Motes grabbed him by the shoulders and shook him. "What
is that address!" he shouted. "Give me that address!"

Even if Enoch had been sure what the address was, he
couldn't have thought of it then. He could not even stand
up. As soon as Hazel Motes let him go, he fell backward
and landed against one of the white-socked trees. He rolled
over and lay stretched out on the ground, with an exalted
look on his face. He thought he was floating. A long way
off he saw the blue figure spring and pick up a rock, and
he saw the wild face turn, and the rock hurtle toward him;
he shut his eyes tight and the rock hit him on the forehead.

When he came to again, Hazel Motes was gone. He lay
there a minute. He put his fingers to his forehead and then
held them in front of his eyes. They were streaked with
red. He turned his head and saw a drop of blood on the
ground and as he looked at it, he thought it widened like
a little spring. He sat straight up, frozen-skinned, and put
his finger in it, and very faintly he could hear his blood
beating, his secret blood, in the center of the city.

Then he knew that whatever was expected of him was only just beginning.

VI

That evening Haze drove his car around the streets until he found the blind man and the child again. They were standing on a corner, waiting for the light to change. He drove the Essex at some distance behind them for about four blocks up the main street and then turned it after them down a side street. He followed them on into a dark section past the railroad yards and watched them go up on the porch of a box-like two-story house. When the blind man opened the door a shaft of light fell on him and Haze craned his neck to see him better. The child turned her head, slowly, as if it worked on a screw, and watched his car pass. His face was so close to the glass that it looked like a paper face pasted there. He noted the number of the house and a sign on it that said, ROOMS FOR RENT.

Then he drove back down town and parked the Essex in front of a movie house where he could catch the drain of people coming out from the picture show. The lights around the marquee were so bright that the moon, moving overhead with a small procession of clouds behind it, looked pale and insignificant. Haze got out of the Essex and climbed up on the nose of it.

A thin little man with a long upper lip was at the glass ticket box, buying tickets for three portly women who were behind him. "Gotta get these girls some refreshments too," he said to the woman in the ticket box. "Can't have 'em starve right before my eyes."

"Ain't he a card?" one of the women hollered. "He keeps me in stitches!"

Three boys in red satin lumberjackets came out of the foyer. Haze raised his arms. "Where has the blood you think you been redeemed by touched you?" he cried.

The women all turned around at once and stared at him.

"A wise guy," the little thin man said, and glared as if someone were about to insult him.

The three boys moved up, pushing each other's shoulders.

Haze waited a second and then he cried again. "Where has the blood you think you been redeemed by touched you?"

"Rabble rouser," the little man said. "One thing I can't stand it's a rabble rouser."

FLANNERY O'CONNOR

"What church you belong to, you boy there?" Haze asked, pointing at the tallest boy in the red satin lumberjacket.

The boy giggled.

"You then," he said impatiently, pointing at the next one. "What church you belong to?"

"Church of Christ," the boy said in a falsetto to hide the truth.

"Church of Christ!" Haze repeated. "Well, I preach the Church Without Christ. I'm member and preacher to that church where the blind don't see and the lame don't walk and what's dead stays that way. Ask me about that church and I'll tell you it's the church that the blood of Jesus don't foul with redemption."

"He's a preacher," one of the women said. "Let's go."

"Listen, you people, I'm going to take the truth with me wherever I go," Haze called. "I'm going to preach it to whoever'll listen at whatever place. I'm going to preach there was no Fall because there was nothing to fall from and no Redemption because there was no Fall and no Judgment because there wasn't the first two. Nothing matters but that Jesus was a liar."

The little man herded his girls into the picture show quickly and the three boys left but more people came out and he began over and said the same thing again. They left and some more came and he said it a third time. Then they left and no one else came out; there was no one there but the woman in the glass box. She had been glaring at him all the time but he had not noticed her. She wore glasses with rhinestones in the bows and she had white hair stacked in sausages around her head. She stuck her mouth to a hole in the glass and shouted, "Listen, if you don't have a church to do it in, you don't have to do it in front of this show."

"My church is the Church Without Christ, lady," he said. "If there's no Christ, there's no reason to have a set place to do it in."

"Listen," she said, "if you don't get from in front of this show, I'll call the police."

"There's plenty of shows," he said and got down and got back in the Essex and drove off. That night he preached in front of three other picture shows before he went to Mrs. Watts.

In the morning he drove back to the house where the blind man and the child had gone in the night before. It was yellow clapboard, the second one in a block of them, all alike. He went up to the front door and rang the bell.

After a few minutes a woman with a mop opened it. He said he wanted to rent a room.

"What you do?" she asked. She was a tall bony woman, resembling the mop she carried upside-down.

He said he was a preacher.

The woman looked at him thoroughly and then she looked behind him at his car. "What church?" she asked.

He said the Church Without Christ.

"Protestant?" she asked suspiciously, "or something foreign?"

He said no mam, it was Protestant.

After a minute she said, "Well, you can look at it," and he followed her into a white plastered hall and up some steps at the side of it. She opened a door into a back room that was a little larger than his car, with a cot and a chest of drawers and a table and straight chair in it. There were two nails on the wall to hang clothes on. "Three dollars a week in advance," she said. There was one window and another door opposite the door they had come in by. Haze opened the extra door, expecting it to be a closet. It opened out onto a drop of about thirty feet and looked down into a narrow bare back yard where the garbage was collected. There was a plank nailed across the door frame at knee level to keep anyone from falling out. "A man named Hawks lives here, don't he?" Haze asked quickly.

"Downstairs in the front room," she said, "him and his child." She was looking down into the drop too. "It used to be a fire-escape there," she said, "but I don't know what happened to it."

He paid her three dollars and took possession of the room, and as soon as she was out of the way, he went down the stairs and knocked on the Hawkses' door.

The blind man's child opened it a crack and stood looking at him. She seemed at once to have to balance her face so that her expression would be the same on both sides. "It's that boy, Papa," she said in a low tone. "The one that keeps following me." She held the door close to her head so he couldn't see in past her. The blind man came to the door but he didn't open it any wider. His look was not the same as it had been two nights before; it was sour and unfriendly, and he didn't speak, he only stood there.

Haze had got what he had to say in mind before he left his room. "I live here," he said. "I thought if your girl wanted to give me so much eye, I might return her some of it." He wasn't looking at the girl; he was staring at the black glasses and the curious scars that started somewhere behind them and ran down the blind man's cheeks.

"What I give you the other night," she said, "was a looker indignation for what I seen you do. It was you give me the eye. You should have seen him, Papa," she said, "looked me up and down."

"I've started my own church," Haze said. "The Church Without Christ. I preach on the street."

"You can't let me alone, can you?" Hawks said. His voice was flat, nothing like it had been the other time. "I didn't ask you to come here and I ain't asking you to hang around," he said.

Haze had expected a secret welcome. He waited, trying to think of something to say. "What kind of a preacher are you?" he heard himself murmur, "not to see if you can save my soul?" The blind man pushed the door shut in his face. Haze stood there a second facing the blank door, and then he ran his sleeve across his mouth and went out.

Inside, Hawks took off his dark glasses and, from a hole in the window shade, watched him get in his car and drive off. The eye he put to the hole was slightly rounder and smaller than his other one, but it was obvious he could see out of both of them. The child watched from a lower crack. "Howcome you don't like him, Papa?" she asked, "—because he's after me?"

"If he was after you, that would be enough to make me welcome him," he said.

"I like his eyes," she observed. "They don't look like they see what he's looking at but they keep on looking."

Their room was the same size as Haze's but there were two cots and an oil cooking stove and a wash basin in it and a trunk that they used for a table. Hawks sat down on one of the cots and put a cigarette in his mouth. "Goddam Jesus-hog," he muttered.

"Well, look what you used to be," she said. "Look what you tried to do. You got over it and so will he."

"I don't want him hanging around," he said. "He makes me nervous."

"Listen here," she said, sitting down on the cot with him, "you help me to get him and then you go away and do what you please and I can live with him."

"He don't even know you exist," Hawks said.

"Even if he don't," she said, "that's all right. That's howcome I can get him easy. I want him and you ought to help and then you could go on off like you want to."

He lay down on the cot and finished the cigarette; his face was thoughtful and evil. Once while he was lying there, he laughed and then his expression constricted again. "Well, that might be fine," he said after a while. "That might be the oil on Aaron's beard."

"Listen here," she said, "it would be the nuts! I'm just crazy about him. I never seen a boy that I liked the looks of any better. Don't run him off. Tell him how you blinded yourself for Jesus and show him that clipping you got."

"Yeah, the clipping," he said.

Haze had gone out in his car to think and he had decided that he would seduce Hawks's child. He thought that when the blind preacher saw his daughter ruined, he would realize that he was in earnest when he said he preached The Church Without Christ. Besides this reason, there was another: he didn't want to go back to Mrs. Watts. The night before, after he was asleep, she had got up and cut the top of his hat out in an obscene shape. He felt that he should have a woman, not for the sake of the pleasure in her, but to prove that he didn't believe in sin since he practiced what was called it; but he had had enough of her. He wanted someone he could teach something to and he took it for granted that the blind man's child, since she was so homely, would also be innocent.

Before he went back to his room, he went to a dry-goods store to buy a new hat. He wanted one that was completely opposite to the old one. This time he was sold a white panama with a red and green and yellow band around it. The man said they were really the thing and particularly if he was going to Florida.

"I ain't going to Florida," he said. "This hat is opposite from the one I used to have is all."

"You can use it anywheres," the man said; "it's new."

"I know that," Haze said. He went outside and took the red and green and yellow band off it and thumped out the crease in the top and turned down the brim. When he put it on, it looked just as fierce as the other one had.

He didn't go back to the Hawkses' door until late in the afternoon, when he thought they would be eating their supper. It opened almost at once and the child's head appeared in the crack. He pushed the door out of her hand and went in without looking at her directly. Hawks was sitting at the trunk. The remains of his supper were in front of him but he wasn't eating. He had barely got the black glasses on in time.

"If Jesus cured blind men, howcome you don't get Him to cure you?" Haze asked. He had prepared this sentence in his room.

"He blinded Paul," Hawks said.

Haze sat down on the edge of one of the cots. He looked around him and then back at Hawks. He crossed and uncrossed his knees and then he crossed them again. "Where'd you get them scars?" he asked.

The fake blind man leaned forward and smiled. "You still have a chance to save yourself if you repent," he said. "I can't save you but you can save yourself."

"That's what I've already done," Haze said. "Without the repenting. I preach how I done it every night on the . . ."

"Look at this," Hawks said. He took a yellow newspaper clipping from his pocket and handed it to him, and his mouth twisted out of the smile. "This is how I got the scars," he muttered. The child made a sign to him from the door to smile and not look sour. As he waited for Haze to finish reading, the smile slowly returned.

The headline on the clipping said, EVANGELIST PROMISES TO BLIND SELF. The rest of it said that Asa Hawks, an evangelist of the Free Church of Christ, had promised to blind himself to justify his belief that Christ Jesus had redeemed him. It said he would do it at a revival on Saturday night at eight o'clock, the fourth of October. The date on it was more than ten years before. Over the headline was a picture of Hawks, a scarless, straight-mouthed man of about thirty, with one eye a little smaller and rounder than the other. The mouth had a look that might have been either holy or calculating, but there was a wildness in the eyes that suggested terror.

Haze sat staring at the clipping after he had read it. He read it three times. He took his hat off and put it on again and got up and stood looking around the room as if he were trying to remember where the door was.

"He did it with lime," the child said, "and there was hundreds converted. Anybody that blinded himself for justification ought to be able to save you—or even somebody of his blood," she added, inspired.

"Nobody with a good car needs to be justified," Haze murmured. He scowled at her and hurried out the door, but as soon as it was shut behind him, he remembered something. He turned around and opened it and handed her a piece of paper, folded up several times into a small pellet shape; then he hurried out to his car.

Hawks took the note away from her and opened it up. It said, BABE, I NEVER SAW ANYBODY THAT LOOKED AS GOOD AS YOU BEFORE IS WHY I CAME HERE. She read it over his arm, coloring pleasantly.

"Now you got the written proof for it, Papa," she said.

"That bastard got away with my clipping," Hawks muttered.

"Well you got another clipping, ain't you?" she asked, with a little smirk.

"Shut your mouth," he said and flung himself down on the cot. The other clipping was one that said, EVANGELIST'S NERVE FAILS.

"I can get it for you," she offered, standing close to the door so that she could run if she disturbed him too much, but he had turned toward the wall as if he were going to sleep.

Ten years ago at a revival he had intended to blind himself and two hundred people or more were there, waiting for him to do it. He had preached for an hour on the blindness of Paul, working himself up until he saw himself struck blind by a Divine flash of lightning and, with courage enough then, he had thrust his hands into the bucket of wet lime and streaked them down his face; but he hadn't been able to let any of it get into his eyes. He had been possessed of as many devils as were necessary to do it, but at that instant, they disappeared, and he saw himself standing there as he was. He fancied Jesus, Who had expelled them, was standing there too, beckoning to him; and he had fled out of the tent into the alley and disappeared.

"Okay, Pa," she said, "I'll go out for a while and leave you in peace."

Haze had driven his car immediately to the nearest garage where a man with black bangs and a short expressionless face had come out to wait on him. He told the man he wanted the horn made to blow and the leaks taken out of the gas tank, the starter made to work smoother and the windshield wipers tightened.

The man lifted the hood and glanced inside and then shut it again. Then he walked around the car, stopping to lean on it here and there, and thumping it in one place and another. Haze asked him how long it would take to put it in the best order.

"It can't be done," the man said.

"This is a good car," Haze said. "I knew when I first saw

it that it was the car for me, and since I've had it, I've had a place to be that I can always get away in."

"Was you going some place in this?" the man asked.

"To another garage," Haze said, and he got in the Essex and drove off. At the other garage he went to, there was a man who said he could put the car in the best shape overnight, because it was such a good car to begin with, so well put together and with such good materials in it, and because, he added, he was the best mechanic in town, working in the best-equipped shop. Haze left it with him, certain that it was in honest hands.

VII

The next afternoon when he got his car back, he drove it out into the country to see how well it worked on the open road. The sky was just a little lighter blue than his suit, clear and even, with only one cloud in it, a large blinding white one with curls and a beard. He had gone about a mile out of town when he heard a throat cleared behind him. He slowed down and turned his head and saw Hawks's child getting up off the floor onto the two-by-four that stretched across the seat frame. "I been here all the time," she said, "and you never known it." She had a bunch of dandelions in her hair and a wide red mouth on her pale face.

"What do you want to hide in my car for?" he said angrily. "I got business before me. I don't have time for foolishness." Then he checked his ugly tone and stretched his mouth a little, remembering that he was going to seduce her. "Yeah sure," he said, "glad to see you."

She swung one thin black-stockinged leg over the back of the front seat and then let the rest of herself over. "Did you mean 'good to look at' in that note, or only 'good'?" she asked.

"The both," he said stiffly.

"My name is Sabbath," she said. "Sabbath Lily Hawks. My mother named me that just after I was born because I was born on the Sabbath and then she turned over in her bed and died and I never seen her."

"Unh," Haze said. His jaw tightened and he entrenched himself behind it and drove on. He had not wanted any company. His sense of pleasure in the car and in the afternoon was gone.

"Him and her wasn't married," she continued, "and that

makes me a bastard, but I can't help it. It was what he done to me and not what I done to myself."

"A bastard?" he murmured. He couldn't see how a preacher who had blinded himself for Jesus could have a bastard. He turned his head and looked at her with interest for the first time.

She nodded and the corners of her mouth turned up. "A real bastard," she said, catching his elbow, "and do you know what? A bastard shall not enter the kingdom of heaven!" she said.

Haze was driving his car toward the ditch while he stared at her. "How could you be . . . ," he started and saw the red embankment in front of him and pulled the car back on the road.

"Do you read the papers?" she asked.

"No," he said.

"Well, there's this woman in it named Mary Brittle that tells you what to do when you don't know. I wrote her a letter and ast her what I was to do."

"How could you be a bastard when he blinded him . . . ," he started again.

"I says, 'Dear Mary, I am a bastard and a bastard shall not enter the kingdom of heaven as we all know, but I have this personality that makes boys follow me. Do you think I should neck or not? I shall not enter the kingdom of heaven anyway so I don't see what difference it makes.' "

"Listen here," Haze said, "if he blinded himself how . . ."

"Then she answered my letter in the paper. She said, 'Dear Sabbath, Light necking is acceptable, but I think your real problem is one of adjustment to the modern world. Perhaps you ought to re-examine your religious values to see if they meet your needs in Life. A religious experience can be a beautiful addition to living if you put it in the proper prespective and do not let it warf you. Read some books on Ethical Culture.' "

"You couldn't be a bastard," Haze said, getting very pale. "You must be mixed up. Your daddy blinded himself."

"Then I wrote her another letter," she said, scratching his ankle with the toe of her sneaker, and smiling, "I says, 'Dear Mary, What I really want to know is should I go the whole hog or not? That's my real problem. I'm adjusted okay to the modern world.' "

"Your daddy blinded himself," Haze repeated.

"He wasn't always as good as he is now," she said. "She never answered my second letter."

"You mean in his youth he didn't believe but he came to?" he asked. "Is that what you mean or ain't it?" and he kicked her foot roughly away from his.

"That's right," she said. Then she drew herself up a little. "Quit that feeling my leg with yours," she said.

The blinding white cloud was a little ahead of them, moving to the left. "Why don't you turn down that dirt road?" she asked. The highway forked off onto a clay road and he turned onto it. It was hilly and shady and the country showed to advantage on either side. One side was dense honeysuckle and the other was open and slanted down to a telescoped view of the city. The white cloud was directly in front of them.

"How did he come to believe?" Haze asked. "What changed him into a preacher for Jesus?"

"I do like a dirt road," she said, "particularly when it's hilly like this one here. Why don't we get out and sit under a tree where we could get better acquainted?"

After a few hundred feet Haze stopped the car and they got out. "Was he a very evil-seeming man before he came to believe," he asked, "or just part way evil-seeming?"

"All the way evil," she said, going under the barbed wire fence on the side of the road. Once under it she sat down and began to take off her shoes and stockings. "How I like to walk in a field is barefooted," she said with gusto.

"Listenhere," Haze muttered, "I got to be going back to town. I don't have time to walk in any field," but he went under the fence and on the other side he said, "I suppose before he came to believe he didn't believe at all."

"Let's us go over that hill yonder and sit under the trees," she said.

They climbed the hill and went down the other side of it, she a little ahead of Haze. He saw that sitting under a tree with her might help him to seduce her, but he was in no hurry to get on with it, considering her innocence. He felt it was too hard a job to be done in an afternoon. She sat down under a large pine and patted the ground close beside her for him to sit on, but he sat about five feet away from her on a rock. He rested his chin on his knees and looked straight ahead.

"I can save you," she said. "I got a church in my heart where Jesus is King."

He leaned in her direction, glaring. "I believe in a new kind of jesus," he said, "one that can't waste his blood redeeming people with it, because he's all man and ain't got any God in him. My church is the Church Without Christ!"

She moved up closer to him. "Can a bastard be saved in it?" she asked.

"There's no such thing as a bastard in the Church Without Christ," he said. "Everything is all one. A bastard wouldn't be any different from anybody else."

"That's good," she said.

He looked at her irritably, for something in his mind was already contradicting him and saying that a bastard couldn't, that there was only one truth—that Jesus was a liar—and that her case was hopeless. She pulled open her collar and lay down on the ground full length. "Ain't my feet white, though?" she asked raising them slightly.

Haze didn't look at her feet. The thing in his mind said that the truth didn't contradict itself and that a bastard couldn't be saved in the Church Without Christ. He decided he would forget it, that it was not important.

"There was this child once," she said, turning over on her stomach, "that nobody cared if it lived or died. Its kin sent it around from one to another of them and finally to its grandmother who was a very evil woman and she couldn't stand to have it around because the least good thing made her break out in these welps. She would get all itching and swoll. Even her eyes would itch her and swell up and there wasn't nothing she could do but run up and down the road, shaking her hands and cursing and it was twicet as bad when this child was there so she kept the child locked up in a chicken crate. It seen its granny in hell-fire, swoll and burning, and it told her everything it seen and she got so swoll until finally she went to the well and wrapped the well rope around her neck and let down the bucket and broke her neck.

"Would you guess me to be fifteen years old?" she asked.

"There wouldn't be any sense to the word, bastard, in the Church Without Christ," Haze said.

"Why don't you lie down and rest yourself?" she inquired.

Haze moved a few feet away and lay down. He put his hat over his face and folded his arms across his chest. She lifted herself up on her hands and knees and crawled over to him and gazed at the top of his hat. Then she lifted it off like a lid and peered into his eyes. They stared straight upward. "It don't make any difference to me," she said softly, "how much you like me."

He trained his eyes into her neck. Gradually she lowered her head until the tips of their noses almost touched but still he didn't look at her. "I see you," she said in a playful voice.

"Git away!" he said, jumping violently.

She scrambled up and ran around behind the tree. Haze put his hat back on and stood up, shaken. He wanted to get back in the Essex. He realized suddenly that it was parked on a country road, unlocked, and that the first person passing would drive off in it.

"I see you," a voice said from behind the tree.

He walked off quickly in the opposite direction toward the car. The jubilant expression on the face that looked from around the tree, flattened.

He got in his car and went through the motions of starting it but it only made a noise like water lost somewhere in the pipes. A panic took him and he began to pound the starter. There were two instruments on the dashboard with needles that pointed dizzily in first one direction and then another, but they worked on a private system, independent of the whole car. He couldn't tell if it was out of gas or not. Sabbath Hawks came running up to the fence. She got down on the ground and rolled under the barbed wire and then stood at the window of the car, looking in at him. He turned his head at her fiercely and said, "What did you do to my car?" Then he got out and started walking down the road, without waiting for her to answer. After a second, she followed him, keeping her distance.

Where the highway had forked off onto the dirt road, there had been a store with a gas pump in front of it. It was about a half-mile back; Haze kept up a steady fast pace until he reached it. It had a deserted look, but after a few minutes a man appeared from out of the woods behind it, and Haze told him what he wanted. While the man got out his pick-up truck to drive them back to the Essex, Sabbath Hawks arrived and went over to a cage about six feet high that was at the side of the shack. Haze had not noticed it until she came up. He saw that there was something alive in it, and went near enough to read a sign that said, TWO DEADLY ENEMIES. HAVE A LOOK FREE.

There was a black bear about four feet long and very thin, resting on the floor of the cage; his back was spotted with bird lime that had been shot down on him by a small chicken hawk that was sitting on a perch in the upper part of the same apartment. Most of the hawk's tail was gone; the bear had only one eye.

"Come on here if you don't want to get left," Haze said

roughly, grabbing her by the arm. The man had his truck ready and the three of them drove back in it to the Essex. On the way Haze told him about the Church Without Christ; he explained its principles and said there was no such thing as a bastard in it. The man didn't comment. When they got out at the Essex, he put a can of gas in the tank and Haze got in and tried to start it but nothing happened. The man opened up the hood and studied the inside for a while. He was a one-armed man with two sandy colored teeth and eyes that were slate-blue and thoughtful. He had not spoken more than two words yet. He looked for a long time under the hood while Haze stood by, but he didn't touch anything. After a while he shut it and blew his nose.

"What's wrong in there?" Haze asked in an agitated voice. "It's a good car, ain't it?"

The man didn't answer him. He sat down on the ground and eased under the Essex. He wore hightop shoes and gray socks. He stayed under the car a long time. Haze got down on his hands and knees and looked under to see what he was doing but he wasn't doing anything. He was just lying there, looking up, as if he were contemplating; his good arm was folded on his chest. After a while, he eased himself out and wiped his face and neck with a piece of flannel rag he had in his pocket.

"Listenhere," Haze said, "that's a good car. You just give me a push, that's all. That car'll get me anywhere I want to go."

The man didn't say anything but he got back in the truck and Haze and Sabbath Hawks got in the Essex and he pushed them. After a few hundred yards the Essex began to belch and gasp and jiggle. Haze stuck his head out the window and motioned for the truck to come alongside. "Ha!" he said. "I told you, didn't I? This car'll get me anywhere I want to go. It may stop here and there but it won't stop permanent. What do I owe you?"

"Nothing," the man said, "not a thing."

"But the gas," Haze said, "how much for the gas?"

"Nothing," the man said with the same level look. "Not a thing."

"All right, I thank you," Haze said and drove on. "I don't need no favors from him," he said.

"It's a grand auto," Sabbath Hawks said. "It goes as smooth as honey."

"It ain't been built by a bunch of foreigners or niggers

or one-arm men," Haze said. "It was built by people with their eyes open that knew where they were at."

When they came to the end of the dirt road and were facing the paved one, the pick-up truck pulled alongside again and while the two cars paused side by side, Haze and the slate-eyed man looked at each other out of their two windows. "I told you this car would get me anywhere I wanted to go," Haze said sourly.

"Some things," the man said, " 'll get some folks somewheres," and he turned the truck up the highway.

Haze drove on. The blinding white cloud had turned into a bird with long thin wings and was disappearing in the opposite direction.

VIII

Enoch Emery knew now that his life would never be the same again, because the thing that was going to happen to him had started to happen. He had always known that something was going to happen but he hadn't known what. If he had been much given to thought, he might have thought that now was the time for him to justify his daddy's blood, but he didn't think in broad sweeps like that, he thought what he would do next. Sometimes he didn't think, he only wondered; then before long he would find himself doing this or that, like a bird finds itself building a nest when it hasn't actually been planning to.

What was going to happen to him had started to happen when he showed what was in the glass case to Haze Motes. That was a mystery beyond his understanding, but he knew that what was going to be expected of him was something awful. His blood was more sensitive than any other part of him; it wrote doom all through him, except possibly in his brain, and the result was that his tongue, which edged out every few minutes to test his fever blister, knew more than he did.

The first thing that he found himself doing that was not normal was saving his pay. He was saving all of it, except what his landlady came to collect every week and what he had to use to buy something to eat with. Then to his surprise, he found he wasn't eating very much and he was saving that money too. He had a fondness for Supermarkets; it was his custom to spend an hour or so in one every afternoon after he left the city park, browsing around among the canned goods and reading the cereal stories. Lately he had been compelled to pick up a few things here and there that would not be bulky in his pockets, and he wondered if this could be the reason he was saving so much money on food. It could have been, but he had the suspicion that saving the money was connected with some larger thing. He had always been given to stealing but he had never saved before.

At the same time, he began cleaning up his room. It was a little green room, or it had once been green, in the attic of an elderly rooming house. There was a mummified look and feel to this residence, but Enoch had never thought before of brightening the part (corresponding to the head) that he lived in. Then he simply found himself doing it.

First, he removed the rug from the floor and hung it out the window. This was a mistake because when he went to pull it back in, there were only a few long strings left with a carpet tack caught in one of them. He imagined that it must have been a very old rug and he decided to handle the rest of the furniture with more care. He washed the bed frame with soap and water and found that under the second layer of dirt, it was pure gold, and this affected him so strongly that he washed the chair. It was a low round chair that bulged around the legs so that it seemed to be in the act of squatting. The gold began to appear with the first touch of water but it disappeared with the second and with a little more, the chair sat down as if this were the end of long years of inner struggle. Enoch didn't know if it was for him or against him. He had a nasty impulse to kick it to pieces, but he let it stay there, exactly in the position it had sat down in, because for the time anyway, he was not a foolhardy boy who took chances on the meanings of things. For the time, he knew that what he didn't know was what mattered.

The only other piece of furniture in the room was a washstand. This was built in three parts and stood on bird legs six inches high. The legs had clawed feet that were each one gripped around a small cannon ball. The lowest part was a tabernacle-like cabinet which was meant to contain a slop-jar. Enoch didn't own a slop-jar but he had a certain reverence for the purpose of things and since he didn't have the right thing to put in it, he left it empty. Directly over this place for the treasure, there was a gray marble slab and coming up from behind it was a wooden trellis-work of hearts, scrolls and flowers, extending into a hunched eagle wing on either side, and containing in the middle, just at the level of Enoch's face when he stood in front of it, a small oval mirror. The wooden frame continued again over the mirror and ended in a crowned, horned headpiece, showing that the artist had not lost faith in his work.

As far as Enoch was concerned, this piece had always been the center of the room and the one that most connected him with what he didn't know. More than once after a big supper, he had dreamed of unlocking the cabinet and getting in it and then proceeding to certain rites and mysteries that he had a very vague idea about in the morning. In his cleaning up, his mind was on the washstand from the first, but as was usual with him, he began with the least important thing and worked around and in toward the center where the meaning was. So before he tackled the washstand, he took care of the pictures in the room.

These were three, one belonging to his landlady (who was almost totally blind but moved about by an acute sense of smell) and two of his own. Hers was a brown portrait of a moose standing in a small lake. The look of superiority on this animal's face was so insufferable to Enoch that, if he hadn't been afraid of him, he would have done something about it a long time ago. As it was, he couldn't do anything in his room but what the smug face was watching, not shocked because nothing better could be expected and not amused because nothing was funny. If he had looked all over for one, he couldn't have found a roommate that irritated him more. He kept up a constant stream of inner comment, uncomplimentary to the moose, though when he said anything aloud, he was more guarded. The moose was in a heavy brown frame with leaf designs on it and this added to his weight and his self-satisfied look. Enoch knew the time had come when something had to be done; he didn't know what was going to happen in his room, but when it happened, he didn't want to have the feeling that the moose was running it. The answer came to him fully prepared: he realized with a sudden intuition that taking the frame off him would be equal to taking the clothes off him (although he didn't have on any) and he was right because when he had done it, the animal looked so reduced that Enoch could only snicker and look at him out the corner of his eye.

After this success he turned his attention to the other two pictures. They were over calendars and had been sent him by the Hilltop Funeral Home and the American Rubber Tire Company. One showed a small boy in a pair of blue Doctor Denton sleepers, kneeling at his bed, saying, "And bless daddy," while the moon looked in at the window. This was

Enoch's favorite painting and it hung directly over his bed. The other pictured a lady wearing a rubber tire and it hung directly across from the moose on the opposite wall. He left it where it was, pretty certain that the moose only pretended not to see it. Immediately after he finished with the pictures, he went out and bought chintz curtains, a bottle of gilt, and a paint brush with all the money he had saved.

This was a disappointment to him because he had hoped that the money would be for some new clothes for him, and here he saw it going into a set of drapes. He didn't know what the gilt was for until he got home with it; when he got home with it, he sat down in front of the slop-jar cabinet in the washstand, unlocked it, and painted the inside of it with the gilt. Then he realized that the cabinet was to be used FOR something.

Enoch never nagged his blood to tell him a thing until it was ready. He wasn't the kind of a boy who grabs at any possibility and runs off, proposing this or that preposterous thing. In a large matter like this, he was always willing to wait for a certainty, and he waited for this one, certain at least that he would know in a few days. Then for about a week his blood was in secret conference with itself every day, only stopping now and then to shout some order at him.

On the following Monday, he was certain when he woke up that today was the day he was going to know on. His blood was rushing around like a woman who cleans up the house after the company has come, and he was surly and rebellious. When he realized that today was the day, he decided not to get up. He didn't want to justify his daddy's blood, he didn't want to be always having to do something that something else wanted him to do, that he didn't know what it was and that was always dangerous.

Naturally, his blood was not going to put up with any attitude like this. He was at the zoo by nine-thirty, only a half-hour later than he was supposed to be. All morning his mind was not on the gate he was supposed to guard but was chasing around after his blood, like a boy with a mop and a bucket, beating something here and sloshing down something there, without a second's rest. As soon as the second-shift guard came, Enoch headed toward town.

Town was the last place he wanted to be because anything could happen there. All the time his mind had been chasing around it had been thinking how as soon as he got off duty he was going to sneak off home and go to bed.

By the time he got into the center of the business district he was exhausted and he had to lean against Walgreen's window and cool off. Sweat crept down his back and provoked him to itch so that in just a few minutes he appeared to be working his way across the glass by his muscles, against a background of alarm clocks, toilet waters, candies, sanitary pads, fountain pens, and pocket flashlights, displayed in all colors to twice his height. He appeared to be working his way to a rumbling noise which came from the center of a small alcove that formed the entrance to the drug store. Here was a yellow and blue, glass and steel machine, belching popcorn into a cauldron of butter and salt. Enoch approached, already with his purse out, sorting his money. His purse was a long gray leather pouch, tied at the top with a drawstring. It was one he had stolen from his daddy and he treasured it because it was the only thing he owned now that his daddy had touched (besides himself). He sorted out two nickels and handed them to a pasty boy in a white apron who was there to serve the machine. The boy felt around in its vitals and filled a white paper bag with the corn, not taking his eye off Enoch's purse the while. On any other day Enoch would have tried to make friends with him but today he was too preoccupied even to see him. He took the bag and began stuffing the pouch back where it had come from. The youth's eye followed to the very edge of the pocket. "That thang looks like a hawg bladder," he observed enviously.

"I got to go now," Enoch murmured and hurried into the drug store. Inside, he walked abstractedly to the back of the store, and then up to the front again by the other aisle as if he wanted any person who might be looking for him to see he was there. He paused in front of the soda fountain to see if he would sit down and have something to eat. The fountain counter was pink and green marble linoleum and behind it there was a red-headed waitress in a lime-colored uniform and a pink apron. She had green eyes set in pink and they resembled a picture behind her of a Lime-Cherry Surprise, a special that day for ten cents. She confronted Enoch while he studied the information over her head. After a minute she laid her chest on the counter and surrounded it by her folded arms, to wait. Enoch couldn't decide which of several concoctions was the one for him to have until she ended it by moving one arm under the counter and bringing out a Lime-Cherry Surprise. "It's okay," she said, "I fixed it this morning after breakfast."

"Something's going to happen to me today," Enoch said.

"I told you it was okay," she said. "I fixed it today."

"I seen it this morning when I woke up," he said, with the look of a visionary.

"God," she said, and jerked it from under his face. She turned around and began slapping things together; in a second she slammed another—exactly like it, but fresh—in front of him.

"I got to go now," Enoch said, and hurried out. An eye caught at his pocket as he passed the popcorn machine but he didn't stop. I don't want to do it, he was saying to himself. Whatever it is, I don't want to do it. I'm going home. It'll be something I don't want to do. It'll be something I ain't got no business doing. And he thought of how he had had to spend all his money on drapes and gilt when he could have bought him a shirt and a phosphorescent tie. It'll be something against the law, he said. It's always something against the law. I ain't going to do it, he said, and stopped. He had stopped in front of a movie house where there was a large illustration of a monster stuffing a young woman into an incinerator.

I ain't going in no picture show like that, he said, giving it a nervous look. I'm going home. I ain't going to wait around in no picture show. I ain't got the money to buy a ticket, he said, taking out his purse again. I ain't even going to count thisyer change.

It ain't but forty-three cent here, he said, that ain't enough. A sign said the price of a ticket for adults was forty-five cents, balcony, thirty-five. I ain't going to sit in no balcony, he said, buying a thirty-five cent ticket.

I ain't going in, he said.

Two doors flew open and he found himself moving down a long red foyer and then up a darker tunnel and then up a higher, still darker tunnel. In a few minutes he was up in a high part of the maw, feeling around, like Jonah, for a seat. I ain't going to look at it, he said furiously. He didn't like any picture shows but colored musical ones.

The first picture was about a scientist named The Eye who performed operations by remote control. You would wake up in the morning and find a slit in your chest or head or stomach and something you couldn't do without would be gone. Enoch pulled his hat down very low and drew his knees up in front of his face; only his eyes looked at the screen. That picture lasted an hour.

The second picture was about life at Devil's Island Penitentiary. After a while, Enoch had to grip the two arms of his seat to keep himself from falling over the rail in front of him.

The third picture was called, "Lonnie Comes Home Again." It was about a baboon named Lonnie who rescued attractive children from a burning orphanage. Enoch kept hoping Lonnie would get burned up but he didn't appear to get even hot. In the end a nice-looking girl gave him a medal. It was more than Enoch could stand. He made a dive for the aisle, fell down the two higher tunnels, and raced out the red foyer and into the street. He collapsed as soon as the air hit him.

When he recovered himself, he was sitting against the wall of the picture show building and he was not thinking any more about escaping his duty. It was night and he had the feeling that the knowledge he couldn't avoid was almost on him. His resignation was perfect. He leaned against the wall for about twenty minutes and then he got up and began to walk down the street as if he were led by a silent melody or by one of those whistles that only dogs hear. At the end of two blocks he stopped, his attention directed across the street. There, facing him under a street light, was a high rat-colored car and up on the nose of it, a dark figure with a fierce white hat on. The figure's arms were working up and down and he had thin, gesticulating hands, almost as pale as the hat. "Hazel Motes!" Enoch breathed, and his heart began to slam from side to side like a wild bell clapper.

There were a few people standing on the sidewalk near the car. Enoch didn't know that Hazel Motes had started the Church Without Christ and was preaching it every night on the street; he hadn't seen him since that day at the park when he had showed him the shriveled man in the glass case.

"If you had been redeemed," Hazel Motes was shouting, "you would care about redemption but you don't. Look inside yourselves and see if you hadn't rather it wasn't if it was. There's no peace for the redeemed," he shouted, "and I preach peace, I preach the Church Without Christ, the church peaceful and satisfied!"

Two or three people who had stopped near the car started walking off the other way. "Leave!" Hazel Motes cried. "Go ahead and leave! The truth don't matter to you. Listen," he said, pointing his finger at the rest of them, "the truth don't matter to you. If Jesus had redeemed you, what difference would it make to you? You wouldn't do nothing about it. Your faces wouldn't move, neither this way nor that, and if it was three crosses there and Him hung on the middle one, that one wouldn't mean no more to you and me than the other two. Listen here. What you need is something to take the place of Jesus, something that would speak plain. The Church Without Christ don't have a Jesus but it needs one! It needs a new jesus! It needs one that's all man, without blood to waste, and it needs one that don't look like any other man so you'll look at him. Give me such a jesus, you people. Give me such a new jesus and you'll see how far the Church Without Christ can go!"

One of the people watching walked off so there were only two left. Enoch was standing in the middle of the street, paralyzed.

"Show me where this new jesus is," Hazel Motes cried, "and I'll set him up in the Church Without Christ and then you'll see the truth. Then you'll know once and for all that you haven't been redeemed. Give me this new jesus, somebody, so we'll all be saved by the sight of him!"

Enoch began shouting without a sound. He shouted that way for a full minute while Hazel Motes went on.

"Look at me!" Hazel Motes cried, with a tare in his throat, "and you look at a peaceful man! Peaceful because my blood has set me free. Take counsel from your blood and come into the Church Without Christ and maybe somebody will bring us a new jesus and we'll all be saved by the sight of him!"

An unintelligible sound spluttered out of Enoch. He tried to bellow, but his blood held him back. He whispered, "Listen here, I got him! I mean I can get him! You know! Him! Him I shown you to. You seen him yourself!"

His blood reminded him that the last time he had seen Haze Motes was when Haze Motes had hit him over the head with a rock. And he didn't even know yet how he would steal it out of the glass case. The only thing he knew was that he had a place in his room prepared to keep it in until Haze was ready to take it. His blood suggested he just let it come as a surprise to Haze Motes. He began to back away. He backed across the street and over a piece of sidewalk and out into the other street and a taxi had to stop short to keep from hitting him. The driver put his head out the window and asked him how he got around so well when God had made him by putting two backs together instead of a back and a front.

Enoch was too preoccupied to think about it. "I got to go now," he murmured, and hurried off.

IX

Hawks kept his door bolted and whenever Haze knocked
on it, which he did two or three times a day, the ex-
evangelist sent his child out to him and bolted the door
again behind her. It infuriated him to have Haze lurking
in the house, thinking up some excuse to get in and look
at his face; and he was often drunk and didn't want to be
discovered that way.

Haze couldn't understand why the preacher didn't welcome him and act like a preacher should when he sees what
he believes is a lost soul. He kept trying to get into the
room again; the window he could have reached was kept
locked and the shade pulled down. He wanted to see, if
he could, *behind* the black glasses.

Every time he went to the door, the girl came out and
the bolt shut inside; then he couldn't get rid of her. She followed him out to his car and climbed in and spoiled his rides
or she followed him up to his room and sat. He abandoned
the notion of seducing her and tried to protect himself.
He hadn't been in the house a week before she appeared in
his room one night after he had gone to bed. She was holding a candle burning in a jelly glass and wore, hanging onto
her thin shoulders, a woman's nightgown that dragged on
the floor behind her. Haze didn't wake up until she was almost up to his bed, and when he did, he sprang from under
his cover into the middle of the room.

"What you want?" he said.

She didn't say anything and her grin widened in the candle
light. He stood glowering at her for an instant and then he
picked up the straight chair and raised it as if he were going
to bring it down on her. She lingered only a fraction of a
second. His door didn't bolt so he propped the chair under
the knob before he went back to bed.

"Listen," she said when she got back to their room, "nothing works. He would have hit me with a chair."

"I'm leaving out of here in a couple of days," Hawks said,
"you better make it work if you want to eat after I'm gone."
He was drunk but he meant it.

Nothing was working the way Haze had expected it to.
He had spent every evening preaching, but the membership
of the Church Without Christ was still only one person:
himself. He had wanted to have a large following quickly
to impress the blind man with his powers, but no one had

followed him. There had been a sort of follower but that had
been a mistake. That had been a boy about sixteen years old
who had wanted someone to go to a whorehouse with him
because he had never been to one before. He knew where the
place was but he didn't want to go without a person of
experience, and when he heard Haze, he hung around until
he stopped preaching and then asked him to go. But it was
all a mistake because after they had gone and got out again
and Haze had asked him to be a member of the Church
Without Christ, or more than that, a disciple, an apostle, the
boy said he was sorry but he couldn't be a member of that
church because he was a Lapsed Catholic. He said that
what they had just done was a mortal sin, and that should
they die unrepentant of it they would suffer eternal punishment and never see God. Haze had not enjoyed the whorehouse anywhere near as much as the boy had and he had
wasted half his evening. He shouted that there was no such
thing as sin or judgment, but the boy only shook his head
and asked him if he would like to go again the next night.

If Haze had believed in praying, he would have prayed
for a disciple, but as it was all he could do was worry
about it a lot. Then two nights after the boy, the disciple appeared.

That night he preached outside of four different picture
shows and every time he looked up, he saw the same big
face smiling at him. The man was plumpish, and he had
curly blond hair that was cut with showy sideburns. He wore
a black suit with a silver stripe in it and a wide-brimmed
white hat pushed onto the back of his head, and he had on
tight-fitting black pointed shoes and no socks. He looked like
an ex-preacher turned cowboy, or an ex-cowboy turned
mortician. He was not handsome but under his smile, there
was an honest look that fitted into his face like a set of false
teeth.

Every time Haze looked at him, the man winked.

At the last picture show he preached in front of, there
were three people listening to him besides the man. "Do you
people care anything about the truth?" he asked. "The only
way to the truth is through blasphemy, but do you care?
Are you going to pay any attention to what I've been saying
or are you just going to walk off like everybody else?"

There were two men and a woman with a cat-faced baby
sprawled over her shoulder. She had been looking at Haze
as if he were in a booth at the fair. "Well, come on," she

said, "he's finished. We got to be going." She turned away and the two men fell in behind her.

"Go ahead and go," Haze said, "but remember that the truth don't lurk around every street corner."

The man who had been following reached up quickly and pulled Haze's pantsleg and gave him a wink. "Come on back heah, you folks," he said. "I want to tell you all about *me*."

The woman turned around again and he smiled at her as if he had been struck all along with her good looks. She had a square red face and her hair was freshly set. "I wisht I had my gittarr here," the man said, " 'cause I just somehow can say sweet things to music bettern plain. And when you talk about Jesus you need a little music, don't you, friends?" He looked at the two men as if he were appealing to the good judgment that was impressed on their faces. They had on brown felt hats and black town suits, and they looked like older and younger brother. "Listen, friends," the disciple said confidentially, "two months ago before I met the Prophet here, you wouldn't know me for the same man. I didn't have a friend in the world. Do you know what it's like not to have a friend in the world?"

"It ain't no worsen havinum that would put a knife in your back when you wasn't looking," the older man said, barely parting his lips.

"Friend, you said a mouthful when you said that," the man said. "If we had time, I would have you repeat that just so ever'body could hear it like I did." The picture show was over and more people were coming up. "Friends," the man said, "I know you're all interested in the Prophet here," pointing to Haze on the nose of the car, "and if you'll just give me time I'm going to tell you what him and his idears've done for me. Don't crowd because I'm willing to stay here all night and tell you if it takes that long."

Haze stood where he was, motionless, with his head slightly forward, as if he weren't sure what he was hearing.

"Friends," the man said, "lemme innerduce myself. My name is Onnie Jay Holy and I'm telling it to you so you can check up and see I don't tell you any lie. I'm a preacher and I don't mind who knows it but I wouldn't have you believe nothing you can't feel in your own hearts. You people coming up on the edge right on up in here where you can hear good," he said. "I'm not selling a thing, I'm giving something away!" A considerable number of people had stopped.

"Friends," he said, "two months ago you wouldn't know

me for the same man. I didn't have a friend in the world. Do you know what it's like not to have a friend in the world?"

A loud voice said, "It ain't no worsen havinum that would put . . ."

"Why, friends," Onnie Jay Holy said, "not to have a friend in the world is just about the most miserable and lonesome thing that can happen to a man or woman! And that's the way it was with me. I was ready to hang myself or to despair completely. Not even my own dear old mother loved me, and it wasn't because I wasn't sweet inside, it was because I never known how to make the natural sweetness inside me show. Every person that comes onto this earth," he said, stretching out his arms, "is born sweet and full of love. A little child loves ever'body, friends, and its nature is sweetness—until something happens. Something happens, friends, I don't need to tell people like you that can think for theirselves. As that little child gets bigger, its sweetness don't show so much, cares and troubles come to perplext it, and all its sweetness is driven inside it. Then it gets miserable and lonesome and sick, friends. It says, 'Where is all my sweetness gone? where are all the friends that loved me?' and all the time, that little beat-up rose of its sweetness is inside, not a petal dropped, and on the outside is just a mean lonesomeness. It may want to take its own life or yours or mine, or to despair completely, friends." He said it in a sad nasal voice but he was smiling all the time so that they could tell he had been through what he was talking about and come out on top. "That was the way it was with me, friends. I know what of I speak," he said, and folded his hands in front of him. "But all the time that I was ready to hang myself or to despair completely, I was sweet inside, like ever'body else, and I only needed something to bring it out. I only needed a little help, friends.

"Then I met this Prophet here," he said, pointing at Haze on the nose of the car. "That was two months ago, folks, that I heard how he was out to help me, how he was preaching the Church of Christ Without Christ, the church that was going to get a new jesus to help me bring my sweet nature into the open where ever'body could enjoy it. That was two months ago, friends, and now you wouldn't know me for the same man. I love ever'one of you people and I want you to listen to him and me and join our church, the Holy Church of Christ Without Christ, the new church with the new jesus, and then you'll all be helped like me!"

Haze leaned forward. "This man is not true," he said. "I never saw him before tonight. I wasn't preaching this church two months ago and the name of it ain't the Holy Church of Christ Without Christ!"

The man ignored this and so did the people. There were ten or twelve gathered around. "Friends," Onnie Jay Holy said, "I'm mighty glad you're seeing me now instead of two months ago because then I couldn't have testified to this new church and this Prophet here. If I had my gittarr with me I could say all this better but I'll just have to do the best I can by myself." He had a winning smile and it was evident that he didn't think he was any better than anybody else even though he was.

"Now I just want to give you folks a few reasons why you can trust this church," he said. "In the first place, friends, you can rely on it that it's nothing foreign connected with it. You don't have to believe nothing you don't understand and approve of. If you don't understand it, it ain't true, and that's all there is to it. No jokers in the deck, friends."

Haze leaned forward. "Blasphemy is the way to the truth," he said, "and there's no other way whether you understand it or not!"

"Now, friends," Onnie Jay said, "I want to tell you a second reason why you can absolutely trust this church—it's based on the Bible. Yes sir! It's based on your own personal interpitation of the Bible, friends. You can sit at home and interpit your own Bible however you feel in your heart it ought to be interpited. That's right," he said, "just the way Jesus would have done it. Gee, I wisht I had my gittarr here," he complained.

"This man is a liar," Haze said. "I never saw him before tonight. I never . . ."

"That ought to be enough reasons, friends," Onnie Jay Holy said, "but I'm going to tell you one more, just to show I can. This church is up-to-date! When you're in this church you can know that there's nothing or nobody ahead of you, nobody knows nothing you don't know, all the cards are on the table, friends, and that's a fack!"

Haze's face under the white hat began to take on a look of fierceness. Just as he was about to open his mouth again, Onnie Jay Holy pointed in astonishment to the baby in the blue bonnet who was sprawled limp over the woman's shoulder. "Why yonder is a little babe," he said, "a little bundle of helpless sweetness. Why, I know you people aren't going to let that little thing grow up and have all his sweetness pushed inside him when it could be on the outside to win friends and make him loved. That's why I want ever' one of you people to join the Holy Church of Christ Without Christ. It'll cost you each a dollar but what is a dollar? A few dimes! Not too much to pay to unlock that little rose of sweetness inside you!"

"Listen!" Haze shouted. "It don't cost you any money to know the truth! You can't know it for money!"

"You hear what the Prophet says, friends," Onnie Jay Holy said, "a dollar is not too much to pay. No amount of money is too much to learn the truth! Now I want each of you people that are going to take advantage of this church to sign on this little pad I have in my pocket here and give me your dollar personally and let me shake your hand!"

Haze slid down from the nose of his car and got in it and slammed his foot on the starter.

"Hey wait! Wait!" Onnie Jay Holy shouted, "I ain't got any of these friends' names yet!"

The Essex had a tendency to develop a tic by nightfall. It would go forward about six inches and then back about four; it did that now a succession of times rapidly; otherwise Haze would have shot off in it and been gone. He had to grip the steering wheel with both hands to keep from being thrown either out the windshield or into the back. It stopped this after a few seconds and slid about twenty feet and then began it again.

Onnie Jay Holy's face showed a great strain; he put his hand to the side of it as if the only way he could keep his smile on was to hold it. "I got to go now, friends," he said quickly, "but I'll be at this same spot tomorrow night, I got to go catch the Prophet now," and he ran off just as the Essex began to slide again. He wouldn't have caught it, except that it stopped before it had gone ten feet farther. He jumped on the running board and got the door open and plumped in, panting, beside Haze. "Friend," he said, "we just lost ten dollars. What you in such a hurry for?" His face showed that he was in some kind of genuine pain even though he looked at Haze with a smile that revealed all his upper teeth and the tops of his lowers.

Haze turned his head and looked at him long enough to see the smile before it was thrown forward at the windshield. After that the Essex began running smoothly. Onnie Jay took out a lavender handkerchief and held it in front of his mouth for some time. When he removed it, the smile

was back on his face. "Friend," he said, "you and me have
to get together on this thing. I said when I first heard you
open your mouth, 'Why, yonder is a great man with great
idears.' "

Haze didn't turn his head.

Onnie Jay took in a long breath. "Why, do you know who
you put me in mind of when I first saw you?" he asked.
After a minute of waiting, he said in a soft voice, "Jesus
Christ and Abraham Lincoln, friend."

Haze's face was suddenly swamped with outrage. All the
expression on it was obliterated. "You ain't true," he said
in a barely audible voice.

"Friend, how can you say that?" Onnie Jay said. "Why I
was on the radio for three years with a program that give
real religious experiences to the whole family. Didn't you
ever listen to it—called, Soulsease, a quarter hour of Mood,
Melody, and Mentality? I'm a real preacher, friend."

Haze stopped the Essex. "You get out," he said.

"Why friend!" Onnie Jay said. "You ought not to say such
a thing! That's the absolute truth that I'm a preacher and a
radio star."

"Get out," Haze said, reaching across and opening the door
for him.

"I never thought you would treat a friend thisaway,"
Onnie Jay said. "All I wanted to ast you about was this new
jesus."

"Get out," Haze said, and began to push him toward the
door. He pushed him to the edge of the seat and gave him
a shove and Onnie Jay fell out the door and into the road.

"I never thought a friend would treat me thisaway," he
complained. Haze kicked his leg off the running board and
shut the door again. He put his foot on the starter but nothing happened except a noise somewhere underneath him
that sounded like a person gargling without water. Onnie
Jay got up off the pavement and stood at the window. "If you
would just tell me where this new jesus is you was men-
tioning," he began.

Haze put his foot on the starter a succession of times but
nothing happened.

"Pull out the choke," Onnie Jay advised, getting up on the
running board.

"There's no choke on it," Haze snarled.

"Maybe it's flooded," Onnie Jay said. "While we're waiting,
you and me can talk about the Holy Church of Christ Without Christ."

"My church is the Church Without Christ," Haze said. "I've seen all of you I want to."

"It don't make any difference how many Christs you add to the name if you don't add none to the meaning, friend," Onnie Jay said in a hurt tone. "You ought to listen to me because I'm not just an amateur. I'm an artist-type. If you want to get anywheres in religion, you got to keep it sweet. You got good idears but what you need is an artist-type to work with you."

Haze rammed his foot on the gas and then on the starter and then on the starter and then on the gas. Nothing happened. The street was practically deserted. "Me and you could get behind it and push it over to the curb," Onnie Jay suggested.

"I ain't asked for your help," Haze said.

"You know, friend, I certainly would like to see this new jesus," Onnie Jay said. "I never heard a idear before that had more in it than that one. All it would need is a little promotion."

Haze tried to start the car by forcing his weight forward on the steering wheel, but that didn't work. He got out and got behind it and began to push it over to the curb. Onnie Jay got behind with him and added his weight. "I kind of have had that idear about a new jesus myself," he remarked. "I seen how a new one would be more up-to-date."

"Where you keeping him, friend?" he asked. "Is he somebody you see ever' day? I certainly would like to meet him and hear some of his idears."

They pushed the car into a parking space. There was no way to lock it and Haze was afraid that if he left it out all night so far away from where he lived someone would be able to steal it. There was nothing for him to do but sleep in it. He got in the back and began to pull down the fringed shades. Onnie Jay had his head in the front, however. "You needn't to be afraid that if I seen this new jesus I would cut you out of anything," he said. "Why friend, it would just mean a lot to me for the good of my spirit."

Haze moved the two-by-four off the seat frame to make more room to fix up his pallet. He kept a pillow and an army blanket back there and he had a sterno stove and a coffee pot up on the shelf under the back oval window. "Friend, I would even be glad to pay you a little something to see him," Onnie Jay suggested.

"Listen here," Haze said, "you get away from here. I've seen all of you I want to. There's no such thing as any new jesus. That ain't anything but a way to say something."

The smile more or less slithered off Onnie Jay's face. "What you mean by that?" he asked.

"That there's no such thing or person," Haze said. "It wasn't nothing but a way to say a thing." He put his hand on the door handle and began to close it in spite of Onnie Jay's head. "No such thing exists!" he shouted.

"That's the trouble with your innerleckchuls," Onnie Jay muttered, "you don't never have nothing to show for what you're saying."

"Get your head out of my car door, Holy," Haze said.

"My name is Hoover Shoats," the man with his head in the door growled. "I known when I first seen you that you wasn't nothing but a crackpot."

Haze opened the door enough to be able to slam it. Hoover Shoats got his head out the way but not his thumb. A howl arose that would have rended almost any heart. Haze opened the door and released the thumb and then slammed the door again. He pulled down the front shades and lay down in the back of the car on the army blanket. Outside he could hear Hoover Shoats jumping around on the pavement and howling. When the howls died down, Haze heard a few steps up to the car and then an impassioned, breathless voice say through the tin, "You watch out, friend. I'm going to run you out of business. I can get my own new jesus and I can get Prophets for peanuts, you hear? Do you hear me, friend?" the hoarse voice said.

Haze didn't answer.

"Yeah and I'll be out there doing my own preaching to-morrow night. What you need is a little competition," the voice said. "Do you hear me, friend?"

Haze got up and leaned over the front seat and banged his hand down on the horn of the Essex. It made a sound like a goat's laugh cut off with a buzz saw. Hoover Shoats jumped back as if a charge of electricity had gone through him. "All right, friend," he said, standing about fifteen feet away, trembling, "you just wait, you ain't heard the last of me yet," and he turned and went off down the quiet street.

Haze stayed in his car about an hour and had a bad experience in it: he dreamed he was not dead but only buried. He was not waiting on the Judgment because there was no Judgment, he was waiting on nothing. Various eyes looked through the back oval window at his situation, some with considerable reverence, like the boy from the zoo, and some only to see what they could see. There were three

women with paper sacks who looked at him critically as if
he were something—a piece of fish—they might buy, but
they passed on after a minute. A man in a canvas hat looked
in and put his thumb to his nose and wiggled his fingers.
Then a woman with two little boys on either side of her
stopped and looked in, grinning. After a second, she pushed
the boys out of view and indicated that she would climb in
and keep him company for a while, but she couldn't get
through the glass and finally she went off. All this time Haze
was bent on getting out but since there was no use to try, he
didn't make any move one way or the other. He kept expecting Hawks to appear at the oval window with a wrench, but
the blind man didn't come.

Finally he shook off the dream and woke up. He thought
it should be morning but it was only midnight. He pulled himself over into the front of the car and eased his foot on
the starter and the Essex rolled off quietly as if nothing were
the matter with it. He drove back to the house and let himself in but instead of going upstairs to his room, he stood in
the hall, looking at the blind man's door. He went over to it
and put his ear to the keyhole and heard the sound of snoring; he turned the knob gently but the door didn't move.

For the first time, the idea of picking the lock occurred to
him. He felt in his pockets for an instrument and came on a
small piece of wire that he sometimes used for a toothpick. There was only a dim light in the hall but it was
enough for him to work by and he knelt down at the keyhole and inserted the wire into it carefully, trying not to
make a noise.

After a while when he had tried the wire five or six different ways, there was a slight click in the lock. He stood
up, trembling, and opened the door. His breath came short
and his heart was palpitating as if he had run all the way
here from a great distance. He stood just inside the room until
his eyes got accustomed to the darkness and then he moved
slowly over to the iron bed and stood there. Hawks was lying across it. His head was hanging over the edge. Haze
squatted down by him and struck a match close to his face
and he opened his eyes. The two sets of eyes looked at each
other as long as the match lasted; Haze's expression seemed
to open onto a deeper blankness and reflect something and
then close again.

"Now you can get out," Hawks said in a short thick voice,
"now you can leave me alone," and he made a jab at the

face over him without touching it. It moved back, expressionless under the white hat, and was gone in a second.

x

The next night, Haze parked the Essex in front of the Odeon Theater and climbed up on it and began to preach. "Let me tell you what I and this church stand for!" he called from the nose of the car. "Stop one minute to listen to the truth because you may never hear it again." He stood there with his neck thrust forward, moving one arm upward in a vague arc. Two women and a boy stopped.

"I preach there are all kinds of truth, your truth and somebody else's, but behind all of them, there's only one truth and that is that there's no truth," he called. "No truth behind all truths is what I and this church preach! Where you come from is gone, where you thought you were going to never was there, and where you are is no good unless you can get away from it. Where is there a place for you to be? No place.

"Nothing outside you can give you any place," he said. "You needn't to look at the sky because it's not going to open up and show no place behind it. You needn't to search for any hole in the ground to look through into somewhere else. You can't go neither forwards nor backwards into your daddy's time nor your children's if you have them. In yourself right now is all the place you've got. If there was any Fall, look there, if there was any Redemption, look there, and if you expect any Judgment, look there, because they all three will have to be in your time and your body and where in your time and your body can they be?

"Where in your time and your body has Jesus redeemed you?" he cried. "Show me where because I don't see the place. If there was a place where Jesus had redeemed you that would be the place for you to be, but which of you can find it?"

Another trickle of people came out of the Odeon and two stopped to look at him. "Who is that that says it's your conscience?" he cried, looking around with a constricted face as if he could smell the particular person who thought that. "Your conscience is a trick," he said, "it don't exist though you may think it does, and if you think it does, you had best get it out in the open and hunt it down and kill it, because it's no more than your face in the mirror is or your shadow behind you."

He was preaching with such concentration that he didn't notice a high rat-colored car that had been driven around the block three times already, while the two men in it hunted a place to park. He didn't see it when it pulled in two cars over from him in a space that another car had just pulled out of, and he didn't see Hoover Shoats and a man in a glare-blue suit and white hat get out of it, but after a few seconds, his head turned that way and he saw the man in the glare-blue suit and white hat up on the nose of it. He was so struck with how gaunt and thin he looked in the illusion that he stopped preaching. He had never pictured himself that way before. The man he saw was hollow-chested and carried his neck thrust forward and his arms down by his side; he stood there as if he were waiting for some signal he was afraid he might not catch.

Hoover Shoats was walking about on the sidewalk, striking a few chords on his guitar. "Friends," he called, "I want to innerduce you to the True Prophet here and I want you all to listen to his words because I think they're going to make you happy like they've made me!" If Haze had noticed Hoover he might have been impressed by how happy he looked, but his attention was fixed on the man on the nose of the car. He slid down from his own car and moved up closer, never taking his eyes from the bleak figure. Hoover Shoats raised his hand with two fingers pointed and the man suddenly cried out in a high nasal· singsong voice. "The unredeemed are redeeming theirselves and the new jesus is at hand! Watch for this miracle! Help yourself to salvation in the Holy Church of Christ Without Christ!" He called it over again in exactly the same tone of voice, but faster. Then he began to cough. He had a loud consumptive cough that started somewhere deep in him and finished with a long wheeze. He expectorated a white fluid at the end of it.

Haze was standing next to a fat woman who after a minute turned her head and stared at him and then turned it again and stared at the True Prophet. Finally she touched his elbow with hers and grinned at him. "Him and you twins?" she asked.

"If you don't hunt it down and kill it, it'll hunt you down and kill you," Haze answered.

"Huh? Who?" she said.

He turned away and she stared at him as he got back in his car and drove off. Then she touched the elbow of a man on the other side of her. "He's nuts," she said. "I never seen no twins that hunted each other down."

When he got back to his room, Sabbath Hawks was in his
bed. She was pushed over into one corner of it, sitting
with one arm drawn around her knees and one hand holding
onto the sheet as if she meant to hang on by it. Her face
was sullen and apprehensive. Haze sat down on the bed but
he barely glanced at her. "I don't care if you hit me with
the table," she said. "I'm not going. There's no place for me
to go. He's run off on me and it was you run him off. I was
watching last night and I seen you come in and hold that
match to his face. I thought anybody would have seen what
he was before that without having to strike no match. He's
just a crook. He ain't even a big crook, just a little one,
and when he gets tired of that, he begs on the street."

Haze leaned down and began untying his shoes. They were
old army shoes that he had painted black to get the government off. He untied them and eased his feet out and sat there
looking down, while she watched him cautiously.

"Are you going to hit me or not?" she asked. "If you are,
go ahead and do it right now because I'm not going. I ain't
got any place to go." He didn't look as if he were going to
hit anything; he looked as if he were going to sit there until
he died. "Listen," she said, with a quick change of tone,
"from the minute I set eyes on you I said to myself, that's
what I got to have, just give me some of him! I said look at
those pee-can eyes and go crazy, girl! That innocent look
don't hide a thing, he's just pure filthy right down to the guts,
like me. The only difference is I like being that way and he
don't. Yes sir!" she said. "I like being that way, and I can
teach you how to like it. Don't you want to learn how to
like it?"

He turned his head slightly and just over his shoulder he
saw a pinched homely little face with bright green eyes and
a grin. "Yeah," he said with no change in his stony expression, "I want to." He stood up and took off his coat and
his trousers and his drawers and put them on the straight
chair. Then he turned off the light and sat down on the cot
again and pulled off his socks. His feet were big and white
and damp to the floor and he sat there, looking at the two
white shapes they made.

"Come on! Make haste," she said, knocking his back
with her knee.

He unbuttoned his shirt and took it off and wiped his
face with it and dropped it on the floor. Then he slid his
legs under the cover by her and sat there as if he were waiting to remember one more thing.

She was breathing very quickly. "Take off your hat, king of the beasts," she said gruffly and her hand came up behind his head and snatched the hat off and sent it flying across the room in the dark.

XI

The next morning toward noon a person in a long black raincoat, with a lightish hat pulled down low on his face and the brim of it turned down to meet the turned-up collar of the raincoat, was moving rapidly along certain back streets, close to the walls of the buildings. He was carrying something about the size of a baby, wrapped up in newspapers, and he carried a dark umbrella too, as the sky was an unpredictable surly gray like the back of an old goat. He had on a pair of dark glasses and a black beard which a keen observer would have said was not a natural growth but was pinned onto his hat on either side with safety pins. As he walked along, the umbrella kept slipping from under his arm and getting tangled in his feet, as if it meant to keep him from going anywhere.

He had not gone half a block before large putty-colored drops began to splatter on the pavement and there was an ugly growl in the sky behind him. He began to run, clutching the bundle in one arm and the umbrella in the other. In a second, the storm overtook him and he ducked between two show-windows into the blue and white tiled entrance of a drug store. He lowered his dark glasses a little. The pale eyes that looked over the rims belonged to Enoch Emery. Enoch was on his way to Hazel Motes's room.

He had never been to Hazel Mote's place before but the instinct that was guiding him was very sure of itself. What was in the bundle was what he had shown Hazel at the museum. He had stolen it the day before.

He had darkened his face and hands with brown shoe polish so that if he were seen in the act, he would be taken for a colored person; then he had sneaked into the museum while the guard was asleep and had broken the glass case with a wrench he'd borrowed from his landlady; then, shaking and sweating, he had lifted the shriveled man out and thrust him in a paper sack, and had crept out again past the guard, who was still asleep. He realized as soon as he got out of the museum that since no one had seen him to think he was a colored boy, he would be suspected immediately and would have to disguise himself. That was why he had on the black beard and dark glasses.

When he'd got back to his room, he had taken the new jesus out of the sack and, hardly daring to look at him, had laid him in the gilted cabinet; then he had sat down on the edge of his bed to wait. He was waiting for something to happen, he didn't know what. He knew something was going to happen and his entire system was waiting on it. He thought it was going to be one of the supreme moments in his life but apart from that, he didn't have the vaguest notion what it might be. He pictured himself, after it was over, as an entirely new man, with an even better personality than he had now. He sat there for about fifteen minutes and nothing happened.

He sat there for about five more.

Then he realized that he had to make the first move. He got up and tiptoed to the cabinet and squatted down at the door of it; in a second he opened it a crack and looked in. After a while, very slowly, he broadened the crack and inserted his head into the tabernacle.

Some time passed.

From directly behind him, only the soles of his shoes and the seat of his trousers were visible. The room was absolutely silent; there was no sound even from the street; the Universe might have been shut off; not a flea jumped. Then without any warning, a loud liquid noise burst from the cabinet and there was the thump of bone cracked once against a piece of wood. Enoch staggered backward, clutching his head and his face. He sat on the floor for a few minutes with a shocked expression on his whole figure. At the first instant, he had thought it was the shriveled man who had sneezed, but after a second, he perceived the condition of his own nose. He wiped it off with his sleeve and then he sat there on the floor for some time longer. His expression had showed that a deep unpleasant knowledge was breaking on him slowly. After a while he had kicked the ark door shut in the new jesus' face, and then he had got up and begun to eat a candy bar very rapidly. He had eaten it as if he had something against it.

The next morning he had not got up until ten o'clock—it was his day off—and he had not set out until nearly noon to look for Hazel Motes. He remembered the address Sabbath Hawks had given him and that was where his instinct was leading him. He was very sullen and disgruntled at having to spend his day off in such a way as this, and in bad

weather, but he wanted to get rid of the new jesus so that
if the police had to catch anybody for the robbery, they
could catch Hazel Motes instead of him. He couldn't understand at all why he had let himself risk his skin for a dead
shriveled-up part-nigger dwarf that had never done anything
but get himself embalmed and then lain stinking in a museum
the rest of his life. It was far beyond his understanding. He
was very sullen. So far as he was now concerned, one jesus
was as bad as another.

He had borrowed his landlady's umbrella and he discovered as he stood in the entrance of the drug store, trying
to open it, that it was at least as old as she was. When he
finally got it hoisted, he pushed his dark glasses back on his
eyes and re-entered the downpour.

The umbrella was one his landlady had stopped using
fifteen years before (which was the only reason she had lent
it to him) and as soon as the rain touched the top of it, it
came down with a shriek and stabbed him in the back of the
neck. He ran a few feet with it over his head and then
backed into another store entrance and removed it. Then to
get it up again, he had to place the tip of it on the ground
and ram it open with his foot. He ran out again, holding his
hand up near the spokes to keep them open and this allowed
the handle, which was carved to represent the head of a fox
terrier, to jab him every few seconds in the stomach. He
proceeded for another quarter of a block this way before the
back half of the silk stood up off the spokes and allowed
the storm to sweep down his collar. Then he ducked under
the marquee of a movie house. It was Saturday and there
were a lot of children standing more or less in a line in front
of the ticket box.

Enoch was not very fond of children but children always
seemed to like to look at him. The line turned and twenty
or thirty eyes began to observe him with a steady interest.
The umbrella had assumed an ugly position, half up and
half down, and the half that was up was about to come
down and spill more water under his collar. When this happened the children laughed and jumped up and down. Enoch
glared at them and turned his back and lowered his dark
glasses. He found himself facing a life-size four-color picture of a gorilla. Over the gorilla's head, written in red letters
was, "GONGA! Giant Jungle Monarch and a Great Star!
HERE IN PERSON! ! !" At the level of the gorilla's knee,
there was more that said, "Gonga will appear in person in
front of this theater at 12 A.M. *TODAY!* A free pass to the

first ten brave enough to step up and shake his hand!"

Enoch was usually thinking of something else at the moment that Fate began drawing back her leg to kick him. When he was four years old, his father had brought him home a tin box from the penitentiary. It was orange and had a picture of some peanut brittle on the outside of it and green letters that said, A NUTTY SURPRISE! When Enoch had opened it, a coiled piece of steel had sprung out at him and broken off the ends of his two front teeth. His life was full of so many happenings like that that it would seem he should have been more sensitive to his times of danger. He stood there and read the poster twice through carefully. To his mind, an opportunity to insult a successful ape came from the hand of Providence. He suddenly regained all his reverence for the new jesus. He saw that he was going to be rewarded after all and have the supreme moment he had expected.

He turned around and asked the nearest child what time it was. The child said it was twelve-ten and that Gonga was already ten minutes late. Another child said that maybe the rain had delayed him. Another said, no not the rain, his director was taking a plane from Hollywood. Enoch gritted his teeth. The first child said that if he wanted to shake the star's hand, he would have to get in line like the rest of them and wait his turn. Enoch got in line. A child asked him how old he was. Another observed that he had funny-looking teeth. He ignored all this as best he could and began to straighten out the umbrella.

In a few minutes a black truck turned around the corner and came slowly up the street in the heavy rain. Enoch pushed the umbrella under his arm and began to squint through his dark glasses. As the truck approached, a phonograph inside it began to play "Tarara Boom Di Aye," but the music was almost drowned out by the rain. There was a large illustration of a blonde on the outside of the truck, advertising some picture other than the gorilla's.

The children held their line carefully as the truck stopped in front of the movie house. The back door of it was constructed like a paddy wagon, with a grate, but the ape was not at it. Two men in raincoats got out of the cab part, cursing, and ran around to the back and opened the door. One of them stuck his head in and said, "Okay, make it snappy, willya?" The other jerked his thumb at the children and said, "Get back willya, willya get back?"

A voice on the record inside the truck said, "Here's

Gonga, folks, Roaring Gonga and a Great Star! Give Gonga a big hand, folks!" The voice was barely a mumble in the rain.

The man who was waiting by the door of the truck stuck his head in again. "Okay willya get out?" he said.

There was a faint thump somewhere inside the van. After a second a dark furry arm emerged just enough for the rain to touch it and then drew back inside.

"Goddam," the man who was under the marquee said; he took off his raincoat and threw it to the man by the door, who threw it into the wagon. After two or three minutes more, the gorilla appeared at the door, with the raincoat buttoned up to his chin and the collar turned up. There was an iron chain hanging from around his neck; the man grabbed it and pulled him down and the two of them bounded under the marquee together. A motherly-looking woman was in the glass ticket box, getting the passes ready for the first ten children brave enough to step up and shake hands.

The gorilla ignored the children entirely and followed the man over to the other side of the entrance where there was a small platform raised about a foot off the ground. He stepped up on it and turned facing the children and began to growl. His growls were not so much loud as poisonous; they appeared to issue from a black heart. Enoch was terrified and if he had not been surrounded by the children, he would have run away.

"Who'll step up first?" the man said. "Come on come on, who'll step up first? A free pass to the first kid stepping up."

There was no movement from the group of children. The man glared at them. "What's the matter with you kids?" he barked. "You yellow? He won't hurt you as long as I got him by this chain." He tightened his grip on the chain and jangled it at them to show he was holding it securely.

After a minute a little girl separated herself from the group. She had long wood-shaving curls and a fierce tri-angular face. She moved up to within four feet of the star.

"Okay okay," the man said, rattling the chain, "make it snappy."

The ape reached out and gave her hand a quick shake. By this time there was another little girl ready and then two boys. The line re-formed and began to move up.

The gorilla kept his hand extended and turned his head away with a bored look at the rain. Enoch had got over his fear and was trying frantically to think of an obscene remark that would be suitable to insult him with. Usually he didn't have any trouble with this kind of composition but nothing came to him now. His brain, both parts, was completely empty. He couldn't think even of the insulting phrases he used every day.

There were only two children in front of him by now. The first one shook hands and stepped aside. Enoch's heart was beating violently. The child in front of him finished and stepped aside and left him facing the ape, who took his hand with an automatic motion.

It was the first hand that had been extended to Enoch since he had come to the city. It was warm and soft.

For a second he only stood there, clasping it. Then he began to stammer. "My name is Enoch Emery," he mumbled. "I attended the Rodemill Boys' Bible Academy. I work at the city zoo. I seen two of your pictures. I'm only eighteen year old but I already work for the city. My daddy made me com . . ." and his voice cracked.

The star leaned slightly forward and a change came in his eyes: an ugly pair of human ones moved closer and squinted at Enoch from behind the celluloid pair. "You go to hell," a surly voice inside the ape-suit said, low but distinctly, and the hand was jerked away.

Enoch's humiliation was so sharp and painful that he turned around three times before he realized which direction he wanted to go in. Then he ran off into the rain as fast as he could.

By the time he reached Sabbath Hawks's house, he was soaked through and so was his bundle. He held it in a fierce grip but all he wanted was to get rid of it and never see it again. Haze's landlady was out on the porch, looking distrustfully into the storm. He found out from her where Haze's room was and went up to it. The door was ajar and he stuck his head in the crack. Haze was lying on his cot, with a washrag over his eyes; the exposed part of his face was ashen and set in a grimace, as if he were in some permanent pain. Sabbath Hawks was sitting at the table by the window, studying herself in a pocket mirror. Enoch scratched on the wall and she looked up. She put the mirror down and tiptoed out into the hall and shut the door behind her.

"My man is sick today and sleeping," she said, "because he didn't sleep none last night. What you want?"

"This is for him, it ain't for you," Enoch said, handing her the wet bundle. "A friend of his give it to me to give to him. I don't know what's in it."

"I'll take care of it," she said. "You needn't to worry none."

Enoch had an urgent need to insult somebody immediately; it was the only thing that could give his feelings even a temporary relief. "I never known he would have nothing to do with you," he remarked, giving her one of his special looks.

"He couldn't leave off following me," she said. "Sometimes it's thataway with them. You don't know what's in this package?"

"Lay-overs to catch meddlers," he said. "You just give it to him and he'll know what it is and you can tell him I'm glad to get shut of it." He started down the stairs and halfway he turned and gave her another special look. "I see why he has to put theter washrag over his eyes," he said.

"You keep your beeswax in your ears," she said. "Nobody asked you." When she heard the front door slam behind him, she turned the bundle over and began to examine it. There was no telling from the outside what was in it; it was too hard to be clothes and too soft to be a machine. She tore a hole in the paper at one end and saw what looked like five dried peas in a row but the hall was too dark for her to see clearly what they were. She decided to take the package to the bathroom, where there was a good light, and open it up before she gave it to Haze. If he was so sick as he said he was, he wouldn't want to be bothered with any bundle.

Early that morning he had claimed to have a terrible pain in his chest. He had begun to cough during the night—a hard hollow cough that sounded as if he were making it up as he went along. She was certain he was only trying to drive her off by letting her think he had a catching disease.

He's not really sick, she said to herself going down the hall, he just ain't used to me yet. She went in and sat down on the edge of a large green claw-footed tub and ripped the string off the package. "But he'll get used to me," she muttered. She pulled off the wet paper and let it fall on the floor; then she sat with a stunned look, staring at what was in her lap.

Two days out of the glass case had not improved the new jesus' condition. One side of his face had been partly mashed in and on the other side, his eyelid had split and a pale dust was seeping out of it. For a while her face had an empty look, as if she didn't know what she thought about him or didn't think anything. She might have sat there for ten minutes, without a thought, held by whatever it was that was familiar about him. She had never known anyone who looked like him before, but there was something in him of everyone she had ever known, as if they had all been rolled into one person and killed and shrunk and dried.

She held him up and began to examine him and after a minute her hands grew accustomed to the feel of his skin. Some of his hair had come undone and she brushed it back where it belonged, holding him in the crook of her arm and looking down into his squinched face. His mouth had been knocked a little to one side so that there was just a trace of a grin covering his terrified look. She began to rock him a little in her arm and a slight reflection of the same grin appeared on her own face. "Well I declare," she murmured, "you're right cute, ain't you?"

His head fitted exactly into the hollow of her shoulder. "Who's your momma and daddy?" she asked.

An answer came into her mind at once and she let out a short little bark and sat grinning, with a pleased expression in her eyes. "Well, let's go give him a jolt," she said after a while.

Haze had already been jolted awake when the front door slammed behind Enoch Emery. He had sat up and seeing she was not in the room, he had jumped up and begun to put on his clothes. He had one thought in mind and it had come to him, like his decision to buy a car, out of his sleep and without any indication of it beforehand: he was going to move immediately to some other city and preach the Church Without Christ where they had never heard of it. He would get another room there and another woman and make a new start with nothing on his mind. The entire possibility of this came from the advantage of having a car—of having something that moved fast, in privacy, to the place you wanted to be. He looked out the window at the Essex. It sat high and square in the pouring rain. He didn't notice the rain, only the car; if asked he would not have been able to say that it was raining. He was charged with energy and he left the window and finished putting on his clothes. Earlier that morning, when he had waked up for the first time, he had felt as if he were about to be caught by a complete consumption in his chest; it had seemed to be growing hollow all night and yawning underneath him, and he had kept hearing his coughs as if they came from a distance. After a while he had been sucked down into a strengthless sleep, but he had waked up with this plan, and with the energy to carry it out right away.

He snatched his duffel bag from under the table and began plunging his extra belongings into it. He didn't have much and a quarter of what he had was already in. His hand managed the packing so that it never touched the Bible that had sat like a rock in the bottom of the bag for the last few years, but as he rooted out a place for his second shoes, his fingers clutched around a small oblong object and he pulled it out. It was the case with his mother's glasses in it. He had forgotten that he had a pair of glasses. He put them on and the wall that he was facing moved up closer and wavered. There was a small white-framed mirror hung on the back of the door and he made his way to it and looked at himself. His blurred face was dark with excitement and the lines in it were deep and crooked. The little silver-rimmed glasses gave him a look of deflected sharpness, as if they were hiding some dishonest plan that would show in his naked eyes. His fingers began to snap nervously and he forgot what he had been going to do. He saw his mother's face in his, looking at the face in the mirror. He moved back quickly and raised his hand to take off the glasses but the door opened and two more faces floated into his line of vision; one of them said, "Call me Momma now."

The smaller dark one, just under the other, only squinted as if it were trying to identify an old friend who was going to kill it.

Haze stood motionless with one hand still on the bow of the glasses and the other arrested in the air at the level of his chest; his head was thrust forward as if he had to use his whole face to see with. He was about four feet from them but they seemed just under his eyes.

"Ask your daddy yonder where he was running off to—sick as he is?" Sabbath said. "Ask him isn't he going to take you and me with him?"

The hand that had been arrested in the air moved forward and plucked at the squinting face but without touching it; it reached again, slowly, and plucked at nothing and then it lunged and snatched the shriveled body and threw it against the wall. The head popped and the trash inside sprayed out in a little cloud of dust.

"You've broken him!" Sabbath shouted, "and he was mine!"

Haze snatched the skin off the floor. He opened the outside door where the landlady thought there had once been a fire-escape, and flung out what he had in his hand. The rain blew in his face and he jumped back and stood, with a cautious look, as if he were bracing himself for a blow.

"You didn't have to throw him out," she yelled. "I might have fixed him!"

He moved up closer and hung out the door, staring into the gray blur around him. The rain fell on his hat with loud splatters as if it were falling on tin.

"I knew when I first seen you you were mean and evil," a furious voice behind him said. "I seen you wouldn't let nobody have nothing. I seen you were mean enough to slam a baby against a wall. I seen you wouldn't never have no fun or let anybody else because you didn't want nothing but Jesus!"

He turned and raised his arm in a vicious gesture, almost losing his balance in the door. Drops of rain water were splattered over the front of the glasses and on his red face and here and there they hung sparkling from the brim of his hat. "I don't want nothing but the truth!" he shouted, "and what you see is the truth and I've seen it!"

"Preacher talk," she said. "Where were you going to run off to?"

"I've seen the only truth there is!" he shouted.

"Where were you going to run off to?"

"To some other city," he said in a loud hoarse voice, "to preach the truth. The Church Without Christ! And I got a car to get there in, I got . . ." but he was stopped by a cough. It was not much of a cough—it sounded like a little yell for help at the bottom of a canyon—but the color and the expression drained out of his face until it was as straight and blank as the rain falling down behind him.

"And when were you going?" she asked.

"After I get some more sleep," he said, and pulled off the glasses and threw them out the door.

"You ain't going to get none," she said.

XII

In spite of himself, Enoch couldn't get over the expectation that the new jesus was going to do something for him in return for his services. This was the virtue of Hope, which was made up, in Enoch, of two parts suspicion and one part lust. It operated on him all the rest of the day after he left Sabbath Hawks. He had only a vague idea how he wanted to be rewarded, but he was not a boy without ambition: he wanted to become something. He wanted to

better his condition until it was the best. He wanted to be
THE young man of the future, like the ones in the insurance
ads. He wanted, some day, to see a line of people waiting
to shake his hand.

All afternoon, he fidgeted and fooled in his room, biting
his nails and shredding what was left of the silk off the
landlady's umbrella. Finally he denuded it entirely and broke
off the spokes. What was left was a black stick with a sharp
steel point at one end and a dog's head at the other. It
might have been an instrument for some specialized kind of
torture that had gone out of fashion. Enoch walked up and
down his room with it under his arm and realized that it
would distinguish him on the sidewalk.

About seven o'clock in the evening, he put on his coat
and took the stick and headed for a little restaurant two
blocks away. He had the sense that he was setting off to
get some honor, but he was very nervous, as if he were
afraid he might have to snatch it instead of receive it.

He never set out for anything without eating first. The
restaurant was called the Paris Diner; it was a tunnel about
six feet wide, located between a shoe shine parlor and a
dry-cleaning establishment. Enoch slid in and climbed up on
the far stool at the counter and said he would have a bowl
of split-pea soup and a chocolate malted milkshake.

The waitress was a tall woman with a big yellow dental
plate and the same color hair done up in a black hairnet.
One hand never left her hip; she filled orders with the other
one. Although Enoch came in every night, she had never
learned to like him.

Instead of filling his order, she began to fry bacon; there
was only one other customer in the place and he had finished his meal and was reading a newspaper; there was no
one to eat the bacon but her. Enoch reached over the counter
and prodded her hip with his stick. "Listenhere," he said,
"I got to go. I'm in a hurry."

"Go then," she said. Her jaw began to work and she
stared into the skillet with a fixed attention.

"Lemme just have a piece of theter cake yonder," he said,
pointing to a half of pink and yellow cake on a round
glass stand. "I think I got something to do. I got to be
going. Set it up there next to him," he said, indicating the
customer reading the newspaper. He slid over the stools
and began reading the outside sheet of the man's paper.

The man lowered the paper and looked at him. Enoch
smiled. The man raised the paper again. "Could I borrow

some part of your paper that you ain't studying?" Enoch asked. The man lowered it again and stared at him; he had muddy unflinching eyes. He leafed deliberately through the paper and shook out the sheet with the comic strips and handed it to Enoch. It was Enoch's favorite part. He read it every evening like an office. While he ate the cake that the waitress had torpedoed down the counter at him, he read and felt himself surge with kindness and courage and strength.

When he finished one side, he turned the sheet over and began to scan the advertisements for movies, that filled the other side. His eye went over three columns without stopping; then it came to a box that advertised Gonga, Giant Jungle Monarch, and listed the theaters he would visit on his tour and the hours he would be at each one. In thirty minutes he would arrive at the Victory on 57th Street and that would be his last appearance in the city.

If anyone had watched Enoch read this, he would have seen a certain transformation in his countenance. It still shone with the inspiration he had absorbed from the comic strips, but something else had come over it: a look of awakening.

The waitress happened to turn around to see if he hadn't gone. "What's the matter with you?" she said. "Did you swallow a seed?"

"I know what I want," Enoch murmured.

"I know what I want too," she said with a dark look.

Enoch felt for his stick and laid his change on the counter. "I got to be going."

"Don't let me keep you," she said.

"You may not see me again," he said, "—the way I am."

"Any way I don't see you will be all right with me," she said.

Enoch left. It was a pleasant damp evening. The puddles on the sidewalk shone and the store windows were steamy and bright with junk. He disappeared down a side street and made his way rapidly along the darker passages of the city, pausing only once or twice at the end of an alley to dart a glance in each direction before he ran on. The Victory was a small theater, suited to the needs of the family, in one of the closer subdivisions; he passed through a succession of lighted areas and then on through more alleys and back streets until he came to the business section that surrounded it. Then he slowed up. He saw it about a block away, glittering in its darker setting. He didn't cross the street to the side it was on but kept on the far side, moving forward with his squint fixed on the glary spot. He stopped when he was directly across from it and hid himself in a narrow stair cavity that divided a building.

The truck that carried Gonga was parked across the street and the star was standing under the marquee, shaking hands with an elderly woman. She moved aside and a gentleman in a polo shirt stepped up and shook hands vigorously, like a sportsman. He was followed by a boy of about three who wore a tall Western hat that nearly covered his face; he had to be pushed ahead by the line. Enoch watched for some time, his face working with envy. The small boy was followed by a lady in shorts, she by an old man who tried to draw extra attention to himself by dancing up instead of walking in a dignified way. Enoch suddenly darted across the street and slipped noiselessly into the open back door of the truck.

The handshaking went on until the feature picture was ready to begin. Then the star got back in the van and the people filed into the theater. The driver and the man who was master of ceremonies climbed in the cab part and the truck rumbled off. It crossed the city rapidly and continued on the highway, going very fast.

There came from the van certain thumping noises, not those of the normal gorilla, but they were drowned out by the drone of the motor and the steady sound of wheels against the road. The night was pale and quiet, with nothing to stir it but an occasional complaint from a hoot owl and the distant muted jarring of a freight train. The truck sped on until it slowed for a crossing, and as the van rattled over the tracks, a figure slipped from the door and almost fell, and then limped hurriedly off toward the woods.

Once in the darkness of a pine thicket, he laid down a pointed stick he had been clutching and something bulky and loose that he had been carrying under his arm, and began to undress. He folded each garment neatly after he had taken it off and then stacked it on top of the last thing he had removed. When all his clothes were in the pile, he took up the stick and began making a hole in the ground with it.

The darkness of the pine grove was broken by paler moonlit spots that moved over him now and again and showed him to be Enoch. His natural appearance was marred by a gash that ran from the corner of his lip to his collarbone and by a lump under his eye that gave him a dulled insensitive look. Nothing could have been more deceptive for he was burning with the intensest kind of happiness.

He dug rapidly until he had made a trench about a foot long and a foot deep. Then he placed the stack of clothes in it and stood aside to rest a second. Burying his clothes was not a symbol to him of burying his former self; he only knew he wouldn't need them any more. As soon as he got his breath, he pushed the displaced dirt over the hole and stamped it down with his foot. He discovered while he did this that he still had his shoes on, and when he finished, he removed them and threw them from him. Then he picked up the loose bulky object and shook it vigorously.

In the uncertain light, one of his lean white legs could be seen to disappear and then the other, one arm and then the other: a black heavier shaggier figure replaced his. For an instant, it had two heads, one light and one dark, but after a second, it pulled the dark back head over the other and corrected this. It busied itself with certain hidden fastenings and what appeared to be minor adjustments of its hide.

For a time after this, it stood very still and didn't do anything. Then it began to growl and beat its chest; it jumped up and down and flung its arms and thrust its head forward. The growls were thin and uncertain at first but they grew louder after a second. They became low and poisonous, louder again, low and poisonous again; they stopped altogether. The figure extended its hand, clutched nothing, and shook its arm vigorously; it withdrew the arm, extended it again, clutched nothing, and shook. It repeated this four or five times. Then it picked up the pointed stick and placed it at a cocky angle under its arm and left the woods for the highway. No gorilla in existence, whether in the jungles of Africa or California, or in New York City in the finest apartment in the world, was happier at that moment than this one, whose god had finally rewarded it.

A man and woman sitting close together on a rock just off the highway were looking across an open stretch of valley at a view of the city in the distance and they didn't see the shaggy figure approaching. The smokestacks and square tops of buildings made a black uneven wall against the lighter sky and here and there a steeple cut a sharp wedge out of a cloud. The young man turned his neck just in time to see the gorilla standing a few feet away, hideous and black, with its hand extended. He eased his arm from around the woman and disappeared silently into the woods.

She, as soon as she turned her eyes, fled screaming down
the highway. The gorilla stood as though surprised and presently its arm fell to its side. It sat down on the rock where
they had been sitting and stared over the valley at the uneven skyline of the city.

XIII

On his second night out, working with his hired Prophet
and the Holy Church of Christ Without Christ, Hoover
Shoats made fifteen dollars and thirty-five cents clear. The
Prophet got three dollars an evening for his services and
the use of his car. His name was Solace Layfield; he had
consumption and a wife and six children and being a Prophet was as much work as he wanted to do. It never occurred
to him that it might be a dangerous job. The second night
out, he failed to observe a high rat-colored car parked about
a half-block away and a white face inside it, watching him
with the kind of intensity that means something is going to
happen no matter what is done to keep it from happening.

The face watched him for almost an hour while he performed on the nose of his car every time Hoover Shoats
raised his hand with two fingers pointed. When the last
showing of the movie was over and there were no more
people to attract, Hoover paid him and the two of them
got in his car and drove off. They drove about ten blocks
to where Hoover lived; the car stopped and Hoover jumped
out, calling, "See you tomorrow night, friend"; then he went
inside a dark doorway and Solace Layfield drove on. A
half-block behind him the other rat-colored car was following steadily. The driver was Hazel Motes.

Both cars increased their speed and in a few minutes
they were heading rapidly toward the outskirts of town.
The first car cut off onto a lonesome road where the trees
were hung over with moss and the only light came like stiff
antennae from the two cars. Haze gradually shortened the
distance between them and then, grinding his motor suddenly, he shot ahead and rammed the back end of the other car.
Both cars came to a stop.

Haze backed the Essex a little way down the road, while
the other Prophet got out of his car and stood squinting in
the glare from Haze's lights. After a second, he came up to
the window of the Essex and looked in. There was no sound
but from crickets and tree frogs. "What you want?" he said
in a nervous voice. Haze didn't answer, he only looked at

him, and in a second the man's jaw slackened and he seemed
to perceive the resemblance in their clothes and possibly in
their faces. "What you want?" he said in a higher voice. "I
ain't done nothing to you."

Haze ground the motor of the Essex again and shot forward. This time he rammed the other car at such an angle
that it rolled to the side of the road and over into the ditch.

The man got up off the ground where he had been thrown
and ran back to the window of the Essex. He stood about
four feet away, looking in.

"What you keep a thing like that on the road for?" Haze
said.

"It ain't nothing wrong with that car," the man said.
"Howcome you knockt it in the ditch?"

"Take off that hat," Haze said.

"Listenere," the man said, beginning to cough, "what
you want? Quit just looking at me. Say what you want."

"You ain't true," Haze said. "What do you get up on
top of a car and say you don't believe in what you do believe in for?"

"Whatsit to you?" the man wheezed. "Whatsit to you
what I do?"

"What do you do it for?" Haze said. "That's what I asked
you."

"A man has to look out for hisself," the other Prophet
said.

"You ain't true," Haze said. "You believe in Jesus."

"Whatsit to you?" the man said. "What you knockt my
car off the road for?"

"Take off that hat and that suit," Haze said.

"Listenere," the man said, "I ain't trying to mock you.
He bought me thisyer suit. I thrown my othern away."

Haze reached out and brushed the man's white hat off.
"And take off that suit," he said.

The man began to sidle off, out into the middle of the
road.

"Take off that suit," Haze shouted and started the car
forward after him. Solace began to lope down the road, taking off his coat as he went. "Take it all off," Haze yelled,
with his face close to the windshield.

The Prophet began to run in earnest. He tore off his shirt
and unbuckled his belt and ran out of his trousers. He began
grabbing for his feet as if he would take off his shoes too,
but before he could get at them, the Essex knocked him
flat and ran over him. Haze drove about twenty feet and

stopped the car and then began to back it. He backed it over the body and then stopped and got out. The Essex stood half over the other Prophet as if it were pleased to guard what it had finally brought down. The man didn't look so much like Haze, lying on the ground on his face without his hat or suit on. A lot of blood was coming out of him and forming a puddle around his head. He was motionless all but for one finger that moved up and down in front of his face as if he were marking time with it. Haze poked his toe in his side and he wheezed for a second and then was quiet. "Two things I can't stand," Haze said, "—a man that ain't true and one that mocks what is. You shouldn't ever have tampered with me if you didn't want what you got."

The man was trying to say something but he was only wheezing. Haze squatted down by his face to listen. "Give my mother a lot of trouble," he said through a kind of bubbling in his throat. "Never giver no rest. Stole theter car. Never told the truth to my daddy or give Henry what, never give him . . ."

"You shut up," Haze said, leaning his head closer to hear the confession.

"Told where his still was and got five dollars for it," the man gasped.

"You shut up now," Haze said.

"Jesus . . ." the man said.

"Shut up like I told you to now," Haze said.

"Jesus hep me," the man wheezed.

Haze gave him a hard slap on the back and he was quiet. He leaned down to hear if he was going to say anything else but he wasn't breathing any more. Haze turned around and examined the front of the Essex to see if there had been any damage done to it. The bumper had a few splurts of blood on it but that was all. Before he turned around and drove back to town, he wiped them off with a rag.

Early the next morning he got out of the back of the car and drove to a filling station to get the Essex filled up and checked for his trip. He hadn't gone back to his room but had spent the night parked in an alley, not sleeping but thinking about the life he was going to begin, preaching the Church Without Christ in the new city.

At the filling station a sleepy-looking white boy came out to wait on him and he said he wanted the tank filled up, the oil and water checked, and the tires tested for air, that he was going on a long trip. The boy asked him where he was going and he told him to another city. The boy

asked him if he was going that far in this car here and he
said yes he was. He tapped the boy on the front of his
shirt. He said nobody with a good car needed to worry
about anything, and he asked the boy if he understood that.
The boy said yes he did, that that was his opinion too.
Haze introduced himself and said that he was a preacher
for the Church Without Christ and that he preached every
night on the nose of this very car here. He explained that
he was going to another city to preach. The boy filled up the
gas tank and checked the water and oil and tested the tires,
and while he was working, Haze followed him around, telling him what it was right to believe. He said it was not
right to believe anything you couldn't see or hold in your
hands or test with your teeth. He said he had only a few
days ago believed in blasphemy as the way to salvation,
but that you couldn't even believe in that because then
you were believing in something to blaspheme. As for the
Jesus who was reported to have been born at Bethlehem and
crucified on Calvary for man's sins, Haze said, He was too
foul a notion for a sane person to carry in his head, and
he picked up the boy's water bucket and bammed it on the
concrete pavement to emphasize what he was saying. He
began to curse and blaspheme Jesus in a quiet intense way
but with such conviction that the boy paused from his work
to listen. When he had finished checking the Essex, he said
that there was a leak in the gas tank and two in the radiator
and that the rear tire would probably last twenty miles if
he went slow.

"Listen," Haze said, "this car is just beginning its life. A
lightening bolt couldn't stop it!"

"It ain't any use to put water in it," the boy said, "because it won't hold it."

"You put it in just the same," Haze said, and he stood
there and watched while the boy put it in. Then he got a
road map from him and drove off, leaving little bead-chains
of water and oil and gas on the road.

He drove very fast out onto the highway, but once he
had gone a few miles, he had the sense that he was not gaining ground. Shacks and filling stations and road camps and
666 signs passed him, and deserted barns with CCC snuff
ads peeling across them, even a sign that said, "Jesus Died
for YOU," which he saw and deliberately did not read.
He had the sense that the road was really slipping back
under him. He had known all along that there was no more
country but he didn't know that there was not another city.

He had not gone five miles on the highway before he heard a siren behind him. He looked around and saw a black patrol car coming up. It drove alongside him and the patrolman in it motioned for him to pull over to the edge of the road. The patrolman had a red pleasant face and eyes the color of clear fresh ice.

"I wasn't speeding," Haze said.

"No," the patrolman agreed, "you wasn't."

"I was on the right side of the road."

"Yes you was, that's right," the cop said.

"What you want with me?"

"I just don't like your face," the patrolman said. "Where's your license?"

"I don't like your face either," Haze said, "and I don't have a license."

"Well," the patrolman said in a kindly voice, "I don't reckon *you* need one."

"Well I ain't got one if I do," Haze said.

"Listen," the patrolman said, taking another tone, "would you mind driving your car up to the top of the next hill? I want you to see the view from up there, puttiest view you ever did see."

Haze shrugged but he started the car up. He didn't mind fighting the patrolman if that was what he wanted. He drove to the top of the hill, with the patrol car following close behind him. "Now you turn it facing the embankment," the patrolman called. "You'll be able to see better that-away." Haze turned it facing the embankment. "Now maybe you better had get out," the cop said. "I think you could see better if you was out."

Haze got out and glanced at the view. The embankment dropped down for about thirty feet, sheer washed-out red clay, into a partly burnt pasture where there was one scrub cow lying near a puddle. Over in the middle distance there was a one-room shack with a buzzard standing hunch-shouldered on the roof.

The patrolman got behind the Essex and pushed it over the embankment and the cow stumbled up and galloped across the field and into the woods; the buzzard flapped off to a tree at the edge of the clearing. The car landed on its top, with the three wheels that stayed on, spinning. The motor bounced out and rolled some distance away and various odd pieces scattered this way and that.

"Them that don't have a car, don't need a license," the patrolman said, dusting his hands on his pants.

Haze stood for a few minutes, looking over at the scene. His face seemed to' reflect the entire distance across the clearing and on beyond, the entire distance that extended from his eyes to the blank gray sky that went on, depth after depth, into space. His knees bent under him and he sat down on the edge of the embankment with his feet hanging over.

The patrolman stood staring at him. "Could I give you a lift to where you was going?" he asked.

After a minute he came a little closer and said, "Where was you going?"

He leaned on down with his hands on his knees and said in an anxious voice, "Was you going anywheres?"

"No," Haze said.

The patrolman squatted down and put his hand on Haze's shoulder. "You hadn't planned to go anywheres?" he asked anxiously.

Haze shook his head. His face didn't change and he didn't turn it toward the patrolman. It seemed to be concentrated on space.

The patrolman got up and went back to his car and stood at the door of it, staring at the back of Haze's hat and shoulder. Then he said, "Well, I'll be seeing you," and got in and drove off.

After a while Haze got up and started walking back to town. It took him three hours to get inside the city again. He stopped at a supply store and bought a tin bucket and a sack of quicklime and then he went on to where he lived, carrying these. When he reached the house, he stopped outside on the sidewalk and opened the sack of lime and poured the bucket half full of it. Then he went to a water spigot by the front steps and filled up the rest of the bucket with water and started up the steps. His landlady was sitting on the porch, rocking a cat. "What you going to do with that, Mr. Motes?" she asked.

"Blind myself," he said and went on in the house.

The landlady sat there for a while longer. She was not a woman who felt more violence in one word than in another; she took every word at its face value but all the faces were the same. Still, instead of blinding herself, if she had felt that bad, she would have killed herself and she wondered why anybody wouldn't do that. She would simply have put her head in an oven or maybe have given herself too many painless sleeping pills and that would have been that. Perhaps Mr. Motes was only being ugly, for what possible reason could a person have for wanting to destroy their sight? A woman like her, who was so clear-sighted, could never stand to be blind. If she had to be blind she would rather be dead. It occurred to her suddenly that when she was dead she would be blind too. She stared in front of her intensely, facing this for the first time. She recalled the phrase, "eternal death," that preachers used, but she cleared it out of her mind immediately, with no more change of expression than the cat. She was not religious or morbid, for which every day she thanked her stars. She would credit a person who had that streak with anything, though, and Mr. Motes had it or he wouldn't be a preacher. He might put lime in his eyes and she wouldn't doubt it a bit, because they were all, if the truth was only known, a little bit off in their heads. What possible reason could a sane person have for wanting to not enjoy himself any more?

She certainly couldn't say.

XIV

But she kept it in mind because after he had done it, he continued to live in her house and every day the sight of him presented her with the question. She first told him he couldn't stay because he wouldn't wear dark glasses and she didn't like to look at the mess he had made in his eye sockets. At least she didn't think she did. If she didn't keep her mind going on something else when he was near her, she would find herself leaning forward, staring into his face as if she expected to see something she hadn't seen before. This irritated her with him and gave her the sense that he was cheating her in some secret way. He sat on her porch a good part of every afternoon, but sitting out there with him was like sitting by yourself; he didn't talk except when it suited him. You asked him a question in the morning and he might answer it in the afternoon, or he might never. He offered to pay her extra to let him keep his room because he knew his way in and out, and she decided to let him stay, at least until she found out how she was being cheated.

He got money from the government every month for something the war had done to his insides and so he was not obliged to work. The landlady had always been impressed with the ability to pay. When she found a stream of wealth, she followed it to its source and before long, it was not distinguishable from her own. She felt that the money she paid out in taxes returned to all the worthless pockets in the

world, that the government not only sent it to foreign niggers
and a-rabs, but wasted it at home on blind fools and on
every idiot who could sign his name on a card. She felt
justified in getting any of it back that she could. She felt
justified in getting anything at all back that she could, money
or anything else, as if she had once owned the earth and
been dispossessed of it. She couldn't look at anything steadily without wanting it, and what provoked her most was the
thought that there might be something valuable hidden near
her, something she couldn't see.

To her, the blind man had the look of seeing something.
His face had a peculiar pushing look, as if it were going forward after something it could just distinguish in the distance.
Even when he was sitting motionless in a chair, his face had
the look of straining toward something. But she knew he
was totally blind. She had satisfied herself of that as soon
as he took off the rag he used for a while as a bandage. She
had got one long good look and it had been enough to tell
her he had done what he'd said he was going to do. The
other boarders, after he had taken off the rag, would pass
him slowly in the hall, tiptoeing, and looking as long as they
could, but now they didn't pay any attention to him; some of
the new ones didn't know he had done it himself. The Hawks
girl had spread it over the house as soon as it happened.
She had watched him do it and then she had run to every
room, yelling what he had done, and all the boarders had
come running. That girl was a harpy if one ever lived, the
landlady felt. She had hung around pestering him for a few
days and then she had gone on off; she said she hadn't
counted on no honest-to-Jesus blind man and she was home-
sick for her papa; he had deserted her, gone off on a banana
boat. The landlady hoped he was at the bottom of the salt
sea; he had been a month behind in his rent. In two weeks,
of course, she was back, ready to start pestering him again.
She had the disposition of a yellow jacket and you could
hear her a block away, shouting and screaming at him, and
him never opening his mouth.

The landlady conducted an orderly house and she told
him so. She told him that when the girl lived with him, he
would have to pay double; she said there were things she
didn't mind and things she did. She left him to draw his
own conclusions about what she meant by that, but she
waited, with her arms folded, until he had drawn them. He
didn't say anything, he only counted out three more dollars

and handed them to her. "That girl, Mr. Motes," she said, "is only after your money."

"If that was what she wanted she could have it," he said. "I'd pay her to stay away."

The thought that her tax money would go to support such trash was more than the landlady could bear. "Don't do that," she said quickly. "She's got no right to it." The next day she called the Welfare people and made arrangements to have the girl sent to a detention home; she was eligible.

She was curious to know how much he got every month from the government and with that set of eyes removed, she felt at liberty to find out. She steamed open the government envelope as soon as she found it in the mailbox the next time; in a few days she felt obliged to raise his rent. He had made arrangements with her to give him his meals and as the price of food went up, she was obliged to raise his board also; but she didn't get rid of the feeling that she was being cheated. Why had he destroyed his eyes and saved himself unless he had some plan, unless he saw something that he couldn't get without being blind to everything else? She meant to find out everything she could about him.

"Where were your people from, Mr. Motes?" she asked him one afternoon when they were sitting on the porch. "I don't suppose they're alive?"

She supposed she might suppose what she pleased; he didn't disturb his doing nothing to answer her. "None of my people's alive either," she said. "All Mr. Flood's people's alive but him." She was a Mrs. Flood. "They all come here when they want a hand-out," she said, "but Mr. Flood had money. He died in the crack-up of an airplane."

After a while he said, "My people are all dead."

"Mr. Flood," she said, "died in the crack-up of an airplane."

She began to enjoy sitting on the porch with him, but she could never tell if he knew she was there or not. Even when he answered her, she couldn't tell if he knew it was she. She herself. Mrs. Flood, the landlady. Not just anybody. They would sit, he only sit, and she sit rocking, for half an afternoon and not two words seemed to pass between them, though she might talk at length. If she didn't talk and keep her mind going, she would find herself sitting forward in her chair, looking at him with her mouth not closed. Anyone who saw her from the sidewalk would think she was being courted by a corpse.

She observed his habits carefully. He didn't eat much or

seem to mind anything she gave him. If she had been blind, she would have sat by the radio all day, eating cake and ice cream, and soaking her feet. He ate anything and never knew the difference. He kept getting thinner and his cough deepened and he developed a limp. During the first cold months, he took the virus, but he walked out every day in spite of that. He walked about half of each day. He got up early in the morning and walked in his room—she could hear him below in hers, up and down, up and down—and then he went out and walked before breakfast and after breakfast, he went out again and walked until midday. He knew the four or five blocks around the house and he didn't go any farther than those. He could have kept on one for all she saw. He could have stayed in his room, in one spot, moving his feet up and down. He could have been dead and get all he got out of life but the exercise. He might as well be one of them monks, she thought, he might as well be in a monkery. She didn't understand it. She didn't like the thought that something was being put over her head. She liked the clear light of day. She liked to see things.

She could not make up her mind what would be inside his head and what out. She thought of her own head as a switchbox where she controlled from; but with him, she could only imagine the outside in, the whole black world in his head and his head bigger than the world, his head big enough to include the sky and planets and whatever was or had been or would be. How would he know if time was going backwards or forwards or if he was going with it? She imagined it was like you were walking in a tunnel and all you could see was a pin point of light. She had to imagine the pin point of light; she couldn't think of it at all without that. She saw it as some kind of a star, like the star on Christmas cards. She saw him going backwards to Bethlehem and she had to laugh.

She thought it would be a good thing if he had something to do with his hands, something to bring him out of himself and get him in connection with the real world again. She was certain he was out of connection with it, she was not certain at times that he even knew she existed. She suggested he get himself a guitar and learn to strum it; she had a picture of them sitting on the porch in the evening and him strumming it. She had bought two rubber plants to make where they sat more private from the street, and she thought that the sound of him strumming it from behind the rubber plant would take away the dead look he had. She suggested it but he never answered the suggestion.

After he paid his room and board every month, he had a good third of the government check left but that she could see, he never spent any money. He didn't use tobacco or drink whisky; there was nothing for him to do with all that money but lose it, since there was only himself. She thought of benefits that might accrue to his widow should he leave one. She had seen money drop out of his pocket and him not bother to reach down and feel for it. One day when she was cleaning his room, she found four dollar bills and some change in his trash can. He came in about that time from one of his walks. "Mr. Motes," she said, "here's a dollar bill and some change in this waste basket. You know where your waste basket is. How did you make that mistake?"

"It was left over," he said. "I didn't need it."

She dropped onto his straight chair. "Do you throw it away every month?" she asked after a time.

"Only when it's left over," he said.

"The poor and needy," she muttered. "The poor and needy. Don't you ever think about the poor and needy? If you don't want that money somebody else might."

"You can have it," he said.

"Mr. Motes," she said coldly, "I'm not charity yet!" She realized now that he was a mad man and that he ought to be under the control of a sensible person.

The landlady was past her middle years and her plate was too large but she had long race-horse legs and a nose that had been called Grecian by one boarder. She wore her hair clustered like grapes on her brow and over each ear and in the middle behind, but none of these advantages were any use to her in attracting his attention. She saw that the only way was to be interested in what he was interested in. "Mr. Motes," she said one afternoon when they were sitting on the porch, "why don't you preach any more? Being blind wouldn't be a hinderance. People would like to go see a blind preacher. It would be something different." She was used to going on without an answer. "You could get you one of those seeing dogs," she said, "and he and you could get up a good crowd. People'll always go to see a dog.

"For myself," she continued, "I don't have that streak. I believe that what's right today is wrong tomorrow and that the time to enjoy yourself is now so long as you let others do the same. I'm as good, Mr. Motes," she said, "not believing in Jesus as a many a one that does."

"You're better," he said, leaning forward suddenly. "If you believed in Jesus, you wouldn't be so good."

He had never paid her a compliment before! "Why Mr. Motes," she said, "I expect you're a fine preacher! You certainly ought to start it again. It would give you something to do. As it is, you don't have anything to do but walk. Why don't you start preaching again?"

"I can't preach any more," he muttered.

"Why?"

"I don't have time," he said, and got up and walked off the porch as if she had reminded him of some urgent business. He walked as if his feet hurt him but he had to go on.

Some time later she discovered why he limped. She was cleaning his room and happened to knock over his extra pair of shoes. She picked them up and looked into them as if she thought she might find something hidden there. The bottoms of them were lined with gravel and broken glass and pieces of small stone. She spilled this out and sifted it through her fingers, looking for a glitter that might mean something valuable, but she saw that what she had in her hand was trash that anybody could pick up in the alley. She stood for some time, holding the shoes, and finally she put them back under the cot. In a few days she examined them again and they were lined with fresh rocks. Who's he doing this for? she asked herself. What's he getting out of doing it? Every now and then she would have an intimation of something hidden near her but out of her reach. "Mr. Motes," she said that day, when he was in her kitchen eating his dinner, "what do you walk on rocks for?"

"To pay," he said in a harsh voice.

"Pay for what?"

"It don't make any difference for what," he said. "I'm paying."

"But what have you got to show that you're paying for?" she persisted.

"Mind your business," he said rudely. "You can't see."

The landlady continued to chew very slowly. "Do you think, Mr. Motes," she said hoarsely, "that when you're dead, you're blind?"

"I hope so," he said after a minute.

"Why?" she asked, staring at him.

After a while he said, "If there's no bottom in your eyes, they hold more."

The landlady stared for a long time, seeing nothing at all. She began to fasten all her attention on him, to the neglect of other things. She began to follow him in his walks, meeting him accidentally and accompanying him. He didn't seem to know she was there, except occasionally when he would slap at his face as if her voice bothered him, like the singing of a mosquito. He had a deep wheezing cough and she began to badger him about his health. "There's no one," she would say, "to look after you but me, Mr. Motes. No one that has your interest at heart but me. Nobody would care if I didn't." She began to make him tasty dishes and carry them to his room. He would eat what she brought, immediately, with a wry face, and hand back the plate without thanking her, as if all his attention were directed elsewhere and this was an interruption he had to suffer. One morning he told her abruptly that he was going to get his food somewhere else, and named the place, a diner around the corner, run by a foreigner. "And you'll rue the day!" she said. "You'll pick up an infection. No sane person eats there. A dark and filthy place. Encrusted! It's you that can't see, Mr. Motes.

"Crazy fool," she muttered when he had walked off. "Wait till winter comes. Where will you eat when winter comes, when the first wind blows the virus into you?"

She didn't have to wait long. He caught influenza before winter and for a while he was too weak to walk out and she had the satisfaction of bringing his meals to his room. She came earlier than usual one morning and found him asleep, breathing heavily. The old shirt he wore to sleep in was open down the front and showed three strands of barbed wire, wrapped around his chest. She retreated backwards to the door and then she dropped the tray. "Mr. Motes," she said in a thick voice, "what do you do these things for? It's not natural."

He pulled himself up.

"What's that wire around you for? It's not natural," she repeated.

After a second he began to button the shirt. "It's natural," he said.

"Well, it's not normal. It's like one of them gory stories, it's something that people have quit doing—like boiling in oil or being a saint or walling up cats," she said. "There's no reason for it. People have quit doing it."

"They ain't quit doing it as long as I'm doing it," he said.

"People have quit doing it," she repeated. "What do you do it for?"

"I'm not clean," he said.

She stood staring at him, unmindful of the broken dishes

at her feet. "I know it," she said after a minute, "you got blood on that night shirt and on the bed. You ought to get you a washwoman . . ."

"That's not the kind of clean," he said.

"There's only one kind of clean, Mr. Motes," she muttered. She looked down and observed the dishes he had made her break and the mess she would have to get up and she left for the hall closet and returned in a minute with the dust pan and broom. "It's easier to bleed than sweat, Mr. Motes," she said in the voice of High Sarcasm. "You must believe in Jesus or you wouldn't do these foolish things. You must have been lying to me when you named your fine church. I wouldn't be surprised if you weren't some kind of a agent of the pope or got some connection with something funny."

"I ain't treatin' with you," he said and lay back down, coughing.

"You got nobody to take care of you but me," she reminded him.

Her first plan had been to marry him and then have him committed to the state institution for the insane, but gradually her plan had become to marry him and keep him. Watching his face had become a habit with her; she wanted to penetrate the darkness behind it and see for herself what was there. She had the sense that she had tarried long enough and that she must get him now while he was weak, or not at all. He was so weak from the influenza that he tottered when he walked; winter had already begun and the wind slashed at the house from every angle, making a sound like sharp knives swirling in the air.

"Nobody in their right mind would like to be out on a day like this," she said, putting her head suddenly into his room in the middle of the morning on one of the coldest days of the year. "Do you hear that wind, Mr. Motes? It's fortunate for you that you have this warm place to be and someone to take care of you." She made her voice more than usually soft. "Every blind and sick man is not so fortunate," she said, "as to have somebody that cares about him." She came in and sat down on the straight chair that was just at the door. She sat on the edge of it, leaning forward with her legs apart and her hands braced on her knees. "Let me tell you, Mr. Motes," she said, "few men are as fortunate as you but I can't keep climbing these stairs. It wears me out. I've been thinking what we could do about it."

He had been lying motionless on the bed but he sat up suddenly as if he were listening, almost as if he had been alarmed by the tone of her voice. "I know you wouldn't want to give up your room here," she said, and waited for the effect of this. He turned his face toward her; she could tell she had his attention. "I know you like it here and wouldn't want to leave and you're a sick man and need somebody to take care of you as well as being blind," she said and found herself breathless and her heart beginning to flutter. He reached to the foot of the bed and felt for his clothes that were rolled up there. He began to put them on hurriedly over his night shirt. "I been thinking how we could arrange it so you would have a home and somebody to take care of you and I wouldn't have to climb these stairs, what you dressing for today, Mr. Motes? You don't want to go out in this weather.

"I been thinking," she went on, watching him as he went on with what he was doing, "and I see there's only one thing for you and me to do. Get married. I wouldn't do it under any ordinary condition but I would do it for a blind man and a sick one. If we don't help each other, Mr. Motes, there's nobody to help us," she said. "Nobody. The world is a empty place."

The suit that had been glare-blue when it was bought was a softer shade now. The panama hat was wheat-colored. He kept it on the floor by his shoes when he was not wearing it. He reached for it and put it on and then he began to put on his shoes that were still lined with rocks.

"Nobody ought to be without a place of their own to be," she said, "and I'm willing to give you a home here with me, a place where you can always stay, Mr. Motes, and never worry yourself about."

His cane was on the floor near where his shoes had been. He felt for it and then stood up and began to walk slowly toward her. "I got a place for you in my heart, Mr. Motes," she said and felt it shaking like a bird cage; she didn't know whether he was coming toward her to embrace her or not. He passed her, expressionless, out the door and into the hall. "Mr. Motes!" she said, turning sharply in the chair, "I can't allow you to stay here under no other circumstances. I can't climb these stairs. I don't want a thing," she said, "but to help you. You don't have anybody to look after you but me. Nobody to care if you live or die but me! No other place to be but mine!"

He was feeling for the first step with his cane.

"Or were you planning to find you another rooming house?"

she asked in a voice getting higher. "Maybe you were planning to go to some other city!"

"That's not where I'm going," he said. "There's no other house nor no other city."

"There's nothing, Mr. Motes," she said, "and time goes forward, it don't go backward and unless you take what's offered you, you'll find yourself out in the cold pitch black and just how far do you think you'll get?"

He felt for each step with his cane before he put his foot on it. When he reached the bottom, she called down to him. "You needn't to return to a place you don't value, Mr. Motes. The door won't be open to you. You can come back and get your belongings and then go on to wherever you think you're going." She stood at the top of the stairs for a long time. "He'll be back," she muttered. "Let the wind cut into him a little."

That night a driving icy rain came up and lying in her bed, awake at midnight, Mrs. Flood, the landlady, began to weep. She wanted to run out into the rain and cold and hunt him and find him huddled in some half-sheltered place and bring him back and say, Mr. Motes, Mr. Motes, you can stay here forever, or the two of us will go where you're going, the two of us will go. She had had a hard life, without pain and without pleasure, and she thought that now that she was coming to the last part of it, she deserved a friend. If she was going to be blind when she was dead, who better to guide her than a blind man? Who better to lead the blind than the blind, who knew what it was like?

As soon as it was daylight, she went out in the rain and searched the five or six blocks he knew and went from door to door, asking for him, but no one had seen him. She came back and called the police and described him and asked for him to be picked up and brought back to her to pay his rent. She waited all day for them to bring him in the squad car, or for him to come back of his own accord, but he didn't come. The rain and wind continued and she thought he was probably drowned in some alley by now. She paced up and down in her room, walking faster and faster, thinking of his eyes without any bottom in them and of the blindness of death.

Two days later, two young policemen cruising in a squad car found him lying in a drainage ditch near an abandoned construction project. The driver drew the squad car up to the edge of the ditch and looked into it for some time. "Ain't we been looking for a blind one?" he asked.

The other consulted a pad. "Blind and got on a blue suit and ain't paid his rent," he said.

"Yonder he is," the first one said, and pointed into the ditch. The other moved up closer and looked out of the window too.

"His suit ain't blue," he said.

"Yes it is blue," the first one said. "Quit·pushing up so close to me. Get out and I'll show you it's blue." They got out and walked around the car and squatted down on the edge of the ditch. They both had on tall new boots and new policemen's clothes; they both had yellow hair with sideburns, and they were both fat, but one was much fatter than the other.

"It might have uster been blue," the fatter one admitted.

"You reckon he's daid?" the first one asked.

"Ast him," the other said.

"No, he ain't daid. He's moving."

"Maybe he's just unconscious," the fatter one said, taking out his new billy. They watched him for a few seconds. His hand was moving along the edge of the ditch as if it were hunting something to grip. He asked them in a hoarse whisper where he was and if it was day or night.

"It's day," the thinner one said, looking at the sky. "We got to take you back to pay your rent."

"I want to go on where I'm going," the blind man said.

"You got to pay your rent first," the policeman said. "Ever' bit of it!"

The other, perceiving that he was conscious, hit him over the head with his new billy. "We don't want to have no trouble with him," he said. "You take his feet."

He died in the squad car but they didn't notice and took him on to the landlady's. She had them put him on her bed and when she had pushed them out the door, she locked it behind them and drew up a straight chair and sat down close to his face where she could talk to him. "Well, Mr. Motes," she said, "I see you've come home!"

His face was stern and tranquil. "I knew you'd come back," she said. "And I've been waiting for you. And you needn't to pay any more rent but have it free here, any way you like, upstairs or down. Just however you want it and with me to wait on you, or if you want to go on somewhere, we'll both go."

She had never observed his face more composed and she grabbed his hand and held it to her heart. It was resistless and dry. The outline of a skull was plain under his skin and

the deep burned eye sockets seemed to lead into the dark
tunnel where he had disappeared. She leaned closer and
closer to his face, looking deep into them, trying to see how
she had been cheated or what had cheated her, but she
couldn't see anything. She shut her eyes and saw the pin
point of light but so far away that she could not hold it
steady in her mind. She felt as if she were blocked at the
entrance of something. She sat staring with her eyes shut,
into his eyes, and felt as if she had finally got to the
beginning of something she couldn't begin, and she saw
him moving farther and farther away, farther and farther into
the darkness until he was the pin point of light.

WILLIAM STYRON

The Long March
To Hiram Hayden

I

ONE NOON, in the blaze of a cloudless Carolina summer, what was left of eight dead boys lay strewn about the landscape, among the poison ivy and the pine needles and loblolly saplings. It was not so much as if they had departed this life but as if, sprayed from a hose, they were only shreds of bone, gut, and dangling tissue to which it would have been impossible ever to impute the quality of life, far less the capacity to relinquish it. Of course, though, these had really died quickly, no doubt before the faintest flicker of recognition, of wonder, apprehension, or terror had had time to register in their minds. But the shock, it occurred to Lieutenant Culver, who stood in the shady lee of an ambulance and watched the scene, must have been fantastic to those on the periphery of the explosion, those fifteen or so surviving marines who now lay on the ground beneath blankets, moaning with pain and fright, and who, not more than half an hour before, had been waiting patiently in line for their lunch before the two mortar shells, misfired—how? why? the question already hung with a buzzing, palpable fury in the noontime heat—had plummeted down upon the chowline and had deadened their ears and senses and had hurled them earthward where they lay now, alive but stricken in a welter of blood and brain, scattered messkits and mashed potatoes, and puddles of melting ice cream. Moments ago in the confusion—just before he had stolen off from the Colonel's side to go behind a tree and get sick—Lieutenant Culver had had a glimpse of a young sweaty face grimed with dust, had heard the boy's voice, astonishing even in that moment of nausea because of its clear, unhysterical tone of explanation: "Major, I tell you I was on the field phone and I tell you as soon as they come out the tube I knew they were short rounds and so I hollered . . ." Of course it had been an accident. But why? He heard the Major shout something, then Culver had heard no more, retching on the leaves with a sound that, for the moment, drowned out the cries and whines of the wounded and the noise of trucks and ambulances crashing up through the underbrush.

It was not that he had a weak stomach or that he was unacquainted with carnage that allowed him to lose control. If anything, he prided himself on his stomach, and as for blood he had seen a lot spilled on Okinawa and had himself (although through no act of valor whatever) received a shrapnel wound—in the buttocks, a matter which even in retrospect, as he had often been forced to remind his wife, possessed no elements of comedy at all. In this case it was simply that on the one hand he himself had been shocked. The sight of death was the sort of thing which in wartime is expected, which one protects oneself against, and which is finally excused or at least ignored, in the same way that a beggar is ignored, or a head cold, or a social problem. But in training here in the States in peacetime (or what, this sweltering summer in the early 1950s, passed as peacetime) one had felt no particular need for that type of self-defense, and the slick nude litter of intestine and shattered blue bones, among which forks and spoons peeked out like so many pathetic metal flowers, made a crazy, insulting impact at Culver's belly, like the blow of a fist. And on the other hand (and the pulsing ache at his brow now as he vomited helplessly onto his shoes lent confirmation to what he'd been trying to deny to himself for months): he was too old, he was no longer an eager kid just out of Quantico with a knife between his teeth. He was almost thirty, he was old, and he was afraid.

Lieutenant Culver had been called back to the marines early that spring. When, one Saturday morning, his wife had thrown the brown envelope containing his orders onto the bed where he lay sleeping, he experienced an odd distress which kept him wandering about, baffled and mumbling to himself, for days. Like most of his fellow reserves he had retained his commission after the last war. It was an insouciant gesture which he had assumed would in some way benefit him in case of an all-out conflict, say, thirty years hence, but one which made no provisions for such an eventuality as a police action in Korea. It had all come much too soon and Culver had felt weirdly as if he had fallen asleep in some barracks in 1945 and had awakened in a half-dozen years or so to find that the intervening freedom, growth, and serenity had been only a glorious if somewhat prolonged dream. A flood of protest had welled up in him, for he had put the idea of war out of his mind entirely, and the brief years since Okinawa had been the richest of his life. They had produced, among lesser things, a loving, tenderly passionate wife who had passed on to their little girl both some of her gentle nature and her wealth of butter-colored hair; a law degree, the fruits of which he had just begun to realize, even though still somewhat impecuniously, as one of the brightest juniors in a good New York law firm; a friendly beagle named Howard whom he took for hikes in Washington Square; a cat, whom he did not deign to call by name, and despised; and a record-player that played Haydn, Mozart and Bach.

Up until the day that his orders came—the day that he tried to forget and the one that Betsy, his wife, soon bitterly referred to as "the day the roof fell in"—they had been living in a roomy walk-up in the Village and experiencing the prosaic contentment that comes from eating properly, indulging themselves with fair moderation in the pleasures of the city, and watching the growth of a child. This is not to say that they were either smug or dull. They had a bright circle of friends, mostly young lawyers and newspapermen and doctors and their wives. There were parties and occasional week ends in the country, where everyone became frankly drunk. There were the usual household skirmishes, too, but these were infrequent and petered out quickly. Both of them were too sensible to allow some domestic misdemeanor to develop into anything horrible; they were well adjusted and each of them found it easy to admit, long after the honeymoon, that they were deeply in love. Months later at camp, ensnared futilely in the coils of some administrative flypaper, Culver would find himself gazing up from his work and out across the smoky hot barrens of pine and sand, relieving his vast boredom in a daydream of that vanished simplicity and charm. His mind seemed to drift toward one recurrent vision. This was of the afternoons in winter when —bundled to the ears, the baby-carriage joggling bravely in the van and the melancholy beagle scampering at their heels —they took their Sunday stroll. On such days the city, its frantic heartbeat quieted and clothed in the sooty white tatters of a recent snow, seemed to have an Old World calm, and the people that passed them in the twilight appeared to be, like themselves, pink-cheeked and contented, no matter what crimson alarms flowered at the newsstands or what evil rumors sounded from distant radios. For Culver the waning Sunday light had not spelled out the promise of Monday morning's gloom but of Monday's challenge—and this was not because he was a go-getter but because he was happy. He was happy to walk through the chill and leafless dusk with his wife and his child and his dog. And he was happy to return home to warmth and peanut butter and liverwurst, to the familiar delight of the baby's good-night embrace, to the droll combat between beagle and cat, to music before sleep. Sometimes in these reveries Culver thought that it was the music, more than anything, which provided the key, and he recalled himself at a time which already seemed dark ages ago, surrounded by beer cans and attuned, in the nostalgic air of a winter evening, to some passage from some forgotten Haydn. It was one happy and ascending bar that he remembered, a dozen bright notes through which he passed in memory to an earlier, untroubled day at the end of childhood. There, like tumbling flowers against the sunny grass, their motions as nimble as the music itself, two lovely little girls played tennis, called to him voicelessly, as in a dream, and waved their arms.

The sordid little town outside the camp possessed the horror of recognition, for Culver had been there before. They left the baby with a sister and headed South where, on the outskirts of the town, they found a cramped room in a tourist cabin. They were there for two weeks. They searched vainly for a place to live, there was no more room at the camp. They turned away from bleak cell-like rooms offered at five times their value, were shown huts and chicken-coops by characters whose bland country faces could not hide the sparkle, in their calculating eyes, of venal lust. The aging proprietress of the tourist camp was a scold and a cheat. And so they finally gave up. Betsy went home. He kissed her good-by late one rainy afternoon in the bus station, surrounded by a horde of marines and by cheap suitcases and fallen candy wrappers and the sound of fretful children—all of the unlovely mementoes, so nightmarishly familiar, of leave-taking and of anxiety. Of war. He felt her tears against his cheek. It had been an evil day, and the rain that streamed against the windows, blurring a distant frieze of gaunt gray pines, had seemed to nag with both remembrance and foreboding—of tropic seas, storm-swept distances and strange coasts.

II

He had heard the explosion himself. They had been eating
at their own chow-line in a command post set up in a grove
of trees, when the noise came from off to the right, distant
enough but still too close: a twin quick earth-shaking sound
—*crump crump.* Then seconds later in the still of noon
when even the birds had become quiet and only a few murmured voices disturbed the concentration of eating, a shudder
had passed through the surrounding underbrush, like a
faint hot wind. It was premonitory, perhaps, but still no one
knew. The leaves rustled, ceased, and Culver had looked up
from where he squatted against a tree to see fifty scattered
faces peering toward the noise, their knives and forks suspended. Then from the galley among the trees a clatter
broke the silence, a falling pan or kettle, and someone
laughed, and the Colonel, sitting nearby, had said to the
Major—what had he said? Culver couldn't remember, yet
there had been something uneasy in his tone, even then,
before anyone had known, and at least ten minutes before
the radio corporal, a tobacco-chewing clown from Oklahoma
named Hobbs, came trotting up brushing crumbs from his
mouth, a message book clutched in one fat paw. He was
popular in battalion headquarters, one of those favored
men who, through some simplicity or artlessness of nature,
can manage a profane familiarity which in another would be
insubordinate; the look of concern on his clown's face, usually so whimsical, communicated an added dread.

"I gotta flash red from Plumbob, Colonel, and it ain't
no problem emergency. All hell's broke loose over in Third
Battalion. They dropped in some short rounds on a chow-
line and they want corpsmen and a doctor and the chaplain.
Jesus, you should hear 'em down there."

The Colonel had said nothing at first. The brief flicker
of uneasiness in his eyes had fled, and when he put down
his messkit and looked up at Hobbs it was only to wipe his
hands on his handkerchief and squint casually into the sun,
as if he were receiving the most routine of messages. It was
absolutely typical of the man, Culver reflected. Too habitual
to be an act yet still somehow too faintly self-conscious to be
entirely natural, how many years and what strange interior
struggle had gone into the perfection of such a gesture?
It was good, Grade-A Templeton, perhaps not a distinctly
top-notch performance but certainly, from where the critic

Culver sat, deserving of applause: the frail, little-boned, almost pretty face peering upward with a look of attitudinized contemplation; the pensive bulge of tongue sliding inside the rim of one tanned cheek to gouge out some particle of food; small hands working calmly in the folds of the handkerchief—surely all this was more final, more commanding than the arrogant loud mastery of a Booth, more like the skill of Bernhardt, who could cow men by the mystery of her smallest twitch. Perhaps fifteen seconds passed before he spoke. Culver became irritated—at his own suspense, throbbing inside him like a heartbeat, and at the awesome silence which, as if upon order, had fallen over the group of five, detached from the bustle of the rest of the command post: the Colonel; Hobbs; Major Lawrence, the executive officer, now gazing at the Colonel with moist underlip and deferential anxiety; Captain Mannix; himself. Back off in the bushes a mockingbird commenced a shrill rippling chant and far away, amidst the depth of the silence, there seemed to be a single faint and terrible scream. Hobbs spat an auburn gob of tobacco-juice into the sand, and the Colonel spoke: "Let me have that radio, Hobbs, and get me Plumbob One," he said evenly, and then with no change of tone to the Major: "Billy, send a runner over for Doc Patterson and you two get down there with the chaplain. Take my jeep. Tell the Doc to detach all his corpsmen. And you'd better chop-chop."

The Major scrambled to his feet. He was youthful and handsome, a fine marine in his polished boots, his immaculate dungarees—donned freshly clean, Culver had observed, that morning. He was of the handsomeness preferred by other military men—regular features, clean-cut, rather athletic—but there was a trace of peacetime fleshiness in his cheeks which often lent to the corners of his mouth a sort of petulance, so that every now and again, his young uncomplicated face in deep concentration over some operations map or training schedule or order he looked like a spoiled and arrogant baby of five. "Aye-aye, sir," he said and bent over the Colonel, bestowing upon him that third-person flattery which to Culver seemed perilously close to bootlicking and was thought to be considerably out of date, especially among the reserves. "Does the Colonel want us to run our own problem as ordered, sir?" He was a regular.

Templeton took the headset from Hobbs, who lowered the radio down beside him in the sand. "Yeah, Billy," he said, without looking up, "yeah, that'll be all right. We'll run her on time. Tell O'Leary to tell all companies to push off at thirteen-hundred."

"Aye-aye, sir." And the Major, boots sparkling, was off in a puff of pine needles and dust.

"Jesus," Mannix said. He put down his messkit and nudged Culver in the ribs. Captain Mannix, the commanding officer of headquarters company, was Culver's friend and, for five months, his closest one. He was a dark heavy-set Jew from Brooklyn, Culver's age and a reserve, too, who had had to sell his radio store and leave his wife and two children at home. He had a disgruntled sense of humor which often seemed to bring a spark of relief not just to his own, but to Culver's, feeling of futility and isolation. Mannix was a bitter man and, in his bitterness, sometimes recklessly vocal. He had long ago given up genteel accents, and spoke like a marine. It was easier, he maintained. "Je-*sus*," he whispered again, too loud, "what'll Congress do about this? Look at Billy chop-chop."

Culver said nothing. His tension eased off a bit, and he looked around him. The news had not seemed yet to have spread around the command post; the men began to get up and walk to the chow-line to clean their messgear, strolled back beneath the trees and flopped down, heads against their packs, for a moment's nap. The Colonel spoke in an easy, confidential voice with the other battalion commander: the casualties were confined, Culver gathered, to that outfit. It was a battalion made up mostly of young reserves and it was one in which, he suddenly thanked God, he knew no one. Then he heard the Colonel go on calmly—to promise more aid, to promise to come down himself, shortly. "Does it look rough, Luke?" Culver heard him say, "Hold on tight, Luke boy"—all in the cool and leisurely, almost bored, tones of a man to whom the greatest embarrassment would be a show of emotion, and to whom, because of this quality, had been given, in the midst of some strained and violent combat situation long ago, the name "Old Rocky." He was not yet forty-five, yet the adjective "old" applied, for there was a gray sheen in his hair and a bemused, unshakable look in his tranquil eyes that made him seem, like certain young ecclesiastics, prematurely aged and perhaps even wise. Culver saw him put the headset down and get up, walking off toward the operations tent with a springy, slim-hipped, boyish stride, calling out over his shoulder as he went: "Mannix." Simply that: Mannix. A voice neither harsh nor peremptory nor, on the other hand, particularly gentle. It was merely a voice which expected to be obeyed, and Culver felt Mannix's big weight against him as the Captain put a hand on his shoulder and pried himself up from the ground, muttering, "Jesus, lemme digest a bit, Jack."

Mannix despised the Colonel. Yet, Culver thought, as the Captain hulked stiff-kneed behind the Colonel and disappeared after him into the operations tent, Mannix despised everything about the Marine Corps. In this attitude he was like nearly all the reserves, it was true, but Mannix was more noisily frank in regard to his position. He detested Templeton not because of any slight or injustice, but because Templeton was a lieutenant colonel, because he was a regular, and because he possessed over Mannix—after six years of freedom —an absolute and unquestioned authority. Mannix would have hated any battalion commander, had he the benignity of Santa Claus, and Culver, listening to Mannix's frequently comical but often too audible complaints, as just now, was kept in a constant state of mild suspense—half amusement, half horror. Culver settled himself against the tree. Apparently there was nothing, for the moment at least, that he could do. Above him an airplane droned through the stillness. A truck grumbled across the clearing, carrying a group of languid hospital corpsmen, was gone; around him the men lay against their packs in crumpled attitudes of sleep. A heavy drowsiness came over him, and he let his eyes slide closed. Suddenly he yearned, with all of the hunger of a schoolboy in a classroom on a May afternoon, to be able to collapse into slumber. For the three days they had been on the problem he had averaged only four hours of sleep a night —almost none last night—and gratefully he knew he'd be able to sleep this evening. He began to doze, dreaming fitfully of home, of white cottages, of a summer by the sea. *Long walk tonight.* And his eyes snapped open then—on what seemed to be the repeated echo, from afar, of that faint anguished shriek he had heard before—in the horrid remembrance that there would be no sleep tonight. For anyone at all. Only a few seconds had passed.

"Long walk tonight," the voice repeated. Culver stared upward through a dazzling patchwork of leaves and light to see the broad pink face of Sergeant O'Leary, smiling down.

"Christ, O'Leary," he said, "don't remind me."

The Sergeant, still grinning, gestured with his shoulder in the direction of the operations tent. "The Colonel's really got a wild hair, ain't he?" He chuckled and reached down and clutched one of his feet, with an elaborate groan.

Culver abruptly felt cloaked in a gloom that was almost tangible, and he was in no mood to laugh. "You'll be ready holding that foot tomorrow morning," he said, "and that's no joke."

The grin persisted. "Ah, Mister Culver," O'Leary said, "don't take it so hard. It's just a little walk through the night. It'll be over before you know it." He paused, prodding with his toe at the pine needles. "Say," he went on, "what's this I heard about some short rounds down in Third Batt?"

"I don't know from nothing, O'Leary. I just read the papers." Another truck came by, loaded with corpsmen, followed by a jeep in which sat the helmeted Major Lawrence, a look of sulky arrogance on his face, his arms folded at his chest like a legionnaire riding through a conquered city. "But from what I understand," Culver went on, turning back, "quite a few guys got hurt."

"That's tough," O'Leary said. "I'll bet you they were using that old stuff they've had stored on Guam ever since '45. Jesus, you'd think they'd have better sense. Why, I seen those shells stacked up high as a man out there just last year, getting rained on every day and getting the jungle rot and Jesus, they put tarps over 'em but five years is one hell of a long time to let 81-shells lay around. I remember once . . ." Culver let him talk, without hearing the words, and drowsed. O'Leary was an old-timer (though only a few years older than Culver), a regular who had just signed over for four more years, and it was impossible to dislike him. On Guadalcanal he had been only a youngster, but in the intervening years the Marine Corps had molded him—perhaps by his own unconscious choice—in its image, and he had become as inextricably grafted to the system as any piece of flesh surgically laid on to arm or thigh. There was great heartiness and warmth in him but at the same time he performed all infantry jobs with a devoted, methodical competence. He could say sarcastically, "The Colonel's really got a wild hair, ain't he?" but shrug his shoulders and grin, and by that ambivalent gesture sum up an attitude which only a professional soldier could logically retain: I doubt the Colonel's judgment a little, but I will willingly do what he says. He also shared with Hobbs, the radioman, some sort of immunity. And thus it had been last night, Culver recalled, that upon the Colonel's announcement about this evening's forced march—which was to take thirteen hours and extend the nearly thirty-six miles back to the main base—O'Leary had been able to give a long, audible, incredulous whistle, right in the Colonel's face, and elicit from the Colonel an indulgent smile; whereas in the same blackout tent and at virtually the same instant Mannix had murmured, "Thirty-six miles, Jesus Christ," in a tone, however, laden with no more disbelief or no more pain than O'Leary's whistle, and Culver had seen the Colonel's smile vanish, replaced on the fragile little face by a subtle, delicate shadow of irritation.

"You think that's too long?" the Colonel had said to Mannix then, turning slightly. There had been no hostility in his voice, or even reproof; it had, in fact, seemed merely a question candidly stated—although this might have been because two enlisted men had been in the tent, O'Leary, and some wizened, anonymous little private shivering over the radio. It was midsummer, but nights out in the swamps were fiercely, illogically cold, and from where they had set up the operations tent that evening—on a tiny patch of squashy marshland—the dampness seemed to ooze up and around them, clutching their bones in a chill which extra sweaters and field jackets and sweatshirts could not dislodge. A single kerosene pressure-lamp dangled from overhead—roaring like a pint-sized, encapsuled hurricane; it furnished the only light in the tent, and the negligible solace of a candlelike heat. It had the stark, desperate, manufactured quality of the light one imagines in an execution chamber; under it the Colonel's face, in absolute repose as he stared down for a brief, silent instant and awaited Mannix's reply, looked like that of a mannequin, chalky, exquisite, solitary beneath a store-window glare.

"No, sir," Mannix said. He had recovered quickly. He peered up at the Colonel from his camp stool, expressionless. "No, sir," he repeated, "I don't think it's too long, but it's certainly going to be some hike."

The Colonel did something with his lips. It seemed to be a smile. He said nothing—bemused and mystifying—wearing the enigma of the moment like a cape. In the silence the tempestuous little lamp boiled and raged; far off in the swamp somewhere a mortar flare flew up with a short, sharp crack. O'Leary broke the quietness in the tent with a loud sneeze, followed, almost like a prolongation of the sneeze, by a chuckle, and said: "Oh boy, Colonel, there're gonna be some sore feet Saturday morning."

The Colonel didn't answer. He hooked his thumbs in his

belt. He turned to the Major, who was brooding upward from the field desk, cheeks propped against his hands. "I was sitting in my tent a while ago, Billy," the Colonel said, "and I got to thinking. I got to thinking about a lot of things. I got to thinking about the Battalion. I said to myself, 'How's the Battalion doing?' I mean, 'What kind of an outfit do I have here? Is it in good combat shape? If we were to meet an Aggressor enemy tomorrow would we come out all right?' Those were the queries I posed to myself. Then I tried to formulate an answer." He paused, his eyes luminous and his lips twisted in a wry, contemplative smile as if he were indeed, again, struggling with the weight of the questions to which he had addressed himself. The Major was absorbed; he looked up at Templeton with an intent baby-blue gaze and parted mouth, upon which, against a pink cleft of the lower lip, there glittered a bead of saliva. "Reluctantly," the Colonel went on slowly, "reluctantly, I came to this conclusion: the Battalion's been doping off." He paused again. "Doping off. Especially," he said, turning briefly toward Mannix with a thin smile, "a certain component unit known as Headquarters and Service Company." He leaned back on the camp stool and slowly caressed the pewter-colored surface of his hair. "I decided a little walk might be in order for tomorrow night, after we secure the problem. Instead of going back to the base on the trucks. What do you think, Billy?"

"I think that's an excellent idea, sir. An excellent idea. In fact I've been meaning to suggest something like that to the Colonel for quite some time. As a means of inculcating a sort of group *esprit*."

"It's what they need, Billy."

"Full marching order, sir?" O'Leary put in seriously.

"No, that'd be a little rough."

"Aaa-h," O'Leary said, relieved.

Suddenly Culver heard Mannix's voice: "Even so—"

"Even so, what?" the Colonel interrupted. Again, the voice was not hostile, only anticipatory, as if it already held the answer to whatever Mannix might ask or suggest.

"Well, even so, Colonel," Mannix went on mildly, while Culver, suddenly taut and concerned, held his breath, "even without packs thirty-six miles is a long way for anybody, much less for guys who've gone soft for the past five or six years. I'll admit my company isn't the hottest outfit in the world, but most of them are reserves—"

"Wait a minute, Captain, wait a minute," the Colonel said.

Once more the voice—as cool and as level as the marsh, ground upon which they were sitting—carefully skirted any tone of reproach and was merely explicit: "I don't want you to think I'm taking it out on the Battalion merely because of you, or rather H & S Company. But they aren't reserves. They're *marines. Comprend?*" He arose from the chair. "I think," he went on flatly, almost gently, "that there's one thing that we are all tending to overlook these days. We've been trying to differentiate too closely between two particular bodies of men that make up the Marine Corps. Technically it's true that a lot of these new men are reserves —that is, they have an 'R' affixed at the end of the 'USMC.' But it's only a technical difference, you see. Because first and foremost they're *marines.* I don't want my marines doping off. They're going to *act* like marines. They're going to be *fit.* If they meet an Aggressor enemy next week they might have to march a long, long way. And that's what I want this hike to teach them. *Comprend?*" He made what could pass for the token of a smile and laid his hand easily and for a lingering second on Mannix's shoulder, in a sort of half-gesture of conciliation, understanding—something—it was hard to tell. It was an odd picture because from where he sat Culver was the only one in the tent who could see, at the same instant, both of their expressions. In the morbid, comfortless light they were like classical Greek masks, made of chrome or tin, reflecting an almost theatrical disharmony: the Colonel's fleeting grin sculpted cleanly and prettily in the unshadowed air above the Captain's darkened, downcast face where, for a flicker of a second, something outraged and agonized was swiftly graven and swiftly scratched out. The Colonel's smile was not complacent or unfriendly. It was not so much as if he had achieved a triumph but merely equilibrium, had returned once more to that devout, ordered state of communion which the Captain's words had ever so briefly disturbed. At that moment Culver almost liked the Colonel, in some negative way which had nothing to do with affection, but to which "respect," though he hated the word, was the nearest approach. At least it was an honest smile, no matter how faint. It was the expression of a man who might be fatuous and a ham of sorts, but was not himself evil or unjust—a man who would like to overhear some sergeant say, "He keeps a tight outfit, but he's straight." In men like Templeton all emotions—all smiles, all anger—emanated from a priest-like, religious fervor, throbbing inwardly with the cadence of parades and booted footfalls. By that passion rebels are ordered into quick damnation but simple doubters sometimes find indulgence—depending upon the priest, who may be one inclined toward mercy, or who is one ever rapt in some litany of punishment and court-martial. The Colonel was devout but inclined toward mercy. He was not a tyrant, and his smile was a sign that the Captain's doubts were forgiven, probably even forgotten. But only Culver had seen the Captain's face: a quick look of both fury and suffering, like the tragic Greek mask, or a shackled slave. Then Mannix flushed. "Yes, sir," he said.

The Colonel walked toward the door. He seemed already to have put the incident out of his mind. "Culver," he said, "if you can ever make radio contact with Able Company tell them to push off at 0600. If you can't, send a runner down before dawn to see if they've got the word." He gave the side of his thigh a rather self-conscious, gratuitous slap. "Well, good night."

There was a chorus of "Good night, sirs," and then the Major went out, too, trailed by O'Leary. Culver looked at his watch: it was nearly three o'clock.

Mannix looked up. "You going to try and get some sleep, Tom?"

"I've tried. It's too cold. Anyway, I've got to take over the radio watch from Junior here. What's your name, fellow?"

The boy at the radio looked up with a start, trembling with the cold. "McDonald, sir." He was very young, with pimples and a sweet earnest expression; he had obviously just come from boot camp, for he had practically no hair.

"Well, you can shove off and get some sleep, if you can find a nice warm pile of pine needles somewhere." The boy sleepily put down his earphones and went out, fastening the blackout flap behind him.

"I've tried," Culver repeated, "but I just can't get used to sleeping on the ground any more. I'm getting old and rheumatic. Anyway, the Old Rock was in here for about two hours before you came, using up my sack time while he told the Major and O'Leary and me all about his Shanghai days."

"He's a son of a bitch." Mannix morosely cupped his chin in his hands, blinking into space, at the bare canvas wall. He was chewing on the butt of a cigar. The glare seemed to accentuate a flat Mongoloid cast in his face; he looked surly and tough and utterly exhausted. Shivering, he pulled his field jacket closer around his neck, and then, as Culver watched, his face broke out into the comical, exasperated smile which always heralded his bitterest moments of outrage—at the Marine Corps, at the system, at their help-less plight, the state of the world—tirades which, in their unqualified cynicism, would have been intolerable were they not always delivered with such gusto and humor and a kind of grisly delight. "Thirty . . . six . . . *miles*," he said slowly, his eyes alive and glistening, *"thirty . . . six . . . miles!* Christ on a crutch! Do you realize how far that is? Why that's as far as it is from Grand Central to Stamford, Con-necticut! Why, man, I haven't walked a hundred consecutive yards since 1945. I couldn't go thirty-six miles if I were sliding downhill the whole way on a sled. And a *forced* march, mind you. You just don't stroll along, you know. That's like running. That's a regulation two-and-a-half miles per hour with only a ten-minute break each hour. So H & S Company is fouled up. So maybe it is. He can't take green troops like these and do that. After a couple of seven- or ten- or fifteen-mile conditioning hikes, maybe so. If they were young. And rested. Barracks-fresh. But this silly son of a bitch is going to have all these tired, flabby old men flap-ping around on the ground like a bunch of fish after the first two miles. Christ on a frigging crutch!"

"He's not a bad guy, Al," Culver said, "he's just a regular. Shot in the ass with the Corps. A bit off his nut, like all of them."

But Mannix had made the march seem menacing, there was no doubt about that, and Culver—who for the moment had been regarding the hike as a sort of careless abstrac-tion, a prolonged evening's stroll—felt a solid dread creep into his bones, along with the chill of the night. Involun-tarily, he shuddered. He felt suddenly unreal and disori-ented, as if through some curious second sight or seventh sense his surroundings had shifted, ever so imperceptibly, into another dimension of space and time. Perhaps he was just so tired. Freezing marsh and grass instead of wood be-neath his feet, the preposterous cold in the midst of summer, Mannix's huge distorted shadow cast brutishly against the impermeable walls by a lantern so sinister that its raging noise had the sound of a typhoon at sea—all these, just for an instant, did indeed contrive to make him feel as if they were adrift at sea in a dazzling, windowless box, ig-norant of direction or of any points of the globe, and with no way of telling. What he had had for the last years—wife and child and home—seemed to have existed in the infinite past or, dreamlike again, never at all, and what he had done yesterday and the day before, moving wearily with this tent from one strange thicket to a stranger swamp and on to the green depths of some even stranger ravine, had no sequence, like the dream of a man delirious with fever. All time and space seemed for a moment to be enclosed within the tent, itself unmoored and unhelmed upon a dark and compassless ocean.

And although Mannix was close by, he felt profoundly alone. Something that had happened that evening—something Mannix had said, or suggested, perhaps not even that, but only a fleeting look in the Captain's face, the old compressed look of torment mingled with seething outrage— something that evening, without a doubt, had added to the great load of his loneliness an almost intolerable burden. And that burden was simply an anxiety, nameless for the moment and therefore the more menacing. It was not merely the prospect of the hike. Exhaustion had just made him vulnerable to a million shaky, anonymous fears—fears which he might have resisted had he felt strong and refreshed, or younger. His age was showing badly. All this would have been easy at twenty-three. But he was thirty, and seventy-two virtually sleepless hours had left him feeling bushed and defeated. And there was another subtle difference he felt about his advanced age—a new awakening, an awareness— and therein lay the reason for his fears.

It was simply that after six years of an ordered and sympathetic life—made the more placid by the fact that he had assumed he had put war forever behind him—it was a shock almost mystically horrifying, in its unreality, to find himself in this new world of frigid nights and blazing noons, of disorder and movement and fanciful pursuit. He was insecure and uprooted and the prey of many fears. Not for days but for weeks, it seemed, the battalion had been on the trail of an invisible enemy who always eluded them and kept them pressing on—across swamps and blasted fields and past indolent, alien streams. This enemy was labeled Aggressor, on maps brightly spattered with arrows and symbolic tanks and guns, but although there was no sign of his aggression he fled them nonetheless and they pushed the sinister chase, sending up shells and flares as they went. Five hours' pause, five hours in a tent somewhere, lent to the surrounding grove of trees a warm, homelike familiarity that was almost like permanence, and he left each command post feeling lonely and uprooted, as they pushed on after the spectral foe into the infinite strangeness of another swamp or grove. Fatigue pressed down on his shoulders like strong hands, and he awoke in the morning feeling weary, if he ever slept at all. Since their constant movement made the sunlight come from ever-shifting points of the compass, he was often never quite sure—in his steady exhaustion—whether it was morning or afternoon. The displacement and the confusion filled him with an anxiety which would not have been possible six years before, and increased his fatigue. The tent itself, in its tiny, momentary permanence, might have had all of the appeal of the home which he so desperately hungered for, had it not been so cold, and had it not seemed, as he sat there suddenly shivering with fear, so much more like a coffin instead.

Then it occurred to him that he was actually terrified of the march, of the thirty-six miles: not because of the length —which was beyond comprehension—but because he was sure he'd not be able to make it. The contagion of Mannix's fear had touched him. And he wondered then if Mannix's fear had been like his own: that no matter what his hatred of the system, of the Marine Corps, might be, some instilled, twisted pride would make him walk until he dropped, and his fear was not of the hike itself, but of dropping. He looked up at Mannix and said, "Do you think you can make it, Al?"

Mannix heavily slapped his knee. He seemed not to have heard the question. The giddy sensation passed, and Culver got up to warm his hands at the lamp.

"I'll bet if Regiment or Division got wind of this they'd lower the boom on the bastard," Mannix said.

"They have already. They said fine."

"What do you mean? How do you know?"

"He said so, before you came in. He radioed to the base for permission, or so he said."

"The bastard."

"He wouldn't dare without it," Culver said. "What I can't figure out is why Regiment gave him the O.K. on it."

"The swine. The little swine. It's not on account of H & S Company. You know that. It's because it's an exploit. He wants to be known as a tough guy, a boondocker."

"There's one consolation, though," said Culver, after a pause, "if it'll help you any."

"What, for God's sake?"

"Old Rocky, or whatever they call him, is going to hike along, too."

"You think so?" Mannix said doubtfully.

"I know so. So do you. He wouldn't dare not push along with his men."

Mannix was silent for a moment. Then he said viciously, as if obsessed with the idea that no act of Templeton's could remain untainted by a prime and calculated evil: "But the son of a bitch! He's made for that sort of thing. He's been running around the boondocks for six years getting in shape while sane people like you and me were home living like humans and taking it easy. Billy Lawrence, too. They're both gung ho. These fat civilians can't take that sort of thing. My God! Hobbs! Look at that radioman, Hobbs. That guy's going to keel over two minutes out—" He rose suddenly to his feet and stretched, his voice stifled by the long, indrawn breath of a yawn. "Aaa-h, fuck it. I'm going to hit the sack."

"Why don't you?"

"Fine bed. A poncho in a pile of poison ivy. My ass looks like a chessboard from chigger bites. Jesus, if Mimi could see me now." He paused and pawed at his red-rimmed eyes. "Yeah," he said, blinking at his watch, "I think I will." He slapped Culver on the back, without much heartiness. "I'll see you tomorrow, sport. Stay loose." Then he lumbered from the tent, mumbling something: *be in for fifty years.*

Culver turned away from the lamp. He sat down at the field desk, strapping a black garland of wires and earphones around his skull. The wild, lost wail of the radio signal struck his ears, mingling with the roar, much closer now, of the lamp; alone as he was, the chill and cramped universe of the tent seemed made for no one more competent than a blind midget, and was on the verge of bursting with a swollen obbligato of demented sounds. He felt almost sick with the need for sleep and, with the earphones still around his head, he thrust his face into his arms on the field desk. There was nothing on the radio except the signal; far off in the swamp the companies were sleeping wretchedly in scattered squads and platoons, tumbled about in the cold and the dark, and dreaming fitful dreams. The radios were dead everywhere, except for their signals: a crazy, tortured multitude of wails on which his imagination played in exhaustion. They seemed like the cries of souls in the anguish of hell, if he concentrated closely enough, shrill crackling, whines, barks and shrieks—a whole jungle full of noise an inch from his eardrum and across which, like a thread of insanity, was strung the single faint fluting of a dance-band clarinet—blown in from Florida or New York, someplace beyond reckoning. His universe now seemed even more contained: not merely by the tiny space of the tent, but by the almost tangible fact of sound. And it was impossible to sleep.

Besides, something weighed heavily on his mind; there was something he had forgotten, something he was supposed to do . . .

Then suddenly he remembered the Colonel's instructions. He cleared his throat and spoke drowsily into the mouthpiece, his head still resting against his arms. "This is Bundle Three calling Bundle Able. This is Bundle Three calling Bundle Able. This is Bundle Three calling Bundle Able. Do you hear me? Over . . ." He paused for a moment, waiting. There was no answer. He repeated: "This is Bundle Three calling Bundle Able, this is Bundle Three calling Bundle Able, this is. . . ." And he snapped abruptly erect, thinking of Mannix, thinking: to hell with it: simply because the words made him feel juvenile and absurd, as if he were reciting Mother Goose.

He *would* stay awake. And he thought of Mannix. Because Mannix would laugh. Mannix appreciated the idiocy of those radio words, just as in his own crazy way he managed to put his finger on anything which might represent a symbol of their predicament. Like the radio code. He had a violent contempt for the gibberish, the boy-scout passwords which replaced ordinary conversation in the military world. To Mannix they were all part of the secret language of a group of morons, morons who had been made irresponsibly and dangerously clever. He had despised the other side, also —the sweat, the exertion, and the final danger. It had been he, too, who had said, "None of this Hemingway crap for me, Jack"; he was nobody's lousy hero, and he'd get out of this outfit some way. Yet, Culver speculated, who really was a hero anyway, any more? Mannix's disavowal of faith put him automatically out of the hero category, in the classical sense, yet if suffering was part of the hero's role, wasn't Mannix as heroic as any? On his shoulder there was a raw, deeply dented, livid scar, made the more conspicuous and, for that matter, more ugly, by the fact that its evil slick surface only emphasized the burly growth of hair around it. There were smaller scars all over his body. About them Mannix was neither proud nor modest, but just frank, and once while they were showering down after a day in the field, Mannix told him how he had gotten the scars, one day on Peleliu. "I was a buck sergeant then. I got pinned down in a shell hole out in front of my platoon. Christ knows how I got there but I remember there was a telephone in the hole and—whammo!—the Nips began laying in mortar fire on the area and I got a piece right here." He pointed to a shiny, triangular groove just above his knee. "I remember grabbing that phone and hollering for them to for Christ's sake get the 81s up and knock out that position, but they were slow, Jesus they were slow! The Nips were firing for effect, I guess, because they were coming down like rain and every time one of the goddam things went off I seemed to catch it. All I can remember is hollering into that phone and the rounds going off and the zinging noise that shrapnel made. I hollered for 81s and I caught a piece in my hand. Then I hollered for at least a goddam rifle grenade and I caught a piece in the ass, right here. I hollered for 60s and guns and airplanes. Every time I hollered for something I seemed to catch some steel. Christ, I was scared. And hurting! Jesus Christ, I never hurt so much in my life. Then I caught this one right here"—he made a comical, contorted gesture, with a bar of soap, over his shoulder—"man, it was lights out then. I remember thinking, 'Al, you've had it,' and just before I passed out I looked down at that telephone. You know, that frigging wire had been blasted right out of sight all that time."

No, perhaps Mannix wasn't a hero, any more than the rest of them, caught up by wars in which, decade by half-decade, the combatant served peonage to the telephone and the radar and the thunderjet—a horde of cunningly designed, and therefore often treacherous, machines. But Mannix had suffered once, that "once" being, in his own words, "once too goddam many, Jack." And his own particular suffering had made him angry, had given him an acute, if cynical, perception about their renewed bondage, and a keen nose for the winds that threatened to blow up out of the oppressive weather of their surroundings and sweep them all into violence. And he made Culver uneasy. His discontent was not merely peevish; it was rocklike and rebellious, and thus this discontent seemed to Culver to be at once brave and somehow full of peril.

He had first seen Mannix the revolutionary five months ago, soon after they had been called back to duty. He hadn't known him then. There were compulsory lectures arranged at first, to acquaint the junior officers with recent developments in what had been called "the new amphibious doctrine." The outlines of these lectures were appallingly familiar: the stuffy auditorium asprawl with bored lieutenants and captains, the brightly lit stage with its magnified charts and graphs, the lantern slides (at which point, when the lights went out, it was possible to sneak a moment's nap, just as in officers' school seven years ago), the parade of majors and colonels with their maps and pointers, and their cruelly tedious, doggedly memorized lectures: the whole scene, with its grave, professorial air, seemed seedily portentous, especially since no one cared, save the majors and colonels, and no one listened. When Culver sat down, during the darkness of a lantern slide, next to the big relaxed mass which he dimly identified as a captain, he noticed that it was snoring. When the lights went up, Mannix still slept on, filling the air around him with a loud, tranquil blubber. Culver aroused him with a nudge. Mannix grumbled something, but then said, "Thanks, Jack." A young colonel had come onto the stage then. He had made many of the lectures that week. He had a curiously thick, throaty voice which would have made him sound like a yokel, except that his words were coolly, almost passionately put, and he bent forward over the lectern with a bleak and solemn attitude—a lean, natty figure, with hair cut so close to his head that he appeared to be, from that distance, nearly bald. "An SS man," Mannix whispered, "he's gonna come down here and cut your balls off. You Jewish?" He grinned and collapsed back, forehead against his hand, into quiet slumber. Culver couldn't recall what the colonel talked about: the movement of supplies, logistics, ship-to-shore movement, long-range planning, all abstract and vast, and an ardent glint came to his eyes when he spoke of the "grandiose doctrine" which had been formulated since they, the reserves, had been away. "You bet your life, Jack," Mannix had whispered out of the shadows then. He seemed to have snapped fully awake and, following the lecture intently, he appeared to address his whispers not to Culver, or the colonel, but to the air. "You bet your life they're grandiose," he said, "even if you don't know what grandiose means. I'll bet you'd sell your soul to be able to drop a bomb on somebody." And then, aping the colonel's instructions to the corporal—one of the enlisted flunkies who, after each lecture, passed out the reams of printed and mimeographed tables and charts and résumés, which everyone promptly, when out of sight, threw away—he whispered in high, throaty, lilting mockery: "Corporal, kindly pass out the atom bombs for inspection." He smacked the arm of his seat, too hard; it could be heard across the auditorium, and heads turned then, but the colonel had not seemed to have noticed. "Jesus," Mannix rumbled furiously, "Jesus Christ almighty," while the colonel droned on, in his countrified voice: "Our group destiny," he said, "amphibiously integrated, from any force thrown against us by Aggressor enemy."

Later—toward the end of that week of lectures, after Mannix had spoken the calm, public manifesto which at least among the reserves had made him famous, and from then on the object of a certain awe, though with a few doubts about his balance, too—Culver had tried to calculate how he had gotten by with it. Perhaps it had to do with his size, his bearing. There was at times a great massive absoluteness in the way he spoke. He was huge, and the complete honesty and candor of his approach seemed to rumble forth, like notes from a sounding board, in direct proportion to his size. He had suffered, too, and this suffering had left a persistent, unwhipped, scornful look in his eyes, almost like a stain, or rather a wound, which spells out its own warning and cautions the unwary to handle this tortured parcel of flesh with care. And he was an enormous man, his carriage was formidable. That skinny, bristle-haired colonel, Culver finally realized, had been taken aback past the point of punishment, or even reprimand, merely because of the towering, unavoidable, physical fact that he was facing not a student or a captain or a subordinate, but a stubborn and passionate man. So it was that, after a lecture on transport of supplies, when the colonel had called Mannix's name at random from a list to answer some generalized, hypothetical question, Mannix had stood up and said merely, "I don't know, sir." A murmur of surprise passed over the auditorium then, for the colonel, early in the hour, had made it plain that he had wanted at least an attempt at an answer—a guess—even though they might be unacquainted with the subject. But Mannix merely said, "I don't know, sir," while the colonel, as if he hadn't heard correctly, rephrased the question with a little tremor of annoyance. There was a moment's silence and men turned around in their seats to look at the author of this defiance. "I don't know, sir," he said again, in a loud but calm voice. "I don't know what my first consideration would be in making a space table like that. I'm an infantry officer. I got an 0302." The colonel's forehead went pink under the glare of the lights. "I stated earlier, Captain, that I wanted some sort of answer. None of you gentlemen is expected to know this subject pat, but you can essay *some kind of an answer*." Mannix just stood there, solid and huge, blinking at the colonel. "I just have to repeat, sir," he said finally, "that I don't have the faintest idea what my first consideration would be. I never went to cargo-loading school. I'm an 0302. And I'd like to respectfully add, sir, if I might, that there's hardly anybody in this room who knows that answer, either. They've forgotten everything they ever learned seven years ago. Most of them don't even know how to take an M-1 apart. They're too old. They should be home with their family." There was passion in his tone but it was controlled and straightforward—he had managed to keep out of his voice either anger or insolence—and then he fell silent. His words had the quality, the sternness, of an absolute and unequivocal fact, as if they had been some intercession for grace spoken across the heads of a court-room by a lawyer so quietly convinced of his man's inno-cence that there was no need for gesticulations or frenzy. The colonel's eyes bulged incredulously at Mannix from across the rows of seats, but in the complete, astounded hush that had followed he was apparently at a loss for words. A bit unsteadily, he called out another name and Mannix sat down, staring stonily ahead.

It had been perhaps a court-martial offense, at least worthy of some reprimand, but that was all there was to it. Nothing happened, no repercussions, nothing. The thing had been forgotten; either that, or it had been stored away in the uni-versal memory of colonels, where all such incidents are sorted out for retribution, or are forgotten. Whatever effect it had on the colonel, or whatever higher, even more im-portant sources got wind of it, it had its effect on Mannix. And the result was odd. Far from giving the impression that he had been purged, that he had blown off excess pres-sure, he seemed instead more tense, more embittered, more in need to scourge something—his own boiling spirit, au-thority, anything.

Culver's vision of him at this time was always projected against Heaven's Gate, which was the name—no doubt iron-ically supplied at first by the enlisted men—of the pleasure-dome ingeniously erected amid a tangle of alluvial swamp-land, and for officers only. He and Mannix lived in rooms next to each other, in the bachelor quarters upstairs. The entire area was a playground which had all the casual opu-lence of a Riviera resort and found its focus in the sparkling waters of a swimming pool, set like an oblong sapphire amid flowered walks and a fanciful growth of beach umbrellas. There, at ten minutes past four each day, Mannix could be found, his uniform shed in an instant and a gin fizz in his hand—a sullen, mountainous figure in a lurid sportshirt, across which a squadron of monstrous butterflies floated in

luminous, unmilitary files. Both Mannix and Culver hated
the place—its factitious luxury, its wanton atmosphere of
alcohol and torpid ease and dances, the vacant professional
talk of the regular officers and the constant teasing presence
of their wives, who were beautiful and spoke in tender drawls
and boldly flaunted at the wifeless reserves—in a proprietary,
Atlanta-debutante fashion—their lecherous sort of chastity.
The place seemed to offer up, like a cornucopia, the fruits
of boredom, of footlessness and dissolution. It was, in Mannix's words, like a prison where you could have anything
you wanted except happiness, and once, in a rare midnight
moment when he allowed himself to get drunk, he got paper
and wood together from his room and announced to Culver
in an unsteady but determined voice that he was going to
burn the place down. Culver held him off, but it was true:
they were bound to the pleasures of the place by necessity—
for there was no place to go for a hundred miles, even if
they had wanted to go—and therefore out of futility. "Goddam, it's degrading," Mannix had said, making use of an
adjective which indeed seemed to sum it all up. "It's like
sex now. Or the lack of it. Now maybe it's all right for a kid
to go without sex, but it's degrading for someone like me
almost thirty to go without making love for so long. It's
simply degrading, that's all. I'd go for one of these regulars'
pigs if it wasn't for Mimi. . . . This whole mess is degrading. I know it's my own fault I stayed in the reserves, Jack,
you don't have to tell me that. I was a nut. I didn't know I
was going to get called out for every frigging international
incident that came along. But, goddam, it's degrading"—
and with a glum, subdued gesture he'd down the dregs of his
drink—"it's degrading for a man my age to go sniffing around
on my belly in the boondocks like a dog. And furthermore—"
He looked scornfully about him, at the glitter and chrome,
at the terrace by the pool where Japanese lanterns hung
like a grove of pastel moons, and a girl's shrill and empty
laugh uncoiled as bright as tinsel through the sluggish coast-
al dusk. It was a silent moment in a night sprinkled with a
dusty multitude of Southern stars, and the distant bleating
saxophone seemed indecisive and sad, like the nation and
the suffocating summer, neither at peace nor at war. "Furthermore, it's degrading to come out of the field each day
and then be *forced* to go to a night club like this, when all
you want to do is go home to your wife and family. Goddam, man, I've *gotta* get out!"

But underneath his rebellion, Culver finally knew, Mannix—like all of them—was really resigned. Born into a generation of conformists, even Mannix (so Culver sensed) was aware that his gestures were not symbolic, but individual, therefore hopeless, maybe even absurd, and that he was trapped like all of them in a predicament which one personal insurrection could, if anything, only make worse. "You know," he said once, "I think I was really afraid just one time last war." The phrase "last war" had had, itself, a numb, resigned quality, in its lack of any particular inflection, like "last week end," or "last movie I went to see." They had been lying on the beach to which they fled each hot week end. In that setting of coast and sea and lugubrious solitude they felt nearly peaceful, in touch with a tranquil force more important, and more lasting (or so it seemed on those sunlit afternoons), than war. Mannix had been, almost for the first time since Culver had known him, rested and subdued, and the sound of his voice had been a surprise after long, sun-laden hours of sleep and silence. "That's the goddam truth," he said thoughtfully, "I was only afraid once. Really afraid, I mean. It was at a hotel in San Francisco. I think I really came closer to dying that night than I ever have in my life. We were drunk, you see, polluted, all of us. I think there were five of us, all of us boots just out of Dago. Kids. We were on the tenth floor of this hotel and in this room and I believe we were about as drunk as anyone could get. I remember going in to take a shower in the bathroom. It was late at night, past midnight, and after I took this shower, you see, I came out into the room buck naked. Two of those drunks guys were waiting for me. They grabbed me and pushed me toward the window. I was so loaded I couldn't battle. Then they pushed me out the window and held me by the heels while I dangled upside-down buck naked in space, ten floors above the street." He paused and sucked at a beer can. "Can you imagine that?" he went on slowly. "How I felt? I got stone-sober in a second. Imagine being that high upside-down in space with two drunks holding onto your heels. I was heavy, man, just like now, you see. All I can remember is those teeny-weeny lights below and the tiny little people like ants down there and those two crazy drunk guys holding onto my wet slippery ankles, laughing like hell and trying to decide whether to let go or not. I just remember the cold wind blowing on my body and that dark, man, infinite darkness all around me, and my ankles beginning to slip out of their hands. I really saw Death then, and I think that all I could think of was that I was going to fall and smash myself on that hard, hard street below. That those crazy bastards were going to let me fall. I was praying, I guess. I remember the blood rushing to my brain and my ankles slipping, and that awful strange noise. And I was reaching out, man, clutching at thin air. Then I wondered what that noise was, that high loud noise, and then I realized it was me, screaming at the top of my voice, all over San Francisco." He stopped talking then and scuffed at the sand with one calloused heel. "They hauled me up somehow. It was those sober guys—I guess they were sober —the other two. They got me up. But every time I remember that moment a great big cold shudder runs up and down my spine." He chuckled and chewed on his cigar but the laugh was half-hearted and listless, and he dug his elbows into the sand and resumed his quiet, placid gaze toward the horizon. Culver watched him: his bitterness dissolved in the hot salty air, slumped in the sand gazing wistfully out to sea, sun-glassed, hairy-chested, a cigar protruding from his face and a beer can warming in his hand, he seemed no longer the man who could sicken himself with resentment, but relaxed, pliable even, like a huge hairy baby soothed by the wash of elemental tides, ready to receive anything, all, into that great void in his soul which bitterness and rebellion had briefly left vacant—all—the finality of more suffering, or even death. War was in the offing. A promenade of waves, snow-crowned like lovely garlands in the dark hair of girls, swelled eastward toward Africa: past those smoky heights, more eastward still, the horizon seemed to give back repeated echoes of the sea, like far-off thunder, or guns. Culver remembered making a quick, contorted motion in the sand with his body, and being swept by a hot wave of anguish. It was loneliness and homesickness, but it was also fright. Across the rim of his memory two little girls playing on the sunny grass waved to him, were gone, pursued by a shower of uncapturable musical sounds. Mannix's resigned silence fed his loneliness. Suddenly he felt, like Mannix, upturned drunkenly above the abyss, blood rushing to his head, in terror clutching at the substanceless night. . . .

In the noonday light Sergeant O'Leary, his face brightly pink, was still talking. Culver snapped awake with a start. O'Leary grinned down at him—"Damn, Lieutenant, you're gonna crap out tonight if you're that tired now"—and Culver struggled for speech; time seemed to have unspooled past him in a great spiral, and for an instant—his mind still

grappling with the memory of a hurried, chaotic nightmare
—he was unable to tell where he was. He had the feeling
that it should be the night before, and that he was still in
the tent. "Did I go to sleep, O'Leary?" he said, blinking upward.

"Yes, sir," O'Leary said, and chuckled, "you sure did."

"How long?"

"Oh, just a second."

"Christ, I *am* tired. I dreamt it was last night," Culver
said. He got to his feet. A truck moved through the clearing
in a cloud of dust. There seemed to be new activity in the
command post, and new confusion. Culver and O'Leary
turned together then toward the operations tent; the Colonel
had come out and was striding toward them, followed by
Mannix.

"Culver, get your jeep and driver," he said, walking toward
the road, not looking up. His voice was briskly matter-of-fact;
he strode past them with short, choppy steps and the swagger
stick in his hand made a quick tattoo, *slap-slap*-slapping
against his dungaree pants. "I want you and Captain Mannix
to go with me down to Third Batt. See if we can help." His
voice faded; Mannix trailed behind him, saying nothing, but
his face seemed to Culver even more exhausted, and even
more grimly taut, than it had been an hour before.

The road was a dusty cart-path that rambled footlessly
across scrubby, fallow farmland. Shacks and cabins, long
ago abandoned, lay along its way. They piled into the jeep,
Mannix and Culver in the back, the Colonel in front next to
the driver. They hadn't far to go—less than a mile—but
the trip felt endless to Culver because the day, by now a fitful carrousel of sleepy sounds, motions without meaning,
seemed wildly, almost dangerously abstracted, as if viewed
through drug-glazed eyes or eyes, like those of a mole, unacquainted with light. Dust billowed past them as they went.
Above them a blue cloudless sky in which the sun, pitched
now at its summit, beat fearfully down, augured no rain
for the day, or for the evening. Mannix said nothing; his
silence prompted Culver to turn and look at him. He was
gazing straight ahead with eyes that seemed to bore through
the Colonel's neck. Tormented beast in the cul-de-sac, baffled fury, grief at the edge of defeat—his eyes made Culver
suddenly aware of what they were about to see, and he
turned dizzily away and watched the wreck of a Negro
cabin float past through the swirling dust: shell-shattered
doors and sagging walls, blasted façade—a target across

which for one split second in the fantastic noon there seemed to crawl the ghosts of the bereaved and the departed, mourning wraiths come back to reclaim from the ruins some hot scent of honeysuckle, smell of cooking, murmurous noise of bees. Culver closed his eyes and drowsed, slack-jawed, limp, his stomach faintly heaving.

One boy's eyes lay gently closed, and his long dark lashes were washed in tears, as though he had cried himself to sleep. As they bent over him they saw that he was very young, and a breeze came up from the edges of the swamp, bearing with it a scorched odor of smoke and powder, and touched the edges of his hair. A lock fell across his brow with a sort of gawky, tousled grace, as if preserving even in that blank and mindless repose some gesture proper to his years, a callow charm. Around his curly head grasshoppers darted among the weeds. Below, beneath the slumbering eyes, his face had been blasted out of sight. Culver looked up and met Mannix's gaze. The Captain was sobbing helplessly. He cast an agonized look toward the Colonel, standing across the field, then down again at the boy, then at Culver. "Won't they ever let us alone, the sons of bitches," he murmured, weeping. "Won't they ever let us alone?"

III

That evening at twilight, just before the beginning of the march, Mannix found a nail in his shoe. "Look at it," he said to Culver, "What lousy luck." They were sitting on an embankment bordering the road. The blue dusk was already scattered with stars, but evening had brought no relief to the heat of the day. It clung to them still, damp and stifling, enveloping them like an overcoat. The battalion, over a thousand men, was ready for the march. It stretched out in two files on either side of the road below them for more than a mile. Culver turned and looked down into Mannix's shoe: sure enough, a nail-end had penetrated the lining at the base of the heel, a sharp pinpoint of torture. Mannix inspected the bottom of his big dirty foot. He pulled off a flake of skin which the nail had already worn away. "Of all the lousy luck," he said, "Gimme a band-aid."

"It'll wear right through, Al," Culver said, "you'd better get another pair of shoes. Try flattening it out with the end of your bayonet."

Mannix hammered for a moment at the nail and then

looked up in exasperation. "It won't go all the way. Gimme that band-aid." A rusty spatter of blood he had picked up at noon was still on the sleeve of his dungarees. He had become nervous and touchy. All that afternoon, after they had come back, he had seemed, like Culver, still shaken by the slaughter, still awed, and rather despondent. Finally, he had alternated moments of remote abstraction with quick outbursts of temper. The shock of the explosion seemed to have set something off in him. His mood had become vague and unpredictable, and he was able to shift from sour, uncommunicative gloom to violent anger in an instant. Culver had never seen him quite so cranky before, nor had he ever seen him so testily at odds with his men, to whom he usually had shown the breeziest good will. All afternoon he'd been after them, nagging, bellowing orders—only to fall suddenly into a profound and brooding silence. As he squatted in the weeds eating his evening meal two hours before, he had hardly said a word, except to murmur—irrelevantly, Culver thought—that his company "had better goddam well shape up." It puzzled Culver; the explosion seemed to have stripped off layers of skin from the Captain, leaving only raw nerves exposed.

Now he had become fretful again, touchily alert, and his voice was heavy with impatience. He mumbled as he plastered the band-aid on his foot. "I wish they'd get this show on the road. That's the trouble with the Marine Corps, you always stand frigging around for half the night while they think up some grandiose doctrine. I wish to Christ I'd joined the Army. Man, if I'd have known what I was getting in for when I went down to that recruiting office in 1941, I'd have run off at the door." He looked up from his foot and down toward the command group nearly at the head of the column. Three or four officers were clustered together on the road. The Colonel was among them, neat, almost jaunty, in new dungarees and boots. On his head there was a freshly clean utility cap with a spruce uptilted bill and a shiny little silver leaf. At his side he wore a pearl-handled .38 revolver, glistening with silver inlay. It was, as usual, loaded, though no one knew why, for he was never known to shoot it; the general feeling seemed to be that it was his emblematic prerogative, no more an affectation, certainly, than a visored hat encrusted with gilt, or grenades worn at the shoulder. The pistol—like the swagger stick; the nickname; the quizzical, almost tenderly contemplative air of authority—was part of the act, and to be sure, Culver reflected, the act was less offensive, less imperious than it might be. One simply learned soon to believe that the pistol "belonged," just as the name "Old Rocky" belonged; if such an act finally did no harm, if it only flattered his vanity, was the Colonel to be blamed, Culver asked himself, if he did nothing to mitigate the total impression?

Mannix watched him, too, watched the Colonel toe at the sand, thumbs hooked rakishly in his belt, a thin gentle smile on his face, adumbrated by the fading light: he looked youthful and fresh, nonchalant, displaying the studied casualness of an athlete before the stadium throng, confident of his own victory long before the race begins. Mannix gnawed at the end of a cigar, spat it out viciously. "Look at the little jerk. He thinks he's gonna have us pooped out at the halfway mark—"

Culver put in, "Look Al, why don't you do something about that nail? If you told the Colonel he'd let you ride in—"

Mannix went fiercely on, in a husky whisper: "Well he's not. He's a little sadist, but he's not gonna have Al Mannix crapped out. I'll walk anywhere that son of a bitch goes and a mile further. He thinks H & S Company's been doping off. Well, I'll show him. I wouldn't ask him to ride in if I'd been walking over broken glass. I'll—"

He paused. Culver turned and looked at him. They were both silent, staring at each other, embarrassed by the common understanding of their gaze. Each turned away; Mannix murmured something and began to tie his shoe. "You're right, Al," Culver heard himself saying. It seemed it was almost more than he could bear. Night was coming on. As in a stupor, he looked down the road at the battalion, the men lounging along the embankments with their rifles, smoking and talking in tired, subdued voices, smoke rising in giant blue clouds through the dusk, where swarms of gnats rose and fell in vivacious, panicky flight. In the swamp, frogs had begun a brainless chorale; their noise seemed perfectly suited to his sense of complete and final frustration. It was almost more than he could bear. So Mannix had felt it, too: not simply fear of suffering, nor exhaustion, nor the lingering horror, which gripped both of them, of that bloody wasteland in the noonday heat. But the other: the old atavism that clutched them, the voice that commanded, once again, *you will*. How stupid to think they had ever made their own philosophy; it was as puny as a house of straw, and at this moment—by the noise in their brains of those words, *you will*—it was being blasted to the winds like dust. They were as helpless as children. Another war, and years beyond reckoning, had violated their minds irrevocably. For six years they had slept a cataleptic sleep, draming blissfully of peace, awakened in horror to find that, after all, they were only marines, responding anew to the old commands. They were marines. Even if they were old. Bank clerks and salesmen and lawyers. Even if, right now, they were unutterably tired. They could no more *not* be determined to walk the thirty-six miles than they could, in the blink of an eye, turn themselves into beautiful nymphs. Culver was afraid he wasn't going to make it, and now he knew Mannix was afraid, and he didn't know what to feel—resentment or disgust—over the fact that his fear was mingled with a faint, fugitive pride.

Mannix looked up from his shoe and at the Colonel. "You're goddam right, Jack, we're going to make it," he said. "My company's going to make it if I have to *drag in their bodies.*" There was a tone in his voice that Culver had never heard before.

Suddenly the Colonel's flat voice broke through the stillness: "All right, Billy, let's saddle up."

" 'Tallion saddle up!" The Major's words were eager and shrill, became multiplied down the long mile. "Smoking lamp's out!" The blue cloud dissolved on the air, the gnats descended in a swarm and the voices passed on—*Saddle up, saddle up*—while the battalion rose to its feet, not all at once but in a steady gradual surge, like rows of corn snapping back erect after the passing of a wind. Mannix got to his feet, began to sideslip in a cloud of dust down the embankment toward his company directly below. It was at the head of the column, right behind the command group. Culver, moving himself now down the hill, heard Mannix's shout. It rang out in the dusk with deliberate authority, hoarse blunt command: "All right, H & S Company, saddle up, saddle up! You people get off your asses and straighten up!" Culver passed by him on his way to the command group: he stood surrounded by a cloud of gnats, hulking enormously above the company, hands balanced lightly on his hips, poised forward badgering the men like some obsessed, rakehell Civil War general before a battle: "All right, you people, we're gonna walk thirty-six miles tonight and I mean walk! First man I see drop out's gonna get police duty for two weeks, and that goes for everybody. You think I'm kidding you wait and see. There's gonna be trucks going in for those that can't make it but I don't want to see anyone from H & S Company climbing on! If an old man with as much flab as

I've got can make it you people can too . . ." There was a
note, almost, of desperation in his voice. Culver, passing
along the line of bedraggled, mournful-looking men, so few
of whom looked like fabled marines, heard the voice rise to
a taut pitch close to frenzy; it was too loud, it worried
Culver, and he wished to caution him: no longer just admonishing the men to a simple duty, it was the voice of a
man wildly fanatic with one idea: to last. "I want to hear
no bitching out of you people! Take it easy on the water.
You get shinsplints or blisters you see the corpsman, don't
come crying to me. When we get in I want to see all of you
people . . ." Not because the hike was good or even sensible,
Culver thought, but out of hope of triumph, like a chain-
gang convict who endures a flogging without the slightest
whimper, only to spite the flogger. Culver joined the command group, heard the Colonel say to the Major: "Looks
like H & S Company's going to make it *en masse*, Billy."
It was just as Culver feared, for although his words were
pleasant enough, his face, regarding Mannix for a brief
moment, had a look of narrow scrutiny, as if he, too, had
detected in the Captain's tone that note of proud and willful
submission, rebellion in reverse. But there was no emotion in
his voice as he turned quickly, with a glance at his watch,
and said, "Let's move out, Billy."

They started out without delay. A jeep, its headlamps
lit, preceded them. The Colonel, in the lead, abreast of the
Major and just ahead of Culver, plunged off into the deep dust
of the road. He walked with a slinky-hipped, athletic stride,
head down between his shoulders and slightly forward, arms
bent and moving methodically; nothing broke the rhythm of
his steps—ruts in the road or the deeply grooved tire tracks
—and Culver became quickly amazed, and rather appalled, at
the pace he was setting. It was the pace of a trained hiker—
determined, unhesitant, much closer to a trot now than a walk
—and only a few minutes passed before Culver was gasping
for breath. Sand lay thick in the road, hindering a natural
step. They had not gone more than a couple of hundred yards;
already he felt sweat trickling down his forehead and beneath
his arms. For a moment fear surged up in him unnaturally,
and a crazy panic. He had been afraid of the march before,
but his fear had been abstract and hazy; now so quickly
fatigued, in what seemed a matter of seconds, he felt surely
(as Mannix had predicted) that he'd be unable to last the first
hour. A panicky wash of blood came to his face and he
struggled for breath, wanting to cry out—it passed. His mind

groped for reason and the terror receded: once he adjusted
to the shock of this pace, he realized, he'd be all right. Then
the panic went away; as it did so, he found himself breathing
easier, freed of that irrational fright. The Colonel pushed
ahead in front of him with the absolute mechanical confidence of a wound-up, strutting tin soldier on a table top.
Culver, panting a bit, heard his voice, as calm and unwinded
as if he were sitting at a desk somewhere, addressed to the
Major: "We shoved off at nine on the dot, Billy. We should
make the main road at ten and have a break." "Yes, sir,"
he heard the Major say, "we'll be ahead of the game." Culver
made a calculation then; by the operations map, which he
knew so well, that was three and a half miles—a mile farther
than the regulation distance for an hour's march. It was,
indeed, like running. Pushing on through the sand, he felt
a wave of hopelessness so giddy and so incomprehensible
that it was almost like exhilaration—and he heard a noise—
half-chuckle, half-groan—escape between his labored breaths.
Three and a half miles: the distance from Greenwich Village
almost to Harlem. In his mind he measured that giddy parade
of city blocks, an exhausting voyage even on wheels. It was
like twisting a knife in his side but he went on with the
mental yardstick—to imagine himself plodding that stretch
up the sandless, comfortably receptive payments of Fifth
Avenue, past Fourteenth Street and the bleak vistas of the
Twenties and the Thirties, hurrying onward north by the
Library, twenty blocks more to the Plaza, and pressing still
onward along the green acres of the Park . . . his thoughts
recoiled. Three and a half miles. In an hour. With more than
thirty-two still to go. A vision of Mannix came swimming
back; Culver stumbled along after the dauntless Colonel,
thinking, Christ on a crutch.

They hastened on. Night had fallen around them, tropic
and sudden, lit now, as they descended across a thicket of
swampy ground, only by the lights of the jeep. Culver had
regained his wind but already his chest and back were
awash in sweat, and he was thirsty. He took a vague comfort
in the fact that others felt the same way, for behind him
he heard canteens being unsnapped from their cases, rattling
out of their cups, and the noise, in mid-march, of drinking—
a choked, gurgling sound—then, faint to the rear, Mannix's
angry voice: "All right, goddammit, I told you people to hold
onto your water! Put those goddam canteens back until the
break!" Culver, craning his neck around, saw nothing—no
Mannix, who had apparently dropped behind—nothing except

a shadowy double line of men laboring through the sand, fading off far down the road into the general blackness. To the rear some marine made a joke, a remark; there was laughter and a snatch of song—*on top of old Smo-oky, all covered* . . . Then Mannix's voice again out of the dark: "O.K. you people can grabass all you want but I'm telling you you'd better save your wind. If you want to talk all the way it's O.K. with me but you're gonna crap out if you do, and remember what I said . ." His tone had become terse and vicious; it could have been the sound of a satrap of Pharaoh, a galley master. It had the forbidding quality of a strand of barbed wire or a lash made of thorns, and the voices, the song, abruptly ceased, as if they had been strangled. Still his words continued to sting and flay them—already, in this first hour, with the merciless accents of a born bully—and Culver, suddenly angered, had an impulse to drop back and try to make him let up.

"You people close it up now! Dammit, Shea, keep those men closed up there. They fall back they're gonna have to run to catch up! Goddammit, close it up now, you hear me! I mean *you*, Thompson, goddammit you aren't deaf! Close it up! *Close it up*, I said!" So it was that the voice, brutal and furious, continued the rest of the way.

And so it was that those first hours Culver recollected as being the most harrowing of all, even though the later hours brought more subtle refinements of pain. He reasoned that this was because during the first few miles or so he was at least in rough possession of his intellect, his mind lashing his spirit as pitilessly as his body. Later, he seemed to be involved in something routine, an act in which his brain, long past cooperation, played hardly any part at all. But during these early hours there was also the fact of Mannix. Superimposed upon Culver's own fantasies, his anger, his despair (and his own calm moments of rationalization, too) was his growing awareness of what was happening to the Captain. Later, Mannix's actions seemed to become mixed up and a part of the general scheme, the nightmare. But here at first Culver's mind was enough in focus for Mannix's transformation to emerge clearly, even if with the chill, unreal outlines of coming doom—like a man conversing, who might turn around briefly to a mirror and see behind him in the room no longer his familiar friend, but something else—a shape, a ghost, a horror—a wild and threatful face reflected from the glass.

They made the highway at ten o'clock, almost to the

minute. When the Colonel looked at his watch and stopped
and the Major raised his arm, shouting, "Breather! Ten minutes!" Culver went over to the side of the road and sat down
in the weeds. Blood was knocking angrily at his temples,
behind his eyes, and he was thirsty enough to drink, with
a greedy recklessness, nearly a third of his canteen. He lit a
cigarette; it tasted foul and metallic and he flipped it away.
His knees and thighs, unaccustomed to so much pounding,
were stiff and fatigued; he stretched them out slowly into the
dewy underbrush, looking upward at a placid cloud of stars.
He turned. Up the road, threading its way through a barrier
of outstretched legs and rifles, came a figure. It was Mannix.
He was still muttering as he lumbered up and sank down
beside him. "Those goddam people, they won't keep it closed
up. I have to dog them every minute. They're going to find
themselves running the whole way if they don't keep closed
up. Gimme a butt." He was breathing heavily, and he
passed the back of his hand over his brow to wipe the sweat
away.

"Why don't you leave them alone?" Culver said. He gave
the captain a cigarette, which he lit, blowing the smoke out
in a violent sort of choked puff.

"Dammit," he replied, coughing, "you *can't* leave them
alone! They don't want to make this lousy hike. They'd just
as soon crap out on the side and let the trucks haul them in.
They'd just as soon take police duty. Man, they're reserves.
They don't care who sees them crap out—me, anybody."
He fell back with a sigh into the weeds, arms over his eyes.
"Fuck it," he said. Culver looked down at him. From the
jeep's headlamps an oblong of yellow slanted across the
lower part of his face. One corner of his mouth jerked nervously—a distasteful grimace, as if he had been chewing
something sour. Exhausted, completely bushed, there was
something in his manner—even in repose—which refused to
admit his own exhaustion. He clenched his teeth con-
vulsively together. It was as if his own fury, his own obsession
now, held up, Atlas-like, the burden of his great weariness.
"Jesus," he murmured, almost irrelevantly, "I can't help thinking about those kids today, lying out there in the weeds."

Culver rested easily for a moment, thinking too. He looked
at his watch, with a sinking sensation: six of their ten minutes had already passed—so swiftly that they seemed not
to have existed at all. Then he said, "Well, for Christ's sake,
Al, why don't you let them crap out? If you were getting
screwed like these enlisted men are you'd crap out too, you

wouldn't care. You don't have to chew them out like you've been doing. Let's face it, you don't really care if they make it. You. Me, maybe. But these guys . . . anybody else. What the hell." He paused, fumbling for words, went on feebly, "*Do* you?"

Mannix rose up on his elbows then. "You're damn right I do," he said evenly. They turned toward the Colonel standing not far away; he and the Major, pointing a flashlight, were bent together over a map. Mannix hawked something up and spat. His voice became more controlled. "You see that little jerk standing there?" he said. "He thinks he's pulling something on us. Thirty-six miles. *No*body walks that far, stateside. *No*body. We never walked that far even with Edson, last war. See, that little jerk wants to make a name for himself—Old Rocky Templeton. Led the longest forced march in the history of the Corps—"

"But—" Culver started.

"He'd just love to see H & S Company crap out," he went on tensely, "he'd *love* it. It'd do something to his ego. Man, I can see him now"—and his voice lifted itself in a tone of sour mockery— " 'Well, Cap'n Mannix, see where you had a little trouble last night getting your men in. Need a little bit more *esprit,* huh?' " His voice lowered, filled with venom. "Well, screw *him,* Jack. I'll get my company in if I have to carry them on my back—"

It was useless to reason with him. Culver let him go on until he had exhausted his bitter spurt of hatred, of poison, and until finally he lay back again with a groan in the weeds —only a moment before the cry came again: "Saddle up! Saddle up!"

They pushed off once more. It was just a bit easier now, for they were to walk for two miles on the highway, where there was no sand to hinder their steps, before turning back onto the side roads. Yet there was a comfortless feeling at the outset, too: legs cramped and aching from the moment's rest, he walked stooped and bent over, at the start, like an arthritic old man, and he was sweating again, dry with thirst, after only a hundred yards. How on earth, he wondered, gazing up for a second at the dim placid landscape of stars, would they last until the next morning, until nearly noon? A car passed them—a slick convertible bound for the North, New York perhaps—wherever, inevitably, for some civilian pleasure—and its fleet, almost soundless passage brought, along with the red pinpoint of its vanishing taillights, a new sensation of unreality to the night, the march: dozing, shrouded by the dark, its people seemed unaware of the shadowy walkers, had sped unceasingly on, like ocean voyagers oblivious of all those fishy struggles below them in the night, submarine and fathomless.

They plodded on, the Colonel pacing the march, but slower now, and Culver played desperately with the idea that the man would, somehow, tire, become exhausted himself. A wild fantasia of hopes and imaginings swept through his mind: that Templeton *would* become fatigued, having overestimated his own strength, *would* stop the march after an hour or so and load them on the trucks—like a stern father who begins a beating, only to become touched with if not remorse then leniency, and stays his hand. But Culver knew it was a hollow desire. They pushed relentlessly ahead, past shadowy pine groves, fields dense with the fragrance of alfalfa and wild strawberries, shuttered farmhouses, deserted rickety stores. Then this brief civilized vista they abandoned again, and for good, when without pause they plunged off again onto another road, into the sand. Culver had become bathed in sweat once more; they all had, even the Colonel, whose neat dungarees had a black triangular wet spot plastered at their back. Culver heard his own breath coming hoarsely again, and felt the old panic: he'd never be able to make it, he knew, he'd fall out on the side like the old man he was—but far back to the rear then he heard Mannix's huge voice, dominating the night: "All right, goddammit, move out! We got sand here now. Move out and close it up! Close it up, I say, goddammit! Leadbetter, get that barn out of your ass and close it up! *Close it up*, I say!" They spurred Culver on, after a fashion, but following upon those shouts, there was a faint, subdued chorus, almost inaudible, of moans and protests. They came only from Mannix's company, a muffled, sullen groan. To them Culver heard his own fitful breath add a groan—expressing something he could hardly put a name to: fury, despair, approaching doom— he scarcely knew. He stumbled on behind the Colonel, like a ewe who follows the slaughterhouse ram, dumb and undoubting, too panicked by the general chaos to hate its leader, or care.

At the end of the second hour, and three more miles, Culver was sobbing with exhaustion. He flopped down in the weeds, conscious now of a blister beginning at the bottom of his foot, as if it had been scraped by a razor.

Mannix was having trouble, too. This time when he came up, he was limping. He sat down silently and took off his

shoes; Culver, gulping avidly at his canteen, watched him.
Both of them were too winded to smoke, or to speak. They
were sprawled beside some waterway—canal or stream; phosphorescent globes made a spooky glow among shaggy Span-
ish moss, and a rank and fetid odor bloomed in the darkness
—not the swamp's decay, Culver realized, but Mannix's feet.
"Look," the Captain muttered suddenly, "that nail's caught
me right in the heel." Culver peered down by the glare of
Mannix's flashlight to see on his heel a tiny hole, bleeding
slightly, bruised about its perimeter and surrounded by a
pasty white where the band-aid had been pulled away.
"How'm I going to do it with that?" Mannix said.

"Try beating that nail down again."

"I tried, but the point keeps coming out. I'd have to take
the whole frigging shoe apart."

"Can't you put a piece of cloth over it or something?"

"I tried that, too, but it puts my foot off balance. It's worse
than the nail." He paused. "Jesus Christ."

"Look," Culver said, "try taking this strip of belt and
putting it over it." They debated, operated, talked hurriedly,
and neither of them was aware of the Colonel, who had
walked over through the shadows and was standing beside
them. "What's the matter, Captain?" he said.

They looked up, startled. Hands hooked as usual—Culver
wanted to say "characteristically"—in his belt, he stood
serenely above them. In the yellow flashlight glow his face
was red from exertion, still damp with sweat, but he appeared no more fatigued than a man who had sprinted a
few yards to catch a bus. The faint smile hovered at the
corners of his lips. Once more it was neither complacent
nor superior but, if anything, almost benevolent, so that
by the unnatural light, in which his delicate features became fiery red and again now, along the borders of his slim
tapering fingers, nearly transparent, he looked still not so
much the soldier but the priest in whom passion and faith
had made an alloy, at last, of only the purest good inten-
tions; above meanness or petty spite, he was leading a march
to some humorless salvation, and his smile—his solicitous
words, too—had at least a bleak sincerity.

"I got a nail in my shoe," Mannix said.

The Colonel squatted down and inspected Mannix's foot,
cupping it almost tenderly in his hand. Mannix appeared to
squirm at the Colonel's touch. "That looks bad," he said
after a moment, "did you see the corpsman?"

"No, sir," Mannix replied tensely, "I don't think there's

anything can be done. Unless I had a new pair of boon-
dockers."

The Colonel ruminated, rubbing his chin, his other hand
still holding the Captain's foot. His eyes searched the dark
reaches of the surrounding swamp, where now the rising
moon had laid a tranquil silver dust. Frogs piped shrilly in
the night, among the cypress and the shallows and closer
now, by the road and the stagnant canal, along which danced
shifting pinpoints of fire—cigarettes that rose and fell in the
hidden fingers of exhausted men. "Well," the Colonel finally
said, "well—" and paused. Again the act: indecision before
decision, the waiting. "Well," he said, and paused again.
The waiting. At that moment—in a wave that came up
through his thirst, his throbbing lips, his numb sense of
futility—Culver felt that he knew of no one on earth he
had ever loathed so much before. And his fury was height-
ened by the knowledge that he did not hate the man—
the Templeton with his shrewd friendly eyes and harmless
swagger, that fatuous man whose attempt to convey some
impression of a deep and subtle wisdom was almost endear-
ing—not this man, but the Colonel, the marine: that was the
one he despised. He didn't hate him for himself, nor
even for his brutal march. Bad as it was, there were no doubt
worse ordeals; it was at least a peaceful landscape they had
to cross. But he did hate him for his perverse and brainless
gesture: squatting in the sand, gently, almost indecently now,
stroking Mannix's foot, he had too long been conditioned by
the system to perform with grace a human act. Too ignorant
to know that with this gesture—so nakedly human in the
midst of a crazy, capricious punishment which he himself
had imposed—he lacerated the Captain by his very touch.
Then he spoke. Culver knew what he was going to say.
Nothing could have been worse.

"Well," he said, "maybe you'd better ride in on one of the
trucks."

If there had been ever the faintest possibility that Mannix would ride in, those words shattered it. Mannix drew his
foot away abruptly, as if the Colonel's hand were acid, or
fire. "No, sir!" he said fiercely—too fiercely, the note of
antagonism, now, was unmistakable— "No, sir! I'll make this
frigging march." Furiously, he began to put on his shoe. The
Colonel rose to his feet, hooked his thumbs in his belt and
gazed carelessly down.

"I think you're going to regret it," he said, "with that foot
of yours."

The Captain got up, limping off toward his company, over his retreating shoulder shot back a short, clipped burst of words at the Colonel—whose eyeballs rolled white with astonishment when he heard them—and thereby joined the battle.

"Who cares what you think," he said.

IV

Had the Colonel entertained any immediate notions of retribution, he held them off, for at a quarter past four that morning—halfway through the march, when the first green light of dawn streaked the sky—Culver still heard Mannix's hoarse, ill-tempered voice, lashing his troops from the rear. For hours he had lost track of Mannix. As for the Colonel, the word had spread that he was no longer pacing the march but had gone somewhere to the rear and was walking there. In his misery, a wave of hope swelled up in Culver: if the Colonel had become fagged, and was walking no longer but sitting in his jeep somewhere, at least they'd all have the consolation of having succeeded while their leader failed. But it was a hope, Culver knew, that was ill-founded. He'd be back there slogging away. The bastard could outmarch twenty men, twenty raging Mannixes.

The hike had become disorganized, no slower but simply more spread out. Culver—held back by fatigue and thirst and the burning, enlarging pain in his feet—found himself straggling behind. From time to time he managed to catch up; at one point he discovered himself at the tail end of Mannix's company, but he no longer really cared. The night had simply become a great solitude of pain and thirst, and an exhaustion so profound that it enveloped his whole spirit, and precluded thought.

A truck rumbled past, loaded with supine marines, so still they appeared unconscious. Another passed, and another— they came all night. But far to the front, long after each truck's passage, he could hear Mannix's cry: "Keep on, Jack! This company's walking in." They pushed on through the night, a shambling horde of zombies in drenched dungarees, eyes transfixed on the earth in a sort of glazed, avid concentration. After midnight it seemed to Culver that his mind only registered impressions, and these impressions had no sequence but were projected upon his brain in a scattered, disordered riot, like a movie film pieced together by an idiot. His memory went back no further than the day before;

he no longer thought of anything so unattainable as home.
Even the end of the march seemed a fanciful thing, beyond
all possibility, and what small aspirations he now had were
only to endure this one hour, if just to attain the micro-
scopic bliss of ten minutes' rest and a mouthful of warm
water. And bordering his memory was ever the violent and
haunting picture of the mangled bodies he had seen—
when? where? it seemed weeks, years ago, beneath the light
of an almost prehistoric sun; try as he could, to dwell upon
consoling scenes—home, music, sleep—his mind was balked
beyond that vision: the shattered youth with slumbering
eyes, the blood, the swarming noon.

Then at the next halt, their sixth—or seventh, eighth,
Culver had long ago lost count—he saw Mannix lying beside
a jeep-towed water-cart at the rear of his company. O'Leary
was sprawled out next to him, breath coming in long asth-
matic groans. Culver eased himself painfully down beside
them and touched Mannix's arm. The light of dawn, a feverish pale green, had begun to appear, outlining on Mannix's
face a twisted look of suffering. His eyes were closed.

"How you doing, Al?" Culver said, reaching up to refill
his canteen.

"Hotsy-totsy," he breathed, "except for my frigging foot.
How you making it, boy?" His voice was listless. Culver
looked down at Mannix's shoe; he had taken it off, to expose
heel and sock, where, soaked up like the wick of a lantern,
rose a dark streak of blood.

"Jesus," Culver said, "Al, for Christ sake now, you'd
better ride in on a truck."

"Nail's out, sport. I finally stole me a pair of pliers, some
radioman. Had to run like hell to catch up."

"Even so—" Culver began. But Mannix had fallen into an
impervious silence. Up the road stretched a line of squatting men, Mannix's company. Most were sprawled in the
weeds or the dust of the road in attitudes as stiff as death, yet
some nearby sat slumped over their rifles, drinking water,
smoking; there was a thin resentful muttering in the air.
And the men close at hand—the faces he could see in the
indecisive light—wore looks of agonized and silent protest.
They seemed to be mutely seeking for the Captain, author
of their misery, and they were like faces of men in bondage
who had jettisoned all hope, and were close to defeat. In
the weeds Mannix breathed heavily, mingling his with the
tortured wheezes of O'Leary, who had fallen sound asleep.
It was getting hot again. No one spoke. Then a fitful rum-

bling filled the dawn, grew louder, and along the line bodies stirred, heads turned, gazing eastward down the road at an oncoming, roaring cloud of dust. Out of the dust came a machine. It was a truck, and it passed them, and it rattled to a stop up in the midst of the company.

"Anyone crapped out here?" a voice called. "I got room for ten more."

There was a movement toward the truck; nearby, half a dozen men got to their feet, slung their rifles, and began to hobble up the road. Culver watched them tensely, hearing Mannix stir beside him, putting his shoe back on. O'Leary had awakened and sat up. Together the three of them watched the procession toward the truck: a straggle of limping men plodding as wretchedly as dogpound animals toward that yawning vehicle in the smoky dawn, huge, green, and possessed of wheels—which would deliver them to freedom, to sleep, oblivion. Mannix watched them without expression, through inflamed eyes; he seemed so drugged, so dumb with exhaustion, that he was unaware of what was taking place. "What happened to the Colonel?" he said absently.

"He went off in a jeep a couple of hours ago," O'Leary said, "said something about checking on the column of march."

"What?" Mannix said. Again, he seemed unaware of the words, as if they—like the sight of this slow streaming exodus toward the truck—were making no sudden imprint on his mind, but were filtering into his consciousness through piles and layers of wool. A dozen more men arose and began a lame procession toward the truck. Mannix watched them, blinking. "What?" he repeated.

"To check the column, sir," O'Leary repeated. "That's what he said."

"He *did?*" Mannix turned with an angry, questioning look. "Who's pacing the march, then?"

"Major Lawrence is."

"He *is?*" Mannix rose to his feet, precariously, stiffly and in pain balancing himself not on the heel, but the toe only, of his wounded foot. He blinked in the dawn, gazing at the rear of the truck and the cluster of marines there, feebly lifting themselves into the interior. He said nothing and Culver, watching him from below, could only think of the baffled fury of some great bear cornered, bloody and torn by a foe whose tactics were no braver than his own, but simply more cunning. He bit his lips—out of pain perhaps, but as likely out of impotent rage and frustration, and he seemed close to tears when he said, in a tone almost like grief: "*He* crapped out! *He* crapped out!"

He came alive like a somnambulist abruptly shocked out of sleep, and he lunged forward onto the road with a wild and tormented bellow. "Hey, you people, get off that goddam truck!" He sprang into the dust with a skip and a jump, toiling down the road with hobbled leg and furious flailing arms. By his deep swinging gait, his terrible limp, he looked no more capable of locomotion then a wheelchair invalid, and it would have been funny had it not seemed at the same time so full of threat and disaster. He pressed on. "Off that truck, goddammit, I say! Off that truck. Saddle up. Saddle up now, I say! On your feet!" he yelled. "Get off that goddam truck before I start kicking you people in the ass!" His words flayed and cowed them; a long concerted groan arose in the air, seemed to take possession of the very dawn; yet they debarked from the truck in terrified flight, scuttling down like mice from a sinking raft. "Move the hell out of here!" he shouted at the truck driver, a skinny corporal, eyes bulging, who popped back into the cab in fright. "Get that heap out of here!" The truck leaped off with a roar, enveloping the scene in blue smoke and a tornado of dust. Mannix, with windmilling arms, stood propped on his toe in the center of the road, urged the men wildly on. "Saddle up now! Let somebody else crap out O.K., but not you people, hear me! Do you hear me! Goddammit, I mean it! Shea, get those people moving out up there! You people better face it, you got eighteen more miles to go . . ." Culver tried to stop him, but they had already begun to run.

Panic-stricken, limping with blisters and with exhaustion, and in mutinous despair, the men fled westward, whipped on by Mannix's cries. They pressed into the humid, sweltering light of the new day. Culver followed; O'Leary, without a murmur, puffed along beside him, while to the rear, with steady slogging footsteps, trailed the remnants of the battalion. Dust billowed up and preceded them, like Egypt's pillar of cloud, filling the air with its dry oppressive menace. It coated their lips and moist brows with white powdery grit, like a spray of plaster, and gave to the surrounding trees, the underbrush and vacant fields, a blighted pallor, as if touched by unseasonable frost. The sun rose higher, burning down at their backs so that each felt he bore on his shoulders not the burden of a pack but, almost worse, a portable oven growing hotter and hotter as the sun came up from behind the sheltering pines. They walked automatically, no longer with that light and tentative step in order to ease the pain in their feet, but with the firm, dogged tread of robots; and if they were all like Culver they had long since parted with a sensation of motion below the hips, and felt there only a constant throbbing pain—of blisters and battered muscles and the protest of exhausted bones.

Then one time Culver saw the Colonel go by in a jeep, boiling along in a cloud of dust toward the head of the column. He caught a glimpse of him as he passed: he looked sweaty and tired, far from rested, and Culver wondered how justified Mannix's outrage had been, assigning to the Colonel that act of cowardice. So he hadn't been pacing the march, but God knows he must have been hiking along to the rear; and his doubts were bolstered by O'Leary's voice, coming painfully beside him: "Old Captain Mannix's mighty pissed off at the Colonel." He paused, wheezing steadily. "Don't know if he's got a right to be that way. Old Colonel ain't gonna crap out without a reason. Colonel's kind of rough sometimes but he'll go with the troops." Culver said nothing. They plodded ahead silently. Culver felt like cursing the Sergeant. How could he be so stupid? How could he, in the midst of this pain, yield up still only words of accord and respect and even admiration for the creator of such a wild and lunatic punishment? Only a man so firmly cemented to the system that all doubts were beyond countenance could say what O'Leary did—and yet—and yet God knows, Culver thought wearily, he could be right and himself and Mannix, and the rest of them, inescapably wrong. His mind was confused. A swarm of dust came up and filled his lungs. Mannix was screwing everything up horribly, and Culver wanted suddenly to sprint forward—in spite of the effort it took—reach the Captain, take him aside and tell him: *Al, Al, let up, you've already lost the battle.* Defiance, pride, endurance—none of these would help. He only mutilated himself by this perverse and violent rebellion; no matter what the Colonel was—coward and despot or staunch bold leader—he had him beaten, going and coming. Nothing could be worse than what Mannix was doing—adding to a disaster already ordained (Culver somehow sensed) the burden of his vicious fury. At least let up, the men had had enough. But his mind was confused. His kidneys were aching as if they had been pounded with a mallet, and he walked along now with his hands on his waist, like a professor lecturing in a classroom, coattails over his arms.

And for the first time he felt intolerably hot—with a heat that contributed to his mounting fury. At night they had sweated more from exertion; the coolness of the evening had been at least some solace, but the morning's sun began to flagellate him anew, adding curious sharp blades of pain to the furious frustration boiling inside him. Frustration at the fact that he was not independent enough, nor possessed of enough free will, was not *man* enough to say, to hell with it and crap out himself; that he was not man enough to disavow all his determination and endurance and suffering, cash in his chips, and by that act flaunt his contempt of the march, the Colonel, the whole bloody Marine Corps. But he was *not* man enough, he knew, far less simply a free man; he was just a marine—as was Mannix, and so many of the others—and they had been marines, it seemed, all their lives, would go on being marines forever; and the frustration implicit in this thought brought him suddenly close to tears. Mannix. A cold horror came over him. Far down, profoundly, Mannix was so much a marine that it could make him casually demented. The corruption begun years ago in his drill-field feet had climbed up, overtaken him, and had begun to rot his brain. Culver heard himself sobbing with frustration and outrage. The sun beat down against his back. His mind slipped off into fevered blankness, registering once more, on that crazy cinematic tape, chaos, vagrant jigsaw images: Mannix's voice far ahead, hoarse and breaking now, then long spells of silence; halts beside stifling, windless fields, then a shady ditch into which he plunged, feverish and comatose, dreaming of a carnival tent where one bought, from a dozen barrels, all sorts of ice, chipped, crushed, and cubed, in various shapes and sizes. He was awakened by that terribly cry—*Saddle up, saddle up!* —and he set out again. The sun rose higher and higher. O'Leary, with a groan, dropped behind and vanished. Two trucks passed loaded with stiff, green-clad bodies motionless as corpses. The canteen fell off Culver's belt, somewhere, sometime; now he found though, to his surprise, that he was no longer thirsty and no longer sweating. This was dangerous, he recalled from some lecture, but at that moment the young marine vomiting at the roadside seemed more important, even more interesting. He stopped to help, thought better of it, passed on—through a strange crowd of pale and tiny butterflies, borne like bleached petals in shimmering slow-motion across the dusty road. At one point Hobbs, the radioman, cruised by in a jeep with a fishpole antenna; he was laughing, taunting the marchers with a song—*I got romance in my pants*—and he waved a jolly fat hand. A tanager rose, scarlet and beautiful, from a steaming thicket and pinwheeled upward, down again, and into the meadow beyond: there Culver thought, for a brief terrified moment, that he saw eight butchered corpses lying in a row, blood streaming out against the weeds. But it passed. Of course, he remembered, that was yesterday—or was it?—and then for minutes he tried to recall Hobbs's name, gave up to effort; it was along about this time, too, that he gazed at his watch, neither pleased nor saddened to find that it was not quite nine o'clock, began to wind it with careful absorption as he trudged along, and looked up to see Mannix looming enormously at the roadside.

"Get up," the Captain was saying. He had hardly any voice left at all; whatever he spoke with gave up only a rasp, a whisper. "Get your ass off the deck," he was saying, "get up, I say."

Culver stopped and watched. The marine lay back in the weeds. He was fat and he had a three-day growth of beard. He held up one bare foot, where there was a blister big as a silver dollar and a dead, livid white, the color of a toadstool; as the Captain spoke, the marine blandly peeled the skin away, revealing a huge patch of tender, pink, virgin flesh. He had a patient hillbilly voice and he was explaining softly, "Ah just cain't go on, Captain, with a foot like this. Ah just cain't do it, and that's all there is to it."

"You *can*, goddammit," he rasped. "I walked ten miles with a nail in my foot. If I can do it you can, too. Get up, I said. You're a marine . . ."

"Captain," he went on patiently, "Ah cain't help it about your nail. Ah may be a marine and all that but Ah ain't no goddam fool . . ."

The Captain, poised on his crippled foot, made a swift, awkward gesture toward the man, as if to drag him to his feet; Culver grabbed him by the arm, shouting furiously: "Stop it, Al! Stop it! Stop it! Stop it! Enough!" He paused, looking into Mannix's dull hot eyes. "Enough!" he said, more quietly. "Enough." Then gently, "That's enough, Al. They've just had enough." The end was at hand, Culver knew, there was no doubt of that. The march had come to a halt again, the men lay sprawled out on the sweltering road-side. He looked at the Captain, who shook his head dumbly and suddenly ran trembling fingers over his eyes. "O.K.," he murmured, "yeah . . . yes"—something incoherent and touched with grief—and Culver felt tears running down his cheeks. He was too tired to think—except: old Al. Mannix. Goddam. "They've had enough," he repeated.

Mannix jerked his hand away from his face. "O.K.," he croaked, "Christ sake, I hear you. O.K. They've had enough, they've had enough. O.K. I heard you the first time. Let 'em crap out! I've did—done—" He paused, wheeled around. "To hell with them all."

He watched Mannix limp away. The Colonel was standing nearby up the road, thumbs hooked in his belt, regarding the Captain soberly. Culver's spirit sank like a rock. Old Al, he thought. You just couldn't win. Goddam. Old great soft scarred bear of a man.

If in defeat he appeared despondent, he retained one violent shred of life which sustained him to the end—his fury. It would get him through. He was like a man running a gauntlet of whips, who shouts outrage and defiance at his tormentors until he falls at the finish. Yet—as Culver could have long ago foretold—it was a fury that was uncontained; the old smoking bonfire had blazed up in his spirit. And if it had been out of control hours ago when he had first defied the Colonel, there was no doubt at all that now it could not fail to consume both of them. At least one of them. Culver, prone on his belly in the weeds, was hot with tension, and he felt blood pounding at his head when he heard the Colonel call, in a frosty voice: "Captain Mannix, will you come here a minute?"

Culver was the closest at hand. There were six more miles to go. The break had extended this time to fifteen minutes—an added rest because, as Culver had heard the Colonel explain to the Major, they'd walk the last six miles without a halt. Another break, he'd said, with a wry weary grin, and they'd never be able to get the troops off the ground. Culver had groaned—another senseless piece of sadism— then reasoned wearily that it *was* a good idea. Probably. Maybe. Who knew? He was too tired to care. He watched Mannix walk with an awful hobbling motion up the road, face screwed up in pain and eyes asquint like a man trying to gaze at the sun. He moved at a good rate of speed but his gait was terrible to behold—jerks and spasms which warded off, reacted to, or vainly tried to control great zones and areas of pain. Behind him most of his men lay in stupefied rows at the edge of the road and waited for the trucks to come. They knew Mannix had finished, and they had crumpled completely. For the last ten minutes, in a listless fashion, he had assembled less than a third of the company who were willing to continue the march—diehards, athletes, and just those who, like Mannix himself, would make the last six miles out of pride and spite. Out of fury. It was a seedy, bedraggled column of people: of hollow, staring eyes and faces green with slack-jawed exhaustion; and behind them the remnants of the battalion made hardly more than two hundred men. Mannix struggled on up the road, approached the Colonel, and stood there propped on his toe, hands on his hips for balance.

The Colonel looked at him steadily for a moment, coldly. Mannix was no longer a simple doubter but the heretic, and was about to receive judgment. Yet there was still an almost paternal reluctance in Templeton's voice as he spoke, slowly and very softly, out of the troops' hearing: "Captain Mannix, I want you to go in on the trucks."

"No, sir," Mannix said hoarsely, "I'm going to make this march."

The Colonel looked utterly whipped; gray bags of fatigue hung beneath his eyes. He seemed no longer to have strength enough to display his odd theatrical smile; his posture was taut and vaguely stooped, the unmistakable bent-kneed stance of a man with blisters, and Culver was forced to concede—with a sense of mountainous despair—that he *had* made the march after all, somewhere toward the rear and for legitimate reasons of his own, even if Mannix now was too blind, too outraged, to tell. *Goddam,* Culver heard himself moaning aloud, *if just he only hadn't made it,* but he heard the Colonel go on coolly: "Not with that foot you aren't." He glanced down. The Captain's ankle had swollen to a fat milky purple above the top of his shoe; he was unable to touch his heel to the ground even if he had wanted to. "Not with that foot," he repeated.

Mannix was silent, panting deeply—not as if taken aback at all, but only as if gathering wind for an outburst. He and the Colonel gazed at each other, twin profiles embattled against an escarpment of pines, the chaste blue sky of morning. "Listen, Colonel," he rasped, "you ordered this goddam hike and I'm going to walk it even if I haven't got one goddam man left. You can crap out yourself for half the march—" Culver wanted desperately, somehow, by any means to stop him—not just because he was pulling catastrophe down on his head but because it was simply no longer worth the effort. Couldn't he see? That the Colonel didn't care and that was that? That with him the hike had had nothing to do with courage or sacrifice or suffering, but was only a task to be performed, that whatever he was he was no coward, he had marched the whole way—or most of it, any idiot could see that—and that he was as far removed from the vulgar battle, the competition, which Mannix had tried to promote as the frozen, remotest stars. He just didn't care. Culver strove, in a sick, heaving effort, to rise, to go and somehow separate them, but Mannix was charging on: "You run your troops. Fine. O.K. But what's all this about crapping out—"

"Wait a minute, Captain, now—" the Colonel blurted ominously. "For your information—"

"*Fuck* you and your information," said Mannix in a hoarse, choked voice. He was almost sobbing. "If you think—"

But he went no further, for the Colonel had made a curious, quick gesture—stage-gesture, fantastic and subtle, and it was like watching an old cowboy film to see the Colonel's hand go swiftly back to the handle of his pistol and rest there, his eyes cool and passionate and forbidding. It was a gesture of force which balked even the Captain. Mannix's face went pale—as if he had only just then realized the words which had erupted so heedlessly from his mouth— and he said nothing, only stood there sullen and beaten and blinking at the glossy white handle of the pistol as the Colonel went on: "For your information, Captain, you aren't the only one who made this march. But I'm not *interested* in your observations. You quiet down now, hear? You march in, see? I order you confined to your quarters, and I'm going to see that you get a court-martial. Do you understand? I'm going to have you tried for gross insubordination. I'll have you sent to Korea. *Keep your mouth shut.* Now get back to your company!" He was shaking with wrath; the hot morning light beat with piety and with vengeance from his gray, outraged eyes. "Get back to your men," he whispered, *"get back to your men!"*

Then he turned his back to the Captain and called down the road to the Major: "All right, Billy, let's saddle up!"

So it was over, but not quite all. The last six miles took until past noon. Mannix's perpetual tread on his toe alone gave to his gait a ponderous, bobbing motion which resembled that of a man wretchedly spastic and paralyzed. It lent to his face too—whenever Culver became detached from his own misery long enough to glance at him—an aspect of deep, almost prayerfully passionate concentration—eyes thrown skyward and lips fluttering feverishly in pain—so that if one did not know he was in agony one might imagine that he was a communicant in rapture, offering up breaths of hot desire to the heavens. It was impossible to imagine such a distorted face; it was the painted, suffering face of a clown, and the heaving gait was a grotesque and indecent parody of a hopeless cripple, with shoulders gyrating like a seesaw and with flapping, stricken arms. The Colonel and the Major had long since outdistanced them, and Culver and Mannix walked alone. When the base came into sight, he was certain they were not going to make it. They trudged into the camp. Along the barren, treeless streets marines in neat khaki were going to lunch, and they turned to watch the mammoth gyrating Captain, so tattered and soiled—who addressed convulsive fluttering prayers to the sky, and had obviously parted with his senses. Then Mannix stopped suddenly and grasped Culver's arm. "What the hell," he whispered, "we've made it."

v

For a long while Culver was unable to sleep. He had lain naked on his bed for what seemed hours, but unconsciousness would not come; his closed eyes offered up only vistas of endless roads, steaming thickets, fields, tents—sunshine and darkness illogically commingled—and the picture, which returned to his mind with the unshakable regularity of a scrap of music, of the boys who lay dead beneath the light of another noon. Try as he could, sleep would not come. So he dragged himself erect and edged toward the window, laboriously, because of his battered feet; it took him a full minute to do so, and his legs, like those of an amputee which possess the ghost of sensation, felt as if they were still in motion, pacing endless distances. He lowered himself into a chair and lighted a cigarette. Below, the swimming pool was grotto-blue, a miniature of the cloudless sky above, lit with shapes of dancing light as shiny as silver dimes. A squad of sunsuited maidens, officers' wives, splashed at its brink or ate ice-cream sundaes on the lawn, and filled the noontime with

their decorous sunny laughter. It was hot and still. Far off
above the pines, in the hot sunlight and over distant peace
and civilization, brewed the smoky and threatful beginnings
of a storm.

Culver let his head fall on his arm. Yes, they had had
it—those eight boys—he thought, there was no doubt of
that. In mindless slumber now, they were past caring, though
diadems might drop or Doges surrender. They were ignorant
of all. And that they had never grown old enough to know
anything, even the tender miracle of pity, was perhaps
a better ending—it was hard to tell. Faint warm winds came
up from the river, bearing with them a fragrance of swamp
and pine, and a last whisper of air passed through the trees,
shuddered, died, became still; suddenly Culver felt a deep
vast hunger for something he could not explain, nor ever
could remember having known quite so achingly before. He
only felt that all of his life he had yearned for something
that was as fleeting and as incommunicable, in its beauty,
as that one bar of music he remembered, or those lovely little
girls with their ever joyful, ever sprightly dance on some far
and fantastic lawn—serenity, a quality of repose—he could
not call it by name, but only knew that, somehow, it had
always escaped him. As he sat there, with the hunger growing and blossoming within him, he felt that he had hardly
ever known a time in his life when he was not marching or
sick with loneliness or afraid.

And so, he thought, they had all had it, in their various
fashions. The Colonel had had his march and his victory,
and Culver could not say still why he was unable to hate
him. Perhaps it was only because he was a different kind of
man, different enough that he was hardly a man at all, but
just a quantity of attitudes so remote from Culver's world
that to hate him would be like hating a cannibal, merely
because he gobbled human flesh. At any rate, he had had it.
And as for Mannix—well, *he'd* certainly had it, there was no
doubt of *that*. Old Al, he thought tenderly. The man with the
back unbreakable, the soul of pity—where was he now,
great unshatterable vessel of longing, lost in the night, astray
at mid-century in the never-endingness of war?

His hunger faded and died. He raised his head and gazed
out the window. Over the pool a figure swan-dived against the
sky, in crucified, graceless descent broke the water with a
lumpy splash. A cloud passed over the day, darkening the
lawn with a moment's somber light. The conversation of the

girls became subdued, civilized, general. Far off above the trees, on the remotest horizon, thunderheads bloomed, a squall. Later, toward sundown, they would roll landward over a shadowing reach of waves, borne nearer, ever more darkly across the coast, the green wild desolation of palmetto and cypress and pine—and here, where the girls pink and scanty in sunsuits would slant their tar-black eyes skyward in the gathering night, abandon pool and games and chatter and with shrill cries of warning flee homeward like gaudy scraps of paper on the blast, voices young and lovely and lost in the darkness, the onrushing winds. One thing, Culver thought, was certain—they were in for a blow. Already there would be signals up and down the coast.

Abruptly he was conscious of a dry, parched thirst. He rose to his feet, put on a robe, and hobbled out into the hallway toward the water cooler. As he rounded the corner he saw Mannix, naked except for a towel around his waist, making his slow and agonized way down the hall. He was hairy and enormous and as he inched his way toward the shower room, clawing at the wall for support, his face with its clenched eyes and taut, drawn-down mouth was one of tortured and gigantic suffering. The swelling at his ankle was the size of a grapefruit, an ugly blue, and this leg he dragged behind him, a dead weight no longer capable of motion.

Culver started to limp toward him, said, "Al—" in an effort to help him along, but just then one of the Negro maids employed in the place came swinging along with a mop, stopped, seeing Mannix, ceased the singsong little tune she was humming, too, and said, "Oh my, you poor man. What you been doin'? Do it hurt?" Culver halted.

"Do it hurt?" she repeated. "Oh, I bet it does. Deed it does." Mannix looked up at her across the short yards that separated them, silent, blinking. Culver would remember this: the two of them communicating across that chasm one unspoken moment of sympathy and understanding before the woman, spectacled, bandannaed, said again, "Deed it does," and before, almost at precisely the same instant, the towel slipped away slowly from Mannix's waist and fell with a soft plop to the floor; Mannix then, standing there, weaving dizzily and clutching for support at the wall, a mass of scars and naked as the day he emerged from his mother's womb, save for the soap which he held feebly in one hand. He seemed to have neither the strength nor the ability to lean down and retrieve the towel and so he merely stood there huge and naked in the slanting dusty light and blinked and sent toward the woman, finally, a sour, apologetic smile, his words uttered, it seemed to Culver, not with self-pity but only with the tone of a man who, having endured and lasted, was too weary to tell her anything but what was true.

"Deed it does," he said.

BIOGRAPHICAL NOTES

HERMAN MELVILLE (1819–91), perhaps the greatest American writer of the nineteenth century, was born in New York City, a descendant of old Dutch and English families of colonial background. His father having gone bankrupt when Melville was but a child, his formal education was cut short at the age of fifteen, and, after working at various clerical jobs, he shipped as a cabin-boy to Liverpool in 1839. Two years later he sailed to the South Seas on a whaling voyage. At the Marquesas he jumped ship and was held captive for a month by the natives of the valley of Typee. Later he enlisted as a seaman on the frigate *United States,* an experience of which he gives a vivid account in *White-Jacket* (1850). His earlier experiences among the savage islanders of the Marquesas are recorded in two books: *Typee* (1846) and *Omoo* (1847). His life as a sailor ended in 1844, and henceforward he turned his hand to literature, with but negative results so far as recognition and success are concerned. His most important work, *Moby Dick,* was published in 1851, his novel *Pierre* in 1851, *Israel Potter* in 1855, *The Piazza Tales* in 1856, and *The Confidence Man* in 1857. Melville is also the author of several volumes of verse, among them *Clarel* (1876) and *John Marr and Other Sailors* (1888). Having failed to earn his living as a writer, he obtained in 1866 an appointment as an outdoor customs inspector in New York City and held this position for nineteen years, living obscurely and virtually cut off from the world of letters. It was not until the 1920's that he was rediscovered and since then he has been the subject of numerous critical studies and scholarly investigations.

HENRY JAMES (1843–1916), regarded in most critical quarters as the most considerable novelist that America has produced, was born in New York City, the son of Henry James, Sr., who was a friend of the writers and philosophers of his time and himself a brilliant though somewhat eccentric writer on moral and theological subjects. The family, remarkable for its intellectual vitality, travelled in Europe a good deal and Henry acquired very early in his life a sense of the Old World as a cultural resource and as a literary theme. He was educated mostly under private auspices until his brief attendance at the Harvard Law School in 1862. He lived with his family in New York City, Newport, and Cambridge; in 1875 he moved permanently to Europe, making his home in England. James was an immensely creative and prolific writer, and he wrote not only fiction but also plays, travel-books, and literary criticism of the finest quality. The prejudice which his expatriation and the difficult manner of his later work aroused in his own country has been overcome in recent decades and he is now recognized as a classic American man of letters. Among his more important works are *A Passionate Pilgrim and Other Tales* (1875), *Daisy Miller* (1879), *Washington Square* (1881), *The Portrait of a Lady* (1881), *The Bostonians* (1886), *The Princess Casamassima* (1886), *The Aspern Papers* (1888), *What Maisie Knew* (1897), *The Wings of the Dove* (1902), *The Ambassadors* (1903), *The Golden Bowl* (1904), and *The American Scene* (1907).

STEPHEN CRANE (1871–1900) is known as one of the pioneers of the naturalist-realist movement in American literature. He was born in Newark, New Jersey, and briefly attended Lafayette College and Syracuse University before moving to New York City to become a free-lance writer and newspaper-reporter. His first novel, *Maggie: A Girl of the Streets* (1893), failed to attract attention and it was not until the publication of his war novel, *The Red Badge of Courage*, in 1895, that his reputation was established. He served as a war-correspondent in Mexico, Cuba, and in Greece. For a time he lived in England, where he developed a number of significant literary and personal relationships with such distinguished writers as Joseph Conrad and Henry James. Crane was in poor health most of his life and died of tuberculosis. Among his more important work are two collections of short stories, *The Open Boat* (1898) and *The Mon-*

ster (1899), as well as two volumes of verse, *The Black Riders* (1895) and *War Is Kind* (1899).

EDITH WHARTON (1862–1937) was born Edith Newbold Jones in New York City of an old and socially eminent New York family and was educated privately in America and abroad. Her early work testifies to the influence of Henry James, but in her more mature fiction she developed a distinctive manner of her own. She wrote mainly about the life of the leisured rich in New York and in Europe, where she lived after 1907. *The House of Mirth* (1905) was her first novel of significant literary value. Other works of lasting value are *Ethan Frome* (1911), *The Custom of the Country* (1913), *The Age of Innocence* (1920), the four novelettes published under the collective title *Old New York,* and her autobiography *A Backward Glance* (1934).

SHERWOOD ANDERSON (1876–1941) was born in Ohio, received no formal education, served in the Spanish-American War, and abandoned a business career to become a writer. He played a very important part in the literary renaissance and revolt against the then prevailing standards of gentility in literature that preceded the full-fledged modern movement of the 1920's. His collection of stories *Winesburg, Ohio* (1919), depicting life in small-town America, won him critical acclaim and a measure of popular success. The more outstanding of his works are *The Triumph of the Egg* (1921), *Horses and Men* (1923), *Many Marriages* (1923), *Dark Laughter* (1925), and a number of autobiographical narratives, such as *A Story-Teller's Story* (1924), *A Midwest Childhood* (1926), and *Memoirs* (1942), which was published posthumously.

WILLIAM FAULKNER (1897–1962), winner of the Nobel Prize in 1950 and famous the world over as the creator of the Yoknapatawpha County saga, was born in New Albany, Mississippi, and grew up in Oxford, Mississippi, the prototype of "Jefferson," the town which serves as the scene of a good many of his novels. He joined the Canadian Air Force during the First World War but saw no active service, as the war ended before he was commissioned. His early novels, *Soldier's Pay* (1926) and *Mosquitoes* (1927), went unnoticed, and it was not until the publication of *The Sound and the Fury* in 1929, a novel radically experimental in technique dealing with the decadent life of an old Southern family, that critical attention began to be focussed on him. The works that followed established his reputation both here and abroad as the greatest American novelist then alive. Of particular importance among his novels are *As I Lay Dying* (1930), *Sanctuary* (1931), *Light in August* (1932), *Absalom, Absalom* (1936), *The Hamlet* (1940) and *Go Down, Moses* (1942).

FLANNERY O'CONNOR (1925–1964) achieved an enviable place among the younger American novelists. In addition to *Wise Blood* she also published a collection of stories, *A Good Man Is Hard to Find* (1955), and a second novel, *The Violent Bear It Away* (1960).

WILLIAM STYRON (1925—) is among the best known of the younger generation of American novelists. He was an editor of *The Paris Review* and won the Prix de Rome for his novel *Lie Down in Darkness* (1952), which was a popular as well as critical success. His second novel, *Set This House on Fire*, appeared in 1960.